TENGU – Winner o
West Coast of Book

Nancy spoke: "The most evil of all the seven Black Kami is called the Tengu. Even the most experienced adepts at the Shinto shrine are warned opening themselves up to the Tengu. It is said that the leader of the shrine had once done so, and had almost been driven mad."

"Nancy, please—" Gerard interrupted.

"No. You must listen to me. The characteristics the Tengu gave to those he possessed included invincible physical strength, the mad strength of the berserk, the ability to stand up to ferocious attack from any kind of weapon. Also, if the person he was possessing was chopped into the tiniest pieces, the pieces would regenerate and grow again into demons even more hideous than the original—"

"Nancy!" Gerard shouted.

"No!" she hissed. "You have to listen because it's true! *They've done it!* They've brought it here, the Tengu, the real Tengu demon! The devil of remorseless destruction!"

Tengu
GRAHAM MASTERTON

SPHERE BOOKS LIMITED

SPHERE BOOKS LTD

Published by the Penguin Group
27 Wrights Lane, London W8 5TZ, England
Viking Penguin Inc., 40 West 23rd Street, New York, New York 10010, USA
Penguin Books Australia Ltd, Ringwood, Victoria, Australia
Penguin Books Canada Ltd, 2801 John Street, Markham, Ontario, Canada L3R
Penguin Books (NZ) Ltd, 182–190 Wairau Road, Auckland 10, New Zealand

Penguin Books Ltd, Registered Offices: Harmondsworth, Middlesex, England

First published in Great Britain by Sphere Books Ltd 1984
Published in the United States of America by Tor Books 1983
Reprinted 1984 (twice), 1986, 1988

This is a work of fiction. All the characters and events portrayed in this book are
fictional and any resemblance to real people or incidents is purely coincidental.

Printed and bound in Great Britain by
Cox & Wyman Ltd, Reading

Naval records show indisputably that the radio monitoring vessel USS *Value* was at Pearl Harbor on July 2, 1945, undergoing routine equipment repairs. There can be no basis whatever for your suggestion that the vessel was anchored at that time off the coast of Japan. Nor can there be any substance in your claim that the USS *Value* was connected with what you call the "Appomattox Situation." The Navy has no record of any file of that title or description.

SEN. NEILSEN (N.J.): Did you at any time prior to this sortie appreciate that you might have to sacrifice the lives of all but one of your fellow operatives in order to achieve a comparatively minor intelligence coup?

LT. COL. KASTNER: Yes, sir. I was conscious of the risks. I might add that my fellow operatives were, too. We were trained.

SEN. NEILSEN: Do you now believe that what you achieved was worth the loss of all those lives, and worth the political risks which Senator Goldfarb has already outlined?

LT. COL. KASTNER: There was a possibility that it might have been, sir. I admit the net result was a disappointment.

SEN. NEILSEN: A disappointment?

LT. COL. KASTNER: Not all such sorties are disappointments, sir. Appomattox was a good example.

SEN. NEILSEN: Appomattox? What was Appomattox?

LT. COL. KASTNER: I have just been given instructions that I am not to respond to that question, sir. It is outside the area of my competence.

SEN. NEILSEN: I think this inquiry deserves some kind of explanation of your remarks, Colonel.

LT. COL. KASTNER: I'm sorry, sir. I have been advised that any kind of response would be a violation of national security.

SEN. NEILSEN: Very well, Colonel. But I intend to take this matter further.

LT. COL. KASTNER: That is your privilege, sir.

MESSAGE RECEIVED FROM APPOMATTOX ONE, JULY 11, 1945

"We've located it, sir. No question about it. We've taken sixteen radio bearings and we have it right on the button."

"In that case (*inaudible*) immediately. I repeat, immediately. You will be picked up at 2125 hours on the 15th on the beach at (*inaudible*.)"

BOOK ONE
BURNED DOVES

CHAPTER ONE

When Sherry Cantor's alarm clock woke her at 7:27 on the morning of August 9 she had twenty-three minutes to live.

That was the most overwhelming fact of her morning. Yet it was the only fact she didn't know.

She knew that her twenty-second birthday was only three days away. She knew that in two weeks she was supposed to drive down to San Diego and spend a week with her brother Manny and his wife Ruth. She knew that she had a date to meet her good-looking new lawyer, Bert Dentz, in thirteen hours and thirty-three minutes for dinner at the Palm Restaurant on Santa Monica Boulevard.

She knew that her savings account at Security Pacific contained $127,053.62, and she knew that last Wednesday's *Variety* had dubbed her "most promising young video star of 1983."

But knowing all that was not enough. Knowing all that could not possibly save her from what was going to happen in twenty-three minutes' time.

After the alarm had woken her up, she lay on her emerald-green satin sheets in her small white California-rococo bedroom, under the framed black-and-white print of yuccas at Santa Barbara. She thought about the dream she had just been dreaming. It had been vivid, almost realer than real, as only early-morning dreams can be. She had imagined herself jumping rope in the front yard of the old white house in Bloomington, Indiana. She had

imagined the leaves falling from the trees like flakes of
rust. She had imagined her mother coming to the door,
and waving her to come in for cookies and milk. . . .

Sherry thought about her dream, and then let it warmly
melt away. Bloomington, Indiana, was five years ago, and
a lifetime away. She stretched on the twisted sheets.

She was a tall, striking girl with rich chestnut hair and a
face that was uncompromisingly European. Her eyes were
wide, and almost amber. She was wide-shouldered, big-
breasted, and narrow-hipped. She slept naked, except for
a small pair of blue satin panties, and her skin was soft and
brown against the shiny sheets.

There was a faded photograph on the sideboard in
Bloomington of Sherry's mother in a transit camp in
Munchen Gladbach, Germany, in 1945. Except for the
puff-sleeved dress and the headscarf, it could have been
Sherry.

At 7:31, with only nineteen minutes left, Sherry sat up
in bed and ran her hands through her tousled hair. On the
bleached calico window blind, the first nodding patterns
of sunlight shone through the fan palms in her garden,
and made a shadow-play.

Somewhere outside, a radio was giving the morning
traffic report. It was bad everywhere.

Sherry climbed out of bed, stood up, stretched, and
stifled a yawn. Then she padded out of the bedroom and
into her kitchenette. She opened the mock Oregon-oak
cupboard and took down a can of Folger's coffee. As she
reached for her percolator, a triangle of sunlight lit her
hair, and then her shoulder, and then her right breast. The
nipple was pale and soft.

While the coffee perked, Sherry poured herself an
orange-juice and stood in the kitchenette drinking it. She
felt hungry. Last night, she'd shared a bottle of tequila
with Dan Mayhew, the curly-haired actor who played her
unhappily married cousin in *Our Family Jones*, and
hangovers always made her feel hungry.

She opened the fridge again. There were two Thomas's

muffins left. She wondered how guilty she would feel if
she toasted one.

It was 7:37. She decided against the muffin. Dan Mayhew hadn't even been worth getting a hangover over, and
so he certainly wasn't worth putting on weight over. Last
week she'd seen him sitting in the studio commissary with
a boy whose pale lemon ballet shoes and surfer's knobs
hadn't exactly reassured her about Dan's essential virility.

It was 7:39. There were eleven minutes of life left.
Sherry left the kitchenette as the coffee began to perk, and
walked into her small bathroom. There were T-shirts and
panties hanging to dry on a line over the tub. She looked
at herself in the mirror, pouted at herself, and pulled
down her eyelids to make sure her eyes weren't too
bloodshot. Lionel—Lionel Schultz, the director of *Our
Family Jones*—always went crazy if anyone arrived on the
floor with reddened eyes.

"What do you think we're shooting here?" he
invariably screamed. "A fucking Dracula picture?"

Lionel Schultz wasn't a gentle man. He wasn't much of
a gentleman, either. But he had a perverse genius for soap
opera, and for provoking believable performances out of
inexperienced actors. It was Lionel Schultz who had shown
Sherry how to develop the dumb, busty part of Lindsay
Jones into a character of sweet and quirky sympathy. And
he hadn't touched her once.

Sherry finished her orange juice and set her glass down
on the basin, next to her cake of herbal soap. She stepped
out of her panties, and sat on the toilet. She could hear the
birds chittering in the garden, and the distant murmur of
the freeways. She closed her eyes, and tried to think what
she felt like wearing today.

It was 7:42. She flushed the toilet, washed her face, and
walked back into the kitchenette naked. The coffee was
popping and jumping. She picked up the folded-back
script that lay on the counter, next to the Popeye cookie
jar, and flicked through two or three pages.

LINDSAY (*sobbing*): Is that really what you think of me? After all those days and nights together? After all those things you said?

MARK: Honey, you don't understand. I had to tell Carla we were finished. I didn't have any other choice.

Riboyne Shel O'lem, thought Sherry. If anyone had shown me this script before I signed up for *Our Family Jones*, I wouldn't have thought it was worth turning up at the studio. I would have stayed as a waitress at Butterfield's, fetching and carrying white wine and cottage cheese salads for pretentious British tax exiles in tinted glasses, and been glad of the work. Who would have guessed that some treacly saga about some even more treacly family would have gotten off the ground for a pilot and two episodes, let alone for two series?

Even more amazing, who would have thought that a Jewish girl from Bloomington, Indiana, would have been picked out of hundreds of would-be starlets for one of the most noticeable roles in the whole drama?

There wasn't any question that *Our Family Jones* had cost Sherry the love of her live-in boyfriend, Mack Holt. Mack was lean and moody, with curly blond hair and a broken nose, and he could swim and ride and fence and dance like Fred Astaire. They had met one evening on the plaza outside of the Security Pacific Bank at Century City, when she had just opened her savings account with $10 her mother had sent her. The shadows of the dying day had been very Bauhaus, and he had crossed the plaza at that trotting pace athletes use when they're just on the point of breaking into a run. She had been putting away her bankbook; dropped her purse; and he had picked it up for her in one fell swoop. After such a meeting, he should have known she would make it in soap opera.

Sherry and Mack had lived for seven months on the second floor of a brown crumbling hacienda off Franklin Avenue, in Hollywood. They had shared their three-room apartment with a lumpy divan, two fraying basketwork chairs, three peeling posters for the Grateful Dead, and a dyspeptic gas stove. They had talked, played records, made love, smoked Mexican grass, argued, gone off to work, brushed their teeth, and finally arrived at the moment when Lionel had called to say Sherry was fabulous, and just had to come down to the studio right away, and Mack, far more talented, but still parking cars for a living, had refused to kiss her and wish her luck.

From then on, it had been nothing but sulks, arguments, and eventually, packed suitcases. Sherry had lived for a while with a plain but friendly girl she knew from Butterfield's, and then taken out a mortgage on this small secluded bungalow at the top of a steeply graded dead end called Orchid Place. She enjoyed the luxury of living alone, with her own small garden, her own wrought-iron fence, her own living room, her own perfect peace. She began to think about who she was, and what she wanted out of her life, and all of her friends said she was much nicer since she'd left Mack, and much more relaxed.

To ease one of the more pressing demands of being single, Sherry had bought, through the mail, a pink vibrator. Most of the time it stayed in her bedside cupboard, next to her Oil of Olay and her Piz Buin sun oil, but occasionally there were nights when fantasies crowded her mind, and the Los Angeles heat almost stifled her, and she used it just to keep herself sane.

It was harder than anyone knew, being the most promising young video star of 1983.

With four minutes left, she poured herself a cup of coffee. She sipped it and repeated her lines under her breath: "Is that really what you think of me? After all those days and nights together? After all those things you said?"

There were three minutes left. One hundred eighty seconds of life. She crossed the living room with her coffee mug in one hand and her script in the other. The sun was shining through the loose-woven yellow drapes drawn across the French doors, and the whole room was suffused in daffodil-colored light. Her bare toes curled into the white shag rug.

"Is that *really* what you think of me?" she repeated.

Two minutes. She switched on the Sony television which
stood in the corner. On top of the television was a sprig of
poinsettia in a glass carafe of water. She had picked it
yesterday evening, before she went out with Dan. On the
wall behind the television was an original studio sketch for
the Jones family parlor, signed by the artist. In a concentrated whisper, Sherry said: "After all those days and
nights together? After all those things you said?"

A commercial for Santa Anita Dodge appeared on the
television screen—a fast-talking man in a powder-blue suit
and a Buddy Holly hairstyle. "When you bring the family
down to Santa Anita Dodge, we'll give each of your
children a free balloon, and your wife will be able to pick
up a free voucher for hairstyling and a beauty treatment.
That's guaranteed, whether you buy a new Dodge or
not."

"Is that *really* what you think of me?"

One minute left. Thirty seconds. Fifteen. Ten. Five.
Sherry turned away from the television to set her mug
down on the glass-and-bamboo coffee table in the middle
of the living room. Her telephone rang, although nobody
ever found out who it was, calling her at 7:49:55 in the
morning.

The noise was so shattering that she thought a bomb
had gone off. Then she thought it must be an earthquake.
But as she turned back toward the French windows, she
saw both huge panes of glass bursting inward, so that the
whole living room was filled with a blizzard of glittering,
tumbling fragments. Next, the metal screens were ripped
away, and the aluminum upright between the broken
windows was smashed aside as if it were cardboard.

She didn't scream. She didn't even understand what
was happening until it was too late. She raised her hands
to protect her face from the flying glass, but the glass was
nothing.

Through the wrecked windowframe stepped a short,

powerfully built man dressed in a strangely tied-up yellow robe. His skull was cropped down to a bristly black brush. His face was covered by a grotesque white mask, expressionless and evil.

Sherry tried to back away, tried to cover her nakedness, but a sharp triangle of glass sliced into the side of her foot, and her hesitation was fatal.

The man seized her left wrist in a grip so hard that it broke both her radius and her ulna. He twisted her fiercely around, and gripped her throat from behind. She gagged and choked, and tried to thrash against him with her legs, but he was impossibly strong.

Without a word, without even a grunt, he went down on one knee and pulled Sherry backward across his thigh. She felt a splitting pain in her spine that was so intense that she passed out. But she instantly regained consciousness and was drowned in scarlet waves of agony. The man was hurting her so much she couldn't even believe it was happening to her.

Her back broke. She felt it snap. She could see the combed-plaster ceiling of her bungalow, and the paper lantern with the flower patterns on it. She couldn't speak, couldn't cry out, couldn't move. It couldn't be real. Things like this didn't happen. She wasn't here at all. She must be someplace else. Asleep. Dreaming.

She could still hear the radio somewhere outside. It was playing "Samba Pa Ti."

Silently, the powerful man gripped the inside of her thighs. Her head was lying back on the rug now, and her hands were clenched in paralysis over her breasts. Her entire nervous system was dislocated, and she was already dying. The man let out a deep, suppressed *hmph*! as he pulled her thighs further and further apart, stretching every muscle and sinew. Through a haze of pain and disbelief, Sherry heard something crack in her groin, although she could no longer feel anything below her waist.

The man let her tumble from his upraised knee onto the

rug. He stood up, keeping a hold on the ankle and the thigh of her right leg. With deliberate care, he planted his black silk slipper on Sherry's pubic bone, to give him balance and leverage, and then he twisted her leg around as if he were trying to tear the leg off a chicken.

She was lucky she couldn't feel it. The ball of her thigh-bone was wrenched out of its socket. Then the skin and flesh were screwed around so tightly that they tore apart, in a grisly welter of burst arteries. The man gave Sherry's leg one more turn, and ripped it right away from her body.

He stepped back, and looked down at her. Her breathing was shallow with shock, and her face was already blue. Her eyes were clouded over. The man wiped his hands, first on his robes, then on the drapes. He didn't seem to know what to do next.

Sherry realized she was dying. She didn't know why. She could see the man looking down at her, and she tried to think how she could ask him. It didn't really matter, of course. Nothing mattered when you were dead.

Her last thought was that she wished she could see her home in Indiana just one more time.

The man in the yellow robe watched her die, his mask impassive. Then he walked back out the broken French window, and stood in the morning sunlight, still and thoughtful, as if he had just returned from a long and unexpected journey.

CHAPTER TWO

As Sherry was dying, Mrs. Eva Crowley was parking her slate-colored Seville Elegante on a red line close to the twin towers of Century Park East. She switched off the motor and sat in the driver's seat for a while, watching her pale blue eyes in the rearview mirror. Well, she thought, this is it. This is where my life is pasted back together again, or lost for good.

She climbed out of the car and locked it. Normally she never bothered, but this morning she felt the need for as many mundane rituals as possible—not only to keep herself from trembling with fear, but to delay the moment when she was going to have to stand face to face with Gerard and tell him: "Choose."

Gerard hadn't come home now for three nights in succession, and Eva Crowley had had enough. She had sworn to herself in the small hours of the morning, as she lay hugging her husband's crumpled pillow, that she was going to finish for good all the pain and humiliation of being a cheated wife. No more evenings with only Dan Rather, a bottle of Jack Daniel's, and her sleeping twin daughters for company. No more false sympathy when Gerard called from the office to say that work had snowed him under again, and I'm sorry, Evie, I just have to keep at it all through the night.

Today, Gerard Crowley, the self-made president of Crowley Tobacco Imports, was going to be forced to make up his mind.

As Eva walked across the plaza toward the entrance of Century Park East, her footsteps echoed on the concrete paving, and she could see a distant and severe image of herself in the glass doors, approaching with all the inevitability of her own fate.

She was a petite, slender woman, with ash-blonde hair drawn back in a bun. Her face was pale and perfectly oval, like a blanched almond. For the frightening and solemn performance which this day demanded of her, she was wearing a dark gray suit with a pencil skirt, and black stiletto shoes. She could have been going to a board meeting, or a funeral.

Eva felt breathless as she waited in the deserted lobby for the elevator to take her to the twenty-seventh floor. She began to bite at her pearl-pink nails, and then stopped herself. She hadn't bitten her nails since she was an overweight young student in New York, plain and agonizingly shy, and hopelessly infatuated with an overbearing slob of a business administration senior called Hank Pretty. Her life in those days had been haunted by slipping grades, headaches, and the vision of spending the rest of her years with a man whose body stank of sweat and whose mind had about as much charm and order as the morning after Mardi Gras.

Eva and Hank had fought. Hank had hit her. She had spat red blood into the rose-colored washbasin, and the whole world had seemed to be coming to a close.

She hadn't attempted suicide, though. Eva had never been the suicidal type. These days, she put on weight when she was anxious, eating too many taco chips and guacamole, and she smoked, too. But she had the painful strength to make appointments with her fears and face up to them, as if her fears were imaginary doctors with bad news about her smear, or phantom dentists with bicuspids to pull.

She sometimes wished she had no strength at all, and could readily sacrifice herself to Gerard's faithlessness without a struggle. But she couldn't, and wouldn't. She was too much like her father. Ornery.

The elevator bell softly chimed the arrival of the twenty-seventh floor. The doors rumbled open and Eva stepped out. On the wall in front of the elevator bank was a brushed-aluminum sign with the inscription CROWLEY TOBACCO IMPORTS, INC. LOS ANGELES—CHICAGO —MIAMI. She stood and looked at it for a moment, because she remembered the day it had first been screwed into place. Then she walked evenly along the corridor toward the tinted glass doors of the office itself.

It was a few seconds before eight o'clock. Gerard had always started work early. When they had first married, nineteen years ago, she had hardly ever seen him in the mornings. He had been out of bed and jogging along Lexington Road well before six, and she had only woken up at seven o'clock when the door of his Riviera slammed and the engine whistled into life. The kitchen would be left like the mess deck of the *Marie Celeste*—half-eaten crispbread, spilled milk, letters ripped open and left on the table—and there would never be any husband around to prove who had done it.

In later years, though, Eva had woken up earlier. Some mornings Gerard had opened his eyes, and she had been lying there watching him. He had mistaken her steady gaze for affection, even for adoration. In fact, she had been considering the empty and ungraspable nature of their marriage, and wondering who he really was.

She loved him. She had always known that. She wanted to stay married to him. But she had never been able to decide whether he loved her in return or simply used her as a hostess, and mother, and occasional bed partner. He always called her "Evie," and for three of their nineteen years she had protested about it. Then she had given up.

She opened the office door. There were decorative plants and white vinyl chairs, and a wide teak desk. There was nobody around. Eva waited for a moment, and then crossed the reception area to the door marked GERARD F. CROWLEY, PRESIDENT. She felt peculiarly numb, and her hesitation in front of the door seemed to last for whole minutes.

Here I am, she thought. *I've seen him so tired that he was weeping. I've seen him laugh. I've seen him sick, and I've seen him happy. I've seen every detail of his naked body. The pattern of moles on his thigh. The curl of his pubic hair. I've borne him twins. And yet I'm standing in front of his office door, almost too frightened to knock.*

She knocked.

There was a pause. Then his voice asked, "Who is that?"

In a dry, tight falsetto, she said, "It's me."

"Evie?" he queried.

She opened the door. The office faced east, and it was suffused with the milky light of morning. Gerard, dark and unshaven, and wearing a black shirt with the sleeves rolled up, was sitting behind his wide white desk. On the corner of the desk, her eyes wide with anticipation, was his receptionist Francesca, auburn-haired, tall, and dressed in skin-tight white cotton jeans and an olive-green silk blouse.

There was a silver cigar box on Gerard's desk. It had been Eva's tenth-anniversary present to him. It was engraved: "With undying love, your Evie." That was how much he had taken her character away from her.

Gerard said, "You're up early."

He was a very lean man, with thick black wiry hair that was just beginning to turn gray. His face was long and angular, with a thin, sharp nose and sharply defined lips. His eyes were deep-set and dark, and yet she had always felt they were oddly lacking in expression. You couldn't look at him for very long without having to glance away in search of something more sympathetic.

Francesca stood up. Eva was conscious of the receptionists's breasts, shifting under the thin silk of her blouse. Thirty-six C cup, she guessed, but definitely braless today. There were cheap silver puzzle rings on the girl's fingers, and Eva could almost picture those fingers clutching Gerard's stiffened penis. The same way any prizewinner holds a trophy.

"I, er—Evie, it's good to see you," said Gerard. He stood up, and came around his desk to greet her. He was far taller than she was, nearly six two, but somehow he seemed shorter today, diminished.

Francesca said uneasily, "I think I'll go make that coffee now."

"Sure," said Gerard, with pretended ease. "Would you

like some coffee, Evie?''

Eva shook her head. "I don't think so, thank you."

There was a moment of tension. Gerard rubbed his hand across his mouth, as if he was unconsciously making sure that there were no traces of strange kisses. "Well," he said, "I kind of guessed that you wouldn't."

Francesca was still standing by the door, and Gerard glanced across at her and closed his eyes briefly in a catlike expression which meant, *You go make coffee, I'll handle this*. Francesca paused, then left, leaving the office door fractionally ajar.

"Sit down, why don't you?" Gerard asked Eva, indicating a white revolving armchair.

Eva said: "No, thank you. I don't think it's going to take me long to ask you where you've been these past three nights."

He was walking back around his desk. He looked up at her, his dark head outlined against a bright golden painting of drying tobacco leaves. "Where I've *been*?" he asked her. "You know damn well where I've been."

"You've been working three days and three nights without sleep?"

"Almost. I had paperwork up to here." He raised his hand up to the level of his eyes.

"The Turkish consignment?"

He narrowed his eyes. "Mostly."

"So David Orlando's lying?"

"David Orlando? David's in Dallas."

Eva lowered her eyes. "I know he is," she said softly. "I called him there yesterday. He told me he handled the Turkish consignment all by himself, and finished up two days ago. He also told me you had almost no work in the office this week, and that you wouldn't be pushed until early next month."

Gerard stared at her for almost half a minute, without speaking. Then he opened his silver cigar box, hesitated, and finally chose a small Havana. He reached for his cutters, snipped the end off the cigar, and placed it with exaggerated precision between his lips. Eva found his silence, his meticulous actions, distinctly unnerving. His eyes seemed less penetrable than ever.

If only she didn't want him so much, and need to know that he still loved her. If only she was weak enough to stay at home and be satisfied with what she had.

Outside, a fire siren warbled and whooped along the Avenue of the Stars. Gerard waited until the echoes had died away, and then he said: "You were that suspicious, huh? Suspicious enough to call up David?"

"What would *you* have done, Gerard, if *I'd* stayed away for three nights?"

He opened a box of kitchen matches. "You forget that you don't have any reason for staying away nights. I do."

She tried to smile, but her mouth couldn't manage it. "That's obvious enough," she said. "But the reason isn't work, is it? It's *her*."

"Her?"

Eva nodded toward the half-open office door. "She's the one, isn't she? Francesca?"

Gerard let out an abrupt, uncertain laugh that was almost a cough. "Evie—" he said, "I don't really think you're being very fair to me here—"

"You don't think I'm *fair*?" Eva interrupted, in an intense whisper. "What the hell do you call *fair*?"

"I mean understanding," protested Gerard. "I mean you don't seem like you're trying to understand what's going down here."

"What's to understand? You're going to bed with your receptionist!"

"Evie," Gerard said, raising his hand, as if he were fending off a flapping bird. "Evie, every human situation has its two sides. You don't seem to understand that."

Eva turned away. "You're just the same, aren't you?" she said. "Always trying to make *me* feel guilty for the things that *you've* done. Well, it won't work this time, Gerard, because I do understand. I understand that you've been leaving me at home to run your house and look after your daughters while you go off fornicating with your twenty-five-year-old receptionist.''

Gerard let out a breath.

"Can you understand that I still love you?" he asked her. "Can you understand that what I feel for Francesca hasn't made the slightest difference to my appreciation of what you are?''

She turned back toward him. She was frowning. "Are you *serious*?" she asked.

"Never more serious in my whole life.''

"My God," she said. "I don't believe you sometimes. You treat love and appreciation as if they were brands of tobacco.''

He struck a match. It flared up, and there was a sharp smell of burned phosphorus. He kept his eyes on her while he lit his cigar. Then he waved the match to extinguish it, and puffed smoke. Eva hated the smell of cigars.

"I love you, Evie. That's all I can say. If you don't believe me, then I'm really sorry. But it's true.''

"Do you love Francesca, too?''

He nodded. "Yes. In a different sort of way.''

"What different sort of way? You mean, more sexually? Is she better in bed than me? She's younger, I suppose? Her breasts are more—I mean, her breasts are firmer? And does she do things I won't do?''

Gerard continued to puff at his cigar. "She's different, that's all. She's a different person.''

"I see. Different. That tells me precisely zilch.''

Gerard held out his hand toward her. She didn't take it. She wished she could. Her anger had almost burned itself out now, and a numb depression was gradually filling her up, as if she were lowering herself into an unpleasantly tepid tub of water. She could feel the tears on her eyelashes, and she knew that if Gerard gave her any sympathy now, any warmth, she was going to be lost.

"Evie," Gerard told her, in a gentle voice, "I'm the kind of man who can never stay still. It's in my nature. You've known that from the start. That was one of the reasons you married me. You knew I wanted to go places, make money, widen my horizons.''

"I didn't think your horizons included other women," said Eva sharply.

"It was inevitable. It's not a disaster. It won't do anything to break us up. I needed a different kind of relationship with a different kind of woman, and I found it with Francesca. That's all. There's no reason why we should have to make a big production out of it. It's happening all the time.''

Eva opened her pocketbook and took out a crumpled piece of tissue. She dabbed at her eyes, and said, "You needn't think I'm crying. I'm angry, that's all.''

"You don't have to be angry.''

"I don't have to be angry? I've found out my husband's unfaithful and all I have to do is congratulate him?''

"You can *accept*, can't you? Take it for what it is?''

Eva looked at him, and slowly nodded. "I can accept, Gerard, but I can't forgive.''

"What does that mean? You want a divorce?''

"I don't know. Yes. I mean, no, I don't.''

He came nearer and held her arms. He gave her a wry, comforting smile, almost sad, and she could hardly believe that he was the same Gerard she'd married, the same earnest, ambitious, courteous young man who had given up his seat on a crosstown bus on a wet day in New York, and then sheltered her under his umbrella all the way back to her apartment door. The same young man who had taken her out to Mexican restaurants, and told her over the enchiladas, by the swiveling light of a tabletop candle, that he was going to be rich and famous, and that he wanted her to marry him and come to live in L.A., so that she could share his wealth and his fame, and his love too.

Here he was—rich, well known in his own business, but distant now, a remote and incomprehensible man who seemed to have sold himself somewhere along the line of their married life to some other idea of what life should really be. He looked the same, and she still adored him the same, but his attention appeared to be focused someplace else.

She saw herself in the amber-tinted mirror on the other side of the office. She looked pale and odd, but far less distraught than she'd imagined. In fact, she was surprised at her calmness. Gerard's back, dark and tall, looked like the back of a complete stranger.

"Well," said Gerard. "What are you going to do? If you're not going to divorce me—what?"

Eva bit her lip.

"You're trying to tell me you won't—"

Francesca came to the door. She wasn't carrying any coffee. Gerard held Eva's arms tightly, and warmly, but he said in his softest voice, "No. I won't give up Francesca."

CHAPTER THREE

A few minutes after ten o'clock that morning, the telephone started ringing in a shady, secluded apartment on the fourth floor of a yellow house on Alta Loma Road, off Sunset Boulevard. It rang and rang for almost five minutes before a sliding door opened somewhere in the apartment, and silk-slippered feet came padding along the polished wood floor of the corridor.

Nancy Shiranuka picked up the telephone with long red-lacquered fingernails. She said, "*Moshi moshi*," in a flat, expressionless voice. Then she said, "Oh, it's you."

She stood silent, listening. She was a small, delicately boned girl, even for a Japanese. Her face had that startling wide-eyed Hokkaido prettiness that Japanese men find devastating, and even Americans consider magnetic, especially if they've served out East. It was an acquired

taste, Nancy's prettiness, like *chazuke*, rice and tuna fish
with green tea poured over them. She wore nothing but a
loose silk robe of glistening black, open at the front. Her
long black hair hung tangled and damp over her
shoulders.

All around her, the apartment was lined with polished
oak paneling, and split-bamboo blinds where drawn over
the windows. There were two or three black and-white silk
cushions on the floor, and a low table of carved black
wood, but apart from these the room was bare. On the
walls were three erotic woodblocks by Settei from the
Onna-shimekawa oshie-fumi, the book of sexual
instruction for women. The sun shone across the room in
narrow stripes.

Nancy asked, "Are you sure this is true? Did Torii tell
you? And what happened afterward?"

She paused, listening, and then said, "I see."

While she was listening, the sliding door opened again,
and there was the sound of bare feet along the corridor. A
very tall American came into the living room, his midriff
wrapped in a towel, and he stood quite close to her,
watching her with hooded eyes. He was gray-haired, at
least sixty-five, and his body was gnarled and muscular and
scarred. His face was composed entirely of angles, like
Abraham Lincoln's image on the side of Mount Rushmore,
and even before you knew who he was you would have
guessed he was a military man.

His name was Ernest Perry Ouvarov, ex-U.S. Naval
Commander. He had distinguished himself at Midway and
Okinawa, and after the signing of the Japanese surrender
on the deck of USS *Missouri*, he had been largely
responsible for the brilliant reorganization of the
American naval administration in the Pacific. Truman had
once called him "the knight of the high seas."

Beneath the glittering armor, however, the knight had
some fatal weaknesses. In 1951, at the peak of his influence within the Navy, a newspaper investigation had
implicated him in a bottomless scandal involving opium,

surplus war materials, and worst of all, the procuring of young Japanese girls, some of them no more than seven years old, for the pleasure of himself and other key naval personnel and politicians.

The corruption had been so deep-laid that Ouvarov had been permitted to resign his command without any formal proceedings against him. As one Pentagon official was heard to remark, "If they court-martial Ouvarov, they'll have to court-martial the whole damned Navy."

Ernest Ouvarov had changed his name, and worked for years in San Francisco for a transshipment company. Most people in San Francisco still called him "Fred Milward," and thought of him as nothing more than the moderately prosperous vice president of Bay Shipping, Inc. Two months ago, though, a young Japanese lady called Nancy Shiranuka had called at his office, and his life had never been the same.

He watched Nancy for a minute or two, and then crossed the bare room to the black table. He opened a lacquered box and took out a cigarette. He came back toward her, tapping the cigarette on his thumbnail.

Nancy said, "Okay, if that's the best you can do. Call me again when you have more news. Yes, I'm sorry, too. Yes. But tell them to keep a real low profile. That's right."

Ernest left the room and went into the kitchen in search of a light. He came back again, smoking with affected indifference. Nancy said, "Call me later," and put down the phone.

"Well," asked Ernest, "what was all that about?"

"I'm not sure yet."

"You're not sure? That was Yoshikazu, wasn't it?"

"Yes," she said. "But he thinks something's gone wrong. The police are everywhere, and he can't get close enough to find out."

"Wrong?" queried Ernest, wrinkling his nose, just the way he used to on the bridge of the USS *Ferndale*. "What the hell could have gone wrong?"

"I don't know. But Yoshikazu's worried."

Ernest sucked fiercely at his cigarette, and then blew out
smoke. "The whole operation was perfectly planned. I
can't believe that anything's gone wrong. Even Yoshikazu
isn't that dumb."

Nancy absentmindedly tied the cord of her silk robe.
The sun shone on her hair. "Perfect planning doesn't
always mean perfect execution. You should know that.
Even when you're dealing with ordinary people, things can
go wrong."

"You don't have to give me a lesson in personnel
management," snapped Ernest. "This whole thing was set
up so tight that nobody had any room to move. Not even
the brightest member of the team had room to think.
There was no improvisation, no contingency plan, nothing
but a sequence of precisely controlled and coordinated
events. It can't have gone wrong."

"Yoshikazu seems to think it has."

"Well, in that case, he's probably talking his usual
gibberish."

"What are you going to do?" smiled Nancy, slyly.
"Clap him in irons? Send him off on the next clipper to
Shanghai?"

Ernest scratched the iron-gray stubble on his angular
chin. He still felt unsettled, working with civilians. His
father had been a naval commander before him, and his
grandfather had been a friend of Teddy Roosevelt, back in
his Rough Rider days. Ernest could only think of life as a
battle plan, and he mentally graded the people he had to
deal with as admirals, fellow officers, or idiots. Each day
presented its difficulties like a fleet of hostile ships, and
each difficulty could only be overcome by classic naval
tactics. He even walked his three retrievers, John, Paul,
and Jones, in line formation.

Only Nancy Shiranuka knew all about those moments
when he disembarked (inside his mind) from his self-im-
posed regime of naval discipline. Those moments when he
sought, perversely and desperately, the consolation of girl-
children, and extraordinary sexual techniques. He called

those moments his "shore leave."

"We need some up-to-date intelligence," he said. "Can't Yoshikazu find out what's happening?"

"He's going to try, Commander. But right now the whole area is crawling with police."

Ernest crushed out his cigarette. "Dammit, I should have entrusted this one to somebody with experience." He added, with expressive contempt: "Yoshikazu. The nearest Yoshikazu's been to Tokyo is the Japanese take-out on Sunset and Fairfax."

"I trust him," said Nancy, pointedly. "I believe it's better if we simply wait."

Ernest looked at her with a testy expression, and then nodded. "All right. We'll give him an hour. If he doesn't report in by then, we'll go take a look for ourselves. Meanwhile, let's keep the television going. They might have a news bulletin."

Nancy gave a sarcastic salute. "Aye, aye, Commander. Anything you say."

The old commander ignored her. "Why don't you have Kimo fix some breakfast? I'm getting damned hungry. Have him fix some of that *dashimaki tamago*."

Nancy paused for a moment, a slight smile on her face. Then she picked up a small square silver bell from the telephone table and tinkled it. After a while, a young Japanese in a white shirt, white jeans, and a white headband came into the room and stood, waiting.

"The commander has a taste for your eggs this morning, Kemo," said Nancy.

Kemo looked across at the commander, and gave a brief, correct nod of his head. If anyone had nodded to him like that in the Navy, the commander would have had him up on a charge of dumb insolence. But Ernest turned irritably away, parted the slatted bamboo blinds with two fingers, and glared out at the trees of Alta Loma Road until Kemo had gone back to his kitchen.

Nancy asked, "What are you thinking about?"

He cleared his throat. "I was just wondering, for the six

hundredth time, whether this whole damned carnival is ever going to work.''

"You're not paid to wonder. You're paid to *make* it work.''

"Correction," said Ernest. "I'm paid to make *my* part of it work. I can't be responsible for the rest of this ragbag collection of Oriental hoodlums.''

Nancy gave a high, tittering laugh. "Sometimes you're so fierce. You're just like Cary Grant in *Destination Tokyo*.''

"You like that movie?'' asked Ernest, surprised.

"It's one of my favorites. I like especially the scene where the Japanese pilot parachutes into the water and stabs to death the American seaman who is trying to pull him out.''

"You would," growled Ernest. "But I never saw anyone, Jap or American, anything but eternally grateful to be hauled out of the drink. Maybe it just appealed to your cruel sense of humor.''

"I thought you enjoyed my cruel sense of humor.''

"Hmh? Well, there's a time and a place for everything.''

Nancy came toward him, raising her arms. The silk sash of her robe slipped apart, revealing her naked body. She was slim and pale, the color of Japanese provincial pottery, and her breasts were tiny and round with dark nipples that always reminded Ernest of those cups that conjurors use to hide dice. Between the thighs of her slim, short legs, her black pubic hair had been trimmed into the shape of a heart.

Ernest raised his skinny, sinewy arm. "Now, you get away, Nancy. It's too early. We've got this whole operation going snafu, we don't know what in hell's going on, and you know as well as I do that we're going to have Gerard Crowley coming down on top of us by the end of the day like fifteen tons of hot shit. The Huck Finn of Beverly Hills.''

Still smiling, Nancy pressed her bare body up against

him, and reached up to ruffle his silver hair. "You shouldn't call him that," she cooed. "You know he doesn't like it."

"What else should I call him? He's a good old country boy, isn't he, if you want it put politely? Now, let go of me, will you?"

"I wonder what you call *me* behind my back," Nancy whispered. "The Dragon Lady?"

Ernest gripped her waist, and twisted her away from him. But then his towel slipped, and he had to release her to save his decency. She tittered again, that high birdlike laugh, and Ernest's neck went red with irritation.

"I should have slammed the door in your face that very first day I saw you," he growled.

"Oh, no, Mr. Milward," Nancy mocked. "That would never have done. Think of what you would have missed."

Kemo appeared in the doorway with a tray of tea. Nancy drew her robe around herself as he sulkily crossed the room and set the delicate cups and teapot down on the low table.

"*Dashimaki tamago* five minutes," he said, and slip-slopped out again.

Ernest sighed and sat creakily down on the floor. Nancy poured out two cups of tea, and then sat down beside him, cross-legged. Her robe was wide open again, and he couldn't help noticing how the heel of her right foot, drawn up under her, parted the bright pink lips of her silk-haired sex. He closed his eyes and inhaled the strange, smoky smell of the Japanese tea.

"You have no need to fear anything," said Nancy, in a quiet, monotonous voice. "Even if things have gone wrong this morning, nobody can possibly trace the Tengu back to us. You know that as well as I. And it had to be done. It is all part of the preparations."

"There could have been some other way. I told Crowley that." Ernest spoke without opening his eyes.

"Crowley wanted to make sure it really worked. And you can scarcely blame him for that, can you, when you think how much money he's spent?''

"I don't know. In my book, the best tactics are those which are mounted in secrecy. Then—when you can't keep the secrecy up any longer—you keep your enemy guessing by laying smoke, and taking up unexpected and confusing positions.''

"Ernest," said Nancy, in the same quiet voice, "we are not fighting frigates. This is not Midway anymore. And what in the world could be more confusing to everybody than what the Tengu was sent out to do this morning?''

Ernest opened his eyes. He peered into his steaming teacup, and watched the dark leaves floating around and around.

"My God," he said, under his breath. "What a strange assortment of lost individuals we are. What a cause we're fighting for.''

"Is money such a terrible cause?" asked Nancy.

Ernest thought, and then grimaced, and shook his head.

Nancy leaned over toward him and kissed the roughness of his cheek. He kept his eyes open, watching her, so that when she came close he was almost squinting. She sat up straight again, and said, "I have a woodblock print somewhere by Eisen, in the style of *Ukiyo-e shunga* prints. It shows a Yoshiwara courtesan anointing her lover's organ with saké before they make love.''

Ernest stared at her suspiciously. But he made no attempt to ward her off when she reached across and loosened his towel. With one tug, she bared his already-stiffened penis and his salt-and-pepper hair.

She uncrossed her legs and knelt beside him. She kissed him again, on the forehead. She smelled slightly of sweat, but mostly of some musky, deep-noted perfume.

"We have no saké," she said. "But we have something that will please you even more.''

With one small hand, she stroked his penis up and down, so slowly and leisurely that he felt like gripping his hand over hers and forcing her to rub him faster. But this was one of those times when she was completely in control.

He had to wait. He had to obey. If he didn't, the spell, and the experience she had in store for him, would be forfeit at once.

He said hoarsely, "Nancy—"

She raised one immaculately lacquered fingertip to her lips. Then, still slowly stroking him, she reached across to the tea tray and picked up one of the small white towels that were laid beside a dish of salted plums.

Ernest felt his heart slow up, then quicken, like a man struggling to keep himself afloat in a heavy sea.

Nancy took the lid off the teapot and lowered the towel into the boiling-hot tea. She swirled it around for a moment, and then lifted it out. Hot tea ran onto the tray and across the table.

Ernest said, "You're not—"

She smiled. She said nothing. With a deft flick of her wrist, she wound the scalding towel around the hard shaft and swollen head of Ernest's penis, and gave him a brief, vicious squeeze.

He burst out with a short, sharp shout of pain. He felt as if his whole erection was exploding. But then the pain seemed to detonate into something else altogether. More than pain. More than pleasure. A brief dark instant of that terrible feeling which he craved and feared like a drug. It seemed as if his insides were boiling, as if his brain were going to burst into thousands of pieces. But then he ejaculated, and his semen fell across the back of Nancy's wrist.

The world and the room gradually refocused, as if he were adjusting a pair of binoculars. Everything returned, almost absurdly, to normal. Nancy wiped her hands and arms with the towel, and pulled her robe around herself with stylized modesty. Ernest, feeling stunned and sore, reached down and slowly gathered up his towel.

"Now you know the meaning of *Ukiyo*," said Nancy. "The floating world of pleasure."

"I also know the meaning of burned balls," Ernest told her in a coarse whisper. "You're a devil, you know that?

Much more of a devil than any of those damned Tengus.''

"Perhaps,'' said Nancy. "But even devils are sometimes obliged to live a symbiotic life. I need you, and you need me, and perhaps we should offer a prayer that we found each other in the prime of life.''

Ernest, wincing, bent forward and took a salted plum from the tray. He chewed it thoughtfully.

"My prime,'' he said, "was when I was standing on the fantail of the USS *Ferndale*, watching the whole Japanese fleet blazing like the Fourth of July.''

Nancy touched his hand consolingly. "I'm sorry I can't give you an action replay here in my living room. But it won't be long, will it, before I can offer you something very much like it?''

Ernest didn't answer. Kemo came in with the Japanese omelets.

CHAPTER FOUR

Sergeant Skrolnik of the Hollywood police department watched with deep moroseness as two medics from the coroner's office lifted the white-sheeted stretcher from the living room floor and took it unsteadily outside through the broken French doors.

The yellow drapes were stirred by the morning breeze as the medics made their way down the path between the fan palms and the poinsettia, and out to the waiting car. The sloping sidewalk was crowded with blank-faced, shuffling spectators.

The day was glaring and hot, and getting hotter. Skrolnik took off his crumpled linen coat and laid it over the back of a chair.

Detective Pullet came through from the bathroom with a pair of small blue satin panties in a self-sealing plastic bag. He stood beside Skrolnik without saying a word, chewing his lip and looking at the wide brown splatter of blood on the rug. There were even splashes of blood up the walls, in the shape of commas and question marks and exclamation points, as if Sherry Cantor's dying struggle had been punctuated like a comic book. Skrolnik offered Pullet a stick of Wrigley's, but Pullet shook his head.

"More hygienic than chewing your damned mouth," said Skrolnik, without any particular rancor.

Pullet nodded.

Skrolnik said, "There are more damned bacteria in the human mouth than down the damned sewer. If you kiss somebody's ass, instead of their mouth, it seems like you're doing yourself a favor."

Pullet nodded again.

The two detectives were noticeably ill matched. Skrolnik was short and heavily built, with fraying hair like fuse wire, and a bulbous Slavic face. When they were younger, his two sons had taken delight in squeezing his nose as if it were the horn on a Model T, and there were still one or two fellow officers who were sorely tempted to give it a quick *parp* when they passed him in the corridor.

But Skrolnik was known as a hard man. He played by the rules, straight down the line, and he made sure that everybody else did too, whether they were prostitutes or politicians, winos or brother lawmen. The bunco squad still talked about the day he had caught his partner taking money from a drug racketeer, and had taken him into an alley and beaten him so hard that the man had taken three weeks' sick leave with broken ribs.

Skrolnik was 41, a career policeman with twenty years of service behind him. His father, a barber, had always wanted him to be a judge. But Skrolnik had known his own limitations, and he was satisfied for the most part with what he was. He could be oddly romantic at times, and he doted on his plump wife Sarah and their two plump children. He liked beer and television and taking his family out to the International House of Pancakes.

Out on the streets, though, Skrolnik was caustic and unforgiving. He was even readier than most to shoot first and discuss the Dodgers afterward. Three of his partners had died in five years, and Skrolnik was quite certain that he didn't want to end up with his face on the road, watching his lifeblood draining away down the gutter.

Pullet, on the other hand, was nervous and erratic. He was tall and skinny, with a great wave of brown hair, loose wrists, and a way of grimacing so violently that people often thought they might have offended him without knowing how. At college in Philadelphia, Pullet's lecturers had marked him for a better-than-average research chemist. But one silent snowy night, Pullet's kindly parents had died in the wreckage of their 1961 Plymouth on the Burlington Pike, and Pullet had given up science and wandered off like a stray dog.

Pullet had traveled west by bus, and stayed for several months in a boarding house in San Francisco, under an assumed name. He had played chess in cafés and thrown pebbles at the ocean. He had eaten more Chinese food than was good for him. He had developed a passion for girls in very short shorts.

Eventually, one foggy fall, he had driven south to Los Angeles in a rented Pinto and signed up as a policeman. He could never say why; he didn't even understand it himself. But his officers found him enthusiastic and occasionally inspired, and they could almost forgive his twitches and his unpolished shoes. Skrolnik tried not to think about him too much, but liked him in a big-brotherly, scruff-of-the-neck fashion, and frequently invited him back to his suburban house in Santa Monica for burned wieners, half-thawed apple pie, and a tumble around the crabgrass with his two children.

Today, however, neither Skrolnik nor Pullet was happy. They had been urgently called off the Santini investigation—an intriguing high-society poisoning with two equally beautiful sisters as prime suspects—and sent up to this bungalow in Hollywood without any warning that they shouldn't have eaten breakfast first.

Sherry Cantor's body had been strewn all over the living room rug. Her right leg had been hanging, bloodied and awkward, over the back of an armchair. Her stomach had been torn open in a pale gleaming slide of intestines. Somebody had gripped her face in one hand, with fingers pushed deep into the sockets of her eyes, and then wrenched most of the skin and flesh away from her skull.

Worst of all, the whole bungalow had been humming with blowflies.

Pullet had gone out into the garden and vomited up two scrambled eggs, Canadian bacon, and a side order of home fries. Skrolnik had lit up a cheap cigar, and then wished he hadn't.

Pullet asked, "Did you ever see anything like this before? Anything so darned *fierce*?"

Skrolnik shook his head.

Pullet said, "You remember the Edgar Allan Poe story? *The Murders in the Rue Morgue*? The one where they found the girl had been strangled by a large fulvous orangutan of the East Indian Islands?"

Skrolnik stared at him. "An orangutan? You think an orangutan did this?"

Pullet looked embarrassed. "I didn't exactly mean that. But I guess we shouldn't discount the possibility. Orangutans are incredibly strong, and you can teach them to do almost anything."

"So," said Skrolnik, pacing around the perimeter of the dark stain on the rug, "we could be looking for an orangutan."

"I didn't exactly mean that."

Skrolnik pretended he hadn't heard. "How do you think the orangutan got here? I mean, nobody walks in L.A. Did he have his own car? Would a taxi driver remember picking him up? Did he have the right change? Did he come dressed, or did he come *au naturel*? You have to ask yourself these questions, Pullet."

"I have already," said Pullet. "But if you'll let me get a word in edgewise, you'll see what I'm trying to say."

"You're trying to say it could have been an orangutan."

"I'm trying to say it's so darned unusual it could have been anything or anybody. Come on, sergeant, we've both seen ax murders, and kitchen-knife murders, and sex murders. But what kind of a murder is this? It looks like the victim was torn to pieces like a telephone directory."

"Yes, you're right," said Skrolnik, chewing gum.

Pullet took out his handkerchief and fastidiously wiped sweat from his narrow forehead. "Of course I'm right. We have to entertain every possibility that anybody ever thought of, and a few more besides. We have to think *lateral*."

"I prefer to think standing up," Skrolnik told him.

Pullet said, "You make fun of orangutans. Okay, maybe orangutans are funny. I admit they are. But we can't discount them."

"Them? You mean there was more than one?"

"I mean somebody could have brought on orangutan, or a gorilla, or some other kind of wild beast right up the road in a truck. They could have let it loose in the victim's house, and then zowie."

Skrolnik chewed patiently for almost half a minute. "That had entered my mind."

"It had?" asked Pullet, surprised.

"Listen," Skrolnik told him, "we're going to have to tackle this homicide a little different from usual. If we don't, I don't believe we're going to be able to solve it."

"That's just what I've been saying."

"I know, and as a matter of fact you're quite right. But this is the way we're going to play it. You're going to think of all the nuttiest possibilities you can. Gorillas, men from Mars, anything you like. You're going to think how they got in here, how they killed the victim, and why. You're going to let your mind run totally loose."

Pullet pulled a face. "Well, that's okay," he said, sounding reassured. "But what are *you* going to do?"

Skrolnik stared down at the blood. "I'm going to get into it systematically, conventionally, and right by the rulebook. I'm going to go through all the clues, and I'm going to interview all Ms. Cantor's friends and relations and whatever lovers she might have had, and I'm going to build up a solid file of established facts."

Skrolnik paused. "If we're lucky," he said, "and I'm talking about *damned* lucky, the time will come when one of your off-the-wall ideas fits my proven evidence, and the other way around. And that's when we'll find out who did this, and for what reason, and where the hell they are."

Pullet blinked. "There has to be some explanation. Even if it's crazy. Remember that guy they pulled apart between two cars?"

There was a polite knock on the open door. It was a young forensic detective called Starkey. He was wearing a sweat-stained T-shirt and very crumpled white slacks, and he sported a small, dark, wispy mustache, which he had obviously grown to make himself look older than 19.

"Sergeant?" he asked.

"What is it, Starkey? Don't tell me you've found an orangutan's toeprint on the path."

"Pardon, sir?"

"Just tell me what you've found, Starkey."

"Well, sir," said Starkey, "it's the wrought-iron gates."

"What about them?"

"You said they must have been opened up with a crowbar, sir, something like that?"

Skrolnik's eyes narrowed. "What are you telling me, Starkey?"

"Well, sir, there's no evidence of that. No paint missing, no place where the crowbar might have been lodged to give it leverage. And so far we haven't found any crowbar, either."

"So," said Skrolnik, "any opinions?"

"It's kind of hard to say, sir. But it looks like the lock was twisted out of place by hand."

"By *hand*?"

Starkey went pink. "I know it's impossible, sir, but that's the way it looks. I'm not saying that's the only explanation. We won't know until we examine the lock for traces of human skin oils and sweat."

Skrolnik looked at Pullet, and for the first time there was something in Skrolnik's expression that made Pullet feel alarmed. The sergeant licked his fingers, took the gum out of his mouth, and wrapped it up in a crumpled Disneyland ticket.

"By *hand*," he repeated. Both Pullet and Starkey watched as he let the thought sink into his mind. Then he raised his eyes and asked, "But what about the French doors here? How were they forced open?"

"That's harder to say, sergeant. All the glass was broken. But the aluminum frame was bent pretty bad, too, and that may give us some answers."

"You haven't checked it yet?"

"No, sir. I was waiting for you to finish in here."

"You were waiting? A young girl's been torn to pieces, and you were waiting? Starkey—there are thousands of other young girls out there, and I'd hate to think that one single one of them has been put at risk just because you were waiting. Wouldn't you?"

"Yes, sir. I'm sorry, sir. I'll get at it right away, sir."

When Starkey had gone, Pullet said, "You shouldn't ride him too rough, sergeant. He's pretty good, in his own way."

"So are you," said Skrolnik harshly. "But that doesn't mean you can treat a serious homicide like a picnic in the park."

"No, sir."

Skrolnik was silent for a moment. Then he said, "Come on—let's go take another look at those gates."

They pushed their way through the flapping drapes and out into the heat. The faces of the silent crowd rippled in the rising air like hot pink pebbles on a seashore. There were five police cars parked across the street, their red lights ceaselessly revolving. Skrolnik wiped his mouth with the back of his hand.

Sherry Cantor's bungalow was set on the side of a steeply angled hill, so the detectives had to lope down a series of winding concrete steps before they reached the street. A high fence of black-painted wrought iron was set in a low stone wall, ostensibly to keep out intruders. At the foot of the path, the double wrought-iron gates were wide open, and there was a cluster of forensic men around them, with their aluminum attaché cases of fingerprint powder and litmus lying open on the path.

"Okay," said Skrolnik, "let's see that lock."

The forensic men stood aside. They all wore dark sunglasses and short-sleeved tennis shirts, and one of them had a bronzed bald head that gave off a dazzling reflection.

Skrolnik and Pullet bent forward and peered at the gate. The lock was a hefty five-lever deadlock with steel plates bolted onto either side to prevent housebreakers from drilling into the mechanism. It was welded into the decorative wrought-iron frame of the gate on all four sides. In normal conditions, Skrolnik would have pronounced it pretty well unbustable.

But this morning, someone or something had bent it inward, so that its reinforced tongue had been pulled clear of the plate on the opposite gate. Not just an inch or two, which would have been quite sufficient to open the gates without any trouble at all, but almost nine inches.

Skrolnik stood straight and glanced toward the sloping street.

"Now, if this lock had been bent *outward*," he said, "I would have guessed that someone tied a rope around it, and fixed the other end to the back of a car. But *inward*—"

"Like it's been pushed," said Pullet. "Or maybe *punched*."

The forensic men looked at each other in their dark glasses. Skrolnik looked at Pullet. The crowd looked at all of them, like baffled spectators at a tennis tournament, and didn't understand for a moment the strange fear they were feeling.

CHAPTER FIVE

The coroner's report was part nightmare, part fact.

It said that Sherry Cantor had probably died from brain damage following irreparable damage to the central nervous system. Any one of her other injuries, however, could have killed her almost immediately. Her right leg had been severed by twisting, and there were bruise marks on the thigh and calf which indicated clearly that the twisting had been done by a man's hands.

Her abdomen had been torn open from her vagina upward, and again the indications were clear that the tearing had been done by hand. Her facial flesh had been pulled clear of the bone in the same manner. The coroner guessed that most of the disfigurement had been done after Sherry Cantor had died. He hadn't been able to resist adding, "Thank God."

That afternoon, the television stations began to carry reports that a "King Kong Killer" was loose in the Hollywood hills, and that single women should take extra care to lock and bolt their apartments at night. Sergeant Skrolnik spent twenty minutes on the telephone to Bloomington, Indiana, and afterward went across the street to Matty's Cocktail Lounge and swallowed two Old Crows, straight up, no ice.

Pullet said, "I can't help thinking about that darned orangutan."

CHAPTER SIX

He was driving back from his weekly hour with the analyst when he turned the corner and found the whole street jammed with police cars and ambulances and jostling crowds. He slowed down, and a policeman came across and told him: "You can't come up here, mister. Not a hope."

"I live here," he said. "What's going on?"

The policeman laid a hand on the windowsill of his car. "Hold it right here," he ordered uninformatively. He beckoned across the street to a young ginger-haired detective in a splashy red-and-yellow Hawaiian shirt. The detective came over and said: "Who's this?"

"I live here. Number Eleven. Would you mind telling me what's going on here?"

The detective took a notebook out of his hip pocket and thumbed through it. "Number Eleven," he repeated. "That's Jerry Sennett, right?"

"That's right," Jerry told him. "Is something wrong?"

The detective put away the notebook. "I have to ask you some questions. Would you care to pull your car into your driveway? The officer will help you through the crowd. Take it slow, please."

Jerry nudged his eleven-year-old Dodge around the cluster of police cars, with the policeman walking in front of him, one hand custodially resting on the front fender. Then Jerry slowly turned into his sloping driveway, which ran alongside the wrought-iron fence of Sherry Cantor's garden next door, nosed the car right up to the low wall at the top of the gradient, and put on the handbrake. He climbed out. His shirt was wrinkled and sweaty at the back.

The detective in the Hawaiian shirt came up the driveway after him, taking off his Ray-Bans. "Do you mind if we go inside?" he asked. "It would give us more privacy."

"Sure," said Jerry. He led the way up the crazy-paving

steps to the front door of his pale-green bungalow. He
couldn't help glancing toward Sherry Cantor's house as he
took out his key and opened the door. There were four or
five men in short-sleeved shirts and sunglasses poking
around in the garden like golfers who had lost their balls.

"Miss Cantor's okay, I hope?" he asked the detective.

The detective said: "Let's just get inside, please."

Jerry walked through to the living room. It was gloomy
and stuffy because the patterned drapes were drawn, and
the air conditioning had been off all morning to save
energy. Saving energy was one of the things that Jerry
believed in, mainly because it saved him money, too. His
service pension didn't stretch too far these days.

Jerry Sennett was fifty-nine, and on the last day of
November he would turn sixty. But he had one of those
lean, gentle, Gary Cooper faces that had improved with
middle age. His eyes had an experienced, slightly sorrow-
ful look about them, which always impressed the younger
women he met at neighborhood parties. His hair was
peppery and cut short. He stooped a little, and sometimes
his movements seemed hesitant, but that was only because
he was tall and rangy, and prone to knocking highball
glasses off tables if he didn't make a deliberate effort to
coordinate his movements.

His living room reflected his character. There were two
frayed armchairs, a sofa with a wine stain on one cushion, a
big old television set. On the walls were three prints of
Connecticut in the summer. A 1950's style liquor cabinet,
all veneer and pink-tinted mirrors, stood in the far corner.

He asked, "Do you want a drink? I have 7-Up here if
you're not allowed alcohol on duty."

"Thanks," said the detective.

Jerry opened the cabinet and poured himself a Chivas
Regal, and a 7-Up for the detective. "By the way," he
said, coming across with the drinks, "did I ask to see your
badge?"

"Do you want to?"

"Why not?"

The detective took his badge out of his shirt pocket and held it out. Jerry peered at it nearsightedly, and then nodded. "They tell you to check out the freezer repairman, so I guess it's doubly important to check out detectives."

The detective gave a humorless smile. His name was Arthur, and he'd been working under Sergeant Skrolnik long enough to have lost his sense of fun. He said, "Do you mind if we sit down?"

"Go ahead," Jerry told him, and sat down himself, crossing his long legs. He was wearing sandals, and there was a large Band-Aid on the end of his big toe.

"I have to tell you that Ms. Cantor has been the victim of a homicide," said Detective Arthur. "It happened this morning, around eight o'clock."

Jerry stared at him. "Sherry Cantor's *dead*?"

Detective Arthur nodded. "I'm sorry." He didn't sound particularly sorry.

Jerry let out a long breath. "That's terrible. My God, that's absolutely terrible. What happened? It wasn't a shooting, was it? I didn't have any idea."

"Someone broke into her bungalow and attacked her. I guess you'll hear it on the news in any case. She was kind of mauled."

"*Mauled*? What does that mean?"

Detective Arthur doodled with his pencil on the corner of his notebook. "Whoever it was, they must have been pretty crazy. She was just about torn into bits."

Jerry took a drink. His hand was trembling. "Do you have any idea who might have done it? Jesus—how can anyone *do* something like that?"

"We don't know yet. There are plenty of clear prints, stuff like that."

"My God," whispered Jerry. "She was so goddamned pretty."

"Did you know her well?"

Jerry looked up. "Hardly at all. She left for work real early, and I never get out of the sack before nine. But we waved to each other over the fence sometimes, and I talked to her once at a neighborhood party."

"What kind of a girl would you say she was?"

"Hard-working. Career-minded. Who knows—I didn't really think about it. I guess I saw her on television more often than I did in the flesh."

Detective Arthur sniffed. Jerry had turned on the air conditioning, and the flying fluff was getting to his sinus condition. "Did you see any men friends coming and going next door?"

Jerry thought about it, then shook his head. "Nobody special. One or two friends, yes, but it seemed like they came in groups, mostly. I never saw her with one special man."

"What about you? Did she ever invite you next door?"

"Once, to a party, but I couldn't go. My son was down here for his vacation, and I'd promised to take him to a movie. He's here now, as a matter of fact. I have to go pick him up at two-thirty. He's playing baseball with some friends. You know how sociable kids are these days."

Detective Arthur said, "Do you mind if I ask you one or two personal questions, Mr. Sennett?"

"I'm sure you're going to anyway, whether I mind or not."

"You're a widower, right?"

"That's right. My wife died six years ago come September."

"And you're an architect, retired?"

"I still design an occasional gazebo. How come you know so much about me?"

"Neighbors."

"You mean my neighbors know that much about me? My God, even loggias have ears."

Detective Arthur jotted down a couple of notes. Then he said, "I understand you're undergoing analysis."

"Isn't everybody?"

"Can you tell me why?"

Jerry sipped his drink and looked at Detective Arthur

over the rim of his glass.

"You're not trying to prove that I'm crazy, I hope?"

"I have to be thorough, Mr. Sennett."

"Yes," said Jerry, "I guess you do."

He stood up and walked across to the windows. He parted the drapes, so that a bright triangle of sunshine fell across the worn-out rug. "I had a bad experience during the war," he said quietly. "It didn't make me crazy, but it left a lasting impression that sometimes makes me wonder if it's really worth carrying on."

"Suicidal?"

"No, not exactly. Despairing, if you can call it anything."

"Can you give me the name of your analyst?"

"Doctor Grunwald. His office is on El Camino Drive."

"Expensive, huh?" asked Detective Arthur.

Jerry turned away from the window. "With analysis, like everything else, you get what you pay for."

"What sort of progress are you making? I'm going to have to check that out with Doctor Grunwald in any case."

"Progress? Some, I guess. I'm keeping happy. But I don't expect to get over it completely. When you've seen what men are really capable of doing to other men—well, that's an experience it's hard to live with."

Detective Arthur said, "If that's the way you feel, it's probably just as well you didn't see Sherry Cantor this morning."

Jerry finished his drink. "Yes. It probably is."

"You didn't hear anything? Any shouting? Any breaking glass?"

"Not a thing."

"You didn't hear any cars? Maybe an engine revving up?"

"I'm sorry. I woke up at nine, or maybe a few minutes after. I fixed breakfast for David and me, and then I took him straight down to the Whartons' house on Rosewood. You can check the time I got there. After that, I drove over to Beverly Hills."

Detective Arthur read back his notes to himself. Then he said, "I guess that's going to be all for the time being. Sergeant Skrolnik may want to come around and ask you a few more questions, so I'd appreciate it if you stayed around."

"I wasn't planning on going anyplace," said Jerry.

Jerry escorted Detective Arthur to the door. They walked down the driveway together to the sidewalk and stood for a moment by the gate. Most of the police cars had left now, and the crowd had dwindled down to a few teenagers sitting on the curb drinking Coke and a couple of elderly women with nothing better to do.

It was grillingly hot.

Detective Arthur said, "Well, thanks for your help," and walked off.

Jerry stayed where he was for a while, feeling emotionally empty and upset. The men in sunglasses were still in Sherry Cantor's garden, searching the flowering bushes, and occasionally calling out to one another when they thought that might have come across something interesting.

On the low stone wall that Jerry's house shared with Sherry's bungalow, a lizard basked between the two numerals that made up the number 11.

After a few minutes, Jerry climbed back up his driveway and into the house. He went into the living room and fixed himself another whiskey and he stood by the liquor cabinet drinking it and thinking. The air conditioning whirred and gurgled, and he thought, without much conviction, that he ought to have it serviced.

He remembered the day that Rhoda had died, of cancer. It had been as hot as this. He had taken a walk in Hancock Park, and then sat on a bench in the shade of a tree and wondered how everything could be so damned normal, how traffic could come and go, how people could laugh and talk as if nothing had happened. Today, at eight o'clock, Sherry Cantor had died, and yet the sun was still shining, and the supermarkets were still open, and you could still take a drive to the ocean and paddle your toes.

Even *Our Family Jones* would go on without her. The scriptwriters would simply think of some reasonable excuse for writing Lindsay Jones out. They were probably thinking about it right now. She had already vanished, as if she had never been.

Jerry checked his watch. It was almost time to go fetch David. Quite honestly, he would be glad of the company. He sometimes thought that he was spending too much time alone these days. He wondered if David would like to take a drive out to Griffith Park this afternoon, and practice his pitching.

Doctor Grunwald had told him this morning, just as he'd told him dozens of times before, that he ought to stop feeling so guilty about what had happened. It hadn't been *his* fault, after all. But when the sun was shining like this, and when a pretty girl had died, the same way all those others had died, for no apparent reason—well, it was difficult not to feel responsible. Even now, all these years later.

"You didn't *know* what they were going to do," Doctor Grunwald had insisted. "You didn't *know*."

"No," Jerry had told him. "But I didn't question it, either. My sin was that I didn't even question it."

He went into the kitchen. It was narrow, tiled in blue, and it bore all the hallmarks of a man living alone. The catsup bottles were still on the table after this morning's breakfast, the counter beneath the toaster was strewn with crumbs, and the pans that hung underneath the wall cupboards had only been scoured in the middle, where it was essential. He opened the huge refrigerator and took out a pack of bologna sausage. He didn't really feel hungry after hearing about Sherry Cantor, but he knew that he would need the energy if he was going to take David out this afternoon.

He started to build himself a sandwich, with bologna and sliced pickle. He tried not to think about that hot day, thirty-four years ago, when he had first realized the enormity of what he had done. A radio was playing "You Don't Bring Me Flowers" somewhere outside, and he raised his eyes and looked out of the kitchen window toward the street.

A man in a white wide-brimmed hat and a white suit was standing not far away from Jerry's gate. Spanish, maybe, or Mexican. Although the shadow of the midday sun obscured his face, the man appeared to be looking up toward the house. His hands were pushed deeply into the pockets of his coat, and he was smoking a cigarette. There was something about him that was oddly unsettling, as if he were a leftover from some black-and-white private-eye movie of the 1950's.

Jerry watched him for a minute or two. He couldn't understand why the man's appearance disturbed him so much. The man stood quite still, his cigarette between his lips. Then he crossed the street and walked downhill toward the corner of La Sonoma Avenue. In a moment, he was gone.

Jerry looked down at his hands. His fists were clenched so tightly that his knuckles showed white through the tan.

CHAPTER SEVEN

By four that afternoon, Eva Crowley was quite drunk. She was lying on the white leather couch of her tenth-floor apartment in the better part of West Los Angeles, wearing nothing but her black silk underwear, her hair tousled into a fright wig and her face flushed.

A bottle of Tanqueray gin stood on the glass-topped Italian table beside her, and it was two fingers away from empty.

Eva's black maid Matilda had put her head around the door at about two o'clock that afternoon, but Eva had sent her away. This particular pain she wanted to nurse on her own. She wanted no sympathy, no help. She was determined to fight for Gerard, and she was determined to win him back. But just for a few self-indulgent hours, she needed to wallow in her own sense of loss.

She sat up. Her head felt like a hot-air balloon. All around her, the stylish living room tilted and swayed. She picked up the gin bottle, frowned at it, and then emptied the last dregs into her lipstick-smeared highball glass. She wished she didn't feel so suffocated and sick.

After this morning's row, the opulent décor of their apartment seemed even colder than ever. She had always thought Gerard's taste was sterile. He chose tables made of chrome and gray smoked glass, tapestries woven in bland abstract patterns, and chairs upholstered in neutral-colored leather. There was no emotional commitment in Gerard's surroundings. No warmth. He was an empty man with an empty mind.

She wondered, as she swallowed the oily-smelling gin, why she loved him at all. She only knew that she did, and that she didn't want to lose him. To lose Gerard would mean the loss of her dignity, her femininity, and her pride.

To lose Gerard would mean that her mother had been right all along, that Eva was "born to be unlovable."

She climbed unsteadily to her feet and balanced her way across the polished parquet floor to the liquor cabinet. There didn't seem to be very much left. A bottle of tequila. A bottle of strega. Quarter of a bottle of Jack Daniel's. Maybe she ought to mix herself a combined cocktail out of all of them and drink herself into total unconsciousness.

She was just trying to focus her eyes and her brain when there was a soft chime at the door. She stood up straight, one hand on the cabinet for support. It must be the twins, back from school. She stared at her Cartier wristwatch.

They were at least twenty minutes early.

"Coming!" she said, in a husky, high-pitched voice. She made her way out into the cream-painted hall with its bonsai plants and Spanish rugs, and unlocked the safety chain on the door.

"You're early," she said, opening the door and turning back into the hall. "How did you—"

She paused. Something was wrong. It wasn't the twins at all. Standing in the cool darkness of the hall was a swarthy, smartly dressed man in a white suit and striped maroon tie. He took off his hat and inclined his head slightly. He didn't attempt to come in.

"You must be Mrs. Crowley," he said, in a cultured South American accent. He emphasized *Mrs.* as if he was already well acquainted with *Mr.* Crowley. "I'm sorry if I—"

Eva clutched her hands over her breasts. Until the man had apologized, she'd forgotten that she was wearing nothing but a black transparent bra, black panties, and a black garterbelt and stockings. Her face felt suddenly hot, and she said, flustered: "Please—please wait there—I'll just get my robe—"

"Of course," smiled the man. But he didn't avert his eyes.

She retreated into the bedroom, colliding with the doorframe in her drunkenness and bruising her upper arm. She found her robe on the floor where she had left it that morning and struggled into it. She tried to remember where she had taken off her gray suit, but she couldn't. She couldn't even remember driving back from Gerard's office.

There were only fragments. Pushing past Francesca. Slamming the office door. Standing in the crowded elevator trying not to sob out loud.

She belted her robe and went back to the front door. The man was still politely waiting there, his hat in his hand, a small enigmatic smile on his face. He was short and lightly built, and the shoes that peeped out from

under his unfashionably wide-bottomed pants were made
of white kid, and as small as a tightrope walker's. His hair
was oiled back into curls over his ears, and he wore a thin
clipped mustache.

"Your husband isn't here?" he asked her.

"Gerard? He doesn't usually get back until late. Sometimes he doesn't get back at all."

"He hasn't called you? We had an appointment, you
see. I was supposed to meet him at the office, but when I
went there, his secretary told me that he'd already left for
the day. I thought he might have come home."

Eva shook her head. There was an awkward pause.

"Do you think there's any point in my waiting for
him?" asked the man, raising his hat as if he wanted to
hang it up somewhere.

"Well," said Eva, "I don't know. He may be coming
back. He may not. He hasn't told me."

"I'm very impertinent," said the man. "Here I am
pushing myself on you like this, and I haven't even introduced myself." He inclined his head once again, like a
respectable parrot. "My name is Esmeralda. I am a
business acquaintance of Mr. Crowley. We are almost
friends."

"Almost?" asked Eva.

The man smiled. "Nobody in business can really afford
to have friends. Friends are a luxury."

Eva swayed a little. "Well, Mr. Esmeralda, since you're
almost a friend of Gerard's, I guess it wouldn't do any
harm to invite you in."

"You don't have to. I may be a robber. Or a rapist."

Eva took a deep breath. "The way I feel right now, Mr.
Esmeralda, that'll be your lookout. Please come in."

She led the way into the living room, and Mr. Esmeralda
closed the front door behind him. He hesitated in the hall
for a moment, and then hung his white hat on top of
Gerard's golf clubs. He followed Eva into the pale Italian-
styled room, shooting his startlingly white cuffs and
adjusting his necktie. Eva clumsily collected her empty gin

bottle and smeary glass, but Mr. Esmeralda seemed to take that in his stride.

"Would you care for a cocktail?" asked Eva, blurrily. "I'm afraid I only have tequila or strega. Or maybe some bourbon, if you feel like it."

"I don't drink, as a rule," smiled Mr. Esmeralda. He paced over to the window with mesmerically precise steps and stood for a while admiring the Crowleys' two-thousand-dollar-a-month view of the Rancho golf courses. "You have a pleasant apartment here."

"Thank you," said Eva, sitting on the far end of the couch and tugging her wrap around her knees. "Actually, it's all Gerard's taste, not mine." She paused. "If I'd had my way, we would have furnished it in elegant Colonial."

Mr. Esmeralda smiled briefly. His smiles came and went like shadows on a cloudy day.

"I feel that you're not happy with the world today," he told her.

She frowned at him. Then she ran her hand through her hair. "I don't know what makes you feel that. Happiness is only relative, after all. At least I have a roof over my head, and enough to eat. And nearly enough to drink."

"You mustn't think that I'm being inquisitive," said Mr. Esmeralda.

Eva gave a dismisive wave of her hand. "I don't mind. I don't even know why I went to all the trouble of getting drunk. It hasn't made anything better, and it hasn't made anything worse. Getting drunk, Mr. Esmeralda, is only a way of deferring the pain until tomorrow."

Mr. Esmeralda turned and faced her. "No pain can be deferred without paying interest, Mrs. Crowley. Tomorrow, you will pay for these hours of forgetfulness with your hangover. Life is a business, like any other."

Eva thought about that, and then nodded. "Some business," she said, not particularly to her unexpected guest. Not even to herself.

There was another pause. Mr. Esmeralda walked across the living room, his tiny shoes clicking on the floor. He picked up a nautilus shell from a side table, and turned it over and over in his hands.

"Did you know something?" he asked quietly. "The first sailors who found these shells said that if you put your ear against them, you would hear the cries of every sailor who had ever drowned."

He inclined his head toward the open shell and listened. Then he set it down on the table again.

"Did you hear anything?" asked Eva.

He shook his head. "Only the sound of a woman in distress."

Eva looked away. "It's really not very interesting, you know."

"Your husband?"

She gave a humorless laugh, which turned into a cough. "Of course. What other kind of problems do women of my age and background ever have? We're too trusting to take lovers. We're certainly too conventional to fall in love with other women. Or dogs. Or whatever."

Mr. Esmeralda nodded. "You wait patiently at home, hoping that your spouses will have sufficient loyalty to keep away from pretty young receptionists."

Eva stared at him. "You know about Francesca?"

"Of course. I have taken your husband and Francesca to dinner on several occasions."

"I don't believe it," Eva whispered.

"Oh, I'm afraid it's true," Mr. Esmeralda told her. "But you don't have very much to fear. At the end of the day, Francesca is far more interested in disco music and fashionable clothes than she is in your husband. In time, their relationship will collapse of its own accord."

Eva licked her lips nervously. Mr. Esmeralda paced around the couch, this way and that, around and around, and he kept appearing on one side or the other, and disappearing again, as if there were three of him, three dapper triplets, all with maroon ties.

"Are you in tobacco, Mr. Esmeralda?" asked Eva, in a much higher voice than she'd meant to.

"I was once," said Mr. Esmeralda. "But times change, you know how it is. These days, I'm in this and that."

"I see," said Eva faintly. "Mr. Esmeralda—"

"Yes?"

"Well, I hope you don't mind, but—would you care to sit down? You're making me rather confused. Rather giddy."

Mr. Esmeralda stopped pacing. Then he said: "My dear Mrs. Crowley, of course," and sat down on the opposite end of the couch with all the grace of a settling butterfly. He laced his fingers together and smiled at her. He wore no rings.

"Gerard has never mentioned you," said Eva.

"No," said Mr. Esmeralda, "I don't suppose he has."

"You're very—"

She stopped what she was saying. She wasn't at all sure what she had been going to say anyway. She wanted to tell Mr. Esmeralda that she thought he was very soigné, very together, and really very clean. She had never seen such clean cuffs and fingernails before. But you couldn't say that to a total stranger.

Mr. Esmeralda said, "Go on," coaxingly, but she shook her head.

"Well," he said, leaning back on the cushions of the couch, "whatever you were going to say, it couldn't possibly have affected the way I think about you."

"About me? You scarcely know me."

"I know you, my dear Mrs. Crowley, as well as any unhappy woman needs to be known. In fact, my own view is that unhappy women hardly need to be known at all. Only two things matter. Their unhappiness, and their beauty. You have both."

She looked toward the liquor cabinet. She bit her lip. Then she looked back at Mr. Esmeralda.

"Are you trying to make a pass?" she asked him.

He smiled silently for a moment, and then he let out a sharp little bark of laughter.

"I don't see what's so funny," she said. She could hear

how much her voice was slurring.

"Nothing is funny," said Mr. Esmeralda. "And then again, everything is funny. Yes, I am trying to make a pass."

She blinked at him. "Why?"

"*Why*? That is one question that no woman has ever asked me before. My dear Mrs. Crowley, don't you *know* why?"

"Perhaps. But I want to hear you say it."

"Then I shall. I am trying to make a pass at you because you are a delicate, beautiful woman. You are sad, and you are drunk. Your husband has temporarily deserted you for a receptionist with a noticeable bust but no IQ, and therefore you are prey to any man who makes you feel attractive and confident once again."

Eva pressed the heels of her hands against her forehead. Mr. Esmeralda sat with his legs neatly crossed, watching her.

Eva said, "You must think I'm a fool."

He shook his head. "Not at all. There are only two fools in this ménage. Your husband, for rejecting you; and me, for laying my heart so openly on the line. I risk frightening you away. I know that. But if I don't make love to you now—who knows, your husband may decide to come back tomorrow, and my chance will be gone."

"You want to make love to me *now*?"

"I'm rushing you?"

She threw her head back and tried to laugh, but all that came out was a strangled, high-pitched *hih-hih-hih*. She turned to him, her eyes watering and her hand pressed over her mouth.

"I amuse you?" Mr. Esmeralda asked.

"No," she said. "No, you don't amuse me."

"You laughed," he pointed out.

"Yes." Then, more softly, "Yes."

She stood up. "I laughed because you frighten me."

He watched her carefully. "I told you I might be a robber," he said. "Or a rapist."

She didn't answer. She couldn't understand the feelings rising inside her stomach. What was she doing here? Where was this place, with its intolerable afternoon light and its pale furnishings?

She said, without looking at him, "The twins will be home in a quarter of an hour."

He didn't move. His eyes were liquid and dark; the eyes of a conjuror, or a fairground hypnotist.

"We can't," she whispered hoarsely. "There isn't time."

Mr. Esmeralda thought about that for a while, and then nodded. Eva crossed the room and sat down opposite him, on a natural-colored canvas chair with X-shaped chrome legs. She hated the chair, but somehow her discomfort in it made her feel better. More real.

She said, "I need to know who you are."

He lifted an eyebrow.

"I don't mean that's a *prerequisite*," she added, hurrying her words. "I mean—I'm not saying that if I know who you are, if you tell me—that I'll—"

Mr. Esmeralda nodded again. "I understand."

She breathed out. She could smell the gin on her own breath. "I'm afraid you've caught me at a bad time," she said. She hated the sound of apology in her voice. After all, this was her apartment. This was her marriage. Her pain. But somehow Mr. Esmeralda was the kind of man who invited apologies. He was so calm, so self-possessed, that she couldn't imagine him ever having done anything wrong. Not socially, anyway.

Even his seduction had been a model of politeness.

They waited in silence. The apartment began to fade as the afternoon light faded. They could even hear the sound of the elevators rising and falling through the building.

Eventually Mr. Esmeralda stood up. He said, "You will allow me to call you, then? One evening, when your husband is engaged with work."

"You can call, yes," she said, her mouth dry.

"Perhaps dinner, a few cocktails. Dancing."

"Perhaps."

He smiled. The same smile. He bowed his head.

"I shall look forward to it, my dear Mrs. Crowley, in the same way that the night sky looks forward to the lighting up of the stars."

She lowered her eyes. "That's the first sham sentiment you've uttered."

"Yes," he agreed. "But I am a Colombian, and all Colombians are permitted one sham sentiment per day."

She said nothing more. He waited a while longer, and then left. His shoes clicked on the floor. He closed the apartment door behind him.

She sat in the X-legged chair, staring unblinkingly at the opposite wall and wondering if this was the way all marriages ended.

CHAPTER EIGHT

Sergeant Skrolnik pressed the doorbell for the third time. Beside him, Detective Arthur took out a Kleenex that was crumpled into a tiny, tattered ball and wiped his nose. Skrolnik said, "If you could run like your nose, Irving, you'd catch every murderer in town."

Detective Arthur sniffed and didn't answer. There was flowering jasmine tangled around the doorway of this shabby three-story building on Franklin Avenue, and flowering jasmine always got to his sinus. He wished somebody would hurry up and open the door so that he could ask for a fresh Kleenex. With almost masochistic regularity, he forgot to bring along a pack of his own.

"It doesn't look like there's anyone here," said Skrolnik, stepping back onto the cracked concrete path and shading his eyes so that he could peer up at the second-floor windows. "Can you make it back here this afternoon on your own? I have a briefing with Captain Martin."

Detective Arthur shrugged okay and sniffed again, more conclusively this time.

Skrolnik was turning to leave when a downstairs window opened, and a withered old man looked out. "Did you want something?" he asked in a tremulous voice.

Skrolnik turned back and stared at him. "No, no. I was just testing your response to your doorbell. It's a new city ordinance, you mustn't respond to your doorbell for at least ten minutes. But I'm glad to say you've passed with flying colors."

"Doorbell?" queried the old man. "That doorbell hasn't worked in fifteen years. You want anybody, you have to throw stones at the winders."

Skrolnik looked at Detective Arthur, and then back at the old man. "How foolish of me. I didn't realize. Is Mack Holt home?"

"Sure. He's on nights this week. He's probably sleeping."

"Should I throw a stone at his window, or might you come and open this door for me?"

"Maybe he doesn't want to see you."

"Maybe he doesn't have any choice," said Skrolnik, and produced his badge. The old man screwed up his eyes so that he could make out what it was, and then said: "Oh."

It took another two or three minutes before he came shuffling to the door to let them in. Skrolnik said: "Thanks. If you ever need us cops for any reason, I hope we come just as quick."

"It's upstairs," said the old man, oblivious to Skrolnik's sarcasm.

The hallway was dim, and smelled of Lysol and cheap tile polish. The walls were roughly plastered and painted an unpleasant shade of orange. Someone had penciled by the lightswitch: "Sherry: L called, wants to know if you can call back." It was an epitaph to Sherry Cantor's past. It would probably still be there when they tore the building down.

Skrolnik led the way up the noisy stairs. He crossed the landing and knocked loudly on the door numbered 2. Almost immediately, he knocked again. The old man waited downstairs in the hallway. Detective Arthur said, "Beat it."

There was a sound of bolts being shot back. A thin face appeared at the door, with curly blond hair and a slightly twisted nose. Two blue-gray eyes. A lean, brown twenty-five-year-old torso. Bright-green underpants.

"What do you want?"

Skrolnik pushed the door wide open and stepped into the room. It was dark, with all the drapes drawn tight, and smelled of stale marijuana and *frijoles refritos*. Mack Holt said tensely, "What is this? What do you want?"

Skrolnik flipped open his wallet and showed his badge to Mack Holt without even looking at him. His eyes flicked around the room, taking in the sagging basketwork chairs, the stacks of paperback books and magazines, the cut-price Japanese stereo, the posters for rock concerts and bull-fights.

"Is there anybody else here?" asked Skrolnik, nodding toward the half-open bedroom door.

"A friend."

"Go take a look," Skrolnik told Detective Arthur.

Mack Holt said, "Hey, now, hold on there. She's not dressed yet."

"Keep your hands over yours eyes," Skrolnik instructed Detective Arthur. "And no peeking."

Mack asked, "Listen—what is this? Do you have a warrant?"

"A warrant for what?"

"A search warrant. You can't search this place without a warrant."

"Who's searching?"

Skrolnik crossed the room. He touched the corner of the

bandanna that had been hung around the lampshade. He drew it toward him and sniffed it, then let it swing back. "As a matter of scientific fact," he said, "you'll find that Aramis works better than Carven when it comes to masking the smell of grass."

Mack said, "What are you, an aftershave salesman?"

Detective Arthur rapped at the bedroom door. A girl's voice called out, "Mack?"

"It's the heat," Mack called back. Then he looked at Skrolnik's stony expression and added, almost inaudibly, "The police."

"You'll have to wait a moment," said the girl. Skrolnik didn't take his eyes off Mack. Detective Arthur hesitated at the bedroom door.

Mack said quietly, "I suppose you've come about Sherry."

"That's right," nodded Skrolnik. "You were a friend of hers, weren't you?"

"More than a friend. She lived here."

Skrolnik gave the room an exaggerated reappraisal. "She sure took a step up when she moved out."

"Maybe," said Mack defensively.

Skrolnik walked around the room. "When did she leave?"

"Right after they gave her that part in *Our Family Jones*. What was that? Eighteen months ago. Eighteen, nineteen months."

"You've seen her since?"

"Once or twice."

Skrolnik searched systematically through the pockets of his doubleknit coat until he found a stick of gum. He peeled off the wrapper, folded the stick into his mouth, and then said offhandedly, "they tell me you were jealous of her."

"Jealous? What's that supposed to mean?"

"You were two out-of-work actors. She got a plum part and you didn't. Don't tell me that didn't make you jealous."

"I was pleased for her."

"So pleased that she packed her bags and cut out?"

Mack ran his fingers through his tangled blond curls. "All right," he admitted, "I was jealous. What does that prove?"

"You tell me."

Mack folded his arms across his bare chest. Then he raised a finger and said incredulously, "You're not trying to say that *I* killed her?"

Skrolnik stared at him with contempt. "Whoever killed Sherry Cantor was pretty well superhuman. I don't think you're quite in his league. Let's say it's the difference between Arnold Schwarzenegger and Woody Allen."

Mack lowered his head. "Yes," he said. "I heard about it on the news."

"Can you tell me where you were yesterday morning, around eight o'clock?"

The bedroom door opened wider, and Detective Arthur said, "Come on, miss. You don't have to be shy."

"I was here, in bed," said Mack. "Olive will tell you."

Skrolnik raised an eyebrow. Olive was a glittering, glossy-looking black girl, and she stalked into the living room with her dreadlocks shaking and her head held defiantly erect. She was wrapped in a thin flowered-silk sarong which barely concealed her enormous bouncing breasts. She was pretty in a wide-eyed, 1960's Tamla-Motown kind of way, and there were jingling gold bells around her left ankle. She paused, with her hand on her hip, and said, "That's right. He was here, all right."

Skrolnik said, "The poorer the nabes, the fancier the domestic help. What's your name, miss?"

"It's Mrs.," said the black girl. "Mrs. Robin T. Nesmith, Jr. But you can call me Mrs. Nesmith."

"Where's Mr. Nesmith? Hiding under the comforter?"

"Mr. Nesmith is in Honolulu, with the U.S. Navy."

"And this is the thanks he gets, for serving his country?"

"I don't see that it's any of your business," said Olive,

"but Mr. Nesmith knows about it. He reckons it's better the devil you know."

Skrolnik chewed thoughtfully. "Even when the devil's a white devil?"

"Mr. Nesmith is white, too."

"I see. Can anyone else substantiate your whereabouts?"

Mack put his arm around Olive and drew her closer. He said, "A couple of friends called on the telephone just before eight. But that's all."

"Give Detective Arthur their names, will you?" asked Skrolnik.

Detective Arthur took out his notebook and his ballpoint, while Skrolnik turned his back on them and went to investigate the bedroom. There was a wide, sagging bed covered by stained red satin sheets. The room smelled of perfume and sex, and a blue tin ashtray beside the bed exuded its own peculiar fragrance. The walls were papered with faded floribunda roses.

Skrolnik stood there for a while, chewing and thinking. In one corner of the room, on the floor, were a paperback edition of H. R. Haldeman's *The Ends of Power* and a tiny pair of transparent purple panties.

The incongruity of human life, he thought.

He came back into the living room. Olive was sitting on one of the basketwork chairs, and Mack was stepping into a pair of newish Levi's. The jeans were so tight that he had difficulty zipping them up over his cock. Skrolnik said, "Need a shoehorn?"

Mack picked up a T-shirt with *Snoqualmie National Forest* printed on it. "You must be the life and soul of the squadroom."

"Mr. Holt," Skrolnik retorted, "if you saw people torn apart the way that Sherry Cantor was torn apart, then you'd understand just what it is that makes me talk the way I do. After despair, there's nothing left but humor."

Without raising his eyes, Mack asked, "Was she hurt? I mean, do you think she felt anything?"

Olive reached up and held his hand. Skrolnik said, "We don't know."

"I guess you're going to ask me if I knew anyone who could have done something like that," Mack told him. "But I didn't before, and I still don't. She used to get to people sometimes. She used to get to me. But that was only because life seemed so easy for her. There she was, fresh out of Indiana and raw as an onion, and success fell straight in her lap. That was what finished us, in the end, Sherry and me. And what made it worst of all, she was so nice about it. She used to say that success wouldn't change her, and it damn well didn't. She was just so damn *nice*."

"That's what I thought," Skrolnik said, mostly to himself. "And that's what makes it look like this homicide wasn't premeditated. Not for any personal reason, anyhow."

Olive kept hold of Mack's hand and stroked the back of it with her long, dusky fingers. "Do you think you're going to catch the guy who did it?" she asked Skrolnik.

Skrolnik grimaced.

Detective Arthur said, "Where are you working now, Mr. Holt? I have you down as a car-parking jockey at the Old Sonora Restaurant."

"I'm still there," Mack nodded. "The food's better than most."

"Maybe we'll drop by," said Skrolnik. "Meanwhile, I don't want you to leave the city."

Mack looked up. "Okay," he said. Then, hesitantly: "Can you tell me what actually happened? The television news didn't go into a whole lot of detail. Was it really that awful?"

"Mr. Holt," said Skrolnik patiently, "did you love Sherry Cantor?"

"Yes, sir, I did."

Skrolnik put on his hat. "In that case, you'll prefer it if I don't tell you. As it says in the Good Book: 'In much wisdom is much grief: and he that increaseth knowledge increaseth sorrow.' "

Mack stared at him. "You surprise me."

"I surprise myself," said Skrolnik, and pushed Detective Arthur out of the living room ahead of him. At the door, he turned around and said, "I want you to think about Sherry for the next few days. Yes, I'm sorry, Mrs. Robin T. Nesmith, Jr., but it's going to be necessary. I want you to think about every possible angle of what she was, all the people she knew, and everything she said. I want you to sieve through your memory, Mr. Holt, because you're the the only person who can. And if you think of anything unusual, anything that jars, anything that seems out of place, then give me a call."

Skrolnik took a card out of his breast pocket and tucked it in the crevice behind the lightswitch.

"So long," he said. "Pleasant dreams."

He closed the door behind him, and Mack and Olive stayed quite still, like a tableau in a shabby small-town museum, as the detectives' footsteps clattered down the stairs. The front door slammed, and after a while they heard the whinny of a car starter. Mack coughed.

Olive stood up. "Do you want me to go?" she asked Mack in a gentle voice.

He shook his head. "Not if you can stand a little mourning."

She smiled sadly. "I lost my first man in Vietnam. There's nothing you can teach me about mourning."

"You didn't tell me about that."

"There wasn't no need. I don't know nothing about you, and you don't know nothing about me, and that was the way we were meant to be."

Mack laid his hand on her bare shoulder, and leaned forward and kissed her. "You're very good for me. You know that?"

"Yes," she smiled, her eyes glittering.

He was silent for a moment. Then he said, "I guess I'll go out. Maybe get some beer and some food. We could have Dick and Lois around later, if you like."

"Come to bed first," she said. Her beaded black hair

rattled as she shook her head.

"I just got up."

"This is therapy."

"What kind of therapy?"

"Forget-your-sadness therapy. Come on."

She took his wrist and led him back into the bedroom. He stood silent while she tugged his Snoqualmie T-shirt over his head and then unzippered his Levi's. She knelt on the bedroom floor and pulled the pants down his legs.

He felt as if he couldn't catch his breath; the way you feel in a high wind. Olive's perfume was strong and flowery, and there was something about the way her long fingernails grazed over his skin that he found intensely arousing. She guided him toward the bed and gently pushed him backward onto the red satin sheet. He looked up at her, and the muted flare of the sun that shone through the blind behind her made her appear darker and more mysterious than ever.

He wondered if her first lover had been black or white. He wondered how he had died.

She unwrapped her sarong. It fell to the floor, pure silk, silent as a shadow. The soft sunlight gleamed on the brown skin of her impossibly huge breasts, nippled with black. She climbed onto the bed, and her breasts swayed.

"You have to forget everything," she whispered. He wasn't sure if her voice was far or near. The room was dim and warm and funky from their night of love. He felt her tongue run along the sole of his foot, and her teeth nip at his heel. Then she began to lick and kiss him all the way up the inside of his left leg, pausing every now and then to trace with the tip of her tongue a more elaborate pattern, like the shape of a butterfly, or a star. He had thought that last night was enough, but now he could feel himself hardening again, and a deep pulse between his legs.

Olive's searching mouth at last reached his thigh, and then her wet tongue was burrowing between the cheeks of his ass and licking around his tightened balls. He let out a short, tight breath.

Thoughts of Sherry still crowded his mind. Sherry standing in that same bedroom doorway. Sherry lying asleep on that pillow beside him. The unhappiness in him began to overwhelm him, and he could feel himself soften.

But to Olive, achieving this moment of oblivion was vital. Mack had to know that he could turn to her for forgetfulness when his sadness for Sherry was too much to bear. He had to know that she could blot out his grief.

She held him in her hand, her long fingernails gently digging into the flesh of his penis, and she licked his shaft until it stiffened again. Then she kissed and nuzzled the head with her lips, and probed the salty, secret crevice. She felt his thigh muscles tense up, heard him groan.

Olive took him deep into her mouth. Dark lips enclosed white flesh. Her head moved up and down, faster and faster, until her dreadlocks sounded like maracas. Her mind was a jumble of thoughts. Her eyes were tight closed. All she knew was that she wanted to suck out of him all the love she could. She felt his strong, thin fingers clutching at her breast, pulling at her nipple.

There was a long minute of tension. The world had closed its doors to memory, to Sherry, to Hollywood, to everything but one rising and irresistible sensation.

Then Mack said, "Ah," quite softly, and flooded Olive's mouth.

Olive, after a short while, sat up. Her lips shone in the shaded bedroom sun. "How was it?" she asked him, and she wasn't surprised to see tears in his eyes.

CHAPTER NINE

If his wife Nora hadn't given him sliced onion in his liverwurst sandwiches that morning, patrolman Ed Russo wouldn't have died. But the onion had given him heartburn, and he asked his partner Phil Massey to pull the car into the curb at the intersection of Hollywood and Highland so that he could buy himself a pack of Rolaids.

It was four minutes after eleven. Sergeant Skrolnik was just leaving Mack Holt's apartment building on Franklin Avenue. Olive Nesmith was just saying: "Forget-your-sadness therapy. Come on." In West Los Angeles Mrs. Eva Crowley was staring at her face in the mirror and trying to keep herself from throwing up, and Sherry Cantor had been dead for slightly more than twenty-seven hours.

Ed Russo, a slim, soft-spoken man with a heavy brown mustache, walked through the cold air-conditioned drugstore until he found the shelves he wanted. He bought two packs of Rolaids, one to keep in his locker and one for the car. He wouldn't need either of them.

The strawberry-rinsed woman behind the pharmaceutical counter said, "How are you doing?"

Russo held up the Rolaids. "My wife gave me onions today. I love onions, but onions sure hate me."

"Doesn't anybody or anything like cops?" asked the woman. "Even onions?"

Russo smiled, although the gripes in his stomach had twisted up his sense of humor as well. He walked back toward the checkout, juggling the indigestion tablets in his hand.

Through the ad-plastered window of the drugstore, Russo had a view of the traffic signals at the intersection outside. He watched a souped-up Dodge Charger brake at the line as the lights on Hollywood changed to red. The Charger was a pretty slick job, in crimson metallic-flake paint with chromed exhausts. Ed Russo could have done with a car like that himself.

He was only twenty-four, and he still hankered after beach parties and custom cars and big waves at Malibu. But somehow, after he'd married Nora, he'd settled down to a routine of brown-bag lunches, garage auctions, drive-in movies, and washing the car on the weekend. In subtle, unnoticeable stages, in ways that Russo could never quite recall, Nora had altered in three years of married life from a skinny, suntanned, nineteen-year-old nymphet, pretty and shy, into a talkative, opinionated, intolerant young housewife in a lurex headscarf and rollers, organizer of the local church social club, the La Mirada PTA, and a never-ending ten-ring circus of coffee-and-cake mornings, baby showers, and lectures by white-haired evangelists who stank of tobacco.

When Russo looked at Nora over the battlements of Kellogg's Corn Flakes and Post Toasties in the morning, he sometimes wondered if God was punishing him for some sin he couldn't remember committing.

Russo's change clattered into the tray of the change-maker. But as he reached for it, a squittering sound of tires made him look back out of the drugstore window. A dark blue van was driving straight through the red light, swerving to avoid a white Lincoln, and then turning north up Highland Avenue in a cloud of burned rubber.

Russo grabbed his change, pocketed his Rolaids, and ran for the sidewalk. He wrenched open the police car door and yelled to Phil Massey, "Let's get going!"

Their siren whooped as they U-turned on Hollywood, bucking on their suspension. Then they squealed left on Highland, and the V-8 motor roared.

"Did you see that?" asked Massey. He was young and gingery, with a face splattered with freckles. "He could've killed somebody, coming round that corner like that."

"There he is," said Russo.

The van was speeding round the S-curve by the Hughes supermarket. It shot the lights and kept on north toward the Hollywood Freeway, swaying from one side to the other as it overtook cars, trucks, and a northbound bus.

The police siren warbled and howled as Russo and Massey chased after it. They flashed through light, shadow, flickering sunshine.

Weaving through the traffic, the van sped ahead of them onto the glaring concrete of the freeway. But Massey put his foot flat down, and as they sped through the Hollywood hills, they gradually began to overtake the van, coming up on its left side.

Russo wound down his window and unfastened his holster. Then he put his arm out the window and flagged the van down, pointing to the hard shoulder.

At first, the van driver hesitated. But then Russo pointed to the hard shoulder again, fiercely, and the van driver put on his right-hand indicator and began to slow down. Massey slowed the police car, too, and nosed in behind the van as it pulled off the freeway and gradually came to a stop. Through his loudspeaker, Russo ordered: *"Get out of the van slowly and put your hands on the side panels where we can see them."*

Then he said to Massey, "Run a check on his plate, will you?" It was a Florida license. "And see if the Highway Patrol has any backup around."

Russo climbed out of the car and walked toward the van, putting on his cap. It was hot and dusty on the freeway, and he unhooked his sunglasses from his uniform pocket and put them on. The van driver was Japanese. He was standing beside his vehicle with his hands pressed against the dark-blue paneling, and he was watching Russo guardedly.

Russo walked around him and glanced in the driving compartment. It looked empty, except for a tartan holdall with a vacuum flask sticking out of it. He turned back to the driver. Five foot five or six. Late thirties. Dressed in a black satin windbreaker and cheap gray slacks. Cropped black hair, and a slight white scar on the left eyebrow.

Russo said, "Take out your license with one hand. Slowly. And hand it over."

The Japanese reached cautiously into his windbreaker

pocket and took out his license. He held it out, six inches from Russo's outstretched hand. Russo snatched it and stared intently at the Japanese for a moment before he opened it.

"Eric Yoshikazu? Of Emelita Street, Van Nuys?" asked Russo.

The Japanese nodded.

Russo inspected the license closely, and then folded it. "I'm going to have to book you for a serious traffic offense. And for failing to stop when requested to do so by a police officer."

Yoshikazu shrugged.

"You have anything to say about that?" asked Russo.

"I see my lawyer," said Yoshikazu.

Russo took out his citation book. "You can see as many lawyers as you like. That's your right. But it doesn't alter the fact that you ran a red light on Hollywood Boulevard and made an illegal turn and endangered the lives of yourself and innocent people."

"I don't say nothing," said Yoshikazu.

"That's your right," said Russo. He paced round the van and stood at the back for a while, noting down the license number in his book. Yoshikazu watched him all the time. The freeway traffic swished past them, and the air was sparkling with sunlight and grit and fumes.

Russo lifted his pencil and pointed toward the back of the van. "What you got inside there, Mr. Yoshikazu?"

Yoshikazu looked at Russo for a long time. "I don't carry nothing," he said at last.

"Your rear end is well down," commented Russo.

"I get fixed."

"Supposing it doesn't need fixing, Mr. Yoshikazu? Supposing you're carrying something heavy in the back of this van?"

"I don't carry nothing."

"Well, why don't you open it up and let's take a look?"

Yoshikazu thought about that. He wiped sweat away from his upper lip with the back of his hand. "I don't think I want to open," he said.

Russo put away his pencil. "Mr. Yoshikazu, I have the legal right to demand that you open your van. If you fail to do so, then I'm going to arrest you, and your van will be impounded."

"That's not possible," said Yoshikazu. "This van is not mine. I have no entitlement to open."

Russo adjusted his cap. The headband was sweaty. "If you don't open up this van, Mr. Yoshikazu, then I'm going to open it up for you."

"No!" shouted Yoshikazu, with unexpected vehemence. "You not open! I don't carry nothing! *You not open*!"

At that moment, Massey came up with his notebook in his hand. "You having trouble here?" he asked.

"Guy refuses to open the van," said Russo. "What you got?"

Massey held up the notebook. "It's a legitimate vehicle, not reported as stolen or missing. It belongs to the Florida office of the Willis Candy Corporation. Their head office is in Century City."

"You have candy in there?" Russo asked Yoshikazu.

Yoshikazu nodded. "Just gum. That's all. Just five cases gum."

"Good," said Russo. "In that case, you won't mind us taking a look."

There was a tense silence. Yoshikazu looked at the police officers wide-eyed. Russo could almost see the word *desperation* hovering over his head like a bubble in a cartoon. Whatever Yoshikazu was carrying inside this van, he was scared shitless about letting the police take a look at it.

"It's better you don't open," said Yoshikazu breathlessly. "I think I appeal to better nature. Here—I pay you money. You not open. Here—I pay you fifty dollars."

"Keep your hands in sight," snapped Massey, as Yoshikazu reached inside his windbreaker for his billfold. Yoshikazu paused, and then lifted his hands again.

"It's an offense to attempt to bribe a police officer," said Russo. "If you carry on this way, Mr. Yoshikazu, you're going to wind up doing three to five. Now, let's cut the crap and open this van up."

At that instant, there was a loud, hollow, metallic beating noise from inside the van. Yoshikazu went pale. Russo frowned at Massey, and then demanded of Yoshikazu, "What was that? What the hell have you got in there?"

"Waking up," babbled Yoshikazu. "That's why I hurry. That's why I run light. Waking up."

"Waking up? What's waking up?"

In reply, there was another burst of ferocious knocking from inside the van. Someone or something rattled and kicked at the doors, and thundered at the panels. Massey held Russo's arm and pointed to the side of the van. Bulges were appearing in the sheet metal as if the van were being slugged from the inside with a ten-pound hammer. In moments, the whole side of the vehicle was pimpled with them.

Russo took out his revolver.

"All right, Mr. Yoshikazu, I want that van open."

"I not do it!"

"I said open it—and *move*!"

Yoshikazu dropped to his knees on the concrete.

Russo ordered Massey, "Go get the pump shotgun." Massey ran back toward the patrol car, one hand holding his hat on, as if all the dogs of hell were snapping at his heels.

Russo edged up to the back of the van, his pistol raised, and cautiously put his ear to the panel.

"Is there anyone in there?" he shouted.

There was silence.

"I said, Is there anyone in there?"

There was an ear-splitting bang, and the door of the van was punched out into a huge bulge. He jumped back and stood with his gun in both hands ready to fire. But the lock on the van doors held, and whatever it was inside the van

shuffled off toward the front end. Russo could see the
vehicle swaying as it made its way forward.

Massey came panting back with the shotgun. Russo said,
"Give me some cover. I'm going to see if I can get those
doors open."

Massey asked, "What is it in there? Some kind of wild
animal?"

"I'm not sure. And Emperor Hirohito here isn't about
to tell us."

"Maybe I should call the zoo."

"Maybe we should just find out what the hell we're
dealing with. Did you ask for backup?"

"Sure," said Massey. "A couple of minutes, they said.
There's been a multiple pileup on the Ventura Freeway."

"Okay," said Russo, sweating. "Then let's do it."

Russo advanced toward the doors again, his revolver
held out in front of him. The van was motionless, silent.
Russo coughed. Behind him, Massey raised his gun and
clicked off the safety.

Russo reached the van. He glanced sideways at Yoshikazu, but Yoshikazu was still on his knees on the concrete,
his face white and rigid. Russo waited for a short while,
and then tapped on the van doors with the butt of his gun.

Massey said tightly, "It could have gone back to sleep
again."

Russo turned to Yoshikazu. "That possible?" he asked.

Yoshikazu shook his head.

"You have one last chance to tell me what it is," said
Russo.

Yoshikazu whispered, "You not open. I appeal to
better nature. Easy thing, you let me go, say nothing,
forget."

The Japanese was shaking, and his face was jeweled with
sweat.

Russo looked back at Massey. "Now I've heard everything."

Massey grinned. "You have to admire his—"

The rear doors of the van burst open with a devastating

crash, and Russo was hurtled backward across the concrete. Massey fired his shotgun out of nervous reaction, but his shot went wide.

A short, heavily built man in a glaring white mask swung from the back of the van and threw himself on Russo. Russo felt as if a whole bag of cement had been dropped on him from a second-floor window. He pressed the muzzle of his gun against the man's side and screamed, "Get off, or I'll blow your guts out!" But the man seized Russo by the neck with mad, unstoppable ferocity and began to twist.

Russo saw scarlet. Nothing but scarlet. He didn't know where he was or what was happening. He fired his gun and felt the shock of the recoil and the thump of the bullet entering his attacker's body. But the pain didn't stop, and the viselike grip on his neck didn't let up, and he dropped his pistol—a numbness as agonizing and overwhelming as an electric shock stunned his reflexes.

Massey fired again, hitting the masked man in the muscle of the right shoulder. The shot turfed up a bloody lump of flesh, but the man kept on wrenching wildly at Russo's prostrate body as if nothing had happened. Massey ran two or three paces nearer, knelt down, aimed, and fired at pointblank range. There was a deafening report, and he saw the yellow cotton of the man's clothes scorch black where the bullet entered his side.

The masked man lifted his head, turned, and hit out with a swing of his arm that sent Massey sprawling. Massey knocked his head hard on the concrete, and for a moment he was stunned.

The masked man climbed to his feet, his clothes bloody and burned from the gunshots. He picked up Russo as if he were a child, and carried him over to his patrol car.

The masked man gripped Russo by his ankles and swung him around. Russo was choked and only semiconscious, but he was still alive. He could feel the grip on his ankles, and he could feel the world tilting and rushing around him as the man spun him around like a flail.

Then, with all of his terrible strength, the man gave Russo a final swing and smashed him face first into the windshield of his police car. Razor-sharp fragments of glass sliced the flesh away from Russo's cheeks and forehead, and a long sliver stabbed up into the soft skin under his chin and penetrated his tongue.

Russo couldn't scream, or cry, or do anything. He was helpless in the grip of his maddened killer. He could only close his eyes and hope that the pain would end.

The masked man swung him back, out of the shattered windshield, and then around again. He beat him against the police car's hood, and against the headlights, and against the grille, until the car was splattered with blood and jellyish brains, and Russo was crushed and dead. Through the darkness of his concussion, Massey could hear Russo's death as a series of soft, hollow thumps.

The traffic on the freeway passed by and didn't stop. But this was one time when you couldn't blame anybody. There was too much blood. Too much horror. And the sight of a mangled policeman with a head that was nothing more than a smashed watermelon, sliding off the hood of his wrecked car, well, that was reason enough to step on the gas pedal and keep going, trembling, until you reached home in Pasadena.

The masked man turned toward Massey. His breath came in deep, distinct whines. Massey opened his eyes and saw the man standing over him, and he tried to think where his shotgun was, and whether it was even worth struggling. He felt a moment of utter helplessness and fear.

But then the masked man turned away. Unsteadily, uncertainly, as if the pistol bullet and the two shotgun bullets had hurt him at last. He stood by the side of the freeway, rocking on his heels, and then promptly sat down. After another few seconds, he collapsed.

Massey tried to stand up. He had managed to lift himself onto all fours when Yoshikazu came around the van; he had been hiding on its other side. Yoshikazu raised a warning finger, instructing Massey to stay where he was. Then, with great difficulty, he gripped the masked man under the arms and began to drag him across the concrete back toward the van.

Massey watched Yoshikazu for a while. Then he crawled toward his shotgun, picked it up, pumped another round into the chamber, and knelt on the ground, pointing the gun at Yoshikazu's back.

"Don't you make another move," he said.

Yoshikazu turned. "I have to put him back in van. He could revive."

"You heard me," said Massey.

A green Plymouth station wagon slowed down beside the police car, but when the driver saw the blood, and the gun, and Yoshikazu laying the short man down on the concrete, he took off with a shriek of tires.

Massey said, "Stand up slowly and put your hands on top of your head."

Yoshikazu began to raise his hands. But then, quite suddenly, he dropped to the ground and rolled behind the body of the masked man, using him for cover. Massy fired twice. His first bullet hit the short man in the leg, the second ricocheted off the concrete.

Yoshikazu tugged an automatic out of his windbreaker and fired back. The bullet hit Massey in the side of the head, in an extravagant spray of blood. He reeled on his knees and then toppled face first onto the ground.

Yoshikazu scrambled to his feet. His teeth were clenched with tension and fear. He humped the bleeding body of the masked man back up to the van and succeeded in dragging him inside. He wedged the doors together, even though they were twisted, and prayed to the gods of fortune that they would hold. Then he ran forward to the open door of the driving cab and climbed in. Within fifteen seconds, he was off.

In the distance, from the Ventura Freeway, came the howl of sirens as the California Highway Patrol came to answer Massey's backup call.

Phil Massey lay on his face on the concrete and watched his own dark blood trickling into the dust. A few feet away, Ed Russo lay on his back, his hands stiffly clenched in front of his chest, his face already beaded with flies.

CHAPTER TEN

It was almost sunset. In his suite at the Los Angeles Bonaventure Hotel, Gerard Crowley was sitting in a Chinese silk bathrobe smoking a long Havana cigar and watching the CBS News. The suite was suffused with dying golden sunlight; on the double bed, naked, Francesca was stretched out asleep, exactly as he had left her. There was a plum-colored love bite on the side of her neck.

Gerard kept the cigar clenched between his teeth and smoked steadily, as if the cigar were an aqualung, essential to his survival. He always smoked that way. Once he lit a cigar, he puffed it furiously down to a finish and then stubbed it out. He treated his friends and his lovers in the same way. The only exception, ever, had been Evie.

On the television, a frowning commentator was saying, ". . . *throughout the Tennessee Valley area, and caused widespread damage to homes, shopping centers, and factories. . .*"

Gerard testily blew out smoke. On the rear bumper of his car was a sticker which read *God Bless America . . . She Needs It.* That was more than slightly ironic, considering what he was getting into now. But Gerard's life had always been haunted by religion, and by irony.

He thought about the pain and the hard work that had finally brought him to this thick-carpeted suite. He thought about Evie. He turned his head and looked at

Francesca, at her unconsciously parted thighs, and he thought about her too.

He should be feeling aggressively confident now. Macho, fit, on top of the world. But for some reason he didn't fully understand, he felt afraid.

Maybe his terror of his father still pursued him. His father had been a grocery-store owner in Westville, Virginia—a tall, spare, uncompromising man who had believed in work for its own sake and the severity of the Lord. After school, young Gerard had stacked shelves and weighed out bags of sugar until nine or ten o'clock at night; and before school in the morning he had bicycled around town and delivered orders. The only free time his father had allowed him was Saturday afternoon, after a whole morning of serving behind the counter.

Those Saturday afternoons had been golden and precious. Gerard had walked almost every week to the tobacco plantation outside of town, meeting his friend Jay Leveret for hours of games and adventures. They had played the Green Hornet in and out of the long pungent sheds where the tobacco leaves were hanging to cure; and they had run for miles across the fields, under skies that Gerard always remembered as indelibly blue.

When Saturday afternoon was over, Jay Leveret would return to the big white plantation house, to warmly lit lamps and the bright sound of laughter, while Gerard would trudge home along the dusty twilit road for a silent supper of fatback and beans with his parents, always concluded by a doleful hour of reading from the Bible.

His first introduction to drink had been a mouthful of surgical spirits in the back of the store. His first sexual experience had been with Ada Grant, a cheerful big-breasted woman whose husband had left her to go pick oranges in California, and who gladly took young boys into her high brass bed for three dollars.

Until he was sixteen, Gerard had been a hick. Rural-minded easygoing, and innocent. But on his sixteenth birthday, his life had been turned upside down. Jay

Leveret's father had written to say that there was a place for him on his tobacco plantation, if he cared for it. But Gerard's father had sourly refused. Gerard was to work in the store. Never mind if it was hard and unprofitable. To labor without reward was a blessing of the Lord.

After three miserable weeks of sweeping up, unloading sacks, and scooping beans, Gerard had had enough. One chilly mid-September dawn had found him thumbing a ride on the highway south. He had been bound for Florida, and eventually for Cuba. He didn't think about those years of his life very often. Not these days. He talked about them even less. But it was during those years that he had begun to make his money, first by fixing boats on the Florida keys, and later, in the last days of President Batista, by dealing in drugs and girls in Havana.

In six years, he had grown from a hick to a hard and knowledgeable young wheelerdealer. He had been shot at, stabbed in the left thigh, and beaten up. He had contracted gonorrhea eight times. He had spent days dead drunk in shanty whorehouses on the outskirts of Havana, days which in later years would wake him up at night, sweating and shaking. He had put his life and his determination on the line, and at the end of it all he had built up Crowley Tobacco into what it was today—a tight-knit, highly profitable corporation with a reputation for tackling unusual and different orders. Not all of those orders were concerned with tobacco. Some of the most successful deals were those Gerard called "capers."

Gerard's father, embittered by his son but well prepared for the Lord, had died of emphysema in 1958. Gerard had attended the funeral, although his mother had refused to speak to him. Four years later, she had died, too. Gerard had become an orphan. A wealthy, experience-hardened orphan.

On the bed, Francesca stretched. Her sex parted like a pink flower. Gerard continued to listen to the news. A busload of old folks had dropped off the edge of Slumgullion Pass, Colorado.

Francesca sat up and pulled at her tangled hair. "What time is it?" she asked.

"Seven-thirty," said Gerard, without taking his cigar out of his mouth.

"I must have fallen asleep."

"Uh-huh."

She yawned. "Do you mind if I call room service and get some Perrier water? I have an unnatural craving for Perrier water these days."

"You're not pregnant, are you?" Gerard asked her.

She laughed. Her breasts bounced. "Don't you know the rhyme? There was a little goil, and she had a little coil, right where it mattered most."

"I don't know why you're laughing," said Gerard. "I wouldn't mind if you were pregnant."

"You don't want another child," she said, although it was more of a question than a statement.

"No, I don't. But I still wouldn't mind if you were pregnant."

Francesca stood up. "Are you more chauvinistic than flesh and blood can stand, or am I missing something?"

"You're missing something."

She leaned over and kissed him on the parting of his dark hair. He smelled of cigars and medicated shampoo. "I could be persuaded to love you," she said.

He smiled.

She walked across the bedroom and picked up a pack of cigarettes from the windowsill. She took one out, lit it, and stood looking out through the nylon net drapes at the sparkling dusky lights of downtown Los Angeles. Gerard watched her appreciatively. She was an unusual girl. Not clever, but strong-willed almost to the point of ruthlessness. And pretty, and unquenchably fierce in bed, and to Gerard that was all that mattered. She appeared so aloof and elegant. She always dressed in pure silk. And yet she would do anything, and take it anywhere. That turned Gerard on.

She said, as calmly as if she were asking him what he

wanted to eat for supper, "Have you decided what you're
going to do about Evie yet?"

Gerard took out his cigar. "Do?" he asked her. "What
do you mean?"

"Well, she's not going to let you get away with it."

Gerard shrugged. "What can she do? She can only
divorce me, and she won't do that. She's too insecure; too
dependent."

"She seemed very upset."

"She'll cool down. She'll drink the house dry, and then
have a damned good weep, and that'll be it."

"Do you *want* her to cool down?"

Gerard looked at Francesca closely. She had wide green
eyes. Green as glass.

"Yes," he said in a measured voice. "Of course I want
her to cool down."

"So you want to stay with her?"

"Does it make any difference if I do?"

"Of course it does. Your home is still with her, instead
of with me."

Gerard watched her for a while. Then he said: "As far as
I'm concerned home is where I spend the most time. You
and I see each other all day, we spend two or three nights a
week together. We go to the theater. We have dinner."

"But you belong to her."

"That's where you're wrong," replied Gerard. "Evie
belongs to me."

Francesca drew on her cigarette. "I don't really see the
distinction. A slaveowner has just as many responsibilities
to his slave as his slave has to him. And besides, you still
sleep with her."

Gerard set his cigar down in the ashtray and stood up.
Francesca came nearer, and he rested his hands on her bare
shoulders. He was smiling at her, and yet his eyes were so
remote and expressionless that she was unable to smile
back.

"You're jealous," he said. She wasn't at all sure if he
was joking or not.

"No," she whispered. "I'm just demanding."

"Demanding?"

"I want you. I want your time."

He ran his fingers down the length of her naked back. He cupped one cheek of her bottom in his hand, so that his fingertips just touched her in a sensitive place. He kissed her, so lightly that their lips scarcely grazed.

"Right at the moment, my time is preempted," he said.

"I know. By Esmeralda."

He nodded. "Esmeralda is just as demanding as you. *More* demanding, if anything. He seems cute, and old-fashioned, but underneath that bandleader's clothing he's a goddamned man-eating alligator."

She turned her face away. "He frightens me."

"He frightens me, too. But his money's good."

Gerard thought of Esmeralda, the very first day that Esmeralda had come into his office, and the arrogant way in which the Colombian had carefully tugged up one trouser leg so that he could perch himself on the edge of Gerard's desk. "I have a proposal for you, Mr. Crowley," Esmeralda had said. "Very unusual, but very profitable."

Gerard had eyed Esmeralda coldly. "I'm too busy for any new contracts. I'm sorry."

Esmeralda had smiled warmly. "You weren't too busy last October 24th to run twenty cases of AK-47 Russian machine guns into San Salvador, were you?"

Gerard had remained hard-faced; but he had been deeply disturbed. He was relying heavily these days on a confidential government contract to supply the rebels in Afghanistan with ammunition for their M-60 machine guns, smuggling them over the Pakistani border in convoys of jeeps, and the very last thing he needed was a public revelation that he had also armed Marxist-Leninist guerrillas in El Salvador.

"What do you want?" he had asked Esmeralda pointedly. "No screwing around. What do you want?"

"It's very simple," Esmeralda had smiled. "I have a

Japanese client who is looking for research facilities in California . . . somewhere private where he can undertake a little medical work.''

"What kind of medical work? What are you talking about?''

"Well, it's not much more than a health farm, really. Perhaps a *little* bit more than a health farm. You see, my client is a physiologist; and he discovered during the Tokyo Olympics that a certain combination of chemicals and anabolic steroids could develop an *ordinary* athlete into a *super* athlete . . . tireless, aggressive, and un-stoppable.''

"I thought anabolic steroids were banned by most athletics associations,'' Gerard had interrupted.

"They are,'' Esmeralda had agreed. "Yes, they are. But my client has been clever enough to apply his knowledge to another field, a field of prime concern in the United States, and in many parts of the Middle East, and that is *personal security*. Using the techniques he developed at the Tokyo Olympics, my client now wishes to develop a stable of bodyguards, superbodyguards, who will be rented out to anybody who needs them. They will be available to protect industrialists, politicians, even senior *mafiosi*. They will be bodyguards of invincible strength, crushing capabilities. If Reagan had only had one when John Hinckley shot at him, Hinckley would have been torn to tiny shreds! You can call them killer bodyguards, if you like. They will terrify anyone who comes near them.''

Gerard had said, "I stopped believing in fairy stories when I was seven years old, Mr. Esmeralda.''

"You think I'm telling you a fairy story? You want some kind of proof?''

"I don't want anything from you. I just want you to leave.''

"Look at this,'' Esmeralda had said, and produced from the inside pocket of his coat a manila envelope. He had opened it, and taken out a 5 x 4 glossy black-and-white print, which he had passed over to Gerard in a hand that trembled ever so slightly.

Gerard had not looked down at the picture at first: but then he had slowly lowered his eyes and taken in a blurred, overexposed scene of a short, stocky man holding something up over his head. The picture must have been taken in the mountains somewhere: the ground was sloping, and there were conifer trees and rocks. It was only when Gerard had peered closer, though, that he had begun to understand what it was that the stocky man was holding up. It was a deer, or the remains of a deer, which looked as if it had been torn apart like a gory telephone directory. Its guts hung between the man's outstretched arms, and its head was falling back at a grotesque angle.

"This could have been staged," Gerard had said cautiously.

"Of course it could." Esmeralda had smiled. "But it was not. That man tore that deer to pieces with his bare hands."

Gerard had handed the photograph back and looked at Esmeralda with great suspicion. He had not yet wholly believed. But he had been prepared to listen.

Esmeralda had admired his well-polished fingernails, and then added, "My client needs somebody who can manage his interests in California. Someone to help him with organization and transportation; someone to fetch and carry. Someone sophisticated and unscrupulous. And that someone will be you."

Gerard had stood up and thrust his hands into his trouser pockets. "Mr. Esmeralda," he said fiercely, "I want you to get out of my office."

"Of course you do." Esmeralda had smiled, and his voice had been as oily and soothing as warm coconut milk. "But you've been running risks for years now, selling arms and drugs to whichever client will pay you the most money, and there always comes a time in lives like yours when chickens come home to roost. This is it, Mr. Crowley. This is when your chickens come home."

Gerard had slowly closed the door of his office, and then

he and Esmeralda had talked in private for three hours. At the end of that time, Gerard had agreed, grudgingly but curiously, to supervise the day-to-day fetching and carrying that was going to be needed by the men who were running the program, and to liaise with whomever else Esmeralda might appoint to assist him. "I have already chosen an interpreter, a Japanese woman," Esmeralda had informed him. "Also, a traffic-control expert, a retired naval commander. You will be in excellent company."

As he had adjusted his hat in front of the mirror in preparation for leaving, Esmeralda had added, "The super bodyguards will be called Tengus, after the Japanese word for powerful devils. You like that word, Tengus? They will be volunteers, each one of them . . . young Japanese men who are already physically fit and extremely strong. They know the risks of the drugs they will be taking, the steroids and so forth, and you will have to get used to the idea that some of them may become temporarily . . . well, unstable. My client's experiments are still in their early days."

He had opened the door, so that Francesca could hear what he was saying. "I want you to know, Mr. Crowley that this program is worth millions of dollars—millions. You understand me? You will get your share when the time comes, but only if you do exactly what you are told to do, and behave yourself. And there is one more thing."

"What's that?" Gerard had asked him flatly, annoyed that he had opened the door.

"You must know that the program has some enemies . . . people who look down on this kind of thing. Health officials, bleeding hearts. You know who I mean. After all, some of the drugs that my client will be using won't exactly be . . . *approved*, if you understand me. So, there may be people who have to be warned off, decisively."

Gerard had opened his cigar box and taken out a fresh cigar. He knew exactly what "warned off, decisively," meant. He was quite fluent in the euphemisms of smuggling and arms running. He took out a match, struck it, and looked at Esmeralda through the smoke and the flame. "All right," he had said. "We'll talk about that when the time comes."

Now, the time had come, and their attempt to "warn off" one of the program's enemies had ended in chaos and complications. Francesca could sense the unease and tension in Gerard's body, and she touched his forehead, stroked the backs of his hands, kissed him.

"Money isn't everything, Gerard," she said.

"I don't think I'm involved with Esmeralda for the money," Gerard told her. "In fact, I don't know why I'm involved with Esmeralda at all."

Francesca said, with unexpected softness, "I don't want you to get hurt."

"I've been hurt plenty of times," he said, kissing her quickly. "Once more wouldn't make any difference. Not that I *intend* to get hurt. I don't intend to get anything but very much richer."

The telephone warbled. Gerard picked it up. He listened, but didn't speak. Then he put the receiver down again.

"Put something on," he told Francesca. "Nancy Shiranuka's coming up."

Francesca took a pair of tight white corduroy jeans from the back of the bedroom chair and stepped into them. Then she buttoned a blood-red silk blouse over her bare breasts and ran her hands through her hair. She looked like a woman who had been making love for most of the afternoon. She smelled of sex and Chanel.

Gerard went into the living room and switched on the lamps. He called, "When you get through to room service, have them send up a couple of bottles of California chablis and some potato chips. Maybe some beer."

"When you entertain, you really go to town, don't you?" she said sarcastically, tucking her blouse into her jeans.

Gerard didn't answer. He had opened the drawer in the writing desk, and he was looking inside as intently as if he had found the dead body of a poisonous spider in there. Lying among the Hotel Bonaventure writing paper and postcards was a .357 Python revolver.

He didn't touch the gun. He knew it was loaded. He just wanted to make sure it was still there. Quietly, he closed the drawer.

"Is the commander coming up, too?" asked Francesca.

The door chimes rang. Gerard said: "He's staying out at the ranch for tonight. He's arranging to get Yoshikazu over the border."

He put his eye to the peephole in the door. Then he loosened the chain and opened it. Nancy Shiranuka stalked in, dressed in an olive-green safari shirt and slacks, and wearing a wide-brimmed straw hat. She took off her hat, tossed her long black hair, and looked around the suite disdainfully.

"For two hundred a night, you think they'd give you some decent prints on the walls," she said.

"I don't usually come here to look at the pictures," Gerard told her. He said it without humor.

"I know what you come here for," said Nancy blandly. "But sex is art, and art is sex. If they put up one or two Sugimura prints of ten-year-old courtesans, don't you think the room would look much better? And don't you think it would be a more stimulating place to take your lady-love?"

"Unfortunately, I don't think Westin Hotels have any leeway in their decorating budget for rare Japanese pornography," said Gerard.

Nancy sat down on the mock-antique sofa and elegantly crossed her legs. "Of course not. It's the great Caucasian failing. Budgets before art, budgets before sex, budgets before anything."

Gerard said, "And what about the great Oriental failing?"

His voice was quiet, but acidly sharp. Nancy sensed the change in tone.

"Have you heard from Ernest?" she asked him.

"I talked to Ernest an hour ago."

"Then he probably told you they've already disposed of the van."

"Yes."

"Well," said Nancy edgily, "I don't have much more to tell you."

"What did Doctor Gempaku say?" asked Gerard. "He was too busy when I called."

"He's not very hopeful. The Tengu was shot by the police several times, and he's still in a coma."

"What will Gempaku do if he can't be revived?"

Nancy opened her pocketbook and took out a green lacquered cigarette case. "The same as our noble employers do to *anyone* who doesn't fit in happily with their business schemes, I suppose" she said.

Gerard pursed his lips. He was angry, but controlled. He knew that most of what had happened had been ridiculous bad luck, and that Nancy wasn't really to blame. But now there had been two foulups in two days, two serious and disabling setbacks, and even if the caper hadn't been completely written off, it had certainly been delayed.

Worse, it had shaken Gerard's credibility, and with Esmeralda breathing so closely down his neck, Gerard needed all the credibility he could muster. Working for Esmeralda was all bluff and double bluff, and living on your nerves.

Gerard said, "I suppose Yoshikazu knows how much this has cost us."

"Of course he does. But it wasn't his fault."

"He ran a red light right in front of a police car, and it wasn't his fault?"

"What else was he supposed to do?" Nancy demanded. "The Tengu was going mad. He couldn't sit in traffic while the whole van was torn to pieces around him." She lit her cigarette. Then she added, "Yoshikazu did very well. This has cost us, but it hasn't cost us everything."

"Not unless the police trace the van. Not unless the

customs people pick him up at the border. Not unless some smartass with a long memory puts six and seven together and comes up with unlucky thirteen.

"I think you're fretting too much about what your precious Mr. Esmeralda thinks of you," said Nancy. "Don't worry about him. You know the police won't trace the van. You also know that Ernest will get Yoshikazu safely into Mexico."

"That's two problems out of three," put in Gerard. "But what about our friend Sennett? The one for whom that sad young starlet died in vain?"

"That's up to Esmeralda, not to me."

"He made it *our* responsibility," Gerard insisted.

"It's not a responsibililty I want to accept."

"You'll have to. If you don't, this entire scheme is going to collapse like a half-cooked soufflé."

"I didn't accept this job to murder people," snapped Nancy.

"It's too late for that, my dear. You're an accessory already. And what did you think you were letting yourself in for, really, when Esmeralda told you he was building up a crack stable of killer bodyguards?"

Nancy said, "I'm beginning to wonder if *any* of us is safe. If Esmeralda can order one man killed, why not another? Why not us? Why did he chose any of us in the first place? Because we are all magnificently unprincipled, and because we all have connections in the grubbiest places? Or because, if any of this business goes wrong, we can all be dropped quietly into the ocean without anybody making too much noise about it?"

Gerard nodded. The cold smile was back on his lips. "My thoughts exactly," he said.

Francesca came into the room, her hair brushed and shining. "That wine's taking its time," she remarked.

Gerard said, "They're probably waiting for it to become a respectable vintage."

"Are you going out to the ranch yourself?" Francesca asked him.

"In a couple of days. Once, I get all this administrative mess sorted out. And replace Yoshikazu."

"You could try Kemo," suggested Nancy.

"Kemo? Your houseboy?"

"That's right. He's quick, he's eager, and he's got a good head on his shoulders."

"As long as he doesn't object to having it knocked off."

"He knows the risks."

Gerard pinched the bridge of his nose tiredly. He was beginning to feel that maybe he wasn't as energetic as he had been two or three years ago. A whole afternoon of drinking and lovemaking was more than he could comfortably manage, especially if he wanted to stay alert during the evening. "Okay," he said, "I'll have a talk with him. Now, what other problems do you have for me?"

"Only details. They spotted a couple of prowlers around the ranch yesterday afternoon, but they turned out to be hippies looking for a place to crash. Doctor Gempaku says he needs more power, perhaps another generator, and maybe you can arrange for a temporary stopgap. A mobile generator maybe."

"What's he running out there?" Gerard demanded. "A sound-and-light show?"

"He's hoping to open the new center in six weeks. He has to do it, Gerard, or he'll never meet the deadline."

"All right," said Gerard. "I'll get on it. Francesca?"

Francesca made a scribbled note on the hotel pad, and pulled a tight, unhelpful expression which Gerard recognized as trouble.

CHAPTER ELEVEN

Jerry and David ate breakfast together in silence; a cup of black coffee for Jerry and a bowl of Lucky Charms for David. On the radio, they were still talking about the white-masked copkiller, but by now the story had been chewed over by so many expert opinions and so much tough talk from the Hollywood police that it bore little resemblance to the violent event it had actually been.

David was as rangy as his father; a long-legged, untidy boy of fourteen; but he had inherited, unmistakably, his mother's forehead and eyes. Jerry could stare at him sometimes, when he was watching television or doing his math homework, and see Rhoda, exactly as she had been before the cancer had dulled and wasted her and at last taken her away.

"That's some weird murder,' huh?" asked David. "Do you hear what they said? Some guy in a white mask swinging this cop around by the ankles."

"Sure," said Jerry unenthusiastically. "Real weird."

David said, "You're okay, aren't you, Dad?"

"What makes you ask that?"

"I don't know. You seem like you're down."

Jerry shrugged. "I don't know. I don't know what it is. I just get the feeling there's something strange going on. You know that feeling you get just before an electric storm? Kind of a *tension*. Like two magnets when you try to push them together and they resist each other."

David finished his cereal, drained his glass of orange juice, and then went to the sink to wash his dishes. "Are you seeing Doctor Grunwald today?" he asked matter-of-factly. Dad's continuing analysis was a part of daily life which he had grown to accept as quite normal; besides, half the kids in his class had parents undergoing psychiatric treatment. Kim Pepper's mother had taken an overdose last month and nearly died. It was nearly as fashionable to attempt suicide as it was to Sierra-Stone your poolside.

Jerry said, "Maybe. I mean, yes, I probably will."

David stood by the sink, in his T-shirt and faded Levi's, and looked at his father with a mixture of sorrow and exasperation. "You don't really need him, you know. You could manage on your own, if you tried."

Jerry gave his son a quick and vinegary smile. "Day-to-day living I can manage on my own. *You* I can manage on my own. The only thing I can't manage on my own is Japan."

David was quiet for a long time, but then he said, "That all happened thirty-eight years ago, Dad. You know? Thirty-eight years."

"I know, David. But memories aren't necessarily erased by passing years. Sometimes, they grow more relevant, sharper, more disturbing. And now there's something in the air . . . this tension. . . . It kind of reminds me of Japan. I don't know why. But it has the same feeling of complete doom."

"*Doom*?" repeated David, with exaggerated wide-eyed emphasis. "Jesus, Dad, only comic strip characters say 'doom'!"

Jerry glanced up at David wryly. "Maybe that's my real problem. Maybe, in reality, I'm a comic strip character. Jerry and the Pirates."

David said, "Never," and gave his father a friendly cuff on the arm.

Jerry drove David to school, dropping him outside the gates. Then he cruised slowly back home to Orchid Place, listening to Hilly Rose on KMPC 710 and thinking about Japan.

Japan . . . and those hot still days in the Chugoku Sanchi, under a sky the color of melted lead, hidden deeply in a camouflaged crevice of the forest, with no sound but the chirruping of insects and the endless warbling of the radio. He pulled up at an intersection, and for a split second he didn't know where he was. A garbage truck pulled up behind him and gave him a noisy blast on its horn to remind him that he was back in the present day.

On the radio, Hilly Rose was talking to Sergeant Skrolnik. "Is there anything apart from the white mask which connects these two murders? Any other clue whatsoever? I mean, are we dealing with a *single* murderer here, or a look alike?"

Sergeant Skrolnik was on his best media behavior, and his voice sounded strangled. "The connections are many and varied. You understand what I mean. It's not just the mask. The *modus operandi* is strikingly similar, in that both victims were wrenched apart by bare hands. No sign of any kind of blunt instrument, or weapon of any description. This is a job committed by somebody of almost superhuman strength."

"Somebody crazy, perhaps?" asked Hilly Rose. "Somebody with lunatic strength?"

"Lunatic strength is a myth," said Skrolnik. "What we're dealing with here is somebody who naturally and normally possesses unusual physical power; and that's who we're looking for. Somebody who trains day and night in karate, something like that. Maybe a bodybuilder."

"What about this white mask?"

"We don't have any clues about the mask so far . . . but a police artist has been reconstructing the mask based on the evidence supplied to us by witnesses who passed the homicide location on the Hollywood Freeway, and we hope to be able to show that mask on television tonight, in the hope that it's going to jog somebody's memory. All I can say about it so far is that it's dead white, kind of expressionless . . . and probably varnished. One eyewitness said that it had some kind of pattern on it, on the forehead, but for tonight's reconstruction we're omitting that detail because nobody else saw it, and the witness admits that it might have been a fleck on his own windshield. . . ."

Jerry thought, *White, expressionless. . . .* There was something about the way in which Sergeant Skrolnik was trying to describe the murderer that made his stomach turn over, something which disturbed old memories. . . .

*We've located it, sir. No question about it. We've taken
sixteen radio bearings and we have it right on the button.*

*In that case, withdraw immediately. I repeat, immedi-
ately. You will be picked up at 2125 hours on the 15th on
the beach at Kokubu.*

"Yes, sir," Jerry whispered to himself, aloud, as he
turned into the driveway of his home.

He climbed out of the car. A young man in a sleeveless
T-shirt and shorts was sitting on the wall, smoking and
obviously waiting for him. The young man was blond and
curly, and looked as if he spent most of his day down at the
beach or sunning himself on a flat roof somewhere. Jerry
said flatly, "Good morning. You looking for me?"

"You're Mr. Jerry Sennett?"

"That's right. Who wants to know?"

"Mack Holt's my name. I used to be Sherry's boyfriend.
Sherry Cantor? That was in the days before *Our Family
Jones*. But we broke up when she got into that."

Jerry slung his jacket over his shoulder and climbed up
to his front door. "You broke up, huh?" he asked, as he
took out his key. "What happened? Was she spoiled by
success?"

"She wasn't, but I was. I was a would-be actor in those
days, too. And I can tell you, it wasn't easy, parking cars
for a living while she was the toast of the town. And it isn't
easy to accept her death. That's why I came to see you, I
guess. You're her neighbor, after all."

"Do you want a drink?"

"If it's not imposing on you."

Jerry gave him a wry smile. "*Nothing* imposes on me
these days, young man. I have gradually crystallized into a
kind of emotional rock formation, upon which nothing
can make the slightest impression, let alone impose."

Mack, following Jerry into the living room, gave an uncomfortable laugh.

"Quiet kind of place you've got here," he said.

"Quiet, well, that's the word for it," nodded Jerry.
"What'll you have? There's Chivas Regal or Chivas
Regal."

"I'll have a Chivas Regal," said Mack, sitting down on the sofa.

"What happened to Sherry, that was a great shock to us here," said Jerry. "She was a nice girl. Friendly, pretty. Always bouncing and full of life. I wish now that I could have gotten to know her better."

"She was somebody special," said Mack. "Maybe too special."

Jerry gave Mack a drink and then walked across to the window. "I don't think we're talking about the usual kind of Hollywood nut murder here," he said. "Not a Charles Manson, or anything like that."

Mack said, "She was torn apart, you know. Literally torn apart."

"Yes," agreed Jerry. "But who uses a Sherman tank to crush a peanut?"

"You're a military man?" asked Mack guardedly.

Jerry came away from the window. "Used to be, in the days when it meant anything. Naval intelligence group."

"Now you're . . . ?" asked Mack, indicating the living room with his glass in his hand.

"Now I'm semiretired," Jerry told him. "Living off my investments and a little part-time architectural work. Oh, yes, I used to be an architect, too. But it was the intelligence group that made the big impression on me, made me what I was. You don't get hardened designing duplexes in Westwood. Not hardened the way I am."

In that case, withdraw immediately. I repeat, immediately.

Mack said, "You think they'll ever catch him? Not that it matters."

Jerry stared at him, unfocused. "Catch him? Well, they might. I don't know. I always get the feeling that the police are satisfied with anybody who's prepared to confess, whether he happens to be the real criminal or not."

Mack sipped his whiskey, shuddered, and then said, "You've got some kind of feeling about this, right? I mean, about what happened to Sherry?"

Jerry nodded. "I don't know why. But I noticed it this morning. There's something in the air. Something tense. I don't know what it is. I don't have a clue. But I think it's tied up with what happened to Sherry. And there's something else, too."

Mack sat and waited for Jerry to say what this "something else" was. A minute, two minutes passed, and in the end, Mack said, "What? What else?"

"Well . . . let me try an experiment," said Jerry. "I don't know whether you were listening to the radio this morning or not, but the detective who's handling Sherry's murder said that a police artist is busy reconstructing the same kind of mask that the killer wore, based on descriptions from witnesses, and that tonight it would be shown on television."

"I didn't know that," said Mack. He didn't. This morning, he'd been too busy with Olive. Not making love, but arguing about Sherry, arguing about his unwillingness to give himself to Olive while he mourned.

"I'll tell you what," Jerry said quietly, raising one finger. "I'll show you a mask I brought back from Tokyo after the war; and then you watch television tonight, and if you think the mask they show is similar—maybe not the same, but similar—then you call me. I'll be watching too."

Mack said uneasily, "You're not pulling my leg about this? I mean, you're not. . . ."

"I have a mask that happens to sound like the police description on the radio," said Jerry. "White, expressionless. But that doesn't mean that I had anything to do with Sherry being murdered. I can promise you, I wasn't even here at the time. And besides . . ." He looked down at his hands. "I'm too weak these days to lift a box of groceries. I'm getting old. And I think I did enough killing in the war to satisfy the most bloodthirsty killer's most bloodthirsty dreams."

Mack was quiet for a long time, watching Jerry suspiciously at first, then more sympathetically. The man was old, and deeply upset by what had happened to Sherry, he could see that. He could also see that there were shadows crossing his mind, shadows he would probably prefer to forget.

We've located it, sir. No question about it. No question about it. No question about it.

Mack said, "Sherry once said to me, before she got famous, 'I think that I'll love you forever.' And I said, 'What makes you think that?' and she said, 'Because everything you feel, you feel forever.' "

Jerry said, "What are you trying to tell me, Mack? Can I call you Mack?"

Mack said, "I'm trying to tell you that she still loved me when she was dying. You know that? When she was dying, she still loved me. And that makes me part of what happened. That makes me responsible."

Jerry swilled the whiskey around in his glass, without taking his eyes off this young curly-haired L.A. bum with the raggedy shorts and the tears in his eyes. "You're crying," he said baldly.

"Yes," said Mack miserably.

"Well," said Jerry, "that's a start."

After a while, Jerry left Mack to finish his drink and went down into the cellar. It was dusty and untidy, stacked with tea chests and packing cases and crumpled-up copies of the *Los Angeles Examiner* for the day he had moved in eight years ago. But once he had shifted two stacks of cord-wood and a broken bicycle, he found the varnished trunk with the rusted iron bands which had followed him from apartment to bungalow to hillside house for nearly thirty-five years. He tugged out the six-inch nail which kept the hasp closed, and opened the lid. Inside, like the multi-colored body of a vampire waiting to be revived, lay his remnants of Japan. Kites, fans, *Wajima-nuri* lacquerware, masks, *Arita-yaki* ware, paper flowers.

Mack Holt was sitting on Jerry Sennett's sagging sofa, thinking about Sherry, and about the day they had hurtled on his motorcycle all the way down to Baja California, laughing, ridiculous, loving, and high on the best Mexican grass, when he was abruptly confronted by a ghastly eyeless face, as white as death. He spilled his whiskey and said, "Shit! You scared me!"

Jerry laid the mask carefully on the table. "It's only a mask. I picked it up in Japan after the war."

Mack breathed out unsteadily. "Some mask. But what makes you think it's the same kind of mask that Sherry's killer was wearing?"

"I have a feeling about it, that's all."

"A feeling?"

Jerry stared down at the mask. Its features were blank, apart from a V-shaped black mark which defined the forehead. To anybody who was uninitiated in Japanese demonology, the V looked like a fierce frown. But Jerry knew that it was a representation of the bird's beak which would usually have protruded from such a demon's head. The demon was called a Tengu; and it was supposed to be the supernatural reincarnation of a Shinto monk whose ways had become proud and corrupt. It was the most terrible of all Japanese demons: because it knew heaven as well as hell.

Jerry said, "The Japanese have a phrase: 'The crow kills by day and by night.' These days, they usually use it when they're warning one another to watch out for a particularly aggressive business colleague. In fact, most Japanese have forgotten what it meant originally. But in the old days, the very old days, back in the eighth century, it referred exclusively to the Tengus, the devils of Buddha. They had beaks like crows, which gradually developed into fierce jaws; and they weren't above tearing people to pieces when they felt the urge."

Mack eyed the mask suspiciously. "You're not suggesting that . . ."

"No," said Jerry. "I'm not suggesting anything. It's just that I have a feeling. The Japanese call it 'a cold wind.' "

Mack said nothing for a long time. He looked at Jerry,

and then back at the mask. "This is some kind of a put on, right?" he asked at last, but his voice betrayed his lack of conviction.

"It might sound like it," said Jerry. "I can't find any way to persuade you that it isn't. I'm not even sure about it myself. But the police said that a man in a white mask tore Sherry to pieces, and then assaulted and killed a cop on the Hollywood Freeway."

He swallowed a mouthful of whiskey, and then said, "I'm probably wrong. When they show the mask on television tonight, we'll probably find it's a Casper the Ghost mask from some joke store on Hollywood Boulevard."

"But you can feel 'a cold wind,' " said Mack.

Jerry nodded.

Mack finished his drink, hesitated for a moment, and then stood up. "I'll watch the news, and then I'll call you."

"Even if it turns out to be Casper the Ghost?" asked Jerry dryly.

Mack shook his head. "If it's Casper the Ghost, then I'll simply put you down as a stray fruitcake. And that, believe me, will be the most charitable thing I can do."

Jerry stood in his doorway watching Mack cross the street in the hazy mid-morning sunshine and climb into a dented green Volkswagen Beetle. The engine started up with a clattering roar and a cloud of blue smoke. Jerry closed the door and went back into the living room. The Tengu mask lay on the table where he had left it, staring eyelessly up at the ceiling.

"A stray fruitcake, huh?" Jerry repeated.

No question about it, sir. No question about it.

CHAPTER TWELVE

Mr. Esmeralda had learned very early in life that few people are as deeply despised as those who provide a service for a fee, no matter how exclusive their service, or how rarefied their personal *hauteur*. As a thirteen-year-old boy in Barranquilla, in Colombia, in a crumbling white-stucco mansion enclosed within courtyards and wrought-iron gates, and overshadowed by musty palm trees, he had seen businessmen and entrepreneurs of all persuasions and all nationalities come and go, their suits stained with sweat, seeking assistance and paid favors from his father.

His father had held court on one of the upper balconies—Jesus Esmeralda, one-time Caribbean pirate, famous gunrunner, narcotics smuggler, and spiriter-away of hunted men. If you wanted anything to find its way in or out of Colombia—a packing case crawling with poisonous spiders, a selection of priceless emeralds, a Browning machine gun, a professor of social science who had spoken out once too often against the régime—then Jesus Esmeralda was your man.

But no matter how wealthy he was; in spite of his white Hispano-Suiza and his twenty-two servants; regardless of his talent for procuring faultless cocaine for fashionable parties and tireless young men for Barranquilla's bored middle-aged ladies, he was never accepted into respectable society. Businessmen who had handed Jesus Esmeralda thousands of dollars in used U.S. currency were unlikely to invite him to dinner. Women who knew that he was living off the fear of their husbands and lovers were scarcely inclined to ask him into their beds. He was a lonely, sardonic man, spasmodically wealthy, occasionally hysterical, troubled by coughing fits that he could control only with desperate difficulty, and by extraordinary sexual compulsions that he couldn't control at all. It is sufficient to say that as he grew older and more jaded, he became increasingly obsessed with watching women with animals, and that his son's first glimpse of adult perversion was through the wrought-iron screen of his bedroom window, into the courtyard below, from which the clatter of hoofs and the cries of girls had been disturbing him since ten o'clock. He had seen through the palm trees a small, frisky pony with a long beribboned mane, a gray; and beneath it, naked, on all fours, a young blonde girl of no more than sixteen or seventeen, between whose parted buttocks the pony was thrusting something that looked, to young Esmeralda's, like a rolled-up red umbrella.

Mr. Esmeralda had been nine then. What he had seen had appeared to be magical and mysterious, a peculiar myth brought to life in front of his eyes. He had never forgotten it. It had been early evidence of the enchanted degradation of those who perform for money, their utter enslavement to the will of others. It had both repelled and mesmerized him.

During his schooldays in Colombia, and all through business college in Houston, Texas, Mr. Esmeralda had been friendly, helpful, and sociable. But no matter how many favors he did for his pals, he never accepted anything in return, not even a candy bar, nor a sixpack of root beer, nor the loan of a roommate's T-Bird. The other kids thought him unfailingly trustworthy; and it was on trust that Mr. Esmeralda eventually built his career as a used-car salesman, import-export agent, international entrepreneur, and helper of all those who needed help. He moved from Houston to Cleveland, from Cleveland to Seattle, from Seattle to L.A.

He never made the mistake of asking any of his clients for money, or even of mentioning money. He and his clients remained friends—golfing together, dining together, dating together. The financial side of his business was handled entirely by a pleasant and courteous man called Norris, who had a wonderfully pained and breathy way of pleading with defaulters not to upset Mr. Esmeralda, *please*, he respects and admires you *so much*.

Mr. Esmeralda had never married, although two or three

American ladies had been seen entering and leaving his elegant condominium at The Promenade on Hope and First streets. They were the kind of strawberry-blonde pneumatic 1960's Amazons that Vargas used to airbrush for *Playboy*—girls whom Gerard Crowley had unkindly described as "a greaser's idea of Miss Sexy America."

On the same morning that Mack Holt visited Jerry Sennett, Mr. Esmeralda was being driven in his blue air-conditioned Lincoln Town Car to a house set back among the trees in Laurel Canyon. His chauffeur was a young Chinese girl he had met in Peking two years ago. He had gone there to arrange for the import of forty-five tons of ballbearings and certain unidentified machine spares, many of which had borne an uncanny resemblance to the disassembled components of M-60 general-purpose machine guns. The girl's name was Kuan-yin, and although she looked no more than twenty-one or twenty-two, she claimed that she had once chauffeured Chiang Ching, the widow of Chairman Mao, before the downfall of the Gang of Four. She was calm, pretty, and remote, and Mr. Esmeralda particularly liked her in her severe gray jacket and jodhpurs.

Few of Mr. Esmeralda's colleagues clearly understood his relationship with Kuan-yin. There were stories that he had helped her to escape from Hangzhou during the Cultural Revolution; but why, or how, Mr. Esmeralda would never explain. There was another, less convincing story that he had found her in a Nevada cathouse called the Bucking Horse Ranch, and that she had nursed him through a coronary. But whatever the turth was (and truth, in Mr. Esmeralda's life, was rarely relevant, except on bills of lading), there was a bond between them which, for want of an exact word to describe the magnetism of two isolated and complex and in many ways unpleasant souls, could almost be called affection.

The Lincoln curved up the tree-lined driveway to the front door. A remote-control television camera watched the car suspiciously from its perch in an overhanging spruce. The house was an expensive split-level affair, all triangular rooftops and cedarwood decks, the kind of house that Los Angeles realtors usually describe as "a high-tech home built with old-world craftsmanship," and then price $125,000 over its value. Mr. Esmeralda said to Kuan-yin, "Turn around, and then wait for me. Don't get out of the car. I'll telephone you if they keep me waiting for very long."

In the rearview mirror, Kuan-yin's eyes nodded a passive acknowledgement.

Mr. Esmeralda walked up to the house. Another remote-control television camera, suspended from the eaves, observed his climb up the steps to the front door. He ignored it, and used the large brass knocker.

The door was opened almost instantly. From inside the "tasteful hardwood entryway" came the waft of incense and that other curious smell which always lingered here, and which Mr. Esmeralda had never been able to identify. A Japanese stood before him in black silk robes and a black silk facemask decorated with scarlet and gold thread, and beckoned him inside. The door was quietly and quickly closed behind him.

Mr. Esmeralda had been here three times before, but the strange atmosphere in the house disturbed him just as much today as it had on his previous visits. No electric lights were lit: the only illumination came from small candles placed in flat ceramic dishes of water all the way around the edges of the rooms and corridors. And there was always a faint and distant moaning, almost a keening noise, as if the summer winds were blowing through an abandoned *Koto*, the Japanese harp, or as if a woman were mourning her long-dead husband.

What was even more unsettling, the occupants of the house, of whom Mr. Esmeralda had so far counted eight, were always dressed in black and always masked. He had never even seen the face of the man who called himself *Kappa*, the man he had come to see. But then, Kappa was scarcely a man.

The Japanese who had opened the door for him said, "You will wait now."

"Mr. Esmeralda involuntarily checked his watch. "Is he going to be long? I have a heavy day."

"Kappa pays for your day. If Kappa says wait, then you wait."

"Very well," said Mr. Esmeralda. "Since you put it so persuasively."

"You would care for something to drink?"

"A glass of water would be admirable."

"So it shall be. Now please wait."

While the Japanese went to bring his water, Mr. Esmeralda wandered impatiently into the large empty area which, before this house had been taken over by Kappa and his entourage, must have been the "generous, over-sized family room." Now there was nothing here but bare floor boards and scores of flickering candles. The walls were white and bare, except for three or four sheets of handmade paper on which were written thousands of intricate Japanese characters. Mr. Esmeralda went over and peered at them, as he had peered at them before, and wished he could read Japanese. For all he knew, they were nothing more threatening than Tokyo-Kobe bullet-train timetables.

Upstairs, or next door, or wherever it came from, he could hear that distant moaning sound, and for a moment he held his breath and frowned and listened as hard as he could, trying to make out once and for all what it actually was.

At last, the Japanese came padding back with his glass of water. Mr. Esmeralda drank a little of it and then handed the glass back. "Tepid," he said. The Japanese didn't answer. Then Mr. Esmeralda asked, "Is Kappa going to be very much longer? I am not particularly good at waiting. It doesn't suit my temperament." Still the Japanese didn't answer. "You know, temperament?" repeated Mr. Esmeralda. "I am what they call a man of little patience. I have a short fuse."

A gong rang; a sound more felt than heard. The Japanese said, "Kappa will see you now. Please follow me."

Mr. Esmeralda took out his handkerchief and dabbed at the back of his neck. "Thank God for that." He glanced up at the ceiling and crossed himself quickly. "Thank you," he muttered.

Perhaps the house in Laurel Canyon disturbed him so much because he knew that he was going to have to confront Kappa again. Kappa still gave him occasional nightmares, even though he had seen beggars all over the Middle East, and lepers in Africa, and the deformed victims of mercury pollution at Minamata. Mr. Esmeralda liked to think of himself as a cosmopolitan, a man who could slip comfortably onto a stool at the Oak Bar of the Plaza one week and be greeted by the barman by name; and then be welcomed the next week at a small brothel in Marseilles with the same affability. He couldn't think, offhand, of a country he hadn't visited. He couldn't think of a major international gangster whose hand he hadn't shaken, and whose assistance he couldn't rely on.

But he had never met anything like Kappa; and he nightly prayed to the Virgin Mary that he would never meet anything like Kappa again.

Mr. Esmeralda had become involved with Kappa by accident, on board a ferry that was taking passengers from Tokushima to Wakayama, across the Kii-Suido. The ferry had been elegant, white-painted, and old, with two large paddles which left curling patterns of foam on the silver-gray water. It had been a strange misty afternoon, with the sun as red behind the mist as a Japanese flag, a supernatural scarlet orb. Mr. Esmeralda had been talking to his people in Kochi about heroin. They had left him unsatisfied: there had been a great deal of ceremonial tea-drinking, chanoyu, but very little in the way of firm delivery dates. Mr. Esmeralda was leaning on the rail of the ferry feeling irritated and tired. He often found that the so-called superefficiency of the Japanese was nothing more than an impressive display of Oriental ritual. He enjoyed subtlety in his dealings, but the Kochi people were so suble that they practically disappeared up their own inscrutability.

A voice had said close beside him, "You are Mr. Esmerarda?"

Mr. Esmeralda had shifted sideways to see who was talking to him. Anybody who knew his name was probably police or customs, and he didn't particularly want to speak to either. But, in fact, it had been a young Japanese in a khaki windbreaker and thin beige slacks, unexceptional-looking, the kind of Toyko student type you could have lost in a crowd in Nihonbashi just by blinking.

"Mr. Esmerarda?" the student had repeated.

"What do you want? You had better know that I am very selective when it comes to shipboard romances."

The Japanese student had stared at him unblinkingly. "You must prease accompany me."

"I am here. I am listening. What more do you want?"

"You must accompany me downstairs. Kappa wishes to speak with you."

"Kappa? Who's Kappa?"

The Japanese student had said, "You may have seen him carried on board."

Mr. Esmeralda had said quietly, "You mean the—" and the Japanese student had nodded. Nobody could have failed to notice the long black Toyota limousine that had drawn up to the dock just before the ferry was due to leave, and the extraordinary ensemble which had alighted from it and hurried to the gangway. Four men, hooded and gowned in black, bearing between them a kind of elaborate wickerwork palanquin, in which a diminutive figure nodded and swayed, completely swathed in a white sheet.

When Mr. Esmeralda had seen them come on board, he had crossed himself. Another passenger, an elderly Japanese, had actually disembarked, in spite of the arguments of his relatives, and refused to travel on the ferry in the company of demons. The palanquin had quickly been taken below and the lacquered cabin doors shut behind it, and the ferry had set off on its spectral journey through the mist of the Kii-Suido. But many of the passengers had appeared to be unsettled, and there had been a lot of forced laughter and whiskey-drinking.

Mr. Esmeralda had followed the Japanese student down the companionway to the cabin doors, on which were painted a fleet of fantastic ships and a grisly collection of sea monsters, in the style of the Shijō school. The Japanese student had knocked at the doors and then waited, watching Mr. Esmeralda blandly.

"I don't suppose you're going to tell me what this is all about?" Mr. Esmeralda had asked the student. The student had said nothing, but waited and watched as before, impassive and utterly calm.

The doors to the cabin had been opened. "You may go in now," the student told Mr. Esmeralda.

"You are sure that this is going to be worth my while?" Mr. Esmeralda had asked him.

"Go in," the student had repeated.

A small hand had taken hold of Mr. Esmeralda's wrist as he stepped into the cabin, to guide him down a flight of darkened stairs, and then along the length of an unlit corridor, to a door. It had been immediately opened, and Mr. Esmeralda had found himself in a private stateroom, hot and smoky with dozens and dozens of candles. Behind the swaying flames of the candles, only half-visible through the dazzle and the smoke, Mr. Esmeralda had seen that the basketwork palanquin had been converted into a throne—its bamboo carrying poles having been fixed vertically to the sides of the basket, instead of horizontally. He had shaded his eyes against the candles, but it had been impossible to see clearly who or what it was that was perched in the basket.

Apart from Mr. Esmeralda himself, there were several other people in the stateroom—two or three young Japanese men standing in the shadows, all of them with masked faces—and a very young Japanese girl, wearing

only a red-and-gold silk shirt and an extraordinary lacquered headdress of stylized flowers, similar to the flowers
worn by the Yoshiwara courtesans of the eighteenth
century. From her face, and from her half-developed
breasts, Mr. Esmeralda had guessed that she was only
twelve or thirteen years old.

"I seem to have been sent for," Mr. Esmeralda had said
loudly, in the general direction of the basketwork throne.

"Indeed you have," a voice had replied, slurred and
Japanese, but with a peculiar inflection all its own, as if it
were emerging from the black-haired throat of a tropical
insect. "I know who you are, Mr. Esmeralda, and why you
spent so much time at Kochi, in the company of Katsukawa Shunsho."

"I have many acquaintances in Japan," Mr. Esmeralda
had answered cautiously, screwing up his eyes to see what
this "Kappa" really looked like. "Katsukawa Shunsho is a
trading associate, nothing more."

"You are based in Los Angeles, in America?" the
peculiar voice had asked him.

Mr. Esmeralda felt the first slide of perspiration down
the middle of his back. Suddenly he felt less like the
conjuror than the conjuree, the perplexed victim whose
socks and cufflinks have been removed without his
knowledge. He gave what he hoped was an assured nod,
but he had never felt less assured in his life. "I return there
on Friday," he said. "Air Argentina, flight AX 109.
Perhaps you knew that, too."

"I need a certain task performed for me in Los
Angeles," the voice told him.

Mr. Esmeralda licked his lips. "Certain tasks" usually
turned out to be extremely complicated, costly, and
dangerous. If somebody in Japan wanted a straightforward
favor, they generally asked you for it outright. It was only
when it was unpleasant that they called it "a certain task"
and approached you so obliquely.

"I, er, I regret that *time* will not permit me to accept
any more commissions at present," Mr. Esmeralda had

replied. "I have an art shipment to take care of; a whole freighter loaded with *netsuke*. And I have a meeting in Detroit on Monday morning. And next Wednesday, I must speak to some of my new associates in Cairo. I would have liked to be able to accommodate you, but—" He shrugged, tried to smile.

There had been a second's silence. But then the voice had said, "Mr. Esmeralda, you will not turn me down. I will pay you $1.6 million in U.S. currency, and in return you will give me your absolute obedience. Is that understood?"

"I am not in the habit of performing favors for money," Mr. Esmeralda had replied, although some hint of caution made him add, "Not as a rule, anyway. Well, not often."

Kappa, from behind the swaying candle flames, had said something else hurriedly and authoritatively. Two more Japanese had come forward, both masked, as their colleagues were, dragging a large hardwood block, painted shiny red. Then the young Japanese girl in the headdress had stepped forward, knelt down, and pulled open the zipper of Mr. Esmeralda's white tropical trousers. She had reached inside, wrestled out his penis from his shorts, and tugged it out until it was stretched across the top of the red block.

Mr. Esmeralda had tried to thrash his legs and wriggle from side to side; but the two young Japanese boys had a firm grip on his arms, and the young Japanese girl had an unyielding grip on his penis.

A third Japanese youth had stepped forward, this one clutching a curvy-bladed samurai sword. He had lowered the sword until the sharp edge was just touching the skin of Mr. Esmeralda's penis, not breaking the skin, but resting it there so that Mr. Esmeralda could feel just how keen the blade was.

Then, without warning, the Japanese youth had let out a sharp cry, whipped back the samurai sword, and flashed it down toward the red hardwood block. Mr. Esmeralda had screamed, in spite of himself; in spite of the fact that he was a man of the world.

He had looked down to see that the Japanese youth had somehow managed to stop the blade's descent exactly an inch above the hardwood block. He had cut a thin line across the tip of Mr. Esmeralda's penis, but that was all. Only a scratch, nothing serious. Mr. Esmeralda had closed his eyes, and whispered, "*Madre mia.*"

There had been a lengthy silence. The girl had not released his penis the boy with the sword had not moved away. But the insectlike voice of Kappa had said, "you wish to assist me now."

Mr. Esmeralda had cleared his throat. "I see no reason why not."

"Well, that's excellent," Kappa had told him. "Welcome to the the the Circle of the Burned Doves."

"The Burned Doves?" Mr. Esmeralda had asked.

There had been a short hesitation; then Kappa had whispered, "Come forward. Come nearer. Then you will see what I mean."

Mr. Esmeralda had glanced down at the girl, and then sideways at the boy.

"Let him go," Kappa had ordered, and the girl had stood up and shuffled quickly back into the shadows.

Mr. Esmeralda, zipping up his pants, had made a suspicious circuit of the rows of flickering candles. As he had approached the basketwork throne, a curious smell had reached his nostrils, a sweetish smell that would almost have been alluring if he hadn't been so sure that it was the odor of something curious and frightening. If it had put him in mind of anything at all, it was Japanese seaweed, cloying and slightly briny.

"Come nearer," Kappa had told him, his voice so hoarse and quiet now that Mr. Esmeralda could hardly hear what he was saying. Mr. Esmeralda, sweating in the candlelight, had finally come face to face with the creature that called itself Kappa.

Lying in the basketwork throne on a soiled cushion of

blue Japanese silk was a yellowish thing that looked, at first sight, like a hugely enlarged human embryo. Its head was more than man-sized, but Mr. Esmeralda could see nothing of its features because they were concealed behind a bland yellow-painted mask, a faintly smiling warrior of the reign of the Emperor Kameyama, an uncanny and disturbing masterpiece of Japanese decorative art.

The body, however, was naked, and completely exposed, and it was this grisly collection of distorted flesh and bone that subsequently gave Mr. Esmeralda so many nightmares. There was a narrow chest, which rose and fell as rapidly as that of a suffocating puppy; two tiny arms with budlike nodes instead of fingers; and a bulging stomach. The genitals were even more malformed, a gray and wrinkled array of folds and dewlaps, neither male nor female, which glistened in the candlelight with slippery mucus. The creature had legs of a kind, hunched beneath its genitals, but they were sticklike and obviously powerless.

"You wonder why I hide my face and leave my body exposed?" Kappa had asked Mr. Esmeralda hoarsely, as Mr. Esmeralda stared at him in horror.

Mr. Esmeralda had been unable to answer. His mouth hadn't been able to move itself into any kind of shape at all.

Kappa had watched him for a while through the expressionless eyeholes in his mask. Then he had said, "I hide my face because my face is normal; the face of a normal man. The rest of my body you are welcome to see. I am not ashamed of it. What happened to me was not my fault; nor the fault of my mother. Look at me, and see what the Americans were responsible for, with their atomic bomb. My mother was one month pregnant on August 6, 1945, when the first bomb was dropped on Hiroshima. She was staying with her uncle and aunt in Itsukaichi, but she had traveled to the city the day before to see an old friend of my father, who had been wounded in the Army. She was exposed both to the flash, which burned her, and the gamma rays, which eventually killed her, after eight years. But she was just outside the two-kilometer radius from ground zero within which all pregnant women had miscarriages and even though I was grotesquely premature I was born alive.''

'',The doctors didn't—'' Mr. Esmeralda had begun, his voice thick and choked.

"Think of killing me at birth? No, they didn't do that. My mother was back at Itsukaichi for her confinement. After a while, in a strange way, she became attached to me, and she refused to contemplate euthanasia. She took me every day to water therapy, in the hope that my limbs would grow strong and my body develop. That is why they call me Kappa. It is Japanese for 'water devil'—a nasty little beast that lives in the water and refuses to compromise with anyone.''

Mr. Esmeralda had deliberately turned his back on the revolting spectacle in the basketwork throne, and had made his way unsteadily back through the lines of candles to the far side of the room. During this time, Kappa had said nothing, but had watched him intently through his yellow warrior's mask. Mr. Esmeralda had felt closed-in and nauseous, and the slight roll of the ancient ferry as it had turned on the Pacific swell to dock at Wakayama had unsettled his breakfast, pork leg with mushrooms and too much hot tea.

"What is it you want me to do?" Mr. Esmeralda had asked Kappa at last, clearing his throat.

"A friend of mine, a doctor, must establish himself in America. You will arrange a work permit, and for somewhere private for his research. You can do this kind of thing: Katsukawa Shunsho told me. You have friends who can forge papers, friends who can arrange for green cards. This is so?''

Mr. Esmeralda had nodded queasily.

"You will also bring together four or five people who can help you with the further stages of my scheme. They should be experienced people, people like yourself, preferably with good knowledge of Japan and an understanding of the Japanese way of life. But you must understand that they might have to be dispensed with, especially if anything goes wrong. So I would advise you not to select friends or lovers, or anyone close to you."

Mr. Esmeralda had said, "When you say *dispensed with*, you mean murdered? Or do we speak a different language?"

"Was Hiroshima murder?"

"I am an entrepreneur, not a historical moralist. Hiroshima was war."

There was a long, breathy pause. Then Kappa said, "Pearl Harbor was war; Wake Island was war; Midway was war; Guadalcanal was war. War—men fighting each other like warriors. But Hiroshima was murder. And, for me personally, and all of my brothers and sisters who make up the Circle of the Burned Doves—that is to say, all those innocent children reared in secrecy, who have been born with terrible deformities because of the American atrocity—it has been worse than murder. If there is such a thing as living murder, then we have suffered it."

Mr. Esmeralda had brushed the sleeves of his coat with mock fastidiousness. He didn't intend to argue with Kappa about the morality of revenge. Revenge, as far as he was concerned, was both petulant and boring. Revenge was for cuckolded husbands, rejected wives, and lunatics.

"This doctor friend of yours?" he had said, "What exactly does he want to do in the United States?"

Kappa had been silent for almost a minute. Then he had said, "His name is Sugita Gempaku. He is a doctor of anthropology, not of medicine, a graduate of Keio University in Tokyo. I suppose you could call him something of a revolutionary. I first read about his work in a French science magazine. He was trying to recreate, as a historical experiment, some of the more specialized and arcane defense programs that Emperor Hirohito ordered toward the close of the war.

"One of these programs was an attempt to rediscover a derivative of the Heaven Drug, a kind of sleeping powder which the ancient samurai were said to have burned in censers around their battlegrounds, and which gave their enemies such strange and compelling hallucinations that they simply laid down their weapons and allowed themselves to be beheaded without a fight.

"Another was the Water Flute, a magical wind instrument about which there are many curious legends in Shikoku. Its music was said to induce self-destructive madness; and I can tell you that it was actually tried, during the American landings on Eniwetok atoll. There is no record, however, of its success or failure. Presumably, it failed."

Kappa had paused for a while to regain his breath. He had begun to pant very hard; the young girl had quickly and quietly approached the basketwork throne with a porcelain dish of saké. Mr. Esmeralda had tried to see if he would lift his mask to drink, but the girl had carefully placed herself between him and her master, so that the ritual of his refreshment was completely obscured.

The ferry had docked now at Wakayama, and Mr. Esmeralda glanced up at the ceiling of the cabin as the shuffling footsteps of disembarking passengers crossed the deck. He had been supposed to meet one of his agents on the pier, but he made no attempt to leave the cabin.

At last, Kappa had said, "The most secret and most effective of all the programs, however, was that of the Tengu. It was carried out in Hiroshima in 1945 by Toshiro Mitoma, an extraordinary religious ascetic who believed implicitly in all the magic and demonology of ancient Japan, and who was often consulted during the course of the war by Japanese officers of field and flag rank. Admiral Nagumo trusted him as implicitly as Hitler trusted Dr. Morrell."

"What, exactly, *was* the Tengu?" Mr. Esmeralda had asked.

"The Tengu was—*is*—the most terrible of all Japanese demons. There are stories of Tengus going back to the eighth century, and even earlier. They are related to the

evil which manifests itself in all black birds, like crows and
ravens and rooks. But they are capable of possessing a
man's body, taking him over like a fit of madness, and
giving him extraordinary strength and resistance to attack.
A man possessed by a Tengu could be hacked into tiny
pieces with a sword before he would give up. And even
when they have been destroyed, Tengu-men have remarkable regenerative powers. If you are looking for a Western
comparison, I suppose you could say that the Tengu is like
a zombie, except that a zombie is already dead and a
Tengu can hardly ever be killed.''

Mr. Esmeralda had said, "You'll excuse me for
smiling.''

"You find this difficult to believe?''

"I have my own superstitions. My own little foibles,''
Mr. Esmeralda had said. "I try not to catch sight of the
back of my head in a mirror. I do my best not to spill salt.
But, Mr. Kappa, I really cannot invest any belief in ancient
demons.''

Kappa had said to one of his aides, "Give him the
papers.'' One of the young Japanese had come forward
and silently handed Mr. Esmeralda a plastic envelope containing what looked like a military report sheet.

"What is this?'' Mr. Esmeralda had asked.

"Read it,'' Kappa had insisted.

It was a Xerox copy of a top-secret memorandum from
USMC Intelligence Guam, dated October 17, 1944:

> The failure of the attack on Cape Matatula on
> Tutuila Island on August 25 was due entirely to the
> presence on the Japanese side of no fewer than 10
> but more than 12 individual troops wearing white
> masks and carrying no weapons but swords and
> knives. Reliable reports from five reputable career
> officers have indicated that these individual troops
> were able to walk through heavy enfilading rifle fire
> unharmed, and that they were responsible for the
> deaths of at least 80 of our own men. Some of our

men were killed by the Japanese soldiers' bare hands, extremely brutally, although not in the style generally known as *karate* or *kung fu*. One of the Japanese troops was set afire by a Marine Corps sergeant operating a flame-thrower, and yet he continued to attack our positions and succeeded in strangling and killing two Marines while actually ablaze. Comprehensive accounts of what occurred were obtained from 15 officers and men during debriefing on USS *Oxford*, and these are attached. Meanwhile it is suggested that priority be given to intelligence investigation of these special Japanese troops, whom we have codenamed "Hogs."

Mr. Esmeralda had handed the plastic envelope back without a word.

"Well?" Kappa had asked him breathily.

"Well, what? All that happened a very long time ago. Men make some very strange mistakes when they are fighting battles. Perhaps all this talk of special Japanese soldiers was nothing more than an excuse to cover up the fact that the American Marines lost their nerve under fire, and had to retreat."

Kappa had laughed. "You are being deliberately stubborn."

"Perhaps," Mr. Esmeralda had replied. "But why not? I have nothing to gain by associating myself with you. And, frankly, I find the idea of it extremely unpleasant."

"You forget that I will mutilate you if you refuse," Kappa had whispered.

Mr. Esmeralda had looked around him. The young Japanese in their impenetrable black masks were tense and poised, and he had been in no doubt at all that if he tried to escape they would catch him in a flash, and treat him without hesitation to whatever tortures Kappa might direct. Mr. Esmeralda disliked the idea of working for a shriveled quadriplegic in a basketwork chair; but on the other hand he disliked the idea of being parted from his penis even more.

He had said quietly, "You want me to smuggle your Doctor Gempaku into the United States, and provide him with research facilities? You want me to help him create more of these Tengus, is that it?"

Kappa had said, "I admire your quickness."

"But what is this all in aid of?" Mr. Esmeralda had insisted. "What exactly do you expect these Tengus to do?"

"Just one thing," Kappa had said. "Exact revenge on the American people for what they did in Hiroshima."

Now, at the house in Laurel Canyon, Mr. Esmeralda was once more entering the presence of the malformed Kappa. Here, Kappa had been laid out in a chromium-and-canvas cot, his body mercifully covered by a sheet and his heavy masked head propped up on pillows. There were two televisions suspended from the ceiling on amateurishly homemade gimbals and tape recorders and telephones within easy reach, all adapted for use by someone with the severest of handicaps. The room itself was hung with white cotton drapes and lit only by candles, a nest of them on a small white table. There were no pictures on the walls, no flowers, no miniature trees, none of the decorative art that Mr. Esmeralda expected to see in a Japanese room. And there was that pervasive smell of human flesh that wasn't quite dead but wasn't quite alive, either.

"I hear that things have been going dangerously awry," Kappa said, his eyes glittering through the holes in his mask.

"You could say that things haven't been going as they were planned to go," Mr. Esmeralda replied with great caution. "But, when one is asked to hire dispensable people, one sometimes has to make do with second best. The best people are indispensable."

"Nobody is indispensable," said Kappa.

"Good wheelers and dealers are indispensable," Mr. Esmeralda argued, "Especially when one is obliged to import dozens of illegal Japanese immigrants, along with whole crates of ancient artifacts and God knows how many live Japanese animals and birds. One can't expect miracles, Kapp."

"Do not fail me," whispered Kappa.

Mr. Esmeralda took out a pale lavender handkerchief and patted his sweating neck. "The last time I spoke to Doctor Gempaku, he said that everything was progressing quite well. We had difficulty with the first Tengu, I know, but by definition they aren't easily controllable."

"The man Sennett remains alive."

"It was an understandable mistake. Yoshikazu was given a house number, and it turned out that the number was posted on a concrete pillar between Sennett's house and the girl's house. The Tengu was directed to the wrong house, and there's nothing we can do about it. It's too late."

Kappa was silent for a while. Then he said, "You are sure that Sennett is the last remaining member of the naval intelligence team?"

"Quite sure. The only other person who might conceivably understand what is happening is Admiral Knut Thorson, formerly of the Naval Intelligence Command; and poor Admiral Thorson is currently in an acute-care hospital at Rancho Encino. Everyone else who might have known what happened, and why, is long dead."

"You didn't speak of this Admiral Thorson before."

"There was no need to. He suffered a stroke. His doctors say that he will probably never speak again."

"*Probably*?"

"You don't want me to send a Tengu to a *hospital*, to—"

"Do it," Kappa commanded.

"But—"

"*Do it*! And ensure that you deal with Sennett as well."

Mr. Esmeralda looked around him, unhappy. "All right," he agreed at last. "If you say so. But if your plan works out the way you want it to, it doesn't seem to me that there's going to be very much need to worry about Sennett, or Thorson, or about anybody else."

Kappa rolled his masked head away from Mr. Esmeralda and said in a muffled voice, "What is going to happen to

the United States within the next few weeks must be a devastating mystery. They must never know why it
happened, or how. It must seem like the revenge of God.
If they were to discover that it was I who had initiated it, it
would all seem explicable. They would be able to com-
prehend it; and in comprehending it, they would
gradually be able to repair their morale and their spirit.
That is what I specifically do not wish to happen. I wish
this to be a blow of divine rage, from which the Americans
will take years and years to recover. I want them to feel that
they have been condemned to hell.''

Mr. Esmeralda thoughtfully tugged at his mouth with
his hand. Quite illogically, he found himself thinking
about Eva Crowley. There was something helpless and
bruised about her; something which gave him the urge to
punish her and degrade her even more. But, he knew that
he would have to treat her very carefully. He had other
plans for Eva Crowley, apart from bed and his own
particular brand of Colombian seduction. Eva Crowley was
Mr. Esmeralda's life-insurance policy.

CHAPTER THIRTEEN

Sergeant Skrolnik was dozing over his typewriter that
afternoon when Detective Pullet came into his office,
tripped over the wastebasket, tipped over his styrofoam
cup of cold coffee, and knocked a stack of law books off
the filing cabinet onto the floor.

"What the *hell*?" Skrolnik demanded grumpily. His
eyes were puffy, and he felt as if an armadillo had been
sleeping in his mouth. Then he said, "Oh. It's you."

Pullet dabbed ineffectually at the spilled coffee with a

crumpled-up piece of yellow legal paper. "I'm sorry. I'm sorry. I didn't realize you were resting."

Skrolnik gave Pullet a distinctly old-fashioned look, and sniffed. "I never rest. You should know that by now. I was simply seeking inspiration behind tactically closed eyelids."

"Did you find any?" asked Pullet. He was obviously pleased with himself about something. He picked up the law books, stacked them back on top of the filing cabinet, and frowned in irritation as they all clattered back to the floor again.

"Inspiration? No, not really," said Skrolnik. "But I did mentally marshal a number of interesting facts."

"Tell me," said Pullet. "*Sir*," he added when Skrolnik glanced across at him in disapproval."

"Well," said Skrolnik, "one of the most interesting facts is that when Officer Russo first caught sight of the van on Hollywood Boulevard, it was *already* speeding. That we know from the girl behind the counter at the drugstore where the officer stopped for antacid tablets. Now, why was it speeding, when there was no apparent pursuit, and when it contained a man who obviously wanted to do as little as possible to attract attention—since he had already torn Sherry Cantor into small pieces?"

Pullet nodded, and kept up his "yes, I'm interested" face as brightly as he could, although Skrolnik could sense that he was absolutely bursting to make a startling announcement of his own.

"The point is," Skrolnik went on, "the point is that something must have been *wrong*. So wrong that the driver of the van was prepared to risk almost anything to get our suspect out of town as fast as possible, and off to wherever he was going. That could fit in with your orangutan theory. Maybe the murderer was actually a wild ape, and his tranquilizers were wearing off. But if the orangutan was tranquilized, how did it kill Sherry Cantor? So what we have to look at is this—"

Detective Pullet couldn't contain his excitement any

longer. He reached into his frayed tweed sportscoat and produced, with a flourish, a folded-up poster.

"You told me to think laterally," he said. "Well, this is where lateral thinking got me."

The poster showed a hideous white masklike face, with a grinning red gash of a mouth. Underneath, it said, BRIGHT BROS. GRAND CIRCUS, ONE WEEK ONLY, ANAHEIM.

"A *circus*?" asked Skrolnik, wrinkling up his nose.

"Listen," Pullet enthused, "I thought of every situation in which a man wears or *appears to wear* a white mask. The white mask is crucial. It was seen by three independent witnesses, and all their descriptions are very similiar. Well . . . people don't wear white masks very often. Not full-face masks. A firefighter maybe. A skier. Maybe a ski mask would account for the pattern one of the witnesses said he saw on the suspect's forehead. But then I thought, supposing the mask wasn't a mask at all, but simply makeup, greasepaint? Who wears the white face? The clown in the circus. Where's the nearest circus? Bright Brothers at Anaheim, here this week. Now, you look at the clown's face, and you realize what that pattern probably was—the painted black eyebrows on the clown's forehead."

Skrolnik examined the poster for a long time, chewing his lips. Then he said, "Okay. . . . But you're talking about a clown who can tear a woman to pieces, limb from limb, and then smash a fully grown, fully trained police officer's head in?"

"You don't buy it?"

"I'm not saying I don't *buy* it. I'm just asking a sensible question."

Pullet reached across and tapped some lettering at the foot of the poster. "There's *one* possible answer."

Skrolnik reached into his breast pocket and took out a pair of hornrimmed spectacles. He perched them self-consciously on the end of his snubby nose, and then peered closely at the poster again. It said: EL KRUSHO, THE

STRONGEST MAN IN AMERICA, SEE HIM BEND 1INCH-THICK
STEEL BARS, AS FEATURED IN THE MOVIE *Kung Fu Revenge*.

"El Krusho?" Skrolnik asked, taking off his spectacles.
"I have to go look for a homicide suspect called El Krusho?
How am I going to live it down?"

Pullet shrugged, a little embarrassed. "I know it seems
kind of stupid. But I did some checking with the Screen
Actors' Guild, and a nice lady there told me that El
Krusho is registered with them, and that his real name is
Maurice Needs, and that he comes from Fridley,
Minnesota."

Skrolnik repeated dully, "Fridley, Minnesota? El
Krusho, from Fridley Minnesota? I must be dreaming.
Look, I'm closing my eyes again. Come back into the room
quietly and wake me up, and tell me that I've been
dreaming."

"I'm sorry," said Pullet nasally, a little peeved. "I
know it all sounds peculiar, but you have to admit that it's
a pretty peculiar case. A peculiar case, begging for a
peculiar solution."

Skrolnik sniffed again, stood up, and said, "Why don't
you get some coffee? And bring me a couple of aspirin,
too, while you're at it. I feel like I'm going to have a
terrible headache."

"I think we ought to go down to Anaheim, interview
this guy El Krusho," said Pullet.

Skrolnik stared at him without any expression whatsoever.

"I mean," blustered Pullet, "it does say here that he
can bend inch-thick steel bars, and you remember the
gates at Sherry Cantor's house, the way they were—"

He trailed off. Skrolnik was still staring at him.

"You don't think . . . ?" Pullet began again.

Skrolnik said, "I don't want to belittle your in-
vestigative talents, Detective Pullet. You have true genius
at times. But you mustn't start leaping to conclusions
without sufficient evidence. You've come up with an excellent idea. White greasepaint, clowns, circuses, all that

stuff. It's an idea we're going to have to look into exhaustively. But before we leap into a car and howl down to Anaheim in pursuit of this . . . Maurice Needs . . . well, we're going to have ask *ourselves* a couple of questions, right? Like, how come the strong man is wearing the clown's greasepaint? Like, why would he want to break into Sherry Cantor's house and tear her to pieces? It certainly wasn't for money, nothing was taken. It wasn't a sexual attack, either. It was just *rrrippp*, killing for the sake of it. Dismemberment for the sake of it. So why? Because even if there isn't a reason, there has to be a reason why there isn't a reason. You get me?''

Detective Pullet reached into his coat pocket. ''This is the *pièce de résistance*,'' he said, and laid down on Skrolnik's desk a glossy black-and-white publicity photograph. Skrolnik irritably reached for his glasses again and held the picture up to the light of his desklamp. It showed a young, curly-haired man arm in arm with a hugely built wrestler type. Both of them were grinning at the camera inanely, as if they were slightly high on ganja.

''This curly-headed guy on the left is Mack Holt—Sherry Cantor's ex-boyfriend,'' said Skrolnik slowly.

''And the big muscle bound guy on the right is Maurice Needs, a/k/a El Krusho,'' said Detective Pullet. ''This picture was taken on the set of a movie called *Kung Fu Heroes*, which was the picture that El Krusho made just before *Kung Fu Revenge*. Mack Holt played a young Hell's Angel who appears on the screen just long enough to be smashed to pieces by three crazed exponents of the martial arts.''

Skrolnik sat down again. He stared at the photograph for a little while longer, and then tossed it away across his desk. ''I don't know whether to sing 'God Bless America' or go for a shit,'' he said. ''Forget the coffee. We're going down to Anaheim.''

They spoke very little as they drove through the dusty sunshine toward Anaheim. It was a very hot afternoon, and the Buick's air conditioning was gurgling and splut-

tering with every bump in the Santa Ana Freeway. Skrolnik said from time to time, as if it were the first time he
had ever said it, "El Krusho. Jesus."

Bright Brother Grand Circus had erected its big top just
two blocks south of Lincoln Avenue, on Euclid. Detective
Pullet parked the Buick next to a filthy truck that had
DANGER MAN-EATING LIONS stenciled on the side.
"Your middle name isn't Daniel, by any chance?" asked
Skrolnik, as he stepped out of the car ankle-deep into a dry
sea of popcorn cartons.

It took them nearly a quarter of an hour to find the chief
clown. He was a morose, aging man, with a face like a
canvas bag full of plumbing tools. He was sitting on the
fold-down sofa in his silver Airflow trailer drinking Coor's
and watching baseball on a snowy-screened portable TV.
His lean body was wrapped up in an aquamarine bathrobe.

"Mr. Cherichetti?" asked Skrolnik, tapping on the
open door.

"Who's asking?" demanded the clown.

"Sergeant Skrolnik. Homicide. You got a minute?"

"For what?"

"For questions. Nothing personal. Just a few questions."

Cherichetti sniffed loudly and kept his eyes on the baseball. "I didn't murder anybody, if that's what you're
asking."

"Did I say you murdered anybody?"

"You're from Homicide, right? Detectives from Homicide want to find out who murdered whom. Did you get
that good grammar? Whom, right?"

Sergeant Skrolnik walked along the aisle in the middle
of the trailer and made a show of admiring the Canvas-Tex
reproductions of Olde Masters, including the "Monarch of
the Glen" by Landseer and Boy'a "Maja Nude." He
delicately touched the rim of a blue-and-yellow cut-glass
vase with his fingertips. "Nice place you got here, Mr.
Cherichetti. Tasteful. Can you tell me where you were at

half past seven on the morning of August ninth?''

Cherichetti raised his hooded eyes and looked at Skrolnik with a noticeable lack of clownish humor. "I have to answer that? By law?''

"You don't have to answer anything. It depends whether you want to help me find the guy who tore an innocent young woman into pieces, that's all.''

"Sherry Cantor?''

Skrolnik nodded.

"Well, I seen her once or twice, in the flesh,'' said Cherichetti. "That was before the TV show, you know? Two, three years ago. She used to come to see the circus with Maurice and some other guy.''

"Maurice Needs? El Krusho?''

"El Krusho,'' said Cherichetti with disdain.

Skrolnik raised an eyebrow at Pullet. "Well,'' he said. "Tell me, Mr. Cherichetti, was there ever any evidence in your eyes that Maurice Needs and Sherry Cantor were more than just friends of the same mutual friend? What I mean is, do you think there was any kind of romance between Maurice Needs and Sherry Cantor? Anything like that?''

"Depends what you call romance,'' sniffed Cherichetti. "I don't call it romance, everybody getting into the same bed together.''

Skrolnik gripped Pullet's wrist. For Christ's sake, he thought to himself, this kid Pullet has a nose for homicide like a hunting dog. Needs and Holt and Sherry Cantor all shared the same bed? What a motive for Needs and Holt to tear the poor girl to pieces. What an incredible 100 percent solid brass *motive*. *Both* of them were jealous, loverboy and strongman, and when she left *both* of them to rub shoulders with the glittering and the good-looking, both of them plotted to kill her. And how? With the ready-made weapon of El Krusho's invincible and irresistible hands. What a case! What a fucking gold-plated 100 percent amazing *case*!

"Is El Krusho here today?'' asked Skrolnik. "I'd really like to talk to him.''

Cherichetti shook his head. "He's gone up to Venice to see some girl. He won't be back until tonight's performance, seven o'clock."

"You know *where* in Venice? What kind of car he's driving? Anything like that?"

"He drives a '69 Pontiac, you know, the one with the long pointy hood. Turquoise blue, except for one door, that's beige. The girl lives on Rialto Avenue, pretty girl, he took me around there once to meet her. Her name's Bitzi or Titzi or something like that. Pretty girl."

Detective Pullet said, "Mr. Cherichetti, there's one more thing. Do you happen to have noticed if any of your greasepaint has been missing lately? Any of it been dipped into by somebody else, or maybe stolen?"

Mr. Cherichetti frowned at them. "My slap? Why would anyone want to steal my slap?"

"Well, it could be relevant," said Pullet.

"I don't know," said Cherichetti, slowly shaking his head. "I use so much of the stuff I wouldn't notice."

At that moment, a hefty black-haired woman in a spangled corset and fishnet tights came up the steps of the trailer, patting sweat from her face with a multicolored towel.

"What goes on here?" she asked.

"The police," explained Cherichetti. "They came to see me because they felt like a laugh."

The woman stalked aggressively into the trailer and planted her fists on her spangled hips. "They wasted their time, huh? Nobody gets a laugh from you."

Mr. Cherichetti raised his beercan and said, "This is Josephina, my girlfriend. The most beautiful woman in California, if not the universe."

Skrolnik looked from Josephina to Cherichetti and then back to Josephina again. He gave Cherichetti's shoulder a comforting squeeze. "Good luck," he said. "It looks like you need it. Come on, Pullet, let's go see what the score is in Venice."

CHAPTER FOURTEEN

Jerry Sennett was putting the finishing touches to a homemade pepperoni pizza when the doorbell rang. He dusted the flour off his hands, took a quick swallow of whiskey from the glass beside the pastry board, and then walked through his living room to answer it. It was Mack Holt, in jeans this time, and a T-shirt. He looked hot and agitated.

"Mr. Sennett? Jerry? I'm sorry. I should have called first."

"You saw the news bulletin?"

Mack nodded. "You're right. It's the same mask. The damned same mask! What was that you said about 'a cold wind'? That's like something psychic. Intuition, or something."

"Well, you can call it a hunch, if you want to," said Jerry. "Listen, I've just made a pizza. Do you want to stay and have some? It'll take a little while to bake."

"Pizza? Well, sure. I mean, I don't want to impose on you."

Jerry smiled. "I told you before. I am impervious to imposition. Anyway, my son David's staying with friends this evening out at the beach. He's reached the age when he has a social life of his own, which apparently doesn't include dear old Dad."

No Mom?" asked Mack. It was an innocent question, not prying.

"Mom—my wife, Rhoda—well, she died a few years ago," said Jerry. "Since then I've been trying to bring David up on my own. With varied success, I might tell you. He's cheerful. Ebullient, even. But I sometimes think he lacks the security that a mother could have given him. Do you understand what I mean?"

"I sure do," said Mack. "My parents broke up when I was ten, and I missed my dad like hell. He married some waitress from Albuquerque. Not that I *blame* him, she was half his age and real pretty. I mean, *real* pretty. But, you know, I didn't get any of that friendly cuffing around the head, none of that talk about football and airplanes and cowboys. I used to look at other kids who had two parents, two normal parents, you know, and I used to be so damned *jealous*."

"You're not jealous now, though?" asked Jerry, pouring Mack a drink.

"I don't know. Maybe. Maybe I still envy them their memories."

Jerry sat down on the sofa and crossed his legs, watching Mack with sympathy but also with the perceptiveness of a trained intelligence officer. It was a habit that thirty-eight years had done nothing to erase. Jerry wanted to know things because he had been trained to want to know things. His old instructor had rasped at him, "The intelligence officer who isn't incurably curious isn't worth doodly-squat. Dis-miss!"

Jerry said, "What about Sherry? Did Sherry represent any kind of security for you? Did you ever talk about getting married?"

"We lived together for quite a while," said Mack. "I guess I always assumed that we were going to stay together forever. She was very *warm*, you know. One of these girls you can sit with all evening, and you don't have to say a single word, and you know that you're getting through."

"I think that came over on the TV screen," said Jerry.

Mack swallowed Chivas Regal and shrugged in acknowledgment. "Sure. The trouble was, when everybody else started loving her, I started to feel crowded out."

"You argued?"

"*I* argued. She didn't say anything, just took it, hoping I'd learn to understand. I don't think she really wanted to leave me, but you know what insecure people are like. Forever saying, 'Get out of here, I don't need you,' in the hope that she'll say, 'You may not need me, but I need you.' Classic. She packed and left, and I didn't do anything to stop her. Five minutes later I was banging my head against the wall and wondering why the hell I was so damned stupid.''

Jerry looked across at him carefully. ''Did the police question you?''

''Oh, sure. I'm not supposed to leave the city, and I have to rack my brains to think of anyone who might have killed her.''

''Any ideas?''

Mack tugged his fingers through his blond curls and shook his head. ''Why did Manson's creepie-crawlies kill Sharon Tate? Why does anybody kill anybody? I don't know. This whole town is nutty. I thought *you* were nutty, until I saw that mask on television.''

Jerry stood up again. He needed to stand up to say what he had to say next. ''I *am* nutty,'' he said. ''Well, slightly. I had some bad experiences in Japan during the war, things to do with conscience, and guilt. Things you don't easily forget. You remember Colonel Paul Tibbets, who piloted the *Enola Gay*, the plane that dropped the first atomic bomb on Hiroshima? You remember what happened to him, how he turned into a kelptomaniac, that kind of thing?''

''The same thing happened to you?'' asked Mack.

''I used to steal clocks and turn the hands back to 8 A.M. the minute before they dropped the atom bomb, in the hope that it might never have happened. I don't steal clocks anymore, but I still have dreams about it. That morning, we killed 78,150 people at one stroke, in one instant and burned or injured 37,425. Hundreds of people are still suffering for what we did, even today.''

Mack didn't say anything for a while, but then he suggested gently, ''We were fighting a war, right? A whole lot more people would have died if we hadn't dropped it.''

''You think so? Well, who can say? Yes, you're probably right. My doctor says the same thing. 'You helped to save the lives of countless American troops,' he tells me. 'It was either us, or them.' But that doesn't take away the enormity of what I had to do. That doesn't take away the fact that at one moment in history I was solely responsible for America's decision whether to drop that atomic bomb or not. I've never even told David about it, my own son, I'm so damned *ashamed*.

There was a garlicky smell of baking pizza coming from the kitchen. Mack swallowed a mouthful of whiskey and said, "You picked that mask up in Japan?" It was an obvious attempt to change the subject.

Jerry lifted the mask up from the table. The late-afternoon sun shone brilliantly through its empty eyeholes, giving it a disturbingly triumphant appearance. "You don't believe me?" he asked.

Mack shrugged. "It was Truman who decided to drop the bomb, right?"

Jerry hesitated for a moment, then looked down at his half-empty glass. "Yes, it was Truman who decided to drop the bomb."

Mack looked distinctly uneasy. "Maybe I shouldn't have come."

"Sure, it was Truman who decided to drop the bomb. It was Truman who said go. But Truman wasn't sitting beside me in those mountains by Yuki and Namata, with a high-power receiving set, listening to Japanese intelligence reports from Hiroshima. Truman didn't know whether I was fabricating everything I heard on that radio or not. When I said 'That's it,' Truman said go; but if I *hadn't* said 'That's it,' then Truman would have said forget it. You really believe he was eager to drop that thing? Maybe he was. Who knows?"

Mack finished his drink and put down the glass. "I don't know," he said. "I wasn't even born then."

"Sure," nodded Jerry. "You weren't even born. Well, that lets you out. You can think about Hiroshima with an easy mind."

"Listen," said Mack, "I don't even pretend to understand it. I came here because of the mask; and because of Sherry. I didn't come here for a lecture in moral philosophy, or some kind of psycho confession about World War Two.''

Jerry looked at Mack for a moment, and then nodded. ''You're right. I'm sorry. I'm acting my age. I'm out of date. And I'm even more sorry that I'm having to say sorry.''

Mack said, ''Okay. Listen, I wasn't very understanding. I never had to serve in the Army, you know? I don't even know what I'm talking about. I'm just as sorry as you are.''

Jerry thought for a while, then emptied his glass and set it down on the table beside him. ''You want to talk about the mask?'' he asked Mack.

''Sure. I couldn't believe it when I turned on the television and there it was. The same goddamned mask. I don't think I've ever felt so creepy in my whole goddamned life.''

''You're happy it was the same mask?''

''If happy's the word for it.''

Jerry said, ''Come on into the kitchen. That pizza's going to be ready before you know it.''

Mack perched on a stool while Jerry took the pizza out of the oven and fumbled it onto a wire rack to cool. Jerry said, ''That white mask is similar to those they use in Nō theater, in Japan. There are two main kinds of traditional theater in Japan—Kabuki, which was the dance theater introduced for commoners at the end of the sixteenth century—and Nō, which was reserved for the aristocracy. There was also, of course, the Bugaku theater, which was performed exclusively for the Japanese royal family, and which wasn't seen by the public from the time it began in the seventh century until the end of World War Two. Can you imagine that? A whole art form which was kept secret for 1,300 years. When you start to think about that, you can start to think about what you're really up against when you're competing with the Japanese. I know, I know, you're thinking about Toyotas and Panasonic televisions and Suntory whiskey. But you're missing the point. Everybody's missing the point.

"Japan is a mystical, rigid, highly formalized society; a society in which magic and occult forces have considerably more strength because they're so widely accepted and believed. Japan is the last great magical society of the modern world; and that magic was only slightly diminished by losing the war to the United States. Oh—they were prepared to accept certain superficial changes, after Hiroshima and Nagasaki. There are times when even the dragon is prepared to surrender to the atomic bomb. But Japan remains, and always will. That extraordinary group of islands has a social and religious history more ancient than Americans can imagine. You know something? The city of Nara, that's about 26 miles south of Kyoto, that used to be the capital of Japan, from the year 710 to 784. Can you imagine that? One thousand years before the Declaration of Independence. And that's where the culture that created this mask, the culture that was responsible for Sherry Cantor's murder—that's where this culture began."

Mack said, "I'm not sure that I understand what you're saying."

Jerry began to slice up the pizza. "I'm not sure what I'm saying, either. No masks may make some kind of sense to *me*, but why should they have anything to do with Sherry? Did Sherry ever visit Japan?"

Mack shook his head. "She never traveled farther than Bloomington, Indiana. That's where her mother lived."

"Did she know any Japanese people? Work in a Japanese restaurant?"

"Not that she told me."

Jerry slid a plate out of the cupboard and handed Mack a steaming slice of pizza. "You want a beer?" he asked.

Mack said, "Sure. A light, if you've got it."

They sat side by side at the kitchen counter, devouring the pizza. Every now and then, Mack would stop to fan his mouth with his hand. "This is terrific pizza. I'm going to have a thousand blisters on the roof of my mouth tomorrow."

Jerry said, "We could be making a really bad mistake. I mean, *I* could. When the witnesses said that the murderer was wearing a white mask, they could have been confused. They were all in passing cars, remember. What they saw was probably nothing more than a glimpse. And the guy could have been wearing anything. A white stocking over his face. White makeup. Maybe he was just naturally pale, like an albino."

"But the police drawings," Mack put in. "They look just like that mask."

"Well, sure they do," agreed Jerry. "But what do we have here? Two eyes, a nose, a mouth; and a white, blank face. Not much to go on."

Mack looked up at Jerry narrowly. "That cold wind you talked about. You don't feel it anymore? That intuition?"

Jerry toyed with his last triangle of pizza. "I'm not sure. Once you start analyzing it, once you start thinking about it, you lose it. It was in Kyoto once, after the war, walking along Shijo Street on my way to the Fujii Daimaru department store. I stepped off the curb just opposite the Shiro Karasuma station, and I felt that cold wind like ice. I stepped right back onto the curb again, and an Army truck grazed my hip. Just missed me."

Mack said, "You're sure, aren't you?"

"Sure of what?"

"You're sure that the guy who killed Sherry was wearing a Nō mask."

Jerry thought for a moment. "Yes," he nodded, "I'm sure."

Mack picked up his beer, and then put it down again. "Maybe this isn't relevant," he said.

"Maybe what isn't relevant?"

"Well . . . come with me for a second. I just want to show you something."

Jerry hesitated at first, but then he followed Mack out of the house, leaving the door open behind them, and down the sloping concrete driveway to the street. The day was humid and smoggy, and Jerry wiped his face with his hand to clear away the sweat.

Mack stood on the sidewalk and said, "Take a look at this."

Jerry said, "My house number. What of it?"

"No, but you're *used* to it," said Mack. "When *I* first came up here, I didn't know whether number 11 was your house or Sherry's bungalow next door. The party wall, the angle of the driveway. To someone who isn't familiar with the street, and the way the houses are arranged, it looks like *Sherry's* bungalow is number 11."

Jerry narrowed his eyes, and took a pace or two backward. After a while he said, "You know something? You're right."

Mack stared at Jerry through the sweltering heat of the afternoon. "You know what that could mean, don't you? What with the Japanese mask and everything? It would make more sense."

Jerry felt that cold wind again, blowing around the skirts of his soul. "You're trying to tell me that it would make more sense if the killer had made a mistake, mixed up the houses?"

"Sherry didn't know *anything* about Japanese people. Nothing. I don't think she'd even been to Benihana's. All she was interested in was *Our Family Jones*, and being a terrific television star, and that was it. I'm not sure—and I'm not trying to sound like a jealous ex-boyfriend or anything—but I don't think she was even dating anybody. Not seriously."

Jerry looked back at the low stone wall with 11 on it, and then nodded. "You're saying that the killer was after me, and not Sherry? You're saying that *I'm* the one who should've been torn to pieces?"

"It's only a theory."

"Oh, sure. Some theory."

"Listen," said Mack, "I know there are all kinds of holes in it. Like, how did the killer manage to mistake a young woman for a middle-aged man, and why did he kill her even when he knew that he was attacking the wrong person? But . . . you heard what the police said. The guy was crazy. Only a crazy person could rip the legs right off a girl's body, just for the hell of it. And if he was crazy, then maybe he didn't care too much *who* he killed."

Jerry said, "Let's go back in the house. It's too damned hot out here. And besides, half the blinds in the whole damned street are twitching. They're a nosy bunch up here in Orchid Place. I've been thinking of rechristening it Rubberneck Mountain."

Back in the kitchen, they finished their pizza and drank their beer in silence. Then Mack took out a packet of papers and rolled himself a cigarette.

"The most important clue to this thing is that N̄o mask, isn't it?" he asked Jerry, blowing out smoke.

Jerry wiped beerfoam away from his upper lip. "It could be. I'm not sure. But as far as I know, I'm the only person in this whole street who has ever had anything to do with Japan; and boy, did I have something to do with Japan. It was practically up to me that the whole country got wiped out."

"You think you ought to tell the police?"

"I don't know. I suppose so. It's just that I haven't worked it out in my own head yet, and I think I need to. If I tell the police about it now, that'll kind of take the onus off my own brain, and maybe I'll miss something important, simply because I don't feel I'm responsible for it anymore. I have to admit it, I've got a lazy mind. Old age, I guess."

"Do you think somebody found out what you did in the war? One of these Japanese terrorist groups? Maybe that's it. You remember that trouble they had last year at the Japanese Film Festival, all those fanatical rightwing Japanese students threatening to disembowel themselves all over the place?"

Jerry didn't reply, but swilled the last of his beer around in his glass as if he couldn't decide whether he ought to drink it or not.

Mack said, "It wasn't your fault, you know, what

happened to Sherry. Even if it was all a mistake, and the killer was really looking for you. You can't blame yourself."

Jerry gave Mack a forced smile. "You're just saying that to make me feel better."

"You think so?" said Mack. "I was Sherry's lover. I still am."

Jerry finished his beer, and then said slowly, "That Nō mask, that particular Nō mask, represents the absolute epitome of cruelty. It appears in only one or two traditional plays, and even then it seems to be treated with great ambiguity . . . do you understand? As if the actors themselves can't decide how they ought to react toward it. It's very powerful, very strange . . . as if it's the worst thing the actors could possibly imagine, something they ought to hate and reject, and yet they can't, because it's part of the human condition itself . . . Like, you may detest yourself for being unreasonably angry with somebody at work, or for swearing at somebody who pushes in front of you when you're standing in line, but anger and viciousness are part of what you are, and you can't completely reject them because that means you'd be rejecting part of yourself."

Mack said, "What do they call it? This Nō character?"

Jerry put down his glass. "It has several names. The most common name comes from the Shinto monks who originally staged the Nō drama-dances; and that name is simply used to describe any monk who has sold his soul to total evil. The Tengu, they call him. The carrion monster. The tearer of hearts and souls."

Mack stood up and went across to the table where the mask lay, empty and emotionless, smiling but unsmiling, death without rhyme or reason. "Whatever the police do," he said hoarsely, "you and me, we've got to find this character, the guy who wore this mask; and we've got to take our own revenge."

Jerry said, "Revenge?"

"What would you call it?" asked Mack.

Jerry shrugged. "Justice? I don't know. No, you're right. Not justice. Revenge."

CHAPTER FIFTEEN

Gerard Crowley was sitting in the sauna on the twenty-third floor of Century Park East reading "It Pays to Increase Your Word Power" in the *Reader's Digest* when the telephone rang. He picked it up, sweating, and said, "Yes?"

"Mr. Crowley? This is Mr. Esmeralda."

"Well, good evening to you, Mr. Esmeralda."

"Not so good *yet*, Mr. Crowley. But, if everything goes well . . ."

Gerard took a breath of lung-scorching air. "You want something done, right? I detect that note of lip-licking anticipation."

"You're a good judge of latent emotion, Mr. Crowley. Yes, I want something done. Can we meet?"

Gerard lifted himself up slightly so that he could see the clock on the gymnasium wall through the sauna window. It was 6:47 P.M., and he was due to take Francesca to The Tower at 7:30 for dinner. He said, "Can't we make it tomorrow? I'm really tied up this evening."

"It's urgent, Mr. Crowley. More urgent than dining out with Francesca Allis."

Gerard wiped sweat away from his mouth with the back of his hand. "All right. I'll manage to cancel. Where do you want to meet?"

Mr. Esmeralda cleared this throat. "Meet me at Inca's, 301 North Berendo Street, at eight."

"Inca's?"

"It's a restaurant. South American."

"Listen, Mr. Esmeralda—"

"What is it?" Mr. Esmeralda's voice was calm and cold.

Gerard let out a short, testy sigh. "I'll see you at Inca's, at eight. That's all."

"Goodbye."

Gerard hung up, reached for his towel, and angrily punched open the door of the sauna. Joseph, the coach, was buffing up the chrome on the barbell when Gerard came stalking through to the changing room and banged open the door of his locker.

"You're getting dressed already, Mr. Crowley? Didn't you take a shower? Your pores are going to be way open, Mr. Crowley, like a Swiss cheese."

"Fuck my pores," snapped Gerard, tugging his shirt on to his damp back. Joseph glanced up at Mr. Corrit, from Corrit Film Productions, who was panting into his eighteenth mile on the Puch exercise cycle, and pulled an utterly perplexed face. How could *anybody* who cared *anything* for modern body-toning say anything like "fuck my pores"? It was a total denial of the fitness ethic.

Back at his desk on the twenty-seventh floor, Gerard tucked his shirt untidily into his belt, and called Francis Canu at The Tower. "Francis, I'm sorry. Your restaurant is beautiful. The best. I'm going to remember the Sunset Room when I'm in heaven. Well, wherever. But some other time, you know? Yes. Yes, I know. Well, me too." Then he called Francesca at her studio apartment at Culver and Elenda. "Francesca? Hi. It's Gerard. Yes. Listen, baby—yes, I know—but I have to tell you that tonight's off. No. No, listen, its not Evie. It's nothing to do with Evie. It's business, you got me? Genuine, legitimate business. Well, look. Will you please listen to what I'm telling you? Yes. I'll come by at eleven o'clock if I'm through by then. I should be, sure. And, listen—" He closed his eyes and listened for almost three minutes to a staccato rattle of complaint. Now and then he nodded and began to say something, but it was only when her anger was completely spent that he was able to say, "I'm sorry. You got that? You want me to spell it for you? And I love you, too, regardless. Yes. Well, you can think what you like. But I'm sorry. And I love you. And if I don't see you later tonight I'll see you tomorrow. Yes. Yes. Goodbye. Yes. Goodbye."

He was sweating afresh by the time he put down the phone. He wished—almost, but not really—that he had told Francesca just what to do with her fancy culinary tastes and her wretched language. But the truth was, he did, in his peculiarly self-destructive way, love her. They were right together, she and he, Gerard and Francesca. Suicidal, maybe, like the lovers in "Life in the Fast Lane," by the Eagles, which Gerard played at top volume on his Delco 8-track as he drove to work every morning. *He was brutally handsome . . . and she was terminally pretty. . . .* But wasn't that where he had always needed to be; wasn't that where he had been *born* to be; speeding along in the fast lane, reckless, crazy, high as a kite? He looked at the color photograph of Evie and the twins next to his telephone, and suddenly he knew that he could never go back; security and marriage and Evie's endless attentiveness were like suffocation and slow death. If he was going to die, then he wanted to die fast. So fast that he would never know what hit him.

On his way out of the office, he caught sight of himself in the screen of tinted glass which surrounded his receptionist's desk. He looked not chiseled, but tired; not brutally handsome, but middle-aged. It had never occurred to him before, not with such uncompromising clarity, that he might simply be growing too old for the kind of life he was trying to lead. He started to light up a cigar in the elevator, but a dignified black cleaning woman pointed wordlessly to the notice: NO SMOKING UNDER PENALTY OF LAW.

He had to wait in line for nearly ten minutes before they brought his car up from the underground parking lot, and he drove out of Century City with a shriek of tires and a bad-tempered blast on his horn. He had a stop to make before meeting Mr. Esmeralda.

Outside Nancy Shiranuka's apartment on Alta Loma, he parked his Buick aggressively between two other cars, colliding bumper-to-bumper with both of them, and then he got out and slammed the door. Kemo was waiting for him when he stepped out of the elevator on the fourth floor, impassively holding the door open. "Welcome, Mr. Crowley, he said. "Miss Shiranuka was not expecting you."

"Hi, Kemo," said Gerard, and gripped the boy's arm as he entered the hallway, so that he could balance himself while he slipped off his Bijan loafers. Nancy was sitting cross-legged on one of the black-and-white silk cushions on the living room floor, her eyes closed, listening to a tape of *koto* music. There was sandlewood smoke in the room, and the fragrance of tea. Kemo said to Gerard, "You wish for a drink, Mr. Crowley?"

"Scotch," Gerard told him. "And none of that Japanese stuff you gave me the last time. McKamikaze, or whatever it was called."

"Yes, Mr. Crowley."

Nancy opened her eyes and looked toward Gerard without turning her head. "This is an unexpected delight," she said blandly.

"I've had another call from Esmeralda," Gerard said, dragging over two or three cushions and sitting down closer to Nancy than Nancy obviously thought was comfortable. "I'm supposed to be meeting him at eight at a restaurant downtown called Inca's."

"Do you know what he wants?" asked Nancy. Her eyes were as dark and as reflective as pools of oil. You could have drowned in her eyes—you could have been swallowed up in their Oriental tranquility, but your feathers would have been slicked forever.

Gerard said, "It sounds like something important. Maybe we're going to have to go out to the ranch again.

Personally, I don't know what the hell's going on, and I don't particularly care. As long as Esmeralda keeps the bank deposits coming, that's all that matters.''

"A man of principle," said Nancy, quietly but acidly.

"That's right," Gerard agreed. "And the principle is that I make as much money as I can and stay alive for as long as possible.''

Kemo came in with Gerard's whiskey on a square black-lacquered tray. Gerard took the drink, knocked back half of it, and then said, "one thing, though. It's time we found out who's pulling the strings around here. I mean *really* pulling the strings. If Esmeralda has something particularly important to tell me tonight, and it sounds as if he does, then he's probably going to go straight back to his employers to report that everything's okay, or whatever.''

Nancy nodded almost imperceptibly. "You mean to follow him?" she asked.

"Not me, of course. But Kemo could. If he really wants to take Yoshikazu's place, it's time he statrted getting actively involved.''

"You don't think that it might be excessively dangerous, trying to check up on our employers?" asked Nancy. "Esmeralda did insist from the very beginning, did he not, that we should do nothing except what he told us to do; and that we should refrain from being too inquisitive? And—let us make no bones about it, Gerard, anyone who can create a Tengu, as these people can . . . well, they are not to be played with.''

Gerard said, "Of course it's dangerous. But which is going to be *more* dangerous? That's what we have to ask ourselves. Should we make an attempt to find out who's behind all this—who's giving the orders, who's paying the money? Or should we blindly go on doing all of Esmeralda's dirty work for him, never quite knowing when the police or the FBI or the very people we're working for are going to wipe us out? Just as you said yesterday, my dear, we were all chosen not so much for our individual talents, however sparkling those might be, but because we're all of us *dispensable*. Easy to get rid of. Each one of us has been involved in enough shady little sidelines for the police not to ask too many embarrassing questions if we happened to meet with a nasty and unexpected accident. I used to run guns in Cuba; the commander used to traffic in children; and God only knows what *you* used to be mixed up with, but I can guarantee that it was something less respectable than Sunday-school outings.''

Nancy thought carefully for a while, and then stood up, gracefully slipslopping in silk slippers to the other side of the room, where she switched off her *koto* music and slid a bamboo panel across the stereo equipment.

''I have had a feeling for some time now that we do not know the whole story of what we are doing and why we have been employed,'' she said.

''I've had that feeling from the very beginning,'' said Gerard. ''But when ten thousand dollars is credited to your account every single month, on the first, without fail, then who's arguing?''

''They pay you ten?'' asked Nancy. Her voice was emotionless. The way she said it, Gerard didn't know whether she was getting more than him, or less. Nancy added, ''I wonder where the money is all coming from. I know they are paying the commander seven thousand a month, and Esmeralda has promised him a bonus if he arranges everything to Esmeralda's satisfaction.''

Gerard said, ''Whoever they are, they're obviously loaded.''

''Don't you think, more loaded than this Tengu project warrants? Such an investment, such salaries, all for the sake of bodyguards?''

''Very special bodyguards, so Mr. Esmeralda said. Completely invincible. The kind that a Mafia leader or an Arab oil millionaire would pay up to a couple of million to have beside him.''

''Do you think that really rings true?'' asked Nancy.

''Security is big business these days. There are condominium owners on Wilshire who would pay anything you asked for a bodyguard like one of Esmeralda's Tengus.''

"I don't know..... I find it difficult to be satisfied by what Esmeralda keeps telling us," said Nancy.

"Does it matter?''

"It didn't matter until they sent the Tengu to kill that Sennett man. Now we have two murders on our conscience. That poor actress, and that policeman.''

"On *your* conscience, maybe, but not on mine," said Gerard. He finished his whiskey in one throat-burning swallow, and then held up the glass for Kemo to bring him another one. "Esmeralda said that Sennett used to work in Japan during the war, and that he will guess what the Tengus are all about the minute he hears about them. Gempaku's using some kind of process that isn't strictly in accordance with FDA regulations, you know? Some brand of anabolic steroids to build them up physically, give them muscle. It was either Sennett or us, and that's the hard old story of everyday life and survival. Besides, it gave us a chance to try out the Tengu, didn't it, to see how controllable he was?''

"Not very," said Nancy coolly.

"There was a pharmaceutical problem, that's all. Gempaku used too much stimulant, or so he said. The Tengu woke up in the van and blew his mind. It shouldn't happen again.''

"I don't know," said Nancy. "Esmeralda is always full of explanations, but the *motivations* don't seem right. If you want to develop a team of extra-special bodyguards, why use such clandestine methods? And why use the name of an ancient Japanese demon?''

"You're spooking yourself, that's all," said Gerard. He watched her as she took out her green-lacquered case and lit a cigarette. "As long as we appear to do what we're told, and make sure that Esmeralda never catches us napping, we'll come out of this several hundred thousand dollars richer, and still in one piece.''

Nancy blew two streams of smoke out of her nostrils, and then said quietly, "Let me tell you something, Gerard. I don't know whether Mr. Esmeralda is aware of this or not. It may be the whole reason he approached me and asked me to work for him. But when I was much younger, I belonged for several years to a Shinto shrine in Japan known as the Shrine of the Seven Black *Kami*."

Kemo brought Gerard his Scotch, and Gerard took a large mouthful before he said anything. "The Seven Black *Kami*?" he asked. "What are they?"

"In Shinto, every material object—every mountain, tree, lake, every person, every animal—is seen as a symbol of spiritual power. Everything and everyone has its *kami*, its spiritual essense, which is not so much its 'being' as its 'beingness.' There are evil *kami* as well as good *kami*, and the particular oddity of the Shrine of the Seven Black *Kami* was that its priests revered the seven most terrible of all Japan's ancient spirits, the most evil, in the hope that they would suffer in mind and body, and thereby achieve greater spiritual cleansing."

"I see," lied Gerard.

"Of course you don't see," said Nancy. "There is no way that I can explain the Shinto shrines to a Westerner. Shinto priests believe that the body and the mind are manifestations of spiritual power, and that if they starve themselves for weeks on end, or walk hundreds of miles barefoot, or immerse themselves for hours in freezing water, they will bring themselves closer to a state of purity."

"Not much chance of achieving a state of purity at Inca's," said Gerard, checking his watch.

Nancy sucked at her cigarette and then said, "Shrine Shinto came into being at the end of World War Two, after the abolition of State Shinto. There is also Imperial Shinto, which is forbidden to the public, and centered around the ancient rites performed by the Emperor of Japan; Sect Shinto, based on the thirteen sects which worship a high trinity of great and good *kami*—Amaterasu,

Izanagi, and Izanami; and Folk Shinto, the superstitious customs of the people who live in Japan's remotest rural regions. Shrine Shinto, however, is the most ritualistic and the most mystical.''

Nancy went on, "It was my uncle who introduced me to the Shrine of the Seven Black *Kami*. Before that, I had always gone to the shrine of Fushimi Inari. But he told me that in conjuring up the demons and devils of old Japan, I would experience my inner self in a way that I had never been able to do before. He said, 'You cannot know total spirituality until you have known utter darkness and despair.' ''

"Go on," said Gerard, watching her narrowly.

"I became obsessively involved with the Seven Black *Kami*," said Nancy. Her voice seemed softer and more Japanese-accented than ever. "I went through mental and physical pain such as I had never suffered before and I hope I never suffer again. Whether everything I saw and heard was happening in my mind alone, I shall never know. But I saw demons walking through the streets of Kyoto; real demons such as I can scarcely describe to you. And for night after night I felt myself on the very brink of something I would have to describe to you as hell itself.

"I walked for five miles on shoes that were filled with broken glass. I sat naked in a *karesansui* garden for a day and a night, impaled on a bronze phallus. I learned to talk the language of devils. I have photographs of myself taken when I was seventeen and eighteen years old, and to look at me you would not have thought that I was the same person. You remember the Manson girls? I looked like that."

Gerard said huskily, "What made you give it up?"

Nancy half-smiled at him. "I underwent the greatest of all the mortifications of the spirit and the flesh that a member of the shrine could attempt. I took into my-self—that is, I allowed myself to become possessed—one of the Seven Black *Kami*. Actually *possessed*. The idea was to experience complete evil from the inside; and thereby to conquer it forever.''

She was quiet for a moment. Her long, immaculately painted fingernails traced a pattern on the polished wooden floor. Then she said, ''It took me six years finally to shrug off that demon, and in the end I only managed it because I was taken in by a wise and knowledgeable old Shinto priest called Shizuota-Tani. He had seen me many times in Kyoto during the six years of my possession, and he had gradually come to understand that what I appeared to be was not my true self. I appeared to be a drug addict, a prostitute, and, indirectly, a murderess.''

''A murderess?'' asked Gerard. He felt the skin prickling at the back of his back.

''I procured girls for films which, in Japan, we call sacrifice dramas. In Los Angeles they are commonly known as 'snuff movies.' Films in which girls are involved in sexual orgies, and then, at the height of intercourse, are stabbed or strangled right in front of the camera.''

Gerard said nothing. The room was as silent as a Japanese rock garden.

Nancy said, ''I went through another year in the company of this priest, fighting to find out where, inside myself, my own *kami* had been imprisoned. Then, one night in February, the old priest took me to Nara, the ancient capital, on the evening of the lantern festival at the Kasuga Grand Shrine. I stood in the grounds of the shrine on that evening and saw thousands and thousands of lighted lanterns hanging from the walls and the eaves of the building, bobbing in the wind like the captive souls of happy people. At that moment, without my knowing it, the old priest passed over my head the purification wand, which drives out demons and devils. I fell to the ground as if I had been hit by a truck. They took me to the Kyoto University Hospital, and for three weeks they did not know if I could live. But I survived, and with the help of friends I managed to leave Japan and come here.''

''Why are you telling me this?'' asked Gerard in a harsh, soft voice. ''What does it have to do with Esmeralda?''

"It has everything to do with Esmeralda. The demon which I accepted into myself was Kama Itachi, a kind of weaselike demon which thrives on pain inflicted by knives and blades. There were six other Black *Kami* to which I could have opened myself up: Raiden, the storm demon, for instance, who enters human bodies through the navel, and for fear of whom many Japanese people still sleep on their stomachs during thunderstorms. Kappa, the water demon. Pheng, the bird creature who can eclipse the sun Kami Amaterasu with his wings. Rinjin, the dragon beast, who rejoices in death by fire."

Gerard raised both his hands, a gesture of friendly impatience. "I'm sorry, Nancy, but I'm really not a superstitious guy. I mean, I'm not saying that you didn't experience any of this. I'm not saying that it wasn't as real to you when it happened as anything else you might have experienced. I know how people get when they're on drugs, that kind of thing. But I have to be getting along to see Esmeralda, and I really don't see how this is helping."

Nancy said, very quietly, "The most evil of all the seven Black *Kami* was called the Tengu. Even the most experienced adepts at the shrine were warned opening themselves up to the Tengu. It was said that the leader of the shrine had once done so, and had almost been driven mad. The Tengu had even caused him to bite off his own tongue to prevent him from exorcising the demon, and to curtail his prayers to Amaterasu."

"Nancy, please—" Gerard interrupted.

"*No*," said Nancy. "You must listen to me. The characteristics which the Tengu gave to all the men and women he possessed included invincible physical strength, the mad strength of the berserk; and the ability to stand up to ferocious attack from any kind of weapon. He had another characteristic: if the person he was possessing was chopped into the tiniest pieces, the pieces would regenerate themselves, and grow again into misshapen demons even more hideous than the original. What was more—"

"*Nancy*!" Gerard shouted. "For Christ's sake!"

"*No!*" Nancy hissed back at him. "You have to listen

because it's true! *They've done it*! Don't you understand what I'm saying to you? They're not building up men into bodyguards. They're not using steroids or chemicals or vitamins! They've brought it here, the Tengu, the real Tengu demon!''

She was shaking, and she paced from one side of the room to the other as if she were a madwoman who had been locked up for her own safety. "I didn't believe it at first. I didn't want to believe it. I couldn't! I thought, they are using the name of the Tengu simply because it also means a terrible and powerful being. When Esmeralda said we had to send it out to kill, I had fears enough then. But what happened to that girl, and the way that policeman was smashed to death . . . . That Tengu was no superathlete, no killer bodyguard. Perhaps Esmeralda doesn't even know it himself, but we're helping him to create a race of men who are possessed by the cruelest devil ever known. The Tengu is the devil of remorseless destruction; a god without a conscience and without pity. Those men have him in their souls, and they can *never* get rid of him.''

CHAPTER SIXTEEN

At nine o'clock that evening, Skrolnik and Pullet drew up outside a pink house on Rialto Avenue in Venice, and doused the lights of their car. Across the street, two or three young boys were smoking and playing a guitar and drinking beer. "I could do with a beer myself," growled Skrolnik. "That chili-dog is just about burning me up, from the inside out."

"I could get you a Pepsi," suggested Pullet.

Skrolnik gave Pullet such a withering look in reply that Pullet found himself coughing, looking through his notebook, folding his arms, and finally saying, "Well, I *offered*."

Skrolnik said, "Okay, you offered. Next time, don't offer. Now, how are we going to tackle this El Krusho character? I have a feeling that if we invite him to accompany us back to headquarters, he's going to decline. You know what I mean? Guys with a fifty-pound advantage usually do. So, we're going to have to catch him by surprise. You go round the back of the house. I'll take the front. At nine-fifteen on the button we'll kick open our respective doors and shout '*Freeze, police*'! You got me?"

"Freeze, police?" asked Pullet.

"For Christ's sake," said Skrolnik.

They climbed out of their car and walked side by side across the sidewalk until they reached the low stone wall which surrounded Casita Rosa. Skrolnik hiked his police .38 out of his belt and cocked it. "Just remember," he said. "This guy is totally dangerous. If it looks like he's going for you, armed or not, open fire. Shoot to kill."

"What should I do if it looks like he's going for *you*?"

"Stand by idly and watch him grind me into a Wendy's hamburger," said Skrolnik sarcastically. "What the hell do you think?"

Pullet went around to the back, climbing uncertainly over a wrought-iron fence, while Skrolnik went to the front door, his revolver raised in his right hand, and tentatively rang the bell. There was a long silence, punctuated only by the lonely nighttime sound of a patrol car as it howled its way along Mildred Avenue, answering a call to a supermarket robbery. Skrolnik glanced up at the building and thought for a moment that he could see someone looking down into the street from the third floor, a girl's face. He leaned forward and pressed the bell again.

It was 9:11. If Skrolnik didn't get into the building now, right away, Detective Pullet would inevitably go leaping into the suspect's room, legs bent, revolver held in both hands in the approved Los Angeles Police Academy style, and get the holy shit beaten out of him. Skrolnik yelled, "Somebody open this goddamned door!" but after a whole minute of waiting, nobody did.

Skrolnik propped his back against one of the wooden pillars of the porch, lifted his left leg, and kicked against the lock. There was a loud bang, Kinney town shoe against solid oak, but the door didn't give one fraction of an inch. Skrolnik took a deep breath and kicked again. Nothing. The door was so damned thick that it wouldn't budge.

At that moment, however, there was a clicking noise, like a catch being released, and the door suddenly swung open. An elderly lady in a blue nylon scarf and a blue bathrobe stood there, blinking at Sergeant Skrolnik through bifocals.

"You don't have to *knock*, you know," she told him. She reached across and pointed to the bell. "You can always . . . you know . . . ding-a-ling-a-ling!"

Skrolnik flipped open his badge wallet. "Madam," he said. "I have reason to believe that there may be a dangerous criminal in this building."

"I'm eighty-three years old," the woman said, with a note of triumph.

"That's terrific," Sergeant Skrolnik told her. "Eighty-three! You don't look a day over sixty!"

"Well, you're very flattering," the old lady smiled. Skrolnik checked his watch; it was 9:14.

"Lady," he said, "in one minute flat my partner's going to come busting into the house from the rear, and I've got to be up there to give him some backup. So, will you please . . . ?"

The old lady clutched Skrolnik's sleeve. "Do you know something?" she said. "You remind me so much of my grandson—a fine, well-built fellow, just like you."

"Lady—" said Skrolnik, gently but firmly clutching her wrist and prising her away from him. But it was too late. There was the flat sound of a handgun shot from upstairs, then a scream, a girl's scream, and a door banging open so hard that plaster showered down the stairwell. Skrolnik threw himself against the wall, his .38 raised toward the stairs, his eyes wide.

"Pullet!" he shouted. "Pullet, what the fuck's going on?"

The next instant, a huge man came thundering down the stairs with a noise like an approaching avalanche. Skrolnik shrieked, "Freeze! Police!" but the huge man collided with him as he fired his first shot, and the bullet zonked harmlessly into the plaster.

Skrolnik, however, was a streetfighter, and not so easily put off by one simple dead-end football block. He made a grab for the big man's arm as he galloped for the front door, missed, but ran two steps, jumped, and clung onto the big man's shoulders.

There was a grunting struggle. The big man's hand pushed straight into Skrolnik's face, squashing his nose. Skrolnik punched him in the kidneys, once, twice, three times, and then in the side of the ear. They both toppled and fell over, while the old lady in the blue bathrobe had gone off to fetch a spiky-haired toilet brush, and now was hitting them both violently on the back and the legs.

Skrolnik jerked up the huge man's head and succeeded to getting a wristlock onto his throat, as well as a good firm handful of hair. He banged the head on the green linoleum floor to stun him, and followed that up with another punch in the ear. Then he painfully climbed off, and scrabbled around for his hat, and his glasses, and his .38. He found his gun on the other side of the hallway, wedged behind a cheap Chinese vase with a chipped rim. He picked the gun up, cocked it again, and walked over to the huge man lying half-conscious.

"You have the right to remain silent," he panted. "But you are advised that anything you say can and will be used against you in a court of law."

The huge man lifted his head and saw the muzzle of Skrolnik's revolver pointing at his nose. "All right," he said. "All right."

Skrolnik tugged his handcuffs out and locked the huge man's ankle to the bottom of the newel post. Then he quickly climbed the stairs, calling, "Pullet? Pullet, are you okay?"

The old lady shrilled out, "You can't leave this monster here! Not in my hallway!" and she slapped at the huge man with her toilet brush.

"For Christ's sake," the man complained. "I've surrendered!"

At that moment, one of the doors across the landing opened. Detective Pullet appeared, blushing. Behind him, inside the bedroom, Skrolnik glimpsed somebody bending over, and he pushed past Pullet's foolish grin and threw the door wide. "All right," he demanded. "What goes on here?"

The room was decorated with rose-covered wallpaper, and over the wide bed was a 3-D picture of Jesus the Savior, sad but forgiving, his hand raised, surrounded by a glittering gold chorus of 3-D cherubs. A young girl with very short-cropped blonde hair was sitting on the end of the bed, rolling on a pair of sheer black stockings. Apart from her stockings and a black garter belt, she was naked, small-breasted, suntanned, and Teutonically pretty. A Rhine maiden in shiny nylon.

"Is that your boyfriend, that man-mountain we've got downstairs?" asked Skrolnik. He watched impassively as the girl fastened her stockings and then reached for a sheer black bra. It is a good thing I'm a reliable family man, Skrolnik thought. Because, by God, if I weren't a reliable family man. . . .

"He hasn't *done* anything, has he?" the girl asked, in a snappy East coast accent. "He hasn't broken the *law* or anything?"

"What do you think?" asked Skrolnik. "You probably know him better than we do."

"He's a *real* gentle guy," the girl said. "Most of my girlfriends call him the Gentle Giant."

"Ever known him aggressive? Mad, for any reason? Drunk, maybe?"

The girl reached for a short black dress with a white Peter Pan collar. "Sometimes he gets sore about the whales."

"The whales?"

"You know, the whale-killing, Save the Whale. He hates the Japanese for what they're doing to the whales. And the Russians, he *hates* the Russians. I swear, if he ever saw a Russian, he'd tear him to *pieces*."

Skrolnik nodded. "I see. Is that what he does to people when he's mad at them, tears them to pieces?"

"Oh, sure. I mean, he'd tear *anybody* to pieces."

Detective Pullet was standing by the door with his notebook. Skrolnik turned around and gave him a jaundiced look. "What are you doing, detective? Taking down evidence, or sketching? You heard what the girl said. When he gets mad, he tears people to pieces."

Detective Pullet said, "Oh, sure," and jotted a few notes.

Sergeant Skrolnik looked around the bedroom. "This your room, miss?"

"It's my friend's room. But she lets me use it when I meet Maurice."

"Can you tell me your name please?"

"Oh, sure. Beverly Krauss, Bitzi for short. I live at 1803 Taft Avenue, with my parents. Walter C. Krauss, Consultant Pediatrician."

"Sure. I see. Have you known Maurice long?"

Beverly Krauss shrugged. "I guess a year, almost. Ten months. Maybe longer. I met him at the circus last spring. His circus name is El Krusho the Great."

"Sure. El Krusho."

"You've been lovers all that time?"

Beverly nodded. "Could you do me up, please? This catch is kind of fiddly."

Detective Pullet stepped smartly forward, but Sergeant Skrolnik gave him a sharp stare which sent him smartly

back again. Skrolnik fumbled at the back of Beverly
Krauss's dress with his fat, insensitive fingers, and at last
managed to nudge the hook through the eye.

"Did you ever hear Maurice talk about any of his
previous girlfriends?" asked Skrolnik.

Beverly frowned at him. "Sure. I talked about *my* old
flames, he talked about *his*. What's he supposed to have
done wrong?"

"Just bear with me for one moment," said Skrolnik, as
reassuringly as he could. "Did Maurice ever mention a girl
named Sherry Cantor?"

"Well, sure. I knew Sherry Cantor. I mean, I met her
once or twice. Maurice said that he'd always had a kind of
a crush on her. That was, until he met me."

Skrolnik sniffed dryly. "Did Maurice ever mention to
you that Sherry Cantor and he and another man had all
gone to bed together, a threesome?"

Beverly shook her head. "He never told me anything
like that."

"Did Maurice ever say that he was sorry because he
wasn't seeing Sherry Cantor any longer?"

"Un-unh."

"Did Maurice ever say that he disliked Sherry Cantor for
any reason? Did he ever say anything about her? Anything
at all?"

"Once," she said.

Skrolnik glanced at Pullet. "Can you remember what he
said? This could be very important."

"Well," Beverly hesitated, "I don't really know if it's
relevant or anything. We were sitting watching *Our Family
Jones* because nothing else was on . . . and she came on
the screen, Sherry I mean, and he said it. He was pretty
drunk at the time."

"What did he say?" insisted Skrolnik.

"He said, 'I don't know why *she's* acting so pure and
innocent, I gave it to her up her ass once.' "

Sergeant Skrolnik lowered his head and took a deep
breath. "Miss Krauss," he said, "how old are you?"

"Seventeen, and a week."

"Seventeen and a week," Skrolnik repeated sadly. He wiped his forehead with the back of his hand. It was a warm night, warm and close, and there was no air conditioning in the room. "Well," he said, "I'll call a patrol car and have you taken back to . . . Taft Avenue. Meanwhile, I'm afraid we're going to have to take your boyfriend in."

"Take him in? You mean, arrest him?"

Skrolnik nodded.

"But for *what*—I mean, *why*?"

"Homicide, Miss Krauss. The first-degree murder of Sherry Cantor."

"Are you joking? Maurice could never even—"

"Swat a fly?" said Skrolnik. "Is that what you were going to say? The man who tears people to pieces when he's angry? He could never even swat a fly?"

"But that was only a figure of *speech*," protested Beverly. "I didn't mean he actually *does* it!"

"No, sure," said Skrolnik. "Pullet, will you call up the local cavalry and ask them, nicely, if they could take Miss Seventeen-and-a-Week here home to her folks?"

"But you *can't* arrest Maurice!" cried Beverly. "He hasn't done anything! He never killed anybody!"

Pullet said, "Just watch us."

Skrolnik made a quick check of the bedroom, opening drawers, opening the wardrobe, checking the lipstick and the makeup on the cheap varnished dressing table. He opened one drawer and produced, between two fingers, a white satin G-string.

"Well, what do *you* do to prevent embarrassing panty lines?" Beverly demanded.

Skrolnik grunted. "Seventeen and a week, huh?" he said. He took one last look at the room, and then he went downstairs to the hallway, where Maurice Needs was still lying on the floor, his ankle handcuffed to the newel post. The elderly lady in the blue scarf was standing nearby, sucking nervously at her dentures.

"All right, El Krusho," said Skrolnik. "I'm going to release you now, and I want you to come peacefully with me to the police precinct, where you will have the opportunity to call your lawyer. You understand me?"

Maurice Needs nodded. He was very big—bigger than Skrolnik had imagined he would be, from his photograph. Six foot six, at least, and built like Arnold Schwarzenegger's older brother, all trapezoids and deltoids and overdeveloped triceps. He had dark curly hair, and he was dressed in jeans and a slim-fitting black shirt that probably would have flapped around Skrolnik like a bedouin tent.

Maurice Needs painfully stood up. There was a large red bruise on his forehead, and he had the beginnings of a black eye; but he was a good-looking boy, a mixture of Clark Kent and a young Elvis Presley, with a hint of Clint Walker around the eyes. He hopped a little, and then bent over to massage his ankle.

"Sorry I hurt you," said Skrolnik. "Had to keep you tied down somehow."

El Krusho shrugged. "You needn't have bothered, you know? If I'd wanted to, I'd have torn that newel post out by the roots."

Pullet, coming down the stairs, gave Skrolnik a sick little smile. "Seems we've got our man, sergeant."

Skrolnik said, "Let's go. We can talk about this down at the precinct."

Pullet frowned, and began to say, "You don't think that—?"

"I've charged him now, fuckhead," snarled Skrolnik. "But, no, I don't."

CHAPTER SEVENTEEN

Over Inca's *aji de gallina* and *anticuchos*, Mr. Esmeralda carefully explained to Gerard Crowley about Admiral Thorson.

"He was in Japan during the war, and became very friendly with some of the doctors who later worked on the Tengu program for the Tokyo Olympics. He found out about the research simply by accident. He may suspect nothing, but we cannot risk him blowing the whistle on us."

"What I really want to know is this," Gerard said. "When do we stop killing people, and when do we start getting on with building up this team of bodyguards?"

"We have to take everything by orderly steps," said Mr. Esmeralda. He forked up some of his barbecued beef and chewed it assiduously.

"Nancy Shiranuka is getting distinctly restless," Gerard remarked. "She doesn't like this killing any more than I do. If you were intending to create a hit squad of homicidal maniacs, you should have told us. At least we would have known what we were letting ourselves in for. I'm no angel, Esmeralda, and neither is Nancy Shiranuka; and we all know about the good Commander Ouvarov. But the only reason any of us agreed to submit to your rotten blackmail was because we thought we were in on a shady but highly profitable bit of merchandising. Hired thugs for the protection of the wealthy. *Now* what's happened? We've taken an innocent young actress to pieces, as well as a cop, for no reason at all; and two days later you're asking me to take a Tengu out to Rancho Encino Hospital and rip some poor old retired admiral to shreds."

Mr. Esmeralda pushed his plate away, then changed his mind and drew it back again, so that he could fork up a last piece of beef. He kept his eyes on his food and spoke to Gerard lightly, almost absent-mindedly.

"The very first day I approached you, Mr. Crowley, I warned you that you had very little option but to do as you were told. I also warned you not to question my instructions."

"Maybe you did. But now I'm questioning."

"My clients will not be happy about that," smiled Mr. Esmeralda. "They're very particular people when it comes to secrecy and security."

Gerard snapped his fingers at the waiter and said, "Scotch." Then he folded his arms and leaned forward across the table. "Death comes at a pretty high price in California, Mr. Esmeralda, and I'm beginning to think that perhaps you're not paying enough for it."

"You know what your reward will be when the Tengu program is completed."

"A million six? I'm beginning to wonder whether it's worth it. I'm also beginning to wonder if you've really been giving me the whole picture about these so-called bodyguards."

Mr. Esmeralda watched Gerard carefully. "It does not pay, in your business, Mr. Crowley, to be too curious."

"Is that a statement or a warning?"

"What do you think?"

"I think it sounds like a warning, Mr. Esmeralda, and I also think that I'm beginning to get a hook into you the same way you've got a hook into me. There's such a thing as plea bargaining, you know; and if I were to make a clean breast of everything I happen to know about Sherry Cantor's death to the police . . . well, there's a good chance that I wouldn't get more than one-to-three."

"You are not deceiving me for one instant, Mr. Crowley." Mr. Esmeralda smiled. "Go out to the ranch tomorrow with Kemo and pick up the Tengu. Doctor Gempaku will be waiting for you. Oh—and by the way, we are expecting a new consignment of volunteers on Monday from Kyoto. I will let you know the details tomorrow morning. Fifteen of them. So you can see that the bodyguard program *is* actually getting under way."

"I think I'm dreaming this," said Gerard.

"No," said Mr. Esmeralda, and nodded to the waiter as his dessert—*plátanos fritos*—was set in front of him. "It's not a dream. It's simply a manifestation of the peculiar violence inherent in modern living. The world is in imbalance, Mr. Crowley, between those who have and those who want; and the greater the imbalance, the more violent the confrontation between the two. The people who have the most will always be the prime targets for the people who have the least; and that is why they will pay anything for one of our Tengus. The ultimate weapon is personal security—that is how we are going to advertise them."

Gerard swilled his Scotch around in his glass. "I don't believe you, Mr. Esmeralda. Something's happening here. Some really big caper that you're not telling me about. And, you take notice, sooner or later I'm going to find out what it is."

"I have already taken that into account," said Mr. Esmeralda, thinking of Evie—drunk, in her underwear.

"Well, you take notice," Gerard repeated. "I'm on to you, and if you start pushing me too hard, you're going to regret it. I suspected you from the start. This Tengu thing—if it's such a big secret, why did you tell me so much about it, right from the beginning? This killer-bodyguard story—it's just that, a story. If that was all there was to it, you wouldn't have told me anything about it. But you've told me everything. You've answered every question I might have had about it, even before I've asked them. And that smells to me like a decoy."

"You are drunk," said Mr. Esmeralda. "Why don't you go away now, nurse your hangover, and think about it again in the morning?"

"Oh, don't worry," said Gerard. "I'll do what you want me to do. I'll take out this Thorson character. I'll take him out like a dream. That's always provided the Tengu behaves himself, and goes to the correct address. But take notice that I'm on to you, Mr. Esmeralda. Too much pushing from you, and it's plea-bargain time."

Mr. Esmeralda glanced around the restaurant to make sure that nobody was listening. "You've talked to Nancy?"

Gerard nodded. "Nancy is an interesting lady. More interesting than I first understood."

"Beware of Nancy Shiranuka," said Mr. Esmeralda. "Nancy Shiranuka is by no means everything she appears to be." Mr. Esmeralda ate some of his fried bananas in silence. Then he said, "Mr. Crowley, have you ever heard of a Japanese demon called Kappa?"

"You're the second person who's talked to me about Japanese demons tonight."

"Nancy Shiranuka mentioned them?"

"Nancy Shiranuka's an expert, as far as I can gather. And, yes, she did mention a demon called Kappa. Some kind of water demon, isn't it?"

Mr. Esmeralda nodded. "A small, hideous creature with the limbs of a variety of different creatures, like lobsters and rabbits, all mixed up. A huge, saucer-shaped head. I looked it up in the Huntington Library."

"Why did you do that, Mr. Esmeralda?"

Mr. Esmeralda put down his spoon and laced his fingers together. The band in the restaurant was playing "Samba Pa Ti." "No particular reason. The Tengu, as you know, is named after a Japanese devil. I suppose I was just curious."

"I thought you said that curiosity didn't pay in this business, Mr. Esmeralda."

"Maybe. It depends on the circumstances. But the Kappa is a particularly interesting demon because it has one fundamental weakness."

"What's that, Mr. Esmeralda?" Gerard took out a cigar and clipped the end off it, watching Mr. Esmeralda all the time.

"In its saucer-shaped head, the Kappa keeps a quantity of water, magical water which gives it its strength. The way to defeat the Kappa is to approach it without fear, bow to it, and say, 'Good morning.' In accordance with Japanese custom, it will bow in return, and it will spill the water out of the top of its head, thereby weakening itself so much that you can pass by unscathed.''

Gerard's expression was concealed for a moment behind curls of blue cigar smoke. Then he spat out a fragment of leaf and said, ''What are you trying to tell me, Mr. Esmeralda?''

''I am giving you a chance to save yourself,'' said Mr. Esmeralda. ''I am telling you that the way in which you can survive in this particular adventure is to remain calm and polite, and to observe all the necessary courtesies.''

''In other words?''

Mr. Esmeralda raised a single warning finger. ''In other words, Mr. Crowley, you are in danger of your life, and you ought to be aware of it.''

Gerard thought about that, and then crossed his legs and sniffed. ''What are those bananas like?'' he asked Mr. Esmeralda.

CHAPTER EIGHTEEN

When Mr. Esmeralda left Inca's restaurant at 11:17 P.M., a little over a half-hour after Gerard Crowley's departure, he was watched intently from the shadows of Inca's parking lot by Nancy Shiranuka's houseboy, Kemo. Kemo had been sitting patiently in his red-striped Toyota for almost three hours, smoking menthol cigarettes and listening to a tape of Stomo Yamashta. As soon as Mr. Esmeralda appeared, white-suited, his hair shining in the neon light of a Los Angeles night, Kemo started up his engine and crushed out his latest cigarette.

Mr. Esmeralda's metallic-blue Lincoln appeared from

the darkness on the other side of the parking lot, with
Kuan-yin at the wheel, and Mr. Esmeralda climbed
quickly in. The Lincoln then swerved north on Berendo,
with a squeal of tires, and ran two red lights on its way to
Beverly Boulevard. Kemo, alert and sweating, took a fast
right at 3rd Street, then a left at White House Place, and
managed to end up only two cars behind the Lincoln as it
turned west on Beverly Boulevard and cruised through the
Wilshire Country Club toward Highland Avenue.

Only one car apart, the Lincoln and the Toyota sped
north to Laurel Canyon. Kemo was tense and sweating as
he drove, although the Toyota's air conditioning was set to
cold, and whenever he was forced to slow down, his fingers
drummed impatiently on the wheel.

Follow him closely, Nancy Shiranuka had ordered
Kemo. *Follow him and don't let him go*.

At last, unexpectedly, just past Lookout Mountain
Avenue, the Lincoln screeched off to the right without
making a signal. Kemo, who was being tailgated by an
impatient procession of home-going valley-dwellers, was
forced to drive on for another few hundred yards and make
a right at Willow Glen. He parked his Toyota close to the
side of the road and climbed out, looking nervously from
right to left to make sure nobody had seen him. But why
should anyone have seen him? he asked himself. He was
nothing more than one more pair of headlights in a night
bustling with headlights. He wished he could suppress the
fear which kept rising inside him; the feeling that death
was very close at hand.

Running silently on rope-soled slippers, Kemo went
back down Laurel as far as the driveway where the Lincoln
had turned off. There were no signs there, no house
numbers; only a mailbox with its flap hanging down and
an overgrown hedge of bougainvillea. Kemo squinted up
through the trees and saw a large wooden house in which
two or three lights were shining. He also glimpsed, for an
instant, the Lincoln's taillights, before Kuan-yin switched
them off. He glanced back up the road to make sure that

nobody had been following him; and then, momentarily
concealed by the darkness between two passing cars, he
rolled over sideways into the shrubbery.

It took him nearly a quarter of an hour to get close to the
side of the house. He crept through roots and foilage as
silently and unobtrusively as a lizard. He noted each of the
television cameras as they emotionlessly inspected the
driveway and the surrounding bushes; and he also noted
Mr. Esmeralda's Chinese driver, waiting in his Lincoln
limousine. She was listening to Barry Manilow on the
radio.

At last, he reached the concrete pilings on the south side
of the house, well hidden in darkness, and he lay there
panting quietly for a minute or two before he went on.
Then he skirted around the house to the back, where a
wide patio had been cantilevered out of the side of the
canyon, with huge terra-cotta pots on either side, and
where a silent fountain collected leaves and lichen. He ran
and tumbled from one side of the patio to the other, until
he reached the corner of the house. Kemo was an adept in
judo and in the specialized art of *Noma-oi*, the "wild
horses," in which an opponent was overwhelmed by a
barrage of blows so fast and violent that he looked afterward as if he had been run down by a herd of horses.
Kemo was silent and quick and strong. He had killed a
sailor once, in a bar on Fisherman's Wharf in San
Francisco, with a flurry of blows that nobody else in the bar
had even seen. But Nancy Shiranuka had chosen him more
because he was quiet and self-controlled, and because he
could cook exquisitely, and because he had disciplined
himself to make love for hours and hours on end without
reaching a climax. With Kemo, Nancy had reached what
she described as "the state of the angels."

Kemo waited at the back of the house on Laurel Canyon
for almost ten minutes. Then, silently, he shinned up the
drainpipe to the guttering that surrounded the first-floor
balcony, and swung himself over the cedar railings. The
wide sliding doors to the back bedroom were open a

quarter of an inch, and Kemo slipped his fingers into the
crevice and slid them back just enough to allow him to slip
inside. The bedroom was bare, no drapes and no furnishings, only a *futon* on the floor for someone to sleep on.
There was a smell of candles and incense—a smell that reminded Kemo of Japanese shrines—and something else. A
bitter aroma of death. Kemo waited, motionless. His
hearing was so acute that he could detect the suppressed
sound of someone holding his breath. He decided that it
was safe for him to move quickly forward to the bedroom
door.

With infinite care and in utter silence, he opened the
door and stepped out onto the landing. From here, he
could see down into the hallway where Mr. Esmeralda had
waited only the day before. Mr. Esmeralda was there again
now, his hands in his pockets, sweating in the light of the
candles which flickered along the side of every wall. Kemo
stared down at Mr. Esmeralda, then slipped silently along
the landing to the stairs, keeping himself well back against
the wall.

It took Kemo nearly five minutes to descend the staircase in total silence. He tested every one of the cedar treads
before he put his weight on it, and then he stepped down
so gradually and with such care that not even the mole-
cules in the wood were disturbed. Mr. Esmeralda was still
waiting impatiently in the hall, but Kemo passed him by,
only eight or nine feet away, treading as silently and
swiftly as a draft. Mr. Esmeralda was not even conscious of
his passage. It was a *Noma-oi* technique known as "unseen
shadows."

Kemo found himself in a long corridor. To his left was
the kitchen: he could detect the smell of *Butaniku to
Harusame no Sunomono*, chilled pork with noodles. He
could also hear the sound of knives slicing through fish
and vegetables; and that meant to him that a Japanese of
importance was staying here, a Japanese who could afford
two or three personal cooks. He paused for a moment, and
then padded silently to the end of the corridor, where

there was a door marked with Japanese characters. They were in the old language, but he read them quickly: A SANCTUARY FORBIDDEN TO NONBELIEVERS.

Carefully, Kemo pressed his head against the door, to pick up the vocal vibrations of whoever might be talking in the room beyond. He closed his eyes in concentration, but there was utter silence. Either the room beyond was empty, or those who were in it were silent. Nancy Shiranuka had said, *Find out where he goes, who it is that he sees.* The decision to enter the room or not was not his. He had been told that he must.

Using the *Noma-oi* movement called "the September breeze," Kemo swiftly turned the door handle and opened the door. He paused in the doorway, in a combative stance, but the room was deserted. Three or four cushions, a bird painting on the wall, rows of candles, but nothing else. He crossed the room to the next doorway, his feet as light as a butterfly landing on a leaf, his body as well coordinated as *ikebana*, the arranging of flowers, each muscle tense and disciplined, each nerve sensitive to the dangers of the house.

On the second door was a plaque of iron, engraved with characters which Kemo had never seen before. As far as he could tell, the characters meant "drowning" or "beware of overwhelming water." He touched the plaque with his fingertips, as if to reassure himself. Then he pressed his forehead to the door and closed his eyes, trying to gather voices or breathing, trying to detect the rustle of robes or slippers.

There was somebody in there. Somebody breathing, deeply and noisily. It sounded to Kemo like an invalid, somebody suffering from asthma or a chest infection. He listened again, picking up every single sound and vibration that he could, and after two or three minutes he was sure. There was a sick man in there, but the sick man was probably alone.

Soundlessly, Kemo opened the second door and stepped inside. The inner room was illuminated by hundreds of candles, so many that it was almost impossible to breathe. Kemo dodged to the left and kept close to the wall, touching the door closed behind him with his fingertips, *touch*, silently and gently.

Then he froze, listening, watching, his body rigid as *kokeshi*, the Japanese folk dolls made without arms or legs. All he could hear was the sizzle of the candles as the wicks burned into the wax, and the regular pounding of his own heart.

A voice said, "Who are you? Who let you in?"

Kemo shielded his eyes against the dancing brilliance of the candles. He took one step forward, then another; and gradually he was able to focus on the creature that had spoken to him.

He had been ready to speak: ready to give some spurious explanation about working for Mr. Esmeralda and losing his way. But when he saw the monster in the basketwork throne, the words tangled in his mouth and he was unable to speak at all. And there was that *face*: that yellow-masked face. Unemotional, half-smiling, cruel as death.

There was a moment for Kemo when he felt as if the whole world had tipped off its axis, as if everything were coming to and end. He turned away from the creature in the basketwork throne and stared at the candles as if they could at least offer him sanity. But then the door swung open again, and there was three of them there, black-masked, cloaked in yellow, each of them posed in the martial discipline known as *Oni*, the art of the devils. *Oni* had been forbidden in Japan since the fourteenth century, but Kemo knew it from drawings and paintings. He also knew that its one purpose was to dismember and kill. In *Oni*, death was the only possible outcome.

Kemo wasted no time. He jumped at his three opponents with his hands whirling in the *Noma-oi* "windmill of oblivion." He struck one of his opponents on the neck, his hands blizzarding at 70 or 80 miles per hour, and the man spun away as violently as if he had been hit by an automobile. Then Kemo leaped aside and changed the rhythm of his attack to "the corn-beater," a slower, irregular pattern of hand-fighting which was impossible for any opponent to predict.

The second man went down, whirling to one side as if he had been caught by an exploding grenade. But Kemo was not fast enough for three. The third man, his eyes glittering behind his black silk mask, lashed out with his heel and sent Kemo reeling back against the wall with three ribs broken and two badly cracked.

Kemo heard a high-pitched shriek, almost a cackling sound, from the basketwork throne. Then the third man was on him, in a style of attack for which Kemo could find no defense. A swift lunge with two outstretched fingers rammed into Kemo's eyeballs and burst them both. A fist speeding upward penetrated his abdominal muscles, parted his lungs while they were still breathing, and wrenched his heart away from its moorings in a blast of blood. By the time the third blow hit him, a knuckle-punch which was designed to pulverize the frontal lobes of his brain, Kemo was already dead and collapsing on his feet. The *Oni* adept had killed him in less than three seconds: the same kind of death that Gerard had thought about only a few hours before. So fast that he never knew what hit him.

Mr. Esmeralda came into the room, staring, aghast. He looked down at Kemo's mutilated body, then at Kappa, then at the last remaining *Oni* guard. He started to say something, but then he simply shook his head and stood there in silence.

"You were followed," said Kappa in a hoarse whisper.

"I didn't know," said Mr. Esmeralda. "Believe me, I didn't know."

"You were followed," repeated Kappa. He made the words a chilling indictment.

"Yes," said Mr. Esmeralda. Then, almost inaudibly, "Yes."

CHAPTER NINETEEN

Eva was very drunk when Gerard let himself into their apartment at three o'clock the following morning, turned on all the lights, and began packing a suitcase. She was crouched on the white leather sofa, a bottle of Polish vodka three-quarters empty by her feet. She was wrapped up in one of Gerard's bathrobes, and she looked like the rescued victim of a hotel fire.

"Where are the girls?" Gerard asked her as he walked through the living room to find his cigar case. "Or are you so damned sloshed that you never even noticed they aren't here?"

"They called," said Eva in a blurry voice. "Melanie Radnick invited them to spend the weekend riding."

"Do we know anyone called Melanie Radnick?"

Eva lifted her head and tried to focus on him, but the glaring lights hurt her eyes. "Melanie Radnick is Kelly's best friend. They've been friends for—I don't know, ever since Kelly started going to Seven Hills. The Radnicks have a ranch at La Crescenta."

"That's nice for the Radnicks."

Eva tensely rubbed the side of her face, as if she wanted to reassure herself that she was still real. "George Radnick works in gas, or something like that. Don't you remember him? We met him at the Devoes' anniversary party."

Gerard counted the cigars in his case, and then closed it. "Evie," he said, "go take a shower and sober up. You're a fucking mess."

He walked through to the bedroom again, opening drawers and taking out underwear and handkerchiefs and socks. He finished packing his suitcase neatly and quickly, and then clicked it shut.

Eva was leaning in the doorway now, a smeary vodka glass dangling from one hand, her mascara blotting her eyes like ink on a sentimental letter. She watched him open the glass jar on top of the dressing table, the Steuben

duck that had been given to them by the California
Republicans for the work and the money they had put into
the election of President Reagan, and with conscientious
pain she watched him take out his cufflinks. She said,
"You're leaving me, is that it? You're going off with
her?"

"I should be so lucky," said Gerard sourly.

"Then what? What are you doing? What are you
packing for?"

Gerard said, "I have to go away for the weekend.
Business, that's all. Nothing important. Nothing exciting.
Just business."

"You're taking Francesca?"

"Does it matter if I am? Look at the condition you're
in."

"I don't want you to come back," said Eva. "Just stay
away. The girls and I can survive very well without you."

"You think so?" asked Gerard, absent-mindedly.
"Now, where the hell did I leave my keys?"

"Gerard," insisted Eva.

Gerard pecked her on the cheek as he walked through
the door. "You're a wonderful woman, Evie."

She lost her balance, and snatched at the door frame to
straighten herself up. "I'm in love," she said loudly. "Do
you know that? I'm in love with another man. Not you.
Somebody else. And he loves me too."

"Well, that's good news," said Gerard, taking his coat
out of the hall closet. "Good news for *you*, I mean. Not
for him."

"Gerard—"

Gerard put down his coat and his suitcase, and came
over to Eva and held her shoulders in his hands. She
noticed for the first time that a muscle in his cheek kept
wincing, as if there was an unbearable tension inside him.

"Evie," he said, and for a moment his voice sounded
gentle and almost caring, the way it used to before they
were married. A wave of memory from the days when they
had been lovers came spilling onto the empty beach of

tonight's argument, tonight's drunkenness, and Eva remembered a day at Malibu, swimming, eating lobster, laughing, running.

The wave ebbed away. "You're a bastard," she said quietly. "However sweetly you put it, you're a 110 percent bastard."

"I'm not trying to put it sweetly," he told her. "But just don't forget that it takes two people to make a marriage, and it takes two people to wreck a marriage."

"Three," put in Eva, slurrily but with great vehemence. "You forgot Francesca."

She swayed again, and he held her tighter. "The lovely Francesca," she repeated.

Gerard waited for a moment and then released her. "I'll be back the day after tomorrow," he said, watching her with cold disgust. "Make sure you've sobered up."

"I will," said Eva. "But not for you. By the time you come back the day after tomorrow I shall make love to my lover ten times at least, and probably more." She focused on him sharply, and then said in a voice of pure jealousy and hatred, "If and when you ever want me again, Mr. Gerard Crowley, then you shall have to anoint that precious and unfaithful organ of yours deep in another man's."

Gerard, his eyes telegraphing nothing at all, slapped her fiercely across the face. His wedding ring split her lip, and one side of her face was instantly spotted with blood.

She didn't collapse, though, or even cry. She remained standing where she was, disheveled and bloody, and stared at him with an expression of defiance and contempt that could have turned orange juice to acid. Gerard looked back at her sharply, questioningly, and then picked up his coat and his suitcase, looked again, and made a *hmph* kind of noise, as if he weren't sure that he had really hurt her enough. He opened the door.

"Go," said Eva, through swollen lips. "Don't let me stand in your way."

Gerard hesitated.

"Go," said Eva, and Gerard went, frowning to himself as he closed the door behind him. He whistled an uncomfortable tune as he descended in the elevator to the garage, although the tune died away as he crossed the empty concrete to his car. He opened up the trunk, stowed away his suitcase, and then climbed into the Buick like a man who has a very long distance to travel but doesn't quite know where.

"Shit," he said to himself, thinking about Eva. Then he started up the engine.

It took him less than an hour to drive out to Pacoima Ranch. Although the false dawn was already lightening the eastern sky behind the San Gabriel mountains, the highway was deserted, and the only signs of human life he saw were at San Fernando Airport, where an executive plane was plaintively winking its lights on the runway. He drove past Pacoima Reservoir and then out onto the Little Tujunga Road.

Pacoima Ranch was a ramshackle collection of huts at the end of a twisting, dusty driveway, with corrugated iron rooftops and sagging verandas. The kind of place where unspeakable helter-skelter rituals might have been performed, or where Nancy Drew might have gone in search of ghosts or kidnapers or fugitives from justice.

Gerard turned the car around in front of the main ranch house, and killed the engine. Even before he had fished out his suitcase, two Japanese appeared on the veranda, one of them carrying a Uzi machine gun, both of them masked in black. They watched him, motionless, as he slammed the lid of his trunk and walked toward them. Four or five yards away, he paused.

"Good morning." He smiled at them.

The two Japanese didn't answer, but moved aside to let Gerard cross the veranda and enter the ranch house through the screen door. Gerard asked. "Did the commander get here yet?" and one of the Japanese nodded each pointed upstairs. "Ah," said Gerard. "Sleeping it off, no doubt."

Inside, the ranch house was empty of furniture except for three or four neatly tied-up *futons* in the large living room, but it was scrupulously clean. On the walls were rice-paper scrolls and symbols, and a collection of black silk flags. Gerard had once asked Doctor Gempaku what the flags signified, but Doctor Gempaku had simply told him, "It would take only a minute for me to explain, but twenty years for you to understand."

Gerard left his suitcase in the bare living room, and then walked through to the kitchen. There, sitting on a *zabuton*, a large flat cushion, was Doctor Gempaku himself, eating his breakfast. In the far corner, over the old-fashioned black-iron range, another of the masked Japanese was stirring vegetables in a *donabe*. It was only just past five o'clock in the morning, but Doctor Gempaku always rose early to say his prayers.

"Would you care to eat?" he asked Gerard as Gerard sat down next to him on another *zabuton*. Doctor Gempaku was tall and lean for a Japanese, with a closeshaven head and small, oval-framed spectacles. There was always a certain grace and mystery about him, as if he were living partly in California and partly in some tranquil Japanese garden, a garden of chrysanthemums and golden carp and esoteric riddles.

Gerard peered into Doctor Gempaku's blue-lacquered bowl. "What's on the menu?" he asked.

"*Kitsune udon*," smiled Doctor Gempaku. "In English, that means 'fox noodles.' It is a particularly compelling mystery why a dish of bean curd and noodles should have become historically associated with the fox, which is one of the most evil of Japanese spirits. Some say that the fox was always fond of bean curd. Others say that *kitsune udon* is the last meal you are given before you are sent to everlasting hellfire."

"Do you have any cornflakes?" asked Gerard.

Doctor Gempaku spoke quickly in Japanese, and the black-masked boy came over and set a bowl for Gerard, as well as a paper packet of chopsticks and one of the white china spoons usually used for eating soup.

Before the noodles were served, Gerard observed the small ritual of *oshibori*, wiping his hands with a hot, lightly scented towel. Even at Pacoima Ranch, Doctor Gempaku insisted on the civilized niceties. The black-masked boy filled Gerard's bowl with *kitsune odon*, bowed, and returned to his cooking.

Gerard ate in silence for a while, and then asked, without looking at Doctor Gempaku, "Esmeralda's told you what we're supposed to be doing next?"

"Yes."

"What do you think?"

"I think it is possible. I can have the next Tengu ready by tomorrow night."

"I'm not asking you if it's *possible*. I know it's *possible*. What I'm asking you is, what do you *think*?"

Doctor Gempaku watched Gerard carefully for a moment or two, and then said, "What do you want me to think?"

"I just want your reaction, that's all."

"My moral reaction? Or my philosophical reaction?"

Gerard chased a piece of bean curd around the inside of his bowl. In the end, he gave up and set the half-emptied bowl down on the table.

"We're sending a Tengu out to kill a man. I want to know how you respond to that. Whether you think it's the right thing to do, not just as far as the law is concerned, but as far as the whole project is concerned."

Doctor Gempaku picked up his chopsticks, tested them with his hands, and then snapped them in two. "Japanese esthetics," he said, "are preoccupied with the idea of the perfect moment, the 'accident' that is spontaneous, and yet carefully controlled—so that it takes on an artistic and spiritual deliciousness beyond any experience that occurs either *wholly* accidentally or *wholly* deliberately. To me, this is one of the satisfactions of the Tengu. We have created the strongest and fiercest of human beings, a creature that can terrify and overwhelm anybody and everybody. He obeys our directions, and yet he is also unpredictable. We cannot tell what he might take it into his mind to do, what grisly horrors he might suddenly decide to perpetrate. The death of the girl Sherry Cantor was a perfect example. To the Western mind it seemed like random and brutal murder, purposeless and bloody. To us, however, it was an event of terrible beauty. The Tengu did as he was bidden; and yet the error he made in killing Sherry Cantor added an indefinable ecstasy to the whole event. We are asked to send out a Tengu to deal with Admiral Thorson. Perhaps a smiliar mistake may occur. The only criteria can be destiny and the demands of perfection. So when you ask me, is it *right*? I can only say that it can only be *right* when it actually takes place. Will it be an esthetic event or not? We cannot tell.''

Gerard sat back on his *zabuton* and took out his cigar case. "Are you serious?" he asked Doctor Gempaku.

"Perhaps," said Doctor Gempaku, and smiled.

Gerard clipped the end off a cigar and pasted down a stray piece of broken leaf with saliva. "The Tengu we sent out to deal with Sennett . . . how's he doing? He was shot up pretty bad, wasn't he?"

"He's still in a coma. But most of the body injuries are beginning to heal satisfactorily. You know that a Tengu is so unnaturally strong partly because his metabolism is so drastically accelerated. It gives him a shorter life, of course; but it also means that any wounds or injuries heal themselves with remarkable speed. It's his mental state that concerns me more. Something happened after he killed Sherry Cantor that seriously and dangerously unbalanced him. It seems to me that it was a similar reaction to that of a child whose body temperature rises suddenly and dramatically. A kind of convulsion, or fit.''

"Do you think it might happen again?" asked Gerard. He struck a match and leaned forward slightly to light his cigar.

"I would prefer it if you smoked outside," said Doctor Gempaku. "Tobacco smoke will upset the delicate balance of aromas in this kitchen. It is already bad enough that I can smell it on your clothes and hair.''

Gerard stared at Doctor Gempaku for a moment, and then slowly waved out the match. ''I'll leave the cigar until later,'' he said. ''Let's go take a look at the Tengus.''

Doctor Gempaku clapped his hands, and the black-masked cook removed their bowls. Then the doctor rose from the table, and Gerard followed him through to the front of the house again, where the two black-robed guards were still keeping watch. ''We've had one or two unwelcome intruders lately,'' said Doctor Gempaku as he slipped on his shoes. ''Nobody dangerous, no police or anything like that.''

''Has anybody come up to the house?'' asked Gerard.

Doctor Gempaku shook his head. ''They don't get the chance. Usually I send Frank out with his shotgun to turn them around before they get the idea that anything unusual is happening here. My young *bushi* stay well out of sight.''

The sun was already up and warm as they crossed the yard to what appeared at first sight to be a rundown barn. It was only from close up that it was possible for anyone to see the modern prefabricated building which had been constructed inside the gappy, collapsing timbers, and to hear the deep humming of portable electric generators. Doctor Gempaku led the way through the sagging barn doorway, and then up a short flight of stainless-steel steps that took them to the interior door of the Tengu building. He unlocked the door, using two keys, and when it swung open he rapped on it with his knuckles to show Gerard how solid it was.

''Four-inch carbonized steel,'' he said. ''We fitted it last week.''

''I know,'' Gerard responded coldly. ''I had to pay $7,500 for it. I just hope that it proves to be worth the price.''

Doctor Gempaku smiled. ''If any one of our Tengus goes berserk again, then believe me, it will be worth the price. Not even a Tengu can break his way through four inches of carbonized steel. Well, we hope not.''

Inside the building, which ran nearly 90 feet in length, the only illumination came from tiny, beadlike red safety lights. The temperature was well below 55 degrees, dry and constantly controlled. Doctor Gempaku held Gerard's sleeve while both of them stood in the entrance, waiting for their eyes to become accustomed to the darkness and their skin accustomed to the cold. Gerard felt the sweat in the middle of his back freezing like a cape of ice.

At last, Doctor Gempaku's face began to emerge from the crimson twilight, and Gerard could look around him and see a long, narrow corridor, with doors going off on either side. He had been here before, when the building was just erected, but there were more partitions now, more rooms where Tengus could be concealed. There was also a different resonance, a deep, almost inaudible drumming sound, both irritating and strangely threatening, like the first tremors of an earthquake. A smell, too: of incense and stale flowers and one thing more—sickly and overwhelming, the smell of dried blood.

Gerard said, ''If hell could ever be created in a cabin, then this would be it.''

Doctor Gempaku steered him toward the first door on the right. ''Come see the Tengu we're trying to save. If we have not lost him overnight. A young student of ancient Japanese religion, before he joined us. A very dedicated young man. The sort of personality that refuses to be diverted from the essence of spiritual truth.''

''This is the guy who killed Sherry Cantor?''

Doctor Gempaku nodded. ''He was always our most promising Tengu. But the most promising are usually the most unbalanced. It requires a high level of emotional susceptibility for a man to be suitable for the role of a Tengu, and extreme physical strength and emotional susceptibility are also a volatile mixture. Like nitroglycerin, the Tengu is both powerful and touchy.''

He unlocked the plain metal door and slid it back. It was no lighter on the other side than it had been in the corridor, but Doctor Gempaku guided Gerard into a small antechamber and then swiftly locked the door behind them. "This is always the moment of no return," he said. "If anything should go wrong, it is better for just one or two of us to be slaughtered by the Tengu than to try to give ourselves an escape route and risk letting it out."

"Well," said Gerard, "I would call that a matter of opinion."

"Nothing about the Tengu is a matter of opinion," Doctor Gempaku corrected him, politely but adamantly. "The Tengu represents the ultimate physical power which any human being can achieve, coupled with a spiritual compulsion which is the greatest that any human brain can stand. When we tried out our earliest Tengu program at the Yoyogi Olympic stadium in Tokyo, during the weight-lifting events, a Tengu was able to lift over 430 kilograms. Unfortunately, because our methods were not recognized by the Olympic committee, we were forced to withdraw under conditions of great secrecy."

"Mr. Esmeralda told me about that."

Doctor Gempaku was silent for a second or two. Then he said, "Follow me. But remember to stay quiet. The Tengu is still sensitive to disturbances."

"I'll be quiet," Gerard assured him.

Doctor Gempaku drew aside a curtain of fine jet beads which, in the darkness, Gerard hadn't seen before. Stepping silently on slippered feet, he led the way into a room draped with black silk curtains, a room in which scores of black silk ribbons hung from the ceiling, tied with silver temple bells, birds' feathers, pomanders of cloves and cherry blossoms, bamboo tokens, and *haniwa*, the clay figures usually found in ancient Japanese graves. Gerard, who had been expecting something more like a surgical theater, with cardiopulmonary resuscitators and electronic monitors and oxygen equipment, was considerably taken aback.

"What is that?" he hissed. "Where's the Tengu?"

Doctor Gempaku raised a finger to his lips to indicate

total silence. Then, very gradually, he raised the lighting
in the room with a dimmer switch located behind the
drapes, until Gerard could see the Tengu who had torn
Sherry Cantor to pieces.

The Tengu was suspended from the ceiling, like all the
icons and bells which hung around him; except that he
wasn't tied up by ribbons. He was naked, and he was held
up by fifteen or twenty silver claws, shaped like the hands
of a demon or an old woman, whose long silver nails
actually pierced deep into his flesh. Each of these claws was
tied to a black silk braided cord, and in turn these were all
gathered and knotted close to the ceiling, and attached to
a strange kind of metal frame.

Gerard slowly approached the Tengu, with chilly sweat
sliding down the insides of his armpits and a taste in his
mouth like congealed grease. He had seen many horrors in
Cuba. But for human butchery, he had never seen anything like this, and he could scarcely believe that the mutilated creature hanging in front of him was real.

The Tengu was still masked with his white varnished
mask. He was breathing, in shallow, interrupted gasps,
but Gerard wouldn't have laid money on his survival, especially not hung up like this from the ceiling. The silver
claws had dug so far into his chest muscles that they had
lifted them up in bruised and dead-looking peaks, and the
claws in his buttocks had almost disappeared into the flesh
altogether. There were claws in his leg muscles, in his
shoulders, in his arms. The claws in his feet had gone so
deep that one of them had actually broken right through,
from the sole to the instep. There was even a claw in his
genitals, dragging up his scrotum and piercing his foreskin
so that his penis looked like a hooked eel.

"This is crazy," said Gerard. "What the hell are you
doing here? You're supposed to be making the guy better
and you're injuring him even worse than he was before!"

Doctor Gempaku dimmed the lights again. "What you
are witnessing here is not a traditional Western form of
healing."

"What you're doing here has just about as much to do with the traditional Western form of healing, or *any* form of healing, as Belsen had to do with summer camp," Gerard retorted. "You're going to kill him, doctor; and if you kill him, then more than a few hundred of thousands of dollars are going to be lost with him. Money for which *I* am supposed to be responsible."

Doctor Gempaku took Gerard's arm and guided him back toward the antechamber. "You have nothing to fear, Mr. Crowley. The responsibility for getting the Tengu into the country may have been yours; the responsibility for the building of this center may have been yours; and the day-to-day administration of this plan may be yours. But, don't you see? Everything we are doing here is planned, with great precision; every step I take, whether it is scientific or whether it is spiritual, is taken according to a very careful premeditated scheme."

He unlocked the door, and they emerged into the corridor again. "Do you want to see the Tengu we are preparing for Admiral Thorson?"

Gerard asked, "Is he . . . hung up like the other one?"

"He is undergoing a similar ordeal."

"In that case, no."

Doctor Gempaku said, "They told me you weren't squeamish. They told me you were a man of the world."

Gerard said, "It depends which world you're talking about."

They left the barn and walked back across the yard to the house. Gerard lit up his cigar and took two or three deep puffs. Doctor Gempaku glanced at him from time to time and smiled.

"I don't know what you think is so damned amusing," Gerard snapped as they took off their shoes on the veranda.

"You are like all Occidentals. You are so concerned by the sight of other people undergoing mutilation or pain. It disturbs you, but it also fascinates you. To us, pain is as much a part of existence as happiness. The moment of ex-

quisite, controlled agony can bring on as much heaven as
the moment of sexual climax.''

Gerard said, ''You think I don't know about De Sade,
that stuff? I've spanked a girl or two, had my back
scratched. But what you've got back there, doctor—that's
something else.''

''Something else?''

The guards watched them through the thin slits in their
silk masks as they went upstairs to Doctor Gempaku's
study. Gerard glanced back at them quickly, but by then
they had turned to the window again, in their silent watch
for unwelcome intruders.

Doctor Gempaku's study was simple and silent, *tatami*
mats on the floor, a low table spread with papers, two
scrolls hung on the wall, a framed photograph of *tancho-
zuru*, the Japanese red-crested crane. No family pictures,
no mementoes of the Tokyo Olympics, nothing to show
that Doctor Gempaku had friends or family or even a past.

Gerard picked up the picture of the cranes. ''You're a
bird watcher?'' he asked.

Doctor Gempaku sat down on a cushion. ''I keep that
picture there to remind me of the proverb: 'The crane lives
for a thousand years.' ''

''What does that mean?''

''Many things. It could be a reminder that there are
forces in the universe which live forever, and yet which can
be conjured up in ordinary mortals.''

''You're talking about the Tengu?''

Doctor Gempaku said, ''It does not pay to be too inquisitive about what we are doing here, Mr. Crowley, or
how we do it.''

''Doctor Gempaku,'' said Gerard, taking his cigar out
of his mouth. ''I was shocked back there, I'll admit. Who
wouldn't have been? But believe me, I'm not inquisitive.
I'm just here to do what I've been paid to do. You just go
ahead and do whatever you want, don't mind me.'' Now
Gerard was laying on his down-South good-ole-boy accent
really thickly. ''You can hang fellas up, doctor. You can

prick 'em and pat 'em and mark 'em with T. You do whatever you want. You just go right ahead. Why,'' he said, and now his smile was cold, and he looked at Doctor Gempaku with an expression which anybody from Batista's Havana would immediately have recognized as his 'I've-got-you-sized-up' look, "why, you can even raise the *devil* if the mind takes you. You won't catch me sticking *my* nose in.''

Doctor Gempaku slowly closed the small book which was lying on the table in front of him. He took off his spectacles. Gerard watched him and puffed at his cigar, watched and puffed, while the sun suddenly filled the room with dazzling morning light.

CHAPTER TWENTY

Jerry Sennett was falling asleep in front of the television when the telephone rang. He had been dreaming about Japan, and as he crossed the room to the telephone he was still crossing the Rikugien gardens in Tokyo, under a sky that threatened rain.

"Mr. Sennett? Sergeant Skrolnik, Homicide." The harsh voice brought Jerry back to Orchid Place, and Dan Rather, and a sort of reality.

"Hallo, sergeant.''

"Are you okay?" asked Skrolnik. "You sound like you've got yourself a cold.''

"I was sleeping. Well, nearly.''

"I'm sorry. But we've got ourselves a suspect in custody, and I'd appreciate your coming down to headquarters to take a look at him. You know—see if you recognize him or not.''

"Sergeant, I was out when Ms. Cantor was murdered. I didn't see anybody."

"Sure, I know that," said Skrolnik. "But there's a chance that seeing this guy could jog your memory. You know, maybe you glimpsed him in the locality one day, something like that."

"Can I bring Mr. Holt along with me?"

"Mr. Holt?" asked Skrolnik sharply. "You mean Mack Holt, the victim's last known romantic association?"

Jerry was drinking from a stale glass of whiskey with a sticky rim. He coughed, and almost choked. "If you want to put it so poetically, yes. That's him."

"You're an acquaintance of his?"

"Only since the murder."

"Well . . . okay then, bring him down. Why not? We can kill two birds with one stone."

Jerry went to the kitchen, stuffed a couple of cheese crackers into his mouth, and then, puffing crumbs, switched off all the lights and locked the back door. He pulled on an old plaid jacket, switched off the television, and then went out to his car. He was fumbling for his keys when he became aware of something on the windshield, something white, flapping in the evening breeze.

He approached the car slowly, then picked the sheet of paper out from the windshield wiper. It was thin paper, the kind that Japanese calligraphers used for scrollwork. On it were written, with a brush, the English words "The hawks will return to their roost."

Jerry held the paper up to the streetlight. There was the Japanese character *gwa* watermarked into it, but that was the only identifying mark. He stood silent and alone on the driveway for almost five minutes, holding the paper in his hand, thinking, searching his memory and imagination for what this could mean, and where it could have come from.

It convinced him of one thing: Sherry Cantor's death had really been a mistake, after all. Whoever had smashed his way into her house that morning had been looking for him.

There was nothing about that thought that consoled him. It meant simply that Sherry had died for no reason at all, and that whoever had killed her was still on the loose. Whoever Sergeant Skrolnik was holding down at headquarters, it was unquestionably the wrong man.

The message itself was more subtle. "The hawks will return to their roost." It reminded him of something he had read years and years ago, when he was in Japan. It had an important meaning—he was sure of that. And somebody had taken a considerable risk to tuck it under his windshield wiper. It was a warning of some kind, that was obvious. But against what, and by whom, he was completely at a loss to imagine.

He drove slowly and thoughtfully to Mack Holt's house on Franklin Avenue. Mack was standing in the doorway outside, talking to a shaven-skulled Krishna disciple in saffron robes. When he saw Jerry drawing into the curb, he raised his cigarette hand in salute, and Jerry could see him saying something to the young man in the robes, something which made the young man nod as if he were impressed.

"How are you doing?" asked Jerry as he slammed the car door behind him and walked up the cracked concrete path. It was a warm, dusky evening, and moths were weaving around the naked bulb over the porch.

Mack said, "Okay, how are you?"

"You busy?" asked Jerry.

"Kind of. Depends. Olive's upstairs, and we're expecting some people over later. They've got a pirate videotape of the new *Star Wars* picture, and two gallons of Christian Brothers Pinot Chardonnay."

Jerry glanced up toward the lighted window of Mack's apartment. "I wouldn't keep you long," he said. "It's just that the police have found a suspect, and they'd like us to go to headquarters and take a look at him."

"They've *found* somebody?" asked Mack, as if he had expected that the criminal would disappear int the Xth Dimension, like Dr. Strange.

"They're not sure if it's the right guy," said Jerry. "But

I guess we owe it to Sherry to take a look. Sergeant
What's-his-name, Skrolnik, said we might recognize him
just from some casual encounter in the street.''

"Do you think I could bring Olive?" asked Mack.

Jerry gave him a lopsided shrug.

Mack disappeared upstairs for a minute or two, while
Jerry remained on the stoop, smiling vaguely from time to
time at the shaven-haired Krishna convert and whistling
"The Way We Were." Across the street, a fat strawberry-
blonde woman was trying unsuccessfully to persuade her
pet poodle to do what he had been dragged out of the
house to do.

At last Mack reappeared, closely followed by Olive.
They both looked slightly high. Olive was wearing a
shocking-pink satin jogging vest that did little to conceal
her improbably large breasts, and the tightest of white
satin shorts. Mack said to Jerry, "This is Mrs. Robin T.
Nesmith, Jr. Her husband's in Honolulu, with the Navy."

"Delighted," said Jerry, and shook Olive's hand. "I
was a Navy man once, myself."

"Don't knock them," grinned Olive.

"I hope I'm not spoiling your evening," said Jerry.

"Not at *all*," Olive told him, climbing into the Dodge
beside him and wriggling her hips enthusiastically to make
room for Mack. "I've had enough of videotapes and cheap
wine to last me till Doomsday. It's a change to do something *unpredictable*."

It was dark by the time they reached the police headquarters. A jaded sergeant sat at the desk in the lobby and
regarded them with eyes that had long ago faded into dis-
interest at the sight of oddballs, hookers, pimps, and
general fruitcakes, the flotsam of Hollywood Boulevard
and all parts east. He told them to wait, and they sat side
by side on a patched vinyl bench, tapping their feet and
staring at a poster which reminded them that 10,728
people died in the United States last year as the victims of
handguns. Officers came and went, tired and sweaty from
hours of duty, one or two of them whistling and fooling

around, most of them silent. Mack said to Olive, "This is unpredictable?"

At last, his shoes squeaking on the plastic-tiled floor, Sergeant Skrolnik appeared, with Detective Pullet and Arthur following close behind him. "I'm sorry I kept you good people waiting," said Skrolnik, directing his attention with some humility to Olive's breasts. "Sherry Cantor's case is just one of three similar homicides. I have on my books right now, and I'm afraid that my time is kind of limited."

"You said you've caught somebody," said Jerry. "I didn't hear any announcement on the news."

Skrolnik thrust his hands into his sagging pockets. "That's because I haven't yet announced it to the media. I've detained somebody, yes, and I've charged him with the first-degree homicide of Ms. Sherry Cantor, and the reason I've done that is because I'm not at all sure who *else* apart from this guy could have physically torn a twenty-one-year-old girl to pieces. But I have to tell you that there are doubts in my mind, serious doubts, and that's why I'm looking for all the corroborative evidence I can find. The guy plainly has the capability to inflict serious injuries on people with his bare hands. He had some personal involvement with the victim. But two or three important details still don't seen to add up."

"Does that really bother you, as long as you've made a bust?" asked Mack.

Skrolnik gave him a look of tired disgust. "I want more than an arrest, Mr. Holt. I want to catch the guy who ripped a pretty and innocent young woman into so much raw meat."

Without saying anything else, he squeaked off again along the corridor, and Pullet and Arthur followed. Arthur was busy blowing his nose, but Pullet indicated with a cursory nod of his head that Jerry and Mack and Olive should come along, too.

They were ushered into a small interview room that smelled of stale cigars and Brut 33. On the far wall was a two-way mirror; behind it, disconsolate and edgy, sat Maurice Needs, a/k/a El Krusho, on a cell chair that seemed to be three sizes too small for him. Every now and then he punched his fist into the open palm of his hand, impatiently blew out his cheeks, and looked toward the cell door.

"I don't believe it," said Mack. "That's *Maurice*!"

"That's right," nodded Skrolnik. "Maurice Charles Needs, from Fridley, Minnesota; also known as El Krusho."

"*El Krusho*?" asked Jerry in disbelief.

"My reaction entirely," said Skrolnik. "But in spite of that somewhat fanciful name, he was a close acquaintance and possible lover of Ms. Sherry Cantor. According to two different witnesses, he was involved in a *ménage à trois* with Sherry Cantor and with you, Mr. Holt. Three in a bed, so I'm told."

Olive took Mack's arm, as if to reassure him that whatever had happened in the past wasn't going to affect the strength of their friendship now. Mack said disjointedly, "There was something like that, yes. But not serious, and only one time. It started as a party, and then I guess we all had a little too much wine. There was no bad feeling afterward, no problems."

"You don't think that, having slept with her once, Maurice Needs may have thought that Sherry Cantor was a lover of his? That he might have gotten overpossessive about her? Jealous, even?"

"Look," said Mack, "this is all completely off the wall. Maurice never hurt anyone, never would. We had a scene with Sherry, all right, I admit it, but it was one time only and that was it. We all stayed good friends. Sherry and me used to go down to the circus to see him, and he was always totally friendly. He wouldn't do anything like that, not to anybody, and especially not to Sherry."

"Mr. Sennett?" Skrolnik asked Jerry. "Did you ever see that man before? Lurking around your street maybe?"

Olive said, "That guy couldn't *lurk* if he tried. Look at

the size of him. But don't you think he's *cute*?"

"Don't get ideas," said Mack. "He isn't very big where it really counts. These Muscle Beach types never are."

Sergeant Skrolnik impatiently put in, "Will you take a look at the suspect, please, Mr. Sennett? A real good look?"

Jerry shook his head. "I'm sorry, sergeant. I never saw him before."

"Can we talk to him?" asked Mack. "I mean, you're not going to hold him, are you? Not really?"

Detective Pullet said, "You can talk to him if you want to. But until we have some pretty good evidence that he *didn't* murder Sherry Cantor, he stays right here."

Mack said, "Jerry—Olive—can you wait for me? I'd really like to give the poor guy some encouragement."

"Don't *over*encourage him," said Skrolnik, glancing at Pullet in a way which showed that he didn't really think that allowing Maurice Needs to speak to Mack was a very good idea. But Pullet said, "It could help, right? Anything which gets us nearer to the nub of what actually happened."

"All right," said Skrolnik. "But not longer than five minutes. Then I'm going to have to tell the commissioner we've hauled someone in."

Detective Arthur sneezed loudly.

Outside again, on the vinyl bench, Jerry and Olive waited and smoked while Mack was given time to talk to El Krusho. Olive said, "What were you in the Navy, Jerry? Afloat or ashore?"

"Mostly ashore. Naval Intelligence Department. Nothing very much like the Navy and not very intelligent, either."

"My husband's in Records. Right now he's working on some kind of official history of Midway, something like that."

"Do you miss him?" asked Jerry, looking at her carefully through the winding cigarette smoke.

She nodded. Her eyes gave away just how much she

missed him.

"I can't believe this guy is called El Krusho," Jerry said, to change the subject. "Did Mack ever talk about him before?"

"He did mention he used to know a circus strongman. But that was all."

Jerry said, "He didn't really look the *type* to commit murder, did he? You see the way he kept looking at the door? Sort of soft and hopeless, like he's waiting for his gray-haired momma to come bail him out."

"He looked *strong* enough," remarked Olive.

"Well, sure, and that's obviously one of the reasons they're holding him. But unless he had an accomplice, I don't really believe he did it." He reached into his plaid jacket and took out the sheet of soft scrollwork paper he had found under his windshield wiper. "If anything convinces me that it wasn't him, this does. I found it on my car tonight, just after Sergeant Skrolnik called me."

Olive took the paper and read it carefully, "The hawks will return to their roost?" She frowned. "What the hell does that mean?"

"I don't know. It sounds like an old Japanese proverb. But like all Japanese proverbs, it could have several meanings. Maybe something like 'that which has been troubling you before is going to come back and trouble you again.' On the other hand, it could mean something altogether different."

"Do you know who might have put it on your car?"

Jerry took back the paper, folded it up, and shook his head. "Not a clue. But I think whoever did it knows who killed Sherry Cantor; and whoever did it knows exactly what's going to come down next."

Olive stared at him. "You mean—the murderer's still out there? He could do it again?"

"I hope not," said Jerry dryly. "And the *reason* I hope not is because the next murder could well be mine."

Mack was almost a half-hour. Jerry took a stroll around the hallway, smiling at the impossible desk officer; trying to pat a police dog on the head, going over to talk to a

young blonde woman police officer who was typing up
reports at a desk to one side.

"Hi," he said. "It looks like you're pretty tied up
tonight."

The policewoman looked up at him, sharply. "I'm
sorry," she said, "but visitors are requested to wait over
there."

"Okay," said Jerry. "I was only trying to support my
local police department."

At that moment, however, just as Jerry was turning
away, a lieutenant came up, sweating and paunchy, and
handed the policewoman a sheaf of documents.

"Janice, can you do me a favor and get these sorted out
for me? I mean, real quick. I need them two hours ago."

"Which one's this?" the policewoman asked him,
leafing through the notes.

"The Japanese one. The young guy they found in that
culvert out by West Covina."

"Okay, lieutenant," the policewoman said, and laid
the papers on the edge of her desk.

Jerry didn't ever quite know what led him to do it. But
as the lieutenant headed for the squad room, he turned
around and deliberately knocked against the policewoman's desk, so that all the papers were scattered on the
floor, swooping and tumbling.

"I *asked* you to wait over there!" the policewoman
snapped, getting up from her seat. But Jerry was quicker.
He knelt down and gathered the papers up, and as he did
so he snatched a quick read at every page. A name: *Kemo
Toyama.* Part of a report by the officer who first arrived at
West Covina: *Seriously mutilated, heart dislocated, brain
damaged.* Names of witnesses, no time to read any of
those. And then, like a newsflash, a name and address: *c/o
Nancy Shiranuka, 1114 Alta Loma Road.*

Jerry handed the papers back to the policewoman with a
sheepish smile. "I'm truly sorry. I guess I've always been
clumsy. Can I buy you dinner to make up for my
boobery?"

The policewoman sat down again and zipped a fresh

sheet of paper into her typewriter.

"Just sit down and behave yourself, and I'll resist the temptation to arrest you for interfering with police business," she said.

Jerry saluted. "Yes, ma'am."

CHAPTER TWENTY-ONE

On the way back to Franklin Avenue, Mack said, "The poor guy's completely innocent. I don't even know how they can hold him."

"Does he have an alibi?" asked Jerry.

"He was in bed asleep."

"Alone? Or accompanied?"

"Alone as it happens."

Jerry made a face. "Lying alone in your own bed, no matter how peacefully, is not really much of an alibi. What about the police killing?"

"He doesn't have an alibi then, either. But he couldn't have done either of them. It just isn't in him."

Jerry produced the Japanese paper and handed it across the car. "This is what really convinces me it wasn't him."

"This piece of paper? What does it mean?"

"It's a warning of some sort. It's Japanese. And it must have been attached to my car long after Sergeant Skrolnik locked your friend Maurice Krusho up in the cells."

"Why didn't you show this to Skrolnik?"

"I don't know. I suppose I'm still not sure that what *I* think about Sherry Cantor's death isn't just another manifestation of my neurosis about Japan."

"But if it could have sprung Maurice from jail . . ."

"It's not evidence," said Jerry, taking it back. "Not the

kind of evidence that Skrolnik is looking for.''

"For you, though?"

Jerry tapped his forehead with his finger. "For me, it sets off that cold wind.''

They had reached Mack's apartment, and Jerry drew over to the curb. Mack said, "Are you sure you don't want to stay with us tonight? If there's a killer on the loose and he's looking for you . . . ?"

"I'll be okay," said Jerry. "I've got a Colt automatic in the bedroom and I can still remember some of my judo."

"You're welcome to wine and *Revenge of the Jedi*," smiled Olive.

Jerry shook his head. "Thanks, but I've got to get back for my son. He was supposed to be home a half-hour ago. But let me think this all over tonight, and maybe I'll call you in the morning. There's something real complicated going on here, you know. Something that makes some kind of sense if only we could fit all the pieces together. I just need to get it all assembled in my brain."

It was almost nine o'clock by the time Jerry swung his car into Orchid Place. Considering that David was supposed to have gotten back from the Lechner's by eight o'clock at the latest, he was surprised and concerned to find that the house was still in darkness. He parked his car, locked it, and went to open the front door. It was already two or three inches ajar. He stood and looked at it for a moment, unsure of what to do. Then he reached out with his fingertips and nudged it open.

In the hall, he paused and held his breath. The killer could be waiting for him anywhere, in any shadow. He took two or three steps forward, trying to remember what his old judo instructor had told him. *You are the wind, nothing more. You are the air. When your enemy attacks you, you will become the air, invisible yet strong. You will give way; but in your giving way you will vanquish your enemy instantly.*

Something else came into his mind. An unbidden thought that made him feel cold and alarmed. A single word. *Tengu*.

He called, "David? Are you there, David?" but there was no reply. Either David had come back early and then gone out again when he found that his father wasn't home, leaving the door unlocked by accident, or else—

Jerry reached for the living room light and flicked it on. Everything was in chaos—cushions, chairs, vases, books were scattered all over the rug. Even the liquor cabinet had been wrenched open and its pink-tinted glass smashed. One of the drapes had been pulled down, and there was a smear of blood on the wallpaper.

With stiff, chilled movements, too shocked now to think about judo, Jerry crossed the room. Sprawled on the sofa was a Japanese *Hotei* doll, a puppet of one of the seven gods of fortune. White-faced, cloaked in black, with massive earlobes and the joking, malevolent smile of a trickster. Jerry gently lifted it up, and its head and arms flopped back. Where it had been lying, there was another sheet of scrollwork paper, neatly rolled and tied with string. He opened it up and read, in growing fright, the message: "We have your son. Wait patiently for instructions. Tell nobody."

Beneath the writing was a brushwork picture of a dove with its wings aflame.

Jerry went immediately to the telephone, picked it up, and dialed Sergeant Skrolnik's number. Then, before the police switchboard had answered, he set the phone down again.

He felt at last as if his nightmares had broken through from the past into the present day, like devils crawling and scrambling out of one of those huge pandemonic eggs in a painting by Hieronymus Bosch. He felt as if everything had turned to fire, as if hell had come to life, as if Hiroshima and Nagasaki were again incandescent.

He said, "Oh, God," but the words sounded empty and pitiful.

BOOK TWO
BLAZING EAGLES

CHAPTER ONE

They had expected Admiral Knut S. Thorson to die within hours of his last and most paralyzing stroke. He was 78, after all, and his last ten years of life had been dogged by serious heart disease and delibitating collapses. But "Inch-Thick Thorsen," as the Navy had always nicknamed him, was made of tough, durable stuff, and his hours of life had lengthened into days, then months.

He had lain for nearly a year now inside his oxygen tent at Rancho Encino Hospital, one of the most luxurious acute-care facilities in the whole of southern California, a stumpy little gray-haired man with ferocious eyebrows and a ruddiness in his weathered face which even twelve months of hospitalization had been unable to fade.

Every two days his wife visited and sat watching him breathe inside his plastic cocoon; a plain woman who always wore flowers in her hat. On holidays and anniversaries, his entire family came to Rancho Encino, and stared at him with respect, regret, and boredom. "Inch-Thick" remained with his eyes closed, his heart-beats monitored by the latest and most sensitive of cardio-pulmonary equipment, his brainwaves monitored by electroencephalograph.

His wife was still with him at 9:06 the evening after Jerry Sennett had been asked by Sergeant Skrolnik to come down to police headquarters and look at Maurice Needs. She had said nothing to him for most of the afternoon; but toward nightfall she had recited to him, without any hope

that he could hear or understand her, one of the love
poems he had written to her during the war.

How can a love so gentle be so fierce?
How can a soft caress grip with such strength?
How can your tenderest glance so quickly pierce
My heart its very depth, my life its length?

Admiral Thorson had never written any poetry before
the war; and he never wrote any more afterward. But Mary
Thorson kept in an old ribboned candy box in her
dressing-table drawer a collection of nearly 40 poems that
had expressed his feelings for her in those days when it was
quite possible he would never see her again.

They were the only words of his that she now possessed.

At 9:08, Nurse Abramski, a brusque but charming
woman with a striking resemblance to Mary Tyler Moore,
looked in to check the admiral's heartbeat and drip, and to
ensure that his waste-disposal bags did not need emptying.
She smiled the whole time, but said little; she knew that
Mary Thorson preferred not to chatter. Mary Thorson had
enough to cope with, paying this long drawn-out homage
to her comatose husband and lover.

Nurse Abramski finished in Admiral Thorson's suite at
9:11. At the very moment she closed the door behind her,
a Chevrolet van drew up outside the hospital grounds on
Balboa Boulevard and doused its headlights. Out of the
driver's seat climbed a young Japanese called Masahiro
Yoshino, a *kendo* adept who had arrived in Los Angeles
only four days ago from Kobe. Out of the passenger seat,
puffing slightly, climbed Commander Ernest Perry
Ouvarov, wearing a belted raincoat and chewing an unlit
corncob pipe, an unconscious impersonation of Mac-
Arthur.

The commander took off his tinted glasses and looked
around the hushed hospital grounds. The spreading
California oaks rustled in the warm evening wind, and the
lights from the hospital facility sparkled through their

leaves. "Okay," he said at last, in a hoarse voice. "Let's get it over with."

He and Yoshino went around to the back of the van. Yoshino unlocked it and opened both doors wide. Inside, the van was almost dark, except for a row of beady red safety lights. The walls, floor, and ceiling were padded with black silk quilting. Among these flags, suspended on silver claws, swung the second Tengu, dressed this time in nothing more than a black headband and the tightly bound loincloth of the sumo wrestler. The motion of the van on its way to Encino had caused the silver claws to work their way even more deeply than usual into the Tengu's flesh, and one of them had pierced his thigh muscle completely. The Tengu was not alone: sitting next to him in the darkness were two of Kappa's black-masked disciples. After Yoshino had opened the doors, they quickly and quietly took over, lowering the Tengu to the floor of the van and speaking to him in long, magical murmurings as they raised him up to a sitting position.

Commander Ouvarov said, "We don't have too long, you guys. This place has one of the hottest security patrols going."

The black devil-people didn't turn to look at him. Their concentration was reserved entirely for the Tengu, who was now rhythmically raising and lowering his white-masked face and uttering a high, keening sound that made Commander Ouvarov shiver. It reminded him of a 4.7-inch naval shell screaming high and deadly overhead.

Yoshino glanced at the commander nervously. He was a serious young man, devoted to the samurai ways, a fanatical believer in Japan's ancestral honor. He was close to his gods. But dealing with a Tengu was something different. A Tengu was the fiercest martial horror that ancient Japan and her magical traditions were capable of creating; and until today, Yoshino had never seen one in the flesh.

In Japanese, the black disciples of Kappa incanted, "O great and terrible Tengu, master of all that is evil and frightful, stalker of the night, deathless one, wrencher and devourer of flesh and spirit, use this servant of human clay to revenge our dishonor.''

At last, the Tengu rose jerkily to his feet, the claws still hanging from his body. One by one, the disciples unhooked them, until the Tengu stood free, his muscles still distorted, his body still pierced with ghastly wounds, but breathing strongly now behind his bland white mask, breathing powerfully and harshly like a wolf that rushes up behind you in the night.

''He is ready,'' said the black-masked Japanese, bowing to Commander Ouvarov.

''Yoshino,'' said Commander Ouvarov. ''Wait here with the van. Any trouble, any questions from security guards, tell them you're having a problem with the electrical system, you've called for a tow truck. And, for Christ's sake, *smile* a lot. What's the time?''

Yoshino checked his large stainless-steel wristwatch. ''Nine nineteen, sir.''

''Right, we shouldn't be longer than six or seven minutes. If we're very much longer, or if you hear a disturbance, wait five more minutes and then go straight back to Nancy Shiranuka's. You got me?''

''Yes, sir.''

Quickly now, with Commander Ouvarov leading the way, the four of them crossed the lawns surrounding Rancho Encino Hospital, keeping to the shadows of the trees. Behind him, Commander Ouvarov could hear the Tengu's panting, foul and suppressed. For the first time since he had started working for Nancy Shiranuka and Gerard Crowley, he really understood that he was involved in something far more hair-raising than murdering two or three innocent people for the sake of some rich client's revenge. The discreet disposal of business opponents or political enemies or smart young men who had overplayed their romantic overtures to rich men's daughters—that was all a question of day-to-day American business which Commander Ouvarov could accept.

But this Tengu was something different. Behind that expressionless white mask was the face of a man who was actually *possessed*, body and soul, by something from what Commander Ouvarov could only conceive as hell itself. The Tengu's eyes glowed like blue coals in a midnight furnace, his breath rushed and thundered inside his mask, his nearly naked body was hideous with weals and deep holes that actually bared the fibers of the muscles and the bones themselves.

The Tengu was a demon-creature, a man who had voluntarily given himself to a fate which other men would have happily committed suicide to avoid. Yet, according to Doctor Gempaku, to become a Tengu was a far greater honor than to commit *seppuku*. The *bushi* who committed *seppuku* were simply opening the way for themselves to heaven, those who gave themselves to the Tengu were condemning themselves to eternal life and endless purifying pain. It was the Shinto principle of mortification of the flesh to the nth degree.

That was why the first Tengu mission had been less than a complete success. The Tengu had not had sufficient pain inflicted on him to reach a state of total possession by the ancient demon; he had been halfway between euphoria and utter agony, and when Yoshikazu had tried to drive him back to the ranch, his demon had gradually slipped away from him, leaving him in terrible pain but without the spiritual possession that would have enabled him to endure it. Lying in the van, he had gone partly mad.

This time, with the second Tengu, Doctor Gempaku had taken no such chances. He had suspended the Tengu on hooks until the last possible moment, to maximize his suffering. Beneath the Tengu's loincloth, which was already spotted with fresh blood, a ten-inch-long steel spring, an eighth of an inch in diameter, had been pushed inside his urethra, the length of his penis, into his bladder. The pain from this device alone, Doctor Gempaku had told Commander Ouvarov, would make a god out of anyone.

They reached the corner of the hospital's main administration building. From there, they would skirt around the gardens where the patients sat during the day to the intensive care building. According to the drawings of the hospital Commander Ouvarov had secured yesterday from the Encino planning department, they could gain access to the room where Admiral Thorson lay in his oxygen tent by forcing a pair of double doors, walking the length of a 32-foot corridor, and then turning left.

Close by Commander Ouvarov's shoulder, the Tengu breathed beneath his mask with all the roughness of a creature that knows it is about to kill. Commander Ouvarov took a deep breath himself, to steady his nerves, and then said, "Let's go."

They walked quickly between the rows of flowering bushes; past the ornamental pool and the deck furniture. Their feet were silent on the grass and the patio paving. Only that lascivious breathing betrayed their presence.

Suddenly, with no warning at all, a dazzling security light picked all four of them out in blinding relief. The Tengu stopped, twisting this way and that. But Commander Ouvarov hissed, "Keep going! We've taken them by surprise, so keep going!" A door slammed. A voice shouted, "Mr. Davison—there's someone out there!" Then another door slammed, and there was the sound of running feet.

The four of them had almost crossed the gardens now, and were only twenty feet away from the double doors which would take them into the intensive-care unit. But from both sides of the building, hurrying to intercept them, came two security guards with drawn guns.

"Okay, *freeze!*" one of the guards ordered. "Put your hands *up*," and don't move!"

The black-masked Japanese hardly broke stride. One of them uttered a terrifying screech and rushed forward at the security guard with his arms whirling as fast as helicopter blades. The guard fired one wild shot before the Japanese struck him on the bridge of his nose with a *Oni* move known as "the splinter." The broken cartilage of the guard's nose was rammed upward into his brain, killing him instantly.

The other guard, a heavily built man with a gingery mustache, backed away down the side of the intensive-care block, holding his revolver in both hands.

"Keep back there, or I'm going to blow your head off!" he shouted, his voice high-pitched and frightened. "Keep well back there!"

The second *Oni* adept zigzagged toward him, running in such a fast and complicated dance that the guard could hardly keep his gun trained on him. *Oni* students were taught this evasive running by having to dodge a constant shower of crossbow bolts. But even "the dance of the dragonfly" was not enough to protect the Japanese from an erratic and nervous security guard with a .38 revolver. As he flickered toward the guard like a hovering shadow, the guard fired one shot which hit the Japanese straight in the face. A spray of blood pattered on the paving stones, and the Japanese rolled backward.

The first adept took up where his dead comrade had left off: dodging toward the security guard with his hands flailing. The security guard should have fired a second time, but his nerve and his eye failed him. The Japanese screamed out, "Kappa!" and dropkicked the guard on the side of the head. The guard went down with his neck broken, and lay on the ground twitching like a dead chicken.

Now all the floodlights in the hospital grounds had been switched on, and Commander Ouvarov knew that it would be only minutes before the police arrived. He could cope with a few security guards and frightened nurses, but the police would be altogether different. He rapped out to the one remaining Japanese, "Set him loose! Set the Tengu loose!"

The Japanese uttered a strange, chanting cry. The Tengu, who had been standing a little way behind them, now moved purposefully forward to the double doors of the intensive-care unit and stood in front of them, his mutilated chest rising and falling as he gathered his strength. Each door was glazed with a small circular window, out of which light illuminated the Tengu's white mask. The Japanese called out again, and this time the Tengu lifted both his fists, hesitated, and then plunged them with a slushy crash through the wire-reinforced glass.

Hooking both arms through the broken windows, the Tengu tore the double doors off their hinges and hurled them away across the grass.

Commander Ouvarov waited as long as he dared; but he could already see three more guards making their way, crouched and furtive, across the hospital gardens. He said to the Japanese, "Let's get out of here. I'll give you a hand with your friend." In the distance, police sirens were warbling, and it was becoming more than clear to Commander Ouvarov that the highly sophisticated security which protected most of southern California's wealthier citizens was going to prove a severe obstacle if Gerard Crowley wanted anyone else done away with. He helped the Japanese lift the dead *Oni* adept from the lawn, and between them they dragged him away through the bushes and into the shadows, and began to make their way back to the van.

"We go back for the Tengu?" asked the Japanese.

Commander Ouvarov shook his head. "This has all gotten out of hand. We're going to leave the Tengu behind. If he doesn't, then it's tough luck. But you won't catch me scampering back into the arms of the law, just for the sake of some masochistic Oriental."

The Japanese looked at Commander Ouvarov through the eye-slits of his mask. It was clear that he was uncertain and suspicious.

"We cannot leave the Tengu," he argued. "It is our holy order that we must stay with him, and bring him back."

"I'm in charge of this particular sortie," said Commander Ouvarov, as they dragged the dead Japanese through a low cypress hedge. "If I say we leave the Tengu, then we leave him."

"We must go back," insisted the Japanese. The howling of police sirens was already very close.

Commander Ouvarov let the body of the dead Japanese drop to the grass. "C'mere," he said to the *Oni* adept. "I'll tell you what we'll do."

Commander Ouvarov had learned, more years ago than he could remember, that cunning must always be countered with cunning. He had sent countless irate letters to the Pentagon during the Vietnam War, protesting the way in which American forces had blundered with their bombing and defoliants and armored vehicles into a country of philosophical ruthlessness and extraordinary tactical subtlety. You cannot frighten a man who is not frightened of death, he had told them again and again. You cannot overwhelm an enemy whose dedication to fighting and winning grows fiercer, rather than weaker, the nearer he is to defeat. If you live on steak and French fries, if you drive even a moderately comfortable car, if you sleep in a bed and like beer and television, you cannot possibly confront face to face—and beat—a man who knows and wants nothing more than rice, shoes made out of Goodyear tires, and political independence. Not face to face.

That was why, when the *Oni* adept approached him, a trained killer who could have plunged his fist right into the commander's body and wrenched out his living heart, the commander smiled, and put his arm casually and amicably around the boy's shoulders. The boy didn't even realize that he had walked straight into the five-inch shaft of the commander's open switchblade until the arm around his shoulders abruptly tightened around his neck, and the commander gave a loud grunt of exertion and ripped him upward from his groin to his ribcage.

The Japanese stared at Commander Ouvarov, startled. Then his insides slid out like a bloody fertilized egg yolk sliding off a spoon, and he collapsed on top of them.

Commander Ouvarov snapped his knife shut and began to
hobble and run for the van, hoping that the Tengu would
be causing enough commotion to divert attention from the
front of the hospital. It wasn't the first time he had killed a
man. He had probably killed hundreds, with sixteen-inch
naval shells, from distances of twenty miles away; and once
in Okinawa he had cut the throat of a Indonesian pimp
who had been trying to hustle him over the price of an
eight-year-old girl.

Inside the intensive-care block, the Tengu had reached
the door of Admiral Thorson's suite. It was 9:28, and
inside the suite Mary Thorson had only just become aware
of all the shouting and commotion outside. She put down
the faded poems she had been reading, and stood up to
see what was going on.

With two powerful kicks, the Tengu smashed down the
outside door of the suite and stepped into the chintz-
decorated anteroom. He stood there in his white Nō mask,
both hands raised, turning his head slowly from side to
side as he sensed where to go next. His hearing and eye-
sight were as sharp as samurai sword edges; he was alert to
every shuffle and scrape of everything and everybody
around him. The pain which burned in his body, gave his
senses a demonic acuteness, and he could feel, like a
roaring white fire, the presence within him of the Tengu
itself, the relentless devil of evil and destruction.

As the Tengu stepped forward to Admiral Thorson's
door, he was accompanied by tiny flames that danced in
the air: the foxfire *Kitsune-bi*, the visible evidence of evil.
Foxfire had pursued Yayegaki Hime, one of the characters
in an ancient and still-forbidden Nō play, and it was the
mask of Hime that the Tengu wore tonight. It was Kappa's
idea.

Mary Thorson, terrified by the sound of the anteroom
door being smashed, stood in the middle of the room, her
eyes wide, one hand across her breasts, the other half
raised as if to protect her husband's oxygen tent. "Who's
there?" she demanded. But all she could hear was a

dragging sound, and then a clatter as the Tengu threw aside one of the chairs.

The Tengu kicked at the door once, and splintered it. But just as he was about to kick again, Nurse Abramski came unexpectedly through the shattered doorway into the anteroom. The security guards and the police had seen Commander Ouvarov and the second Japanese *bushi* escape across the gardens, and hadn't realized that the Tengu had actually forced his way into the intensive-care unit.

Nurse Abramski shrieked, "Stop! You mustn't!" and ran forward to seize the Tengu's arm, thinking only that he was small and nearly naked, and that he mustn't disturb Admiral Thorson at any cost.

It was only when she gripped the Tengu's wrist that she understood her mistake. He turned, and his face was blank and white, with eyes that seemed to Nurse Abramski to glow with a fluorescent life of their own. His body was deeply muscular, although it was marked all over with terrible scars and weals, and the loincloth he wore was soaked in crimson blood. It was the sheer *evil* he exuded that terrified Nurse Abramski the most, though. It overwhelmed her like a tide of freezing vomit. She tried to step back, tried to release her grasp, but the evil was so intense that she didn't seem to be able to make her legs move properly, didn't seem to be able to open her mouth and scream for help.

With the bursting, flaring sound of a gas ring lighting, a crown of flames ignited around the Tengu's head. His eyes pulsed a mesmerizing blue. With one hideously powerful movement, he seized the lapels of Nurse Abramski's uniform, and the skin of her collarbone with them, and tore the flesh off her shoulders and ribs. Sternomastoid or cleidomastoid muscles, deltoid muscles, pectoral muscles—all, including her breasts, ripped raw from the bone, all the way down to her abdominal muscles.

Beneath her exposed ribs, her lungs expanded in one last powerful shriek of horror. The realization of death.

Then she dropped to the floor and lay dying of shock in her own blood. The Tengu stared down at her, the foxfire still hovering around him. Then he turned back toward the half-splintered door of Admiral Thorson's suite.

Inside, Mary Thorson knew now that she was in terrible danger. She backed away from the door until she reached the edge of her husband's bed. She glanced behind her. There was a window, and although it was closed she knew that it wasn't locked. But what about Knut? How could she leave Knut, comatose and defenseless, to whatever it was that was rampaging in the next room?

She heard more police sirens warble down Balboa Boulevard; she heard the wail of an ambulance, then another. Then there was another shattering kick at the door, and the top hinge burst free.

Panicking, she stared down at "Inch-Thick" lying with his eyes peacefully closed inside his oxygen tent. The door was kicked again. This time the paneling cracked wide apart, and she saw for the first time her assailant's bare and bloody foot. The cardiopulmonary unit beside her husband's bed bleeped on, unconcerned, and the endless electronic ribbon on the electroencephalograph showed normal, ten alpha waves per second.

She could still have made it to the window. But she was already sure that she wasn't going to try. As fearful as she was, she had stayed with Knut through war and peace, through career struggles and great triumphs, through all of his children and all of his hopes; and through almost a year of unconsciousness. How can a love so gentle be so fierce? she thought. How can a soft caress grip with such strength?

There was one final wrenching noise as the shattered door was hurled across the room; and there in front of her stood the Tengu, his hands gloved in drying blood, his masked face surrounded by floating fires as hot and noisy as blowtorches.

"Oh, my dear Lord," she whispered. "Oh, my dear Lord, save me."

The Tengu stalked forward and tried to thrust her away

from the oxygen tent. The magical instructions he had been given by Kappa's servants were explicit: slay the one in the tent of air. It was the man whose blood he was smelling, the man whose body he wanted to rip to pieces. But the woman clawed and struck and screamed at him, and even when he threw her aside across the room, she climbed painfully to her feet and shrieked at him to stop.

Inside the oxygen tent, miraculously, Admiral Thorson opened his eyes. Mary's screaming had penetrated deep into his comatose sleep, and already the alpha waves on his electroencephalograph were hesitating and jumping. He heard her scream again. He actually *heard* her. He tried to turn his head to see what was happening, but he couldn't. He willed himself, *Turn, turn, turn your head*, but his nervous system wouldn't respond.

The Tengu tore at the plastic tent, and it opened with a soft exhalation, a dying beast. But when Mary Thorson threw herself at him again, screaming and screaming, trying to tear off his mask, scratching and clawing at skin that had already been tortured past human endurance.

Pushing her roughly away from him, the Tengu picked up the chromium stand on which Admiral Thorson's nutritive drip was hanging, and gripped it in both hands like a spear. The foxfire around his head burned even brighter as he took up the *Oni* stance called *Shishi-mai*, the lion dance. Then with a howl that was old as Japan and her demons, a cry that came straight from the mouth of a triumphant devil, he thrust the stand deep into Mary Thorson's stomach and lifted her up on it, struggling and kicking and silent with shock. He rammed the stand straight into the wall, so that she was impaled, alive, with her feet more than two feet from the floor.

Panting harshly, the Tengu turned to Admiral Thorson. But his time had already run out. Three policemen appeared in the doorway, two of them armed with re-volvers and the third with a pump shotgun; while a fourth policeman smashed the window with the butt of a rifle and thrust the muzzle through the shattered frame.

"*Freeze!* Lie flat on the floor with your arms and your legs spread!" one of the officers ordered.

The officer with the pump shotgun, however, wasn't going to wait. He fired one deafening shot and hit the Tengu in the chest. The Tengu pitched around, staggered, but remained upright, his chest smoking, swaying on his feet. The officer reloaded and fired again, and this time blew the Tengu's head apart, so that nothing rose from between his shoulders but the bloody pipe of his neck. As if in nervous reaction, the other officers fired at the headless body too, six or seven times, until it sagged at the knees and dropped heavily to the floor.

Slowly, walking knee-deep through their own glutinous fear, the officers stepped into the room. One of them said, "Jesus H. Christ."

They lifted Mary Thorson down from the wall as carefully as disciples in a religious painting. They looked down at the Tengu, and then looked away again and holstered their guns. They couldn't think of anything to say.

"Will you look at this guy?" one of them said at last. "These goddamned marks all over his body."

After five minutes they declared the room safe for paramedics, medical examiners, forensic staff, TV, press, and anybody else who wanted to mill around and stare at all the blood. A newspaper woman came in, took one look, and hurried outside again to be sick. The medical examiner kept asking for body bags, but nobody seemed to have remembered to bring them. One of the paramedics kept saying, "What is he, Japanese or something? What do you think, Japanese?"

"No head, could be anything," replied a local detective, in a voice as crackly as an old-time radio. "I don't know what kind of *charge* the uniformed guys are putting in their shotguns these days, but you can bet your ass that somebody's going to start an inquiry about it. Look at that, no head. Could have been hit by a fucking cannon."

"Did you bring those bags or didn't you?"

"Speared her, right to the fucking wall."

"Will you move back, please?"

At last, arguing and pushing as he came, Admiral Thorson's personal physician was able to force his way into the room. Dr. Isaac Walach, was a tall, thin, balding man, one of the country's wealthiest and most expert specialists in apoplexy and brain seizures. He ignored the police and the blood and the medical examiners crouched over the corpse of the Tengu, and went straight to Admiral Thorson's bedside. All the monitoring equipment had been torn loose and the oxygen pump disconnected, although one of the policemen had been quickwitted enough to turn off the oxygen supply in case of fire. Doctor Walach made a quick check of the Admiral's pulse rate and vital signs, lifting back his eyelids to check his response to light, listening to his heart. Then he quietly tugged one of the paramedic's sleeves and said, "Help me get this patient out of here, please. He's still alive."

CHAPTER TWO

She came to the door in a black silk robe, painted by hand with modern graphic designs by Shigeo Fukuda, yellow-and-green faces interlinked to form the falling figure of a bird. She said, "Yes, what is it?" in a mystified tone that was strangely attractive.

He recognized her for what she was: Hokkaido Japanese, probably from Sapporo. He said, "My name's Sennett."

"Yes?" she asked.

Jerry hesitated. He had come to Nancy Shiranuka's apartment on Alta Loma Road on nothing more than a hunch: another cold wind that had blown through his mind. He didn't know what he had been expecting to find: David bound and gagged and tied to a chair maybe? He didn't even understand what it was that haunted him so persistently about Japan. Now, here he was, facing a pretty Japanese girl who had asked him what he wanted, and he didn't have the first idea what to say.

"I, er, I heard about Kemo," he told her in a hoarse voice.

She raised one eyebrow. A perfect arch, finely drawn.

"I was down at police headquarters," he said. "They told me there."

"Are you a police officer?"

He shook his head.

There was a lengthy silence. Nancy at last said, "You've come about your son, I suppose?"

"You know where he is? Is he safe?"

Nancy reached out and gently held the sleeve of his jacket. "He's safe for the time being. Come in. There's nobody here at the moment."

Jerry felt as if his head were exploding with questions and anxiety, but he knew Japanese etiquette well enough to hold his tongue, and to follow Nancy into her silent, austere apartment.

"Sit down," said Nancy, indicating a cushion. Jerry eased himself into the cross-legged position which he had once accepted as the only way to sit, but which now required some painful tugging at his shins.

"You're certain he's safe?" he asked.

"Certain," said Nancy. "They have taken him for the express purpose of flushing you out of your home, to entice you to a place where they can easily dispose of you. They will take great care of him until you are dead."

"Who's *they*?" demanded Jerry.

Nancy went across to the liquor cabinet, slid it open, and took out a bottle of Gekkeikan export saké. She poured it carefully into a flask and left it to warm. She said, "I do not know their identity any more than you do. But they are hawks."

"It was you who left that scroll under my windshield?"

"It was a friend who put it there. But the message came from me."

"I should have understood it," said Jerry, with bitter realization. 'The hawks will return to their roost.' To catch the lamb, of course. It's from something by Tanizaki Jun'ichiro. *Chijin no Ai*?"

Nancy said, "You impress me."

"A Westerner shouldn't be conversant with sadistic Japanese literature of the 1920's? Why did you leave me the message if you didn't think that I'd understand it?"

"I hoped you would grasp it intuitively."

Jerry tugged again at his awkwardly folded leg. "As it turned out, I was in too much of a hurry. The police wanted me to look at a suspect they've charged with murdering Sherry Cantor and that police officer out on the Hollywood Freeway."

Nancy poured out a little saké and handed it to Jerry in a fragile porcelain cup. She took some herself, and then sat down close to him. "You are an unusual man," she said. "I sense that there is something hanging over your head."

"A mushroom cloud," he told her wryly, and raised his glass. "*Kampai!*"

"*Kampai!*" she echoed.

They drank, and sat in silence for a while. Then Jerry said, "These people who have taken David—they're the same people who sent that man to murder me?"

Nancy said, "You understand, then, that Sherry Cantor's murder was a mistake?"

"I understood the minute the police described the assailant as wearing a white Nō mask. And—I had a feeling, I guess—something to do with the fact that I've been undergoing psychiatric treatment for years after what happened to me in Japan—and, I don't know. I just guessed."

Nancy reached forward and picked up the saké flask again. Her black robe opened a little, and Jerry was conscious in a way that made him feel curiously old, but also

curiously aroused, that he had glimpsed the dark areola of
her nipple. Underneath that thin silk robe, she must be
naked.

How can I be so anxious about David, he thought of
himself, and still think something like that? But then she
passed him a fresh cup of saké and he remembered that he
was sitting with a Japanese woman. His mind, after all
these years, had slipped back into the timeless traditional
way of observing every ritual scrupulously, whatever its
importance. There was a time for everything, for anxiety,
for passion, for pursuit, and revenge. There was also time
for saké, and quiet intensive conversation, and the studied
but accidental glimpse of a beautiful woman's breast. It
was quite possible she had allowed the accident to happen,
to reassure him.

"Are you one of them?" Jerry asked her.

Nancy stared at him for a moment, as if she were unsure. Then she said, "No, it is impossible to be 'one of
them.' They are not a gang, in the conventional sense of
the word, nor a sect. I am unsure what they are; but I do
now realize that they are evil and powerful. I am employed
by one of their hired running dogs as a translator,
organizer, general drag lady."

She sipped at her drink, and then said, "A few days ago
I became curious about them: why they wanted to kill you,
who they really are. I sent my houseboy Kemo to follow
one of them after a meeting. If you saw my address at the
police headquarters, then you will know what happened to
him."

"I only glimpsed the report," said Jerry, with a dry
mouth. "It seems they tore his heart out."

"It is a technique used in a particular martial art known
as *Oni*, the art of the demons," Nancy explained, almost
as if she were talking to a party of tourists. Then she looked
up at Jerry, and her eyes were hard and dark and unforgiving. "The adept's arm is swung around to gain velocity,
in the same way that a baseball pitcher winds up. By the
time it reaches his intended victim, his hand is formed in

the shape of a chisel, fingers straight, and it is traveling as fast as a bullet train. The technique is to drive the hand right through the muscular wall of the stomach, upward and slightly to the right, and to seize the victim's heart."

Jerry said quietly, "I've heard of *Oni*. But it's forbidden, isn't it? I mean, it's actually illegal."

"Illegality, danger, death, they are all part of what makes the Japanese personality what it is," said Nancy. "You are speaking of the people who invented *seppuku* and *kamikaze* and the rituals of Shrine Shinto. You are speaking of people who eat *fugu* fish not because it tastes better than any other, but because it can kill within minutes. Can you imagine sitting down to a dinner, not knowing if you will ever arise from it alive?"

"Is there any particular reason why I should believe you?" asked Jerry. "Can you give me any *guarantee* that David is unhurt and still alive?"

Nancy Shiranuka watched him for a while, and then said, "No. But if you have only half an understanding of what is happening here, you will know that I am risking my life telling you any of this. If I fail, the next Tengu they send out will be for me."

Jerry lifted one finger, his mouth half open, in sudden and complete understanding. "The Tengu," he whispered. "So I was right."

"You guessed it was the Tengu? That was what they were afraid of. That was why they sent him to kill you. There can be only two or three people in the United States who know what a Tengu is, what a Tengu can do. They wanted to launch their program without anybody knowing what they were doing."

"What program?" Jerry asked her. "What are you talking about?"

"They are creating a corps of killer bodyguards," Nancy told him. "A band of fanatical and superbly fit Japanese who will do whatever they're told to protect their masters. Well, that is what they *claim* they are doing. Whether they are speaking the truth or not, I don't know. That's all they ever tell us. But they may have underestimated what I knew about the Tengu from the days in which I was a disciple of the Seven Black *Kami*. And they may have underestimated my intuition."

"Your cold wind?" asked Jerry gently.

"My cold wind," nodded Nancy. "The cold wind which tells me that if they are creating Tengus, they have more in mind than a mildly profitable scheme to sell killer bodyguards to rich Arabs and Arizona *mafiosi*. If they are creating Tengus, they have only one thing in mind. And that is, apocalypse."

Jerry thought for a long while. Then he said, "Where is my son?"

"They have a ranch out at Pacoima, in the San Gabriel Mountains near San Fernando Airport. That is where they have been keeping the Tengus. I expect they took your son there as well."

Jerry said, "You're not tricking me, are you? This isn't part of a setup, just to get me out to some place where they can kill me quietly and get it over with? Or is it naive to ask?"

She said softly, in her Japanese accent, "I have been through varying degrees of hell in my life, Mr. Sennett. I have committed crimes of greed and crimes of passion and the greatest crime of not taking care of my soul or my body. I can be many things to many different men. I can experience pleasure, and call it pain. I can experience pain, and call it pleasure. I was blackmailed into helping these people. They threatened to turn over to the FBI a file of photographs and documents which would have implicated me in child pornography, abduction, pimping, illegal sexual activities, and manslaughter. At the same time, they offered me a very great deal of money. They told me they required absolute secrecy and absolute devotion. I was to translate technical data for them; arrange house leases and car rentals and hotel facilities; and act as hostess and translator for their employees and guests."

"And they told you they were creating this special team of bodyguards?"

'"That's correct. They said that one of their doctors had discovered a new technique during the Tokyo Olympics for making men stronger and more tolerant to pain. They called the men Tengus—which at first I thought was simply a nickname like calling a baseball team the Red Devils. It was only after they killed that girl, Sherry Cantor, that I began to doubt them. Now, I am quite sure that they have been misleading me.''

Jerry asked, ''Have you told anybody what you think?'' His voice was dull and expressionless.

Nancy said, ''One of them, a man called Gerard Crowley. He is the go-between, the man who arranges for all the Japanese to come into the United States without being stopped by immigration officers; the man who takes care of the finance.''

''What did he say?''

''He didn't know whether to believe me or not. They told him nothing more than they told me. But, he may be sympathetic. I'm not sure. He is a very cold person, very difficult to reach.''

Jerry held out his cup for more saké. He wasn't at all drunk. It usually took more than half a bottle to get him anything near tipsy. He felt highly suspicious of Nancy Shiranuka, and yet he couldn't really see any reason why he should. She had tried to warn him, after all, as subtly as she knew how, and if he hadn't understood her message about the hawks, then it had been his own fault. She certainly hadn't advertised her address, so she couldn't have been prepared for him to come around. The Japanese were always so meticulous: even their accidents didn't happen by accident. But Jerry couldn't believe that he had been afforded a glimpse of Nancy's address by design.

He said, ''You know why they wanted to kill me, don't you?''

Nancy replied. ''It was something to do with the war. Something to do with the fact that, if any of the Tengus had been mentioned in the press or on television, you would have known at once what they were. It was a question of security, they told me.''

"Well, you're partly right," said Jerry. "In fact, they needn't have worried. A Tengu attacked Sherry Cantor next door, quite horribly and spectacularly, and even when I heard what had happened to her, I didn't put two and two together, not at first. It was all too long ago, too far away. The thing still haunts me, still gives me nightmares, but who would have imagined that it would return for real? Not me. I would have been the last one to think of a Tengu, no matter how grotesquely anyone was butchered. It was only the Nō mask that reminded me. The face of the greatest *Oni* of all, the demon of a hundred identities and a million cruel ways."

Nancy said, "You know about the Tengu, don't you?"

Jerry nodded.

"Tell me everything," she said. "I promise we will do whatever we can to find your son. But tell me everything. It could help me to understand what is happening, and who is creating these monsters, and why."

Jerry stood up, and walked across to the window. "I'm not supposed to tell you this," he said. He felt very tired and empty, and somehow his disloyalty to his country's secrets tasted like ashes, as if all the confidential dispatches which had comprised the Appomattox Papers had been burned, as a punishment, on his tongue. "But, during the latter part of the Pacific war, when I was a lieutenant in the Naval Intelligence Command, bright, intelligent, just out of college, I was told that I had volunteered to be parachuted at night into Japan, into the Chugoku Sanchi, not far from Hiroshima, to monitor at close quarters the military radio messages that were being sent to and from Hiroshima to Tokyo."

Nancy said nothing, but lit a cigarette.

Jerry said, "I was the ideal candidate for the job, they told me. I was young and fit. I spoke fluent Japanese. I had worked for nearly two years on Japanese naval codes, and I could put on a headset and understand what the commander of the *Akagi* was saying to the commander of the *Soryu* without even bothering to jot it all down."

He paused for a moment or two, and then he said, "They called the mission 'Appomattox.' They warned me that the chances of my returning to the United States alive were not particularly high; but that what I was going to do was going to be crucial to the entire course of the war. In fact, more than that, to the entire course of twentieth-century history.

"They said that, all across the Pacific theater, U.S. Marines had been suddenly met by fierce opposition from special Japanese troops they had codenamed 'Hogs.' The exact casualty ratio was top secret, they told me, and as far as I'm aware, it still is today. But to give you some idea, five amphibious landings on small Pacific islands yielded a U.S. casualty list of more than twenty-three thousand men dead, and eighteen million dollars of equipment lost, and these were on nothing more than atolls and reefs of minor strategic importance. The island of Pulau Thuap only fell to the Marines after three separate attempts at storming its beaches, and seventeen saturation-bombing missions by B-25's."

"The Tengus," whispered Nancy.

Jerry tiredly rubbed his eyes. "The Japanese were sending Tengus out to every possible location in the Pacific, in a last hopeless attempt to turn the tide of the war. There must have been hundreds of them, even thousands. At that time, it couldn't have been difficult to find enough fanatical young Japanese who were prepared to submit themselves to the pain which was necessary for them to become . . . well, what they became."

"Possessed," Nancy prompted him.

"I don't know," said Jerry. "I wasn't sure then, and I'm still not. After the war was over, and I was sent back to Tokyo, I spent days reading everything I could on ancient Shinto rituals and Japanese demonology. But who knows? The human mind and the human physique are capable of extraordinary things under stress, and in conditions of trance or religious ecstasy. The members of the Pentecostal Holiness Church in Kentucky drink strychnine and burn

their feet with blazing torches, just to show that the Lord
will protect them against harm. I saw a fire-walk myself in
Polynesia, when a man walked twenty yards over white-hot
coals with bare feet and appeared to be unscathed. You
think to yourself, are these people really possessed by
angels, or devils, or are they simply using their ordinary
human capabilities to the utmost—something which most
of us rarely do?''

Nancy said nothing, but waited for Jerry to continue. It
was growing dark outside, and somewhere in that darkness
David was being held captive, for a ransom which
amounted to nothing less than Jerry's own life. The
thought was clinging around his mind like a tangle of
barbed wire, and already his emotions and his desperate
love for David were scratched and bleeding and raw.

''They parachuted six of us into the Chugoku Sanchi at
night, with a high-power Stromberg wireless receiver and
enough food to last us for a week. We set up three base
camps in the mountains and trekked from one to the
other, listening at each one to the military and code
messages that the Japanese were putting out from Hiroshima. Most of the wireless traffic was routine—which
ships were docking, how many troops were being em-
barked for where, how much ammunition was available,
what their civil-defense plans were in case of an American
assault. But after three days we picked up a different batch
of signals from the center of the city, from a building
which we pinpointed on our street plans, by simple
triangulation, near a bridge across the Ota River. All the
signals were related to what they called the Tengus, the
devil-people. We listened for four days and four nights,
and by the end of that time we were absolutely certain that
it was right there, in that building in Hiroshima, that the
Hogs were being trained.''

Jerry came away from the window and sat down again.
Nancy poured him another drink, and watched him with
caution and sympathy. It was clear from the look in his
eyes that he had relived those wartime days in Japan over

and over again, dreaming and awake, and that he would carry the responsibility for what he had done forever.

"They had briefed me, before I was dropped into Japan, that if I found the place where the Hogs were being created, I was going to be giving the President the go-ahead to use a completely new type of bomb, an incredibly devastating firebomb, they told me, which would instantly incinerate the Hogs and give them no chance of survival whatever. They had Japanese experts helping the U.S. Intelligence Commands—experts in Japanese demonology, as I later found out—and it was the opinion of these advisers that the only way in which the Tengus could be eradicated without any fear of their revival would be to vaporize them with an atomic bomb. You know the legends, I expect. If a Tengu is chopped to pieces, even *one* piece, on its own, remains capable of independent life. And so nothing could remain. Not even a fingernail.

"Well, I was sure that I had found the place. Every signal confirmed it. I radioed a message to the USS *Value*, which was waiting off Mi-Shima in the Sea of Japan, and the *Value*, in turn, relayed the message to the U.S. Pacific Fleet. President Truman was at Yalta at the time, with Stalin and Churchill. They gave him the message, and he said go. The official justification was that, if America had the means to bring the war to a swift conclusion, she ought to do so, which as far as it went was quite true. But what they omitted to tell the public and the press was that two or three thousand Tengus could have held up the American advance for five or six years, even longer; and that General MacArthur had already expressed the opinion in a confidential memorandum to President Truman that an invasion of the Japanese mainland would cost an unacceptably high number of American casualties. That is, unless the Tengus were eliminated, totally."

"Which is what you justifiably did," said Nancy.

"Yes," Jerry agreed. "But when I confirmed the position of the Tengu training center, right in the middle of Hiroshima, among ten square kilometers of wooden houses, I didn't understand that our 'incredibly devastating firebomb' was going to be an atomic bomb. I didn't understand that, for the sake of killing three or four hundred fanatical young Japanese soldiers, we were going to wipe out eighty thousand men, women, and children in the space of a split second, and that another sixty thousand were going to die of radioactivity within a year.''

He was silent for a very long while. Then he said, "I didn't *know*."

"And if you *had* known?" asked Nancy.

Again he was silent. "I'm not sure," he replied at last. "When you're in a war, everything looks different. I lost all five of the men who were with me. We got caught in crossfire on the beach at Kokubu, when the landing craft tried to pick us up. Japanese Coast Guardsmen, most of them not much more than sixteen and seventeen years old. They caught us like ducks on a pond. I only got away because I could swim. Five men lost out of six, and I thought it was a massacre.

"Then I heard that they'd dropped the atomic bomb. Compared to that, my massacre was a school picnic."

Nancy allowed Jerry to settle into repose. Then she said, "Nagasaki?"

"I don't know," said Jerry. "They might have suspected another Tengu center there, but I doubt it. They probably realized that the atomic bomb was so damned effective that they could end the war almost immediately. Jesus—once you've killed a hundred and forty thousand people, what does it matter if you kill seventy thousand more?"

Nancy said, "You still blame yourself after all this time?"

"Wouldn't you? I could have sent back a radio message saying that I hadn't found anything."

"Then you would have had to take the responsibility for all of the American soldiers who would have been killed by the Tengus."

Jerry gave her a wry, lopsided smile, the first smile he

had managed since he had heard that David had been kidnapped. "You see my problem," he told her.

Nancy went to her tape deck and switched on a soft recording of *koto* music. There was something about her stillness, something about the peace of her apartment, that made Jerry feel as if whole centuries might have passed by since he had first rung her doorbell.

He said, "I don't know why I've told you all of this. Apart from my shrink, you're the first person I've ever discussed it with. They could put me into jail for twenty years for what I've said to you tonight."

Nancy said, "You want your son back."

"Yes."

"And your son is more important than twenty years in jail?"

"Yes."

"Then you have been justified in telling me about the Tengus, and about the bomb. You and I have more in common than you think."

Jerry reached across and took out one of Nancy's cigarettes. "How's that?" he asked her.

"The Tengus have affected both of our lives. You, because of what you did in the war. Me, because I am now being blackmailed into helping them come back to life. And also because I was once a member of the shrine that worships the Seven Black *Kami*, of whom the Tengu is the greatest and the most terrible."

Jerry said, "I want my son, Miss Shiranuka. What can I do?"

"You can stay here and wait for a while," said Nancy. "Gerard Crowley is due here in just about an hour's time, and you can talk to him."

"It must have been Gerard Crowley who arranged for the Tengu to kill me in the first place. The Tengu who murdered Sherry Cantor."

"It was," said Nancy blandly.

"Then how can I talk to him about David? I mean, how can I—"

"Gerard Crowley has changed a little in the past few days, the same as I have," said Nancy. "Like me, he is beginning to realize that he is extremely dispensible; and that unless he hedges his bets, he may find himself a very bad loser. We are all in fear of our lives."

Jerry said, "Forget it. I'm going straight out to that Pacoima Ranch right now."

"You want to bring your son back alive?"

"Of course I do."

"Then control your anger. Hold back your impatience. Wait and speak with Mr. Crowley. You are up against an enemy which only Presidents and atomic bombs have been able to defeat in the past. You are up against the accumulation of centuries of Japanese history, and a devil that speaks with many voices. Gerard may help. Gerard may tell you how to get your son back. But you must beware, for even Gerard himself may be the devil, or the devil's disciple."

CHAPTER THREE

Mr. Esmeralda heard the news from Rancho Encino at a few minutes after eleven o'clock, on ABC television's evening roundup. He was standing in front of the mirror in his rented house on Camden Drive, fastening his red-and-white silk necktie, in preparation for Commander Ouvarov's imminently expected return from Encino and for the visit he would have to make subsequently to the split-level house in Laurel Canyon, to give Kappa his report that Admiral Thorson had been successfully slain.

Through the half-open bedroom door, he could see Kuan-yin sitting in the parlor in her chauffeur's uniform, her tunic unbuttoned as far as her heavy bronze belt

buckle, her brown-booted legs crossed, reading *TV Guide*.
His Spanish maid, Luisa, was clearing the table from the
evening meal. Then he heard, "From Encino tonight,
we've just heard that a maniac killer—"

"Turn it up!" Mr. Esmeralda demanded. "Quickly,
turn the sound up!"

Kuan-yin reached for the remote control and casually
increased the volume. Mr. Esmeralda walked slowly into
the parlor, his hands still holding his half-fastened
necktie, listening with dreadful attention to the news
which he had feared from the very beginning.

"—examiner says that she died instantly from her injuries, although he would not yet detail what these
actually were. His only comment was that it was a 'terrible
multiple murder, the work of a madman.' The bodies of
two other Japanese were discovered in bushes in the
hospital grounds, one of them shot by security guards, the
other apparently the victim of a knife attack by his
Caucasian associate. Detectives from Hollywood who have
been working on the barehanded killings earlier this week
of *Our Family Jones* star Sherry Cantor and a uniformed
police patrolman by the side of the Hollywood Freeway
have been in close contact with Encino detectives as—"

Mr. Esmeralda scarcely heard the rest of the report. He
sat down on the arm of the sofa and gradually tugged his
necktie loose, twisting it around his hands like a garotte.
So, Commander Ouvarov had failed, and the Tengu had
not only been seen and caught, but killed. He supposed it
wasn't really the commander's fault. Breaking into the
hospital and attempting to silence Admiral Thorson had
been a fanatical idea at best. But Mr. Esmeralda knew that
Kappa would never take the blame for what had
happened, and he also knew that Kappa would lay much
of the blame on *him*.

Worse still, the police would now be in possession of a
wealth of circumstantial and forensic clues which could
lead them, eventually, to an arrest. They were likely to be
questioning the Japanese community already about

unusual comings and goings among Japanese; and if Gerard Crowley had been even slightly careless in his dealings with the immigration authorities, they could pick him up within hours.

He listened to the end of the bulletin, to see if there was any news about Admiral Thorson himself, but the announcer didn't even mention him. That meant the old man was probably still alive; and if that was the case, Kappa's fury would be devastating. Twice the Tengus had been sent out to kill, and twice they have failed. Mr. Esmeralda had warned Kappa again and again about employing unstable people like Gerard Crowley and Ernest Ouvarov, but Kappa had been adamant that their hirelings should not only be dispensable, but "tainted with the breath of evil." Only men and women without any social or sexual morals would be able to undertake the greatest task of all, the task for which the Tengus had been created from the beginning.

Kuan-yin asked Mr. Esmeralda, "It has gone wrong?"

Mr. Esmeralda glanced toward Luisa, to indicate to Kuan-yin that she shouldn't discuss Tengu business in front of the maid. But he nodded and said, "Badly wrong. There will be serious trouble now."

"What will you do?" asked Kuan-yin, when Luisa had gone back down the short flight of stairs that led to the dining room and the kitchen.

"I will have to face them, whatever," said Mr. Esmeralda. "You cannot run away from people like the Circle of Burned Doves. Especially if you want to continue working in Japan."

"They will kill you," said Kuan-yin.

"No," said Mr. Esmeralda. "Not yet. They have gone this far, but they have not yet completed whatever it is they want to do. I think I am comparatively safe until they have accomplished their purpose."

"You have never told me their purpose."

Mr. Esmeralda lifted the points of his collar and began tying his necktie again. "I have not wished to burden you.

What they want to do is utterly catastrophic. If I told you, you would not understand. But, I have committed myself to helping them.''

''Why?'' asked Kuan-yin. In the evening lamplight, her face looked very pretty and serene. ''I always thought you were a man of great independence. The son of the great pirate Jesus Esmeralda.''

Mr. Esmeralda tugged the knot of his necktie straight and examined himself carefully in the gilt-framed mirror that hung on the parlor wall. The shiny hair was perfectly combed back, and the mustache was immaculately scissored. He thought he looked handsome, but also out of date, like a character out of a 1950's movie. If he hadn't been able to play the part of ''Mr. Esmeralda'' as if he were acting, he probably wouldn't have the nerve to survive. The world in which he lived was dangerous and bizarre, where sudden death was considered to be the least of a man's worries.

Kuan-yin stood up and walked across to him, laying her hand on his arm. She said, ''It is years since we were lovers.''

''You cannot measure what I feel for you in years,'' he told her, his dark eyes looking down at her with compelling steadiness. There was a moment of silence, and then Kuan-yin let him go. It was no use. He was the kind of man whose soul lived somewhere else, away from his body. What you saw was suntan and greased-back hair and clipped mustache; a papier-mâché mask with nothing behind it but cocktails, sentimental chatter, and emptiness. The real Mr. Esmeralda was unreachable.

''Do you think you are in very great danger?'' she asked him.

He looked at her unblinkingly, and said, ''It is no time for losing my head. There is too much money at stake. And too many lives. The Japanese are not deterred by such concepts as fairness or justice; and they are certainly not deterred by American law. If they wish to murder me, they will. But they will have to outwit me first.''

When he had finished, he asked Kuan-yin to drive him across to West Los Angeles, to Eva Crowley's apartment. Kuan-yin said nothing, but went to fetch her cap. In the car, while Mr. Esmeralda listened to the radio news in the hope of finding out more about what had happened at Rancho Encino, Kuan-yin remained silent and aloof, although Mr. Esmeralda could see her eyes watching him in the rearview mirror.

"What if Commander Ouvarov comes back and finds that you've gone out?" she asked him at last.

"Commander Ouvarov will never come back. Didn't you hear what they said on the television? One of the Japanese was probably killed by his associate. That means that Commander Ouvarov panicked and ran, but not before he had disposed of anyone who could identify him. In my opinion, he probably killed Yoshikazu in the same way. So much less trouble than taking him all the way down to Mexico and smuggling him over the border. Commander Ouvarov is a profiteer, an opportunist, a murderer, a pimp, and a sexual deviant. He had a reputation for efficient organization, and that is why I asked Nancy Shiranuka to hire him. Maybe I was wrong. Maybe he was too old for the job. It is too late to be concerned about that now, and too late to be concerned about him. He is probably halfway to Mexico already."

"Supposing he goes to the police?"

"Commander Ouvarov has been involved in too many rackets and too many unsavory deals to risk going to the police. He is still wanted in five states, including Washington and Nevada. He is wanted in New York for jumping bail. Commander Ouvarov will never go to the police."

"Not even for a little plea-bargaining?"

Mr. Esmeralda didn't answer. He knew from experience how little honor there was among thieves. And among the motley hirelings he had been obliged to collect for the Tengu project, there was no honor whatsoever. All they had in common was fear and greed, and if someone else could frighten them more, or offer them more money, then their allegiance to Mr. Esmeralda would evaporate like Pacific fog. He had no illusions about them.

Kuan-yin pulled the limousine into the curb outside Eva Crowley's apartment. Mr. Esmeralda said, "Come back for me at six A.M. Bring some hot towels with you, and a change of clothes."

Kuan-yin said, "You're not taking the lady any flowers?"

Mr. Esmeralda smiled at her wryly. "I can do better than that," he said, and took out of his pocket a gold-and-diamond bracelet.

Eva Crowley came to the door in a smart, schoolmarmish blouse with a pleated bib and a severe black pencil skirt. She said breathlessly, "I didn't expect to see you again."

"But, I'm here," said Mr. Esmeralda, with a self-satisfied grin. "Aren't you going to invite me in?"

"The twins are home. We were just about to have a snack. Then we were going to watch a little television and go to bed."

"You don't want me to meet your daughters?"

"Well, it's not that I don't *want* you to . . ."

"Then invite me in." Mr. Esmeralda beamed. He reached through the half-open door and held her wrist. "You can tell them that I am an old friend of your husband's. A cigar exporter from Dominica."

"Well . . ." Eva hesitated.

Mr. Esmeralda reached into his pocket and took out the bracelet, dangling it in front of Eva's eyes. "You won't even let me in if I *bribe* you?" he asked her.

Eva relaxed and smiled. "All right. But only for an hour or so. The girls have to go on a field trip tomorrow for school, and I want them to have a moderately early night."

"Your wish is law," said Mr. Esmeralda, and bowed.

Inside the Crowley's apartment, the mathematical sterility of Gerard's modern Italian décor had already been overwhelmed by dozens of rock records and magazines and

scruffy-looking schoolbooks, as well as two girls' college
sweaters, three fluorescent-yellow sneakers, a pink Fiorucci
bag crammed with hairbrushes and makeup, and a disassembled hair-dryer which looked as if it could never
assembled again. On the Giulini sofa, in tight matador
pants and T-shirts, sat Kathryn and Kelly Crowley, both
17, identical twins, painting their toenails, Kathryn plum
and Kelly green. They were very pretty girls, an inch taller
than their mother, with dark wavy hair and wide slate-and-
lavender-colored eyes.

"We-e-ell," said Kelly saucily, looking up from her toe-
nail painting. "Who's this, Moth-*err*?"

"Don't you be so fresh," Eva Crowley snapped back.
"This is a business colleague of your father's, Mr.
Esmeralda. Mr. Esmeralda, this is Kelly, and this is
Kathryn. Girls, clean up all this mess, will you? Mr.
Esmeralda came by to see your father, but the least we can
do is offer him a drink. Isn't that right, Mr. Esmeralda?"

"It is a great pleasure," replied Mr. Esmeralda, ex-
aggerating his South American accent. "It isn't often that
one sees *one* young girl as beautiful as you, let alone two."

"Do you have a Christian name, Mr. Esmeralda?"
asked Kathryn boldly.

Mr. Esmeralda nodded. "I was baptized Jesus, after my
father. But, for understandable reasons, most of my close
friends call me by second name, Carlos."

"I think I prefer Jesus," said Kathryn.

"Would you like a drink?" Eva interrupted. "I've re-
stocked the cabinet since you were last here."

"Mother's *always* restocking the cabinet." Kelly winked
at Mr. Esmeralda. "She *does* like her little celebration now
and again."

"Thank you, Kelly," said Eva sharply.

Mr. Esmeralda said, "I'll have a negroni, if you don't
mind. Shall I mix my own?"

"Oh, please."

"Can we call you Carlos?" asked Kathryn. "Carlos
Esmeralda, it sounds very romantic. Do you come from

South America, Carlos?''

Mr. Esmeralda took out gin and Campari. "I didn't think for one moment that your daughters would be so grown up," he told Eva. "when you said 'twin daughters,' I imagined two little moppets in ribbons and frills."

"Moppets?" Kathryn exclaimed. "I haven't heard anyone say 'moppets' since I was a moppet. Oh, you're wonderful, Carlos. You're just like Desi Arnaz. Or Ricardo Montalban."

"Kathryn, will you stop being so *personal*," demanded her mother.

"I don't mind," said Mr. Esmeralda, shaking his cocktail in Gerard's most elegant Italian silver shaker. "When you are swarthy, like me, and when you have a South American accent, as I do, you deliberately cultivate a social personality that is halfway between Edmundo Ros and Rudolph Valentino. Perhaps it's outdated, but people like it."

"You're so outdated you make me *dizzy*," said Kelly.

Eva laughed. "I hope you can take all this ribbing," she told Mr. Esmeralda. Mr. Esmeralda poured out his cocktail with all the deftness of a bartender, turned around, raised his glass, and grinned. "From three such beautiful ladies, a man can accept anything."

"*Anything*?" asked Kelly in a deep, melodramatic voice.

Mr. Esmeralda put down his glass. "In actual fact, I came here to invite your mother out.

"We had planned an early evening," said Eva.

"I'm sure your lovely daughters will not miss you," smiled Mr. Esmeralda. "Now please, you cannot refuse me."

Eva smiled and blushed. "I don't know. I shouldn't really."

"Oh, go *on*, Mother," insisted Kelly. "God knows you deserve to have a night out. Especially a really *old-fashioned* night out. What could be better?"

"All right," said Eva, after a moment. "But you'll have

to give me a minute to change."

"Bravo!" said Kathryn, and clapped her hands over her head.

While Eva dressed, Mr. Esmeralda mixed himself another negroni, and told the twins fanciful anecdotes about his life in the Caribbean and the Far East, and a far-fetched story about the time he had agreed to stand up against a wooden fence in Nightmute, Alaska, as the human target for a Canadian bowie-knife thrower. "The sweat froze on my forehead like seed pearls," he said, and the girls giggled in disbelief and delight.

"I can't think why Mother hasn't talked about you *before*," said Kelly.

Mr. Esmeralda gave her a noncommittal shrug. "Sometimes a lady likes to keep certain things to herself. Don't you have secret thoughts, secret ideas, of your own?" He raised one dark, well-combed eyebrow. "Don't you have your own secret desires?"

Kathryn giggled. Mr. Esmeralda was so much of a Latin smoothie that she couldn't decide whether to be amused, amazed, flattered, impressed, or simply skeptical. Yet because he was so stereotypical, because he seemed to have stepped down from the conductor's podium of some cheap rumba band in Rio de Janeiro, she found herself responding to him in a stereotypical way, flirting with him, flashing her eyes at him, metaphorically clutching a rose between bared teeth.

"You won't keep Moth-*err* out too late, will you?" she asked him. "Or maybe you will."

Mr. Esmeralda laughed. It was a laugh as flat and humorless as castanets.

"We'll see," he said. "Life is more exciting when it is uncertain, don't you think? Certainties dull the palate."

Kelly was about to answer when the door opened and her mother reappeared, in the cream-colored Bill Blass cocktail dress she had bought when she first found out about Gerard and Francesca. Her hair was brushed, diamonds sparkled in her ears, she looked prettier and

more confident than she had for months. She came across
and took Mr. Esmeralda's arm. He, in turn, laid his hand
over hers and smiled as possessively as a bridegroom.

"You have beautiful daughters," he told her. "And it
is very easy to see how they inherited their looks."

"You're teasing me," said Eva.

"No," said Mr. Esmeralda. "It is one of the firmest
rules of my life, never to tease."

They were driven by taxi to the Occidental Center on
South Olive. It would have been easier for Kuan-yin to
drive them, but Mr. Esmeralda did not want to risk being
seen too obviously in public with Eva. It was a question of
discretion, rather than absolute secrecy. In the back of the
taxi, Eva said, "I haven't been taken out by a strange man
for years."

"I am so strange?" asked Mr. Esmeralda.

She looked at him. "No," she said. "Not so strange.
Not really."

They knew Mr. Esmeralda well at The Tower; he was
ushered at once to a table by the window, overlooking the
twinkling lights of Greater L.A. He ordered drinks for
both of them and talked fluently and endlessly, about
money, about trading, about the Far East, about the
beauty and perversity of life in Bangkok, Rangoon,
Shanghai and Ho Chi Minh City, once called Saigon.

"You must have known a great many women," Eva
told him gently.

Mr. Esmeralda shook his head. "I am a selective man; not
promiscuous. Of course one could have women, thousands
of them. But that kind of life means nothing to me. What
I have always sought is the woman who can give me a
deep, romantic affair; an affair with roses and wine and
dancing, and expressions of true love. Perhaps not an affair
that lasts forever, but one which ends with no regret, no
bitter feelings, and no promises."

Eva set down her glass, then reached across the table and
took Mr. Esmeralda's hand. She stared into his eyes for a
long time, as if she were searching for reassurance. She

said, "I have to tell you the truth, Carlos. I've never felt this way about anyone else, apart from Gerard. This is the first time in all of my years of marriage that I've actually dared to believe I could be happy."

"Gerard makes you so miserable?"

She looked away. "Gerard still attracts me. Perhaps I'm a masochist. Perhaps I get some painful pleasure out of being cheated. Perhaps I deserve everything I get."

"Would you like to think that you are a martyr? St. Eva the Sanctimonious, broken on the wheel of her husband's inconstancy?"

"That's unfair."

"No," said Mr. Esmeralda. "It is quite true. If you were really angry at Gerard, you would have left him years ago. But you enjoy being degraded. You enjoy catching Gerard with Francesca, and hearing about his passion for her. It excites you. It gives your life some spice, some variety. It makes you believe that Gerard is more exciting then he really is. He must be, if some other girl wants him, too. A pretty young girl like Francesca. The fact is, however, that Gerard is an uninteresting petty criminal; a man whose little struggles with authority have done nothing to mature a personality that is essentially boorish and self-centered and vulgar. Some men, if they had been schooled in the same way that Gerard has, would have become swash-buckling heroes. Gerard has achieved nothing but a condition of abject meanness, both of spirit and of flesh. It is time you recognized it, if you haven't already. And it is time you said to yourself, 'Is this what I really want for the rest of my life? A man like Gerard?''

Eva said in a hushed voice, "Mr. Esmeralda, you're wooing me."

"Wooing?" he asked in surprise. Then, "Yes, if you want to use such a word. Yes, I suppose I am. Wooing.

She stared across the restaurant unashamedly admiring her own reflection in the glass of a picture frame for a long time, while Mr. Esmeralda admired her profile. It was her better profile thank God; and the flickering candlelight gave her looks magic which made her appear younger, more serene, mysterious. She *felt* mysterious, too, which helped. Calm and erotic and mysterious. And drunk.

"I suppose you want to go to bed with me," she said. The words didn't quite come out the way she had meant them to. They sounded squeaky and unbalanced, instead of alluring and Garboesque; but once she'd spoken them it was too late. She turned and stared at him, and he stared back.

"Yes," he said. "Of course."

They were silent in the taxi on the way back to Eva's apartment. They didn't even hold hands. When Eva let them in, they found that the twins had gone to bed. The sitting room was tidied up and in darkness. Mr. Esmeralda loosened his necktie and said, "How much would you like a cocktail?"

Eva came back across the soft white carpet and put her arms around his neck, kissing the tip of his nose. "Not as much as I'd like you."

"Then let's take two cocktails into the bedroom. Do you have any peach brandy? I mix a formidable Fish House Punch."

"A dry martini will do."

Mr. Esmeralda looked down at this woman clinging to his neck, and for one moment he had an almost uncontrollable urge to tug her arms away and slap her into sensibility. But he needed her, and he had learned years and years ago that you never upset anybody you need, no matter how much contempt you might feel for them.

"It will be as quick as my trembling hands will allow," he whispered.

The bedroom, too, was Italian. Mirrors, chrome, and smoked glass. The only touches of human life were a slender vase of lilies, a framed photograph of Gerard after he had won the visitor's golf tournament at San Pedro, and a single white stocking draped over the side of the stainless-steel dressing-table stool.

Mr. Esmeralda took off his jacket and hung it over the

back of a chair. "Gerard is a man who lives inside of himself," he remarked, looking around him. "How can you reach the soul of such a man? I am surprised he loves anybody; although if it has to be anybody, Francesca is the least surprising of all. A chilly, stupid girl. If you knew her better you would like her worse."

Mr. Esmeralda stripped off his tie. Then he approached Eva, and held her in his arms, his eyes liquid and brown and delightfully quizzical. He kissed her, and then began to unzip her dress. She said, "Carlos . . ." but he hushed her and said, "You must call me 'my dear,' and that is all. Names have unhappy memories."

He gently tugged the dress from her shoulders, kissing her face and neck. She felt as if she were afloat, like a balloon. Eva, the Inflatable Woman—so light and heady that the slightest warm breeze could carry her upward into the early-morning smog of West Los Angeles and away across the San Gabriel Mountains.

Mr. Esmeralda unhooked her beige lace bra. Her breasts were firm and full for a woman of her age, and he held them in his hands with obvious pleasure. Her nipples stiffened between his fingers, and he played with them until her wide pink areolas crinkled and she began to feel that tingling which she hadn't felt for so long.

She murmured, "My dear . . ." as if she were quoting from a play. Mr. Esmeralda said, "Sshh." He pushed her gently back onto the bed, onto the white-on-white bedspread, and removed her stockings and sheer panties.

She watched him as he deftly undid his shirt buttons, unbuckled his alligator belt, peeled off his socks. Soon he was kneeling over her naked, his chest shaggy with black hair, his penis rearing from the curly forest between his thighs as purple as an overripe plum."

He gripped her legs and opened them up wide, so that the crimson lips of her vulva parted as stickily as a mouth that has been feeding on cranberry syrup. He lowered his mustachioed face and licked at her clitoris with the tip of his tongue, then probed her urethra so deeply that she shivered. She moaned and twisted her hips, but Mr. Esmeralda clasped her tight, and plunged his tongue into her again and again.

She closed her eyes. She shuddered, deep within herself. She thought, this is mad, and bad. This isn't the way to solve anything. This isn't the way to save my marriage or to salvage my self-esteem. But, God, it feels beautiful.

He rose up at last, and mounted her, his chin shiny and his eyes bright with lust. She reached both her hands down between her legs and opened herself up for him, as wide as she could, so that the very first time he thrust into her, he thrust extravagantly deep, the head of his penis touching the neck of her womb and making her jump in erotic shock.

He thrust again and again, grunting with each thrust; and Eva tugged herself wider and wider, as if she wanted to take all of him inside her, as if she wanted to take so much that he killed her. He was right: she wanted to be martyred. But only to the cause of her own excitement.

She felt herself gradually ascending the foothills of an orgasm. She knew it would come this time, that if she concentrated all her mental and muscular energy, she would climax. She very rarely climaxed with Gerard, only when she was so drunk that she didn't care about his remoteness, or when she knew that he had been with Francesca only hours before. Mr. Esmeralda panted and lowered himself onto her, his hairy chest thick and wiry against her bare breasts, and for a split second she felt an extra-ordinary sense of unreality and alienation, as if she were dreaming that she was making love to some dark-pelted beast.

At eight, Mr. Esmeralda swung himself out of bed and quickly began to dress. Kuan-yin would still be waiting for him outside, and while he had abused her unmercifully as a lover, he didn't like to treat her inconsiderately as an employer. You could only expect so much, even from people who were uncritical and devoted.

As he tied up his necktie, he leaned over the bed and kissed Eva on the ear. "You don't have to open your eyes," he whispered. "If you are awake, I will call you. If you are asleep, I will call you, too. You have been ecstasy beyond belief."

He tiptoed to the hallway, and released the chain on the door. He was just about to close it behind him when he heard a soft voice say, "Mr. Esmeralda?"

He peered back into the apartment through an inch-wide opening in the door. "Who's that?"

"It's me, Kelly." She came up to the door with tangled hair, dressed in a striped nightshirt. "I wanted to say goodbye, and thank you."

"Thank you?"

"I've never seen Mother looking as pleased as when you invited her out last night."

Mr. Esmeralda opened the door a little wider. "Well," he said, "thank you for saying thank you."

"She's our mother," said Kelly. "I know she drinks a lot, and I know she's silly sometimes, but we love her. You will take care of her, won't you?"

"Of course," replied Mr. Esmeralda. He took her hand and kissed it. "She will be marvelously taken care of, I promise."

He left, clicking the apartment door behind him. As he went down in the elevator, he hummed to himself that sentimental old Latin tune, "The Rose of Rio."

Across the street, in a morning that was still chilly, Kuan-yin was sitting behind the wheel of Mr. Esmeralda's limousine, listening to KMPC 710 and eating a cold breakfast of take-out *odamaki mushi*, steamed egg and noodles. Mr. Esmeralda simply said, "Good morning," as he climbed into the back of the car. There were hot-towels waiting for him in an electric steamer, and his shirt and suit were neatly laid out on the seat.

"You looked tired," said Kuan-yin.

"I need some breakfast, that's all," said Mr. Esmeralda, stripping off his jacket, and then gratefully burying his face into the cologne-scented towels. "It's been one of those nights."

"You want to go straight home?"

"No. Take me to Laurel Canyon."

"You're sure?"

"*Now* I'm sure, yes."

Kuan-yin didn't ask what Mr. Esmeralda meant. It wasn't her place to ask, and in any case she wasn't interested. She wasn't a jealous person, but she did expect something more from Mr. Esmeralda than the functional employer-chauffeur relationship they were going through now. Perhaps he would grow softer toward her when he found someone else who could excite him as much as she used to. Perhaps he would always hate her for having summoned up his greatest strengths and for having simulataneously exposed his greatest weaknesses. She knew there was very little left in her life, apart from Mr. Esmeralda and the few Chinese friends she knew in downtown Los Angeles. And the Chinese proverb did say, "When you have only two pennies left, spend one on a loaf of bread, and the other on a lily." She would have to start taking care of herself, both financially and spiritually. She had a feeling that her time with Mr. Esmeralda was coming to an end.

Mr. Esmeralda, buttoning up his clean blue shirt in the back of the limousine, was already sure that the weather was changing, and that a storm was going to break before too long. At least he was prepared for it, as much as anyone who had to deal with a creature like Kappa could ever be prepared. Doctor Gempaku, very early on, when they were first converting the ranch at Pacoima into a center for developing Tengus, had told him, "Once you have instructed a Tengu to kill somebody, then the Tengu *must* kill, whether it is the person you *want* to see killed or not. I suppose the only way to protect yourself against a Tengu is to elect a substitute to be killed in your place. It is written in the old scrolls that if you offer the Tengu the blood of somebody you have lain with—a woman or a man with whom you have had sexual congress—or somebody who owes you a lasting favor, then the Tengu is obliged to accept your offer. Such an offer, after all, heightens the evil of what is about to happen; and no devil as iniquitous as the Tengu could refuse *that*.''

Doctor Gempaku's words had crossed Mr. Esmeralda's mind the very first time he had walked into the Crowleys' apartment and found Eva deserted, half naked, and drunk. Here is a woman who is crying out for consolation, he had thought to himself. Here is a woman who will take me as her lover just to spite her husband. And, quite apart from the fact that taking Eva Crowley to bed will enable me to score a particularly ironic point against that cold and arrogant Gerard Crowley, it will also provide me with a living, loving sacrifice to throw to the Tengus if Kappa ever sends them after me.

This morning, however, Mr. Esmeralda was more than satisfied. This morning, he felt unusually safe. Not only could he offer Eva Crowley to any Tengu which Kappa might direct to kill him; he could also offer Kelly and Kathryn, bound to him by their gratitude. His life-insurance policy had trebled in value in the space of a single night.

CHAPTER FOUR

At the same moment that Mr. Esmeralda closed the door of Eva Crowley's apartment, Sergeant Skrolnik opened the door of El Krusho's cell, folded his arms, took a deep breath, and said, ''It's all right. We've dropped the charges. You can go.''

Maurice had been working out by lifting and lowering his stool with one hand. He blinked at Sergeant Skrolnik and said, ''What?''

Sergeant Skrolnik said, "You deaf or something?"

"I don't know. What? You said I could go?"

"You think I'd leave the fucking cell door wide open if you couldn't? Go. Collect your belongings at the desk."

Maurice looked almost disappointed. "You found out who really did it?" he asked, as he tugged on his T-shirt and tried to straighten his hair in the two-way mirror. Skrolnik watched this impromptu primping with disgust. "We didn't find out who did it," he said. "We just happen to know that it wasn't you. Although, believe it or not, I said from the *beginning* that it wasn't you. I only had to take one look at that sheep's behind of a face of yours, and I knew it wasn't you."

"You really thought I was innocent?"

"You're about as homicidal as a pet llama. Physically, could have taken us both to pieces when we arrested you, but you weren't even angry. You didn't know what you were being arrested for, and you weren't even angry."

Maurice said, "Can I claim compensation?"

"Compensation for what?"

"Well, for spending a couple of nights in the cells. It was pretty uncomfortable. And my mother's totally convinced that I'm a mass murderer."

Sergeant Skrolnik took El Krusho's beefy arm and led him down to the desk to collect his belongings. He said confidentially, "If I were you, I would get the hell out of this place, and not worry about compensation or defamation or any of that shit, because the best place that anyone can ever be is miles and miles away from the law. You got me?"

Maurice counted his $27.76, thrust it into the back pocket of his jeans, and nodded. "I still think there ought to be some kind of compensation. You know, a month's exemption from parking tickets, something like that?"

Just then, the swinging doors of the police headquarters opened and Mack Holt strode in, with Olive close behind him. "Hey, Maurice!" said Mack. "They told me you were sprung."

"You know *why* he was sprung," said Sergeant Skrolnik, poker-faced.

"Well, yes, I'm sorry about that," said Mack. "I guess
I'm just pleased that Maurice is out, that's all. Are you
coming back to my place, Maurice? How about it? A
couple of beers, a steak or two? Fifteen eggs? Maurice has
to keep up his strength," he explained to Sergeant Skrolnik.

"*Why* was I sprung?" asked Maurice, his eyes on
Skrolnik. "You didn't tell me that. You just said I was
free to go."

Mack glanced at Sergeant Skrolnik, then at El Krusho,
and then back again to Sergeant Skrolnik. "Ah," he said
uncomfortably.

But Sergeant Skrolnik said, "You were sprung because I
didn't believe you were guilty, that's all; and because
twelve hours' intensive police work has so far failed to tease
out the slightest evidence that you were the man responsible for Sherry Cantor's murder, or that you were anywhere near the Hollywood Freeway when Patrolman Ed
Russo was killed."

Skrolnik hesitated. Olive started to say something, but
Mack nudged her to keep quiet. This was, after all,
Skrolnik's show; and Mack considered that Skrolnik was
reasonably human. Whatever Mayor Tom Bradley had said
about "the dimensions of violent crime," whatever Sheriff
Peter J. Pitchess had said about everybody in Los Angeles
suffering from a "siege mentality," whatever Governor
Jerry Brown had said about prisoners taking karate lessons
in California's prisons "so that when they get out, they're
more dangerous than ever," it was Sergeant Skrolnik who
had to go out on the streets and track down the killers and
the weirdos and the homicidal freaks, and Mack respected
him for that. If Maurice had actually committed those
murders, Mack wouldn't have gone near Maurice with a
loaded .45 and half a division of the California National
Guard. Yet Skrolnik had arrested Maurice, albeit mis-
takenly, with nobody to help him but Detective Pullet.

Sergeant Skrolnik laid his hand on El Krusho's shoulder and said, "The main reason you were sprung is because last night someone broke into the Rancho Encino Hospital, and tore several people wide apart in the same way that Sherry Cantor was torn apart. The similarities of the killings are overwhelming; and besides that, we have the body of the man who did it. So, what happened at Orchid Place quite obviously wasn't down to you."

"You *caught* the guy?" asked Maurice.

"If you want to know the confidential truth, we caught the guy and blew his fucking head off," said Skrolnik.

"Instant justice," said Olive.

Skrolnik looked at her balefully. This morning she was wearing a thin cheesecloth blouse that dimly revealed the darkness of her nipples and an extremely tight pair of canary-yellow pants. The effect of the pants, as Detective Pullet was to remark afterward in a moment of intense lateral thinking, was to remind him of two bananas side by side.

Mack said, "It's over, then? You've caught him and killed him?"

"*You* think it's over. The *governor* thinks it's over. The *mayor* thinks it's over. Even the police commissioner thinks it's over. But, of course, *we* now have several weeks of intensive and incredibly tedious investigation to carry out to discover who this fruitcake was, and why he committed those killings."

"Isn't that what we pay you for?" asked Olive sharply.

Skrolnik grinned tightly. "You also pay me to keep the *next* murderer away from your door, Mrs. Nesmith. And the next. Hillside Stranglers, Manson gangs, Lawrence Bittakers. Hell's Angels, muggers, intruders, rapists, perverts, sadists, lone headcases. You're not safe now. I'll never pretend that you are. But you're a whole lot safer than if I wasn't here, taking care of you."

El Krusho said, "I could use a beer."

Skrolnik said, "Sign here for your belongings and you can go sink as many beers as you like."

Olive asked, "Where's the body now?"

"What body?" said Sergeant Skrolnik, watching El Krusho sign "M. Needs" in a large, rounded scrawl.

"You said you killed him. The murderer. Where's his body now?"

"They're keeping it on ice for me, in the morgue at Rancho Encino. I'm going up there to collect it later today. The medical examiners can't wait to slice it up and see what made it tick."

Olive said, "I'm sorry."

"Sorry for what?" asked Skrolnik.

"I'm sorry I bugged you. I don't know. Don't press me. Just accept that I'm sorry."

Sergeant Skrolnik put his meaty, red-freckled hands on Olive's bare black shoulders and smiled at her. "Listen," he said, "if only one-tenth of the population said what you just did, *sorry*, then Los Angeles would be a happier city. We make mistakes in the police department. Everybody does. If it costs you, as a taxpayer, then I personally apologize. But it's nice to hear someone say sorry in return. After all, we're all in this thing together."

"This is all getting unnecessarily emotional," said Mack. "Do you think we might leave now?"

"Go ahead," said Skrolnik, and gave Olive a comfortable squeeze on the behind.

"As the criminals get weirder, the cops get weirder," Maurice remarked as they climbed into Mack's battered Volkswagen.

"At least you're out of there," said Mack. He gave Maurice a friendly punch on his muscular arm. "You know, it's fantastic to see you. You're looking great."

"What happened up at Encino?" asked Maurice as Mack started up the Volkswagen's blaring engine, stuck his hand out of the window, and pulled out right in front of a lumbering Hostess Cupcakes truck.

"You shithead!" roared the truck driver.

"I see your driving hasn't improved," Maurice remarked. "Do you remember the time you drove off the edge of that cliff at Santa Barbara?''

"I didn't drive off any cliff," Mack protested. "It was just a *gully*, that's all. Don't give me cliff."

Olive said, "We heard about it on the radio this morning. Some mad guy broke into the hospital at Rancho Encino and ripped a nurse to pieces. Some other people were shot. The police went in there and killed him."

"Was that all?" asked Maurice.

"So far. The cops are being really cagey about giving out information to the media. I guess they don't want to make the same mistake they made with the Hillside Strangler, catching people every two or three days and then having to let them go again."

"If they blew this guy's head off and it's the wrong guy, at least they won't have the problem of letting him go again," said Olive.

Mack said, "Despite her sensitive apologies to Sergeant What's-his-name just now, Olive is still very deeply into citizen's rights vis-à-vis the police and the civil authorities. Olive believes that arrest and trial should be a socio-biological process activated by mutual concern and respect for the general well-being of the human village, rather like eaeting health foods and wearing shoes that are higher at the front than they are at the back."

"We should *absorb* crime, rather than attempt to excise it from our systems," added Olive. "Law and order is a digestive process, not a surgical one."

"Is this lady for real?" Maurice asked Mack. "Digestive? You mean the cops are supposed to eat you, instead of bust you?"

"El Krusho is not known for his sociological perception," Mack said to Olive.

They turned on the radio and tuned it to KABC. There were a few minutes of chatter about sophisticated city dwellers moving out to Santa Ynez to take up farming, then a news bulletin.

"Listen to this," said Olive, turning up the volume.

"Police at Encino have released more details this

morning of the grisly murder at Rancho Encino hospital of Mrs. Mary Thorson, wife of Admiral Knut Thorson. Also the violent slaying of a hospital nurse and two armed security guards. Apparently, the crimes were committed by a multiracial hit team, including at least three Japanese and a Caucasian. The bodies of two of the Japanese were found in the hospital shrubbery after the attack; one obviously slain by a security guard's bullet, the other the apparent victim of his Caucasian colleague. The principle assailant, who was shot and killed by police after his homicidal attack on Mrs. Thorson and on Nurse Ruth Abramski, was also said to be Japanese.

"Admiral Thorson, who survived the attack, has already spoken with the police, although no details have yet been released.

"Chief of Detectives Harry Calsbeek said that the crime was similar in most respects to the recent homicide of television star Sherry Cantor, who played the part of Lindsay in *Our Family Jones*. He is cooperating closely with Hollywood detectives in an attempt to discover why such an attack should have been launched against this luxury private hospital, and by whom. So far, said Calbeek, the butchery remains a mystery."

Mack switched the radio off. "We were right. Did you hear that? We were right from the very beginning."

"*Who* was right?" asked Maurice.

"Me! *I* was right! And Jerry Sennett, the guy who lives in the house next door to Sherry's place, he was right too. He said he was sure that the killer was Japanese, something to do with Japan. You remember that face they showed on television? Well, maybe you didn't see it. But Jerry said it was an ancient Japanese Nō mask. And when I pointed out that it was easy to mistake *his* house number for Sherry's, he agreed that the killer could have been after *him*. And the clincher was that he fought against the Japanese during World War Two, something to do with Naval Intelligence, and as far as I can work out, he was personally responsible for some really important Japanese defeat."

Maurice pulled a face. "This is all beginning to sound extremely complicated. I think I need a beer first."

"It's not complicated at all," said Mack. "I believe that the Japs are getting their revenge on us, that's what. Anybody who did anything really heroic or important during World War Two—the Japs are wiping them out with a hit squad. Don't you think that's *amazing*?"

"I also think it's unbelievable," said Maurice. "Is it very much further? My goddamn neck's aching in the back of this mobile peanut."

They drew up outside Mack's apartment on Franklin Avenue. It was beginning to grow warm. Mack helped El Krusho out of the car and then led the way along the path. Olive said, "It looks like you've got yourself a visitor, Mack."

In the shadow of the porch, unshaven, smoking a cigarette, stood Jerry Sennett, with the look of a man who has had a hard and unsuccessful night.

"Did you hear the news?" Mack asked him as he came up to the door. "Did you hear what happened at Rancho Encino?"

Jerry nodded. "I heard. And that's presumably why they released your friend here?"

"That's right. El Krusho is loose. Maurice, this is Jerry Sennett. Jerry, this is the strongest man south of Visalia."

"Visalia?" asked Jerry, shaking El Krusho's hefty hand.

"We had an interesting evening in Visalia once," explained Mack. "It was something to do with three women and four bottles of Wild Turkey. The rest I forgot."

Olive looked at Jerry and pulled an expression which very clearly meant, "Who are *they* trying to kid?" Jerry smiled back at her, impressed by her wild Rastafarian beauty, and by the tightness of her canary-yellow pants. But there was a frightened ache deep down inside him which wouldn't go away, an ache that made pleasantries impossible.

He said, as steadily as he could manage, "I'm sorry I came around so early. I don't want to break up any parties or anything. But I think I've found out who's behind all these killings, and why they're committing them."

"You have?" asked Mack. "Well, who is it? Have you told the cops?"

Jerry shook his head. "I can't tell the cops. I'm not supposed to tell anyone at all, and I'm only telling you because I can trust you to keep quiet. They've kidnapped my son, David. They're holding him hostage somewhere, so that I'll give myself up to them. They want *me*, because of what I know. That was why they tried to kill me in the first place. And that's why they tried to kill Admiral Thorson out at Rancho Encino. Admiral Thorson directed the same operation during the war that I was involved in, Operation Appomattox."

Olive said, "You'd better come inside. This isn't any kind of a problem to be talking about on the porch."

Jerry was exhausted. After he had spoken to Nancy Shiranuka, he had waited for hours for Gerard Crowley to come around to her apartment. But by four o'clock in the morning, Gerard still hadn't showed, and Nancy, bringing Jerry tea and *anago mushi* she had prepared for him herself had told him softly that it was useless for him to wait any longer. It was the first time that Jerry had eaten steamed egg custard and eel in the small hours of the morning; and the way his stomach felt now, he hoped it would be the last. But he had been afraid to refuse Nancy's hospitality. If he was ever going to have to cultivate Nancy and strengthen her confidence in him. Nancy was as terrified of the Tengus as he was; what she urgently needed was a friend she could trust.

Olive made coffee while Jerry sat on Mack's broken-down sofa and explained what had happened. Mack and Maurice listened intently, and then sat back and sipped their hot coffee and tried to look as if they were thinking extraordinarily hard about some way of rescuing David and destroying the Tengus.

"You really *believe* in these things, these Tengus?" asked Mack.

"President Truman believed in them; enough to drop the first atomic bomb the world had ever seen."

Maurice said, "Let's face it, Mack, I'm strong. But the way those murder victims were torn to pieces, I couldn't do that. That takes somebody superhuman. I couldn't rip your leg off with my bare hands. I couldn't even start. I might *feel* like it but I actually couldn't do it."

"Maurice, those are very comforting words," said Mack. "But what do we do now? What *can* we do? Should we do anything at all? I really think that Jerry should go see Sergeant Skrolnik. I mean it. He's a cop, but he's all there, and and he's only as mean as he needs to be."

"Supposing the kidnappers found out I went to the police?" asked Jerry. "If they can tear a heavily guarded hospital apart, for the sake of trying to kill one poor old retired naval officer in a coma, what the hell do you think they'd do to David? A young, live, alert witness to everything they've been doing?"

"What if you do give yourself up to them?" asked Olive. "What guarantee do you have that they won't kill you both?"

Jerry put down his coffee mug and rubbed his eyes. "No guarantee at all. I don't know whether I'm dealing with criminals or mystics or madmen. Nancy Shiranuka may be double-dealing me, although I can't for the life of me guess why, or what she could conceivably get out of it. I just don't know what to do. It might have been easier to understand if I'd been able to talk to Gerard Crowley."

"Why not talk to him now?" Maurice suggested. "If he's involved in any kind of business, he's probably in the phone book."

Olive clapped her hands. "You see, he's not all muscle. Good thinking, El Krusho!"

Mack picked up his tattered telephone book and thumbed through it. "Here you are," he said at last. "Gerard F. Crowley, Crowley Tobacco Imports, Inc. 2029 Century Park East."

Jerry said, "You really think it's worth a shot?"

"Why not?" said Mack. "You don't have anything to lose. You might get your son back. Look, I'll dial it for you."

It was just nine o'clock, still early for a Los Angeles businessman to be at his desk, but Mack got through to Francesca right away, and Francesca said guardedly, "Yes, Mr. Crowley's here. who is this?"

"Tell him it's Mr. Sennett. Mr. Sennett of 11 Orchid Place."

There was a silence, then Francesca said, "Hold on for just a moment, please," and switched Mack to a holding tape of "Raindrops Keep Fallin' on My Head." Jerry looked quizzical, but Mack held his hand over the receiver and said, "I'm holding."

At last, a tired voice said, "Mr. Sennett?" and Mack passed the phone across to Jerry.

"Mr. Crowley?" said Jerry testily. "I was waiting at Nancy Skiranuka's apartment for you last night. Apparently you were supposed to show up there, but you didn't."

"Well, I was busy," replied Gerard, obviously cautious. "I'm sorry if you had a wasted evening."

"Not evening. *Night.* I waited all goddamned night. I'm still waiting, to hear what you've done with my son."

"Mr. Sennett," said Gerard, "we've got ourselves a critical difficulty here."

"You bet your ass we've got ourselves a critical difficulty," snapped Jerry. "We've got more than that. We've got kidnapping, extortion, blackmail, and murder. That's what we've got. And for some reason this is all connected with what I did in the war, in Japan. I want to know *what*, and *why*, and what the hell I'm supposed to do to get my son back safely."

"Mr. Sennett, I don't really want to talk about this on the telephone," said Gerard. "Apart from the fact that you might be tape-recording this conversation, other people could well be listening in."

"What other people?"

"Believe me, people you wouldn't care to meet."

Jerry said, "All right. Let's meet. Do you know Zucky's, Fifth and Wilshire?"

"I've heard of it. I can find it."

"Meet me there at twelve, for lunch. I'll be sitting in the far corner. I'll leave my name at the counter."

Gerard hesitated for a moment, and then said, "Okay, I'll be there," and put down the phone.

"What did he sound like?" asked Olive. "Suspicious?"

"A little," said Jerry thoughtfully. "But he was much more cooperative than I would have expected. If you ask me, what happened last night at Rancho Encino was a foul-up. They were trying to murder Admiral Thorson, right? And they failed. He's still alive. Better than that, he's out of his coma. What's more, the police have killed the Tengu and recovered the bodies of two Japanese, which means that they could now have a pretty straightforward lead to whoever it is who may be organizing this thing—whatever "this thing" may be. Nancy Shiranuka is convinced that her employers have been trying to do a whole lot more than create a corps of expensive killer bodyguards. Mack here may have come up with a good idea when he suggested that some cranky Japanese outfit is trying to take revenge on American war heroes. Maybe he's right. But, whatever—*something's* happening, something dangerous and volatile and much bigger than it looks. In fact, I think it's so dangerous that Gerard Crowley actually *wants* to talk to me about it. All I can do is wait and see."

"If you're meeting him at Zucky's, try the blintzes," said Maurice.

CHAPTER FIVE

The van drew up by the side of the hot and dusty highway, its right rear tire flapping with a sudden blowout.
The young Japanese switched off the engine and sat back
in his vinyl seat, blowing out his cheeks in exhaustion.
Commander Ouvarov, sitting beside him with his corncob
pipe gritted between his teeth and his .45-caliber Colt
automatic resting loosely on his lap, turned his head and
stared at him with an exaggerated lack of sympathy.

"Well?" he said. "There's a spare in the back."

Yoshino said, "I'm very tired, Commander. Can't we
rest now? Driving for eight hours."

"You were hired as a driver, what do you expect?"

Yoshino wiped his forehead with the back of his hand.
"Please, Commander."

Commander Ouvarov checked his watch. They hadn't
made bad time, considering they had been driving at
night. They had left Encino at high speed; but instead of
making a conventional getaway they had driven just four
or five miles to a nearby Howard Johnson's, where they
had eaten, cleaned themselves up, and gassed up their van
for a long, hard journey. Even as they sat here now, eight
hours later, by the side of the highway which runs just
south of the Superstition Mountains, a few miles east of
Phoenix, Arizona, two police officers were questioning the
manager and the waitresses at Howard Johnson's, trying to
determine which way the fugitives had been heading, and
how much of a head start they had managed to get.

Commander Ouvarov squinted northward through the
August heat haze, towards the broken, uncompromising
outline of the mountains. It was only ten o'clock in the
morning, but the temperature was already into the low
90s. "We can't waste too much time here, Yoshino," he
said. "If we don't make El Paso by evening, we're going to
be in big trouble. That customs officer at El Paso is a close
personal friend of mine; I did him a favor a few years back.

He's the only man who's going to let us through that border without any questions, no matter what."

Yoshino resignedly opened the driver's door and stepped down onto the dusty roadside. There was no traffic in sight for two or three miles in either direction. He walked around to the back of the van and loosened the spare. Commander Ouvarov stayed where he was, his automatic on his lap, listening to the radio. "And now it's 91 degrees at Sky Harbor, with a prospect of 111 to 113 degrees by noon." He knocked the dottle of his pipe out, and meticulously refilled it with Old Geronimo tobacco. He had smoked the same pipe tobacco since 1942.

He felt the van being jacked up beneath him; but he remained where he was, his arms folded, calmly smoking. He felt no guilt about having made a run for it. He'd had his doubts about Mr. Esmeralda and Gerard Crowley right from the very start. Too many sharks in the same pool for Commander Ouvarov's liking, too many people with difficult pasts and uncertain futures. And as for those peculiar Japanese, with their black silk masks, and those tortured Tengus . . . well, the only good Japanese as far as Commander Ouvarov was concerned was a disemboweled Japanese. He hadn't asked too many questions; he'd done whatever they'd asked of him; but the whole plan was ill conceived, badly managed, amateurish, and too damned strange.

He took off his hat and mopped his sweating forehead with his handkerchief. It was a pity about Nancy Shiranuka, he thought. The sensations that Nancy could give to a man, selflessly, purely for the erotic artistry of it, were disturbing enough to haunt him forever. When he was lying on his deathbed, he would remember what she had done to him with a Mexican bead necklace. His last words before he was carried upward by the angels would be, "Nancy, the beads . . ." At least, he fondly imagined they would.

After a quarter of an hour, he felt the van being jacked down onto the road again. He called out, "Yoshino? You through now?'' but he couldn't be sure if Yoshino had heard him.

He opened his door and swung himself heavily out onto the roadside. "Yoshino?" he called.

Yoshino had been packing away the flat. He came around the van, wiping his hands on a rag, his face and chest glossy with sweat. "All done now, Commander. We can go. Make El Paso by dark."

"Good man," said the commander. He turned his back on Yoshino. And that was fatal. The next thing he knew, there was a blinding crunch in his back, as Yoshino drove the sharp end of the van's tire iron between his ribs into his guts.

The commander let out a sharp, barking shout. His hand scrabbled around behind him to tug the tire iron out. But suddenly his nerves went, his coordination froze, and he pitched sideways into the dust.

His brain still worked, but the tire iron had severed vital nerves and left him paralyzed. He watched in glassy, jack-rabbit helplessness as Yoshino bent down and picked up his .45, hesitated for a moment, and then disappeared from view.

Japanese, he thought to himself. Never trust a Japanese. All these years I've preached nothing else. All these years I've been warning them. They never listened. They went their own sweet unconscious way while Datsun and Toyota and Sony and Toshiba took the dollars from under their noses, the bread from their family tables. They're wily by nature, the Japanese. Treacherous by birth. All these years I've said so, and today I forgot my own damned warning; today I neglected my own damned advice. And here I am; helpless and dying on a hot highway in Arizona.

Yoshino climbed into the van and started the engine. Lying on his side by the road, Commander Ouvarov shouted, "No! Don't leave me!" But Yoshino had no intention of leaving him. Instead, carefully watching Commander Ouvarov in his side mirror, he shifted the van into reverse and began to creep back toward him, until

Commander Ouvarov could feel the hot gasoline breath of the exhaust on his neck, and smell the oil and rubber and hydraulic fluid.

With all the precision of an expert driver, Yoshino backed the van up until its rear tire was resting against the side of Commander Ouvarov's head. Commander Ouvarov could feel the wheel pinching his hair, and he wildly tried to heave himself out of its way. But his paralysis was complete. His brain thought *heave*, and nothing happened. His arms remained tangled side by side on the road; his legs seemed to have disappeared altogether. The only feeling he had left was in his face and his head, resting against the gritty pavement.

Yoshino said an ancient Shinto prayer; a prayer for long life, for guidance. Then, with great care, he backed the van over Commander Ouvarov's head.

There was a moment when Commander Ouvarov felt as if his skull could actually withstand the vehicle's two-ton weight. But the pressure built up until it was utterly intolerable, and then his skull collapsed with a snap like a breaking terra-cotta bowl, and his eyes bulged out of their sockets and tumbled bloodily onto the road, promptly followed by a long squirt of brains. He died thinking of nothing but pain. The words "Nancy, the beads . . ." never even occurred to him.

Yoshino shifted the van back into drive, and sped off, leaving behind him a high trail of drifting desert dust and the body of a man who had betrayed himself more than his country. For twenty or thirty yards, the van left a repeated smudge of blood on the road, a telltale tireprint that would have inevitably brought Yoshino to Death Row if his intentions hadn't been different.

After six or seven minutes of driving, he reached a small Exxon station next to a use-car lot, and parked a half-mile out of Apache Junction. He pulled across the road and parked in front of a pump. An old-timer with grizzled white hair and a sport cap was washing the windshield of a Chrysler pickup on the other side of the island. He called out, "Be with you in two shakes there, son."

Yoshino climbed calmly out of the van, unhooked the handle from the nearest pump, started the pump's motor, and dragged the hose across to the van. Then, while the old-timer was busy making change for the driver of the Chrysler, Yoshino sat in the driver's seat, pointed the nozzle of the gas pump toward his chest, and began to splash gasoline over himself, gallons of it. It gushed out all over his clothes, over the seats, over the floor.

It took a moment or two before the old-timer realized what was happening. Then he shouted, "Hey! Goddamn it! What you doing there, son? Hey, stop that!"

Yoshino scarcely heard him. He was already entering the first gate to another world. In his mind he was gliding weightless through one of the *torii* that stand by the shores of the Inland Sea. He lifted the .45, muzzle upward, and tightened his grip on the trigger. This would be an ecstatic way to die.

The old-timer was only five or six feet away when Yoshino fired the automatic, and the interior of the van exploded in a soft, superheated furnace. Yoshino felt nothing but a wave of heat; the old-timer shrieked as he was hurled, blazing, onto the roof of his own gas station.

There was another explosion, louder, as the van's tank blew up. Chunks of burning metal were tossed into the air. A fiery tire careered across the forecourt, bounced across a stretch of grass, and lay there flaring and smoking. Then the station's 500-gallon underground storage tank went up, a blast that demolished the building in a ball of glaring orange fire and set fifteen parked trucks alight in the used-car lot.

The fire burned for hours, sending up a rolling black column of smoke. The police who attended the scene of the explosion were unable to determine the cause, since there were no recognizable survivors. They couldn't even tell that Yoshino was Japanese—not at first, or they might have grasped the irony that all the burning trucks in the lot were Toyotas.

CHAPTER SIX

When Mr. Esmeralda arrived at the house in Laurel Canyon, a few minutes after nine o'clock, he was admitted immediately to Kappa's inner sanctum. Kappa was suspended from a ceiling beam in a basket lined with scarlet silk and padded with cushions. His tiny deformed body was still shining with the scented oils with which his young female attendants had been massaging him, in an attempt to ease his scores and to conceal the odor of his oozing wounds and purulent, convoluted genitalia. He was wearing a different disguise today, a burnished ivory-colored mask that was almost smiling; a face that looked as if it were about to react to a happy surprise.

Mr. Esmeralda was not fooled. The more cheerful the mask Kappa wore, the fouler his temper was likely to be. He had only once seen Kappa wearing a mask that actually laughed, and on that day Mr. Esmeralda had been lucky to escape from the inner sanctum with his life.

He noticed that there were six or seven *Oni* guards in the room today, two or three more than usual, as well as Kappa's half-naked girl assistant. There were scores more candles, too; burning bright and hot in row after row of wrought-iron holders. It was like High Mass in hell.

"Good morning," said Mr. Esmeralda.

Kappa watched him, without blinking, through the eyeholes in his mask. "You have failed me," he said. His voice was more chirrupy and insectlike than ever. "You have failed me *disastrously*."

"Kappa, I said right from the very start that I didn't think it was a good idea to go for Admiral Thorson."

"Thorson knows about the Tengu. Thorson must die."

"You've heard that all the violence in Thorson's room woke him up from his coma?" asked Mr. Esmeralda, perspiring from the heat of the candles. "We're worse off now than we were before."

Kappa was silent, although Mr. Esmeralda was sure that

he could hear a grating sound inside the mask, as if the creature were grinding his teeth.

"We could try to get in to Thorson with just a regular hit man," Mr. Esmeralda suggested, "although I expect that he's pretty heavily guarded at the moment. Or we could just ignore him."

"We cannot ignore him," Kappa whispered. "Fortunately, the Tengu's body is still at the hospital. I have already spoken to Doctor Gempaku, and Doctor Gempaku is sure that he can work the necessary rituals."

"The necessary rituals? The necessary rituals for what?"

"Leave Admiral Thorson to Doctor Gempaku," said Kappa. "I have had enough of your incompetence."

"To be fair, Kappa—"

"To be *fair*, you and our meddling assistants have almost destroyed my dream! Where is Commander Ouvarov now? Where is Gerard Crowley? Who is keeping a watch on Nancy Shiranuka? Your assistants are all as bungling and treacherous as you are. The only reason I am not going to direct my *Oni* to kill you now is because I have no time to find anybody else to replace you. Commander Ouvarov has vanished, nobody knows where, but there is no doubt that he was responsible for murdering Kenji. Yoshino has apparently fled with him."

"They'll be back, I'm sure," said Mr. Esmeralda, trying to sound confident.

Kappa let out a harsh, high-pitched noise that could have been a snarl or a mocking laugh. "If you believe that, Mr. Esmeralda, then you are a bigger fool than I have always thought you to be. They'll never be back. They'll run and hide, in fear of their lives, as very well they might. The influence of the Circle of Burned Doves reaches everywhere, financed and supported by some of the greatest of Japanese businesses. Many of Japan's most eminent financiers and politicians have relations who were deformed or killed by the bombs at Hiroshima and Nagasaki. Twelve thousand people a year are still dying in Japan as a direct effect of America's brutality. The Circle of

Burned Doves is the richest secret society in the world after the American order of Freemasons. We can never forgive, and we can never forget. Usually, our energies are devoted to bringing the United States to her knees economically. All the research that went into microJapanese shipbuilders and electrical manufacturers receive funding from our central bank. Our influence reaches to Canada, Europe, and the Middle East. So wherever your precious Commander Ouvarov tries to hide himself, he will be found and summarily executed for what he did."

Mr. Esmeralda said, "I am impressed. I also regret what occurred. But I did respectfully try to warn you that using the Tengu to assassinate Admiral Thorson was not a good idea. It would have been just as easy to send somebody in to finish him off with a knife. Quiet, no mess, effective."

"What is easy and what is just do not always coincide," whispered Kappa. "Admiral Thorson was in charge of the mission called Appomattox, to discover the training center for the Tengus in 1945 and direct the first atomic bomb onto it, in order that the Tengus might be utterly destroyed. It was simple justice that Admiral Thorson should be killed by the very being which he tried to wipe out forever, especially when you consider how many innocent lives he considered it necessary to extinguish or maim at the same time."

Kappa paused, and then said throatily, "If Japan had possessed the atomic bomb and had dropped it on San Francisco—if that bomb had been exploded in the sky over Telegraph Hill, the most powerful bomb ever used, two thousand times more powerful than anything that had ever been dropped before, the explosive force of 20,320 tons of TNT, coupled with heat and fire and gamma rays that could penetrate the thickest concrete wall as if it didn't exist—what would Americans think today? Even today, thirty-eight years later, they would spit at Japanese in the street. I doubt if the United States, even now, would have resumed diplomatic relations with Japan. Well, many of us Japanese feel the same way, but our nature is less demonstrative than yours. Our emotions and our memories tend to be suppressed, although never forgotten. We borne your occupation of our country with dignity, we accepted the infiltration into our traditional ways of your trashy culture—''

''Please, I am a native of Colombia,'' said Mr. Esmeralda, embarrassed but firm. ''What the Americans did has nothing to do with me.''

Kappa watched him in silence. Then, quietly, he said, ''We will have our revenge, Mr. Esmeralda.''

''What do you propose to do now, if I might ask?'' said Mr. Esmeralda, glancing uncertainly at the black-masked *Oni* guards.

Kappa said something in Japanese to the girl who was standing close by. She came forward with a jar of jade-colored ointment, and began to massage it into the grayish folds between his legs. Mr. Esmeralda felt distinctly nauseated as he watched her slender, well-manicured fingers disappearing into the crevices and dewlaps of Kappa's deformed genitalia, but he swallowed hard and tried to think of Colombia in the summer, the jasmine and the bougainvillea. He tried to think of cigars and good wine, and his father laughing loudly on the balcony.

Kappa said, ''Because of your carelessness and your incompetence, I have brought forward the Day of Fate to the day after tomorrow, fifty-eight hours from now. I have talked to Doctor Gempaku, and he assures me that he can have another Tengu ready by then. I would have liked to have had more than one. I wanted to make absolutely sure that my plan was a success. But we will have to take the risk. The Day of Fate must come.''

''If you say so,'' said Mr. Esmeralda.

''Don't try to mock me,'' snapped Kappa. ''You have angered me enough already to warrant death. And you can be well assured, your incompetent and untrustworthy colleagues will die on the same day.''

Kappa spoke quickly to one of his guards, and the man came forward with a roll of blueprints. Mr. Esmeralda knew what they were: he had obtained them himself, for $2,500, from a disgruntled secretary at the California Center for Nuclear Fusion. They were the detailed plans of the new fusion reactor and power station on the shoreline at Three Arch Bay, just north of Salt Creek and Capistrano Beach, where the southbound Santa Ana Freeway sweeps in a southward curve from San Juan Capistrano toward the Pacific Ocean.

Three Arch Bay Fusion Reactor, one of the world's most advanced nuclear-energy centers, was fueled by deuterium and tritium, processed from the waters of the Pacific itself. Unlike light-water reactors, or their advanced cousins the fast-breeder and thermal reactors, the fusion reactor did not require uranium or other fissionable materials. Deuterium and tritium are both forms of hydrogen, and are present in the world's oceans in an inexhaustible supply, free. All that was required of the Three Arch Bay reactor to tap that was that it should fulfill the two major conditions necessary for a fusion reaction: produce intense confined heat as high as 100 million degrees Celsius, and sustain that temperature for one second.

Kappa had chosen this particular reactor as his target because any intererence in its fusion process would produce an explosion far greater than anything that had ever been witnessed in the world before. He had calculated, with the help of Japanese physicists sympathetic to the cause of the Circle of Burned Doves, that to destabilize the fusion process during the one critical second of 100-million-degree heat would lead to a nuclear detonation with a force equivalent to 150 million tons of TNT—50 million tons greater than the largest hydrogen bomb that the United States or the Soviet Union had ever produced.

Southern California would be devastated. Los Angeles would die instantly. And the winds from the Pacific would carry the radioactivity far across the Midwest, polluting the crops, poisoning the air, and destroying countless millions of Americans for not only months but years to come.

Three Arch Bay, however, was only intended to be the start. Kappa planned to attack one nuclear-power station after another, year by year, until America's spirit was broken and her lands were glowing with radioactivity. She would never rise again. What Kappa wanted to do was to release so much nuclear energy into her atmosphere that her children would be born dead or deformed for centuries to come. It was the least he could do to avenge his mother. It was the least he could do to avenge himself.

Mr. Esmeralda asked, "You have worked out a way for the Tengu to break in?"

Kappa's mask nodded on his shrunken shoulders. "The Tengu will walk straight through the perimeter fence, across the main yard, and break down the doors that lead into the observation room. It is possible that he may be seen by security guards, and it is possible that he may be shot several times. But Doctor Gempaku has promised me that the Tengu he is creating now is his most powerful so far. Nothing short of utter destruction will be able to stop him; a few bullets won't even make him flinch."

Mr. Esmeralda said nothing, but lowered his eyes.

Kappa went on, "The Tengu will start the fusion process. He has been trained how to do it. At the critical moment, he will short-circuit the power supply by ripping out the main control cables—here, and here—and joining them together with his bare hands. The fusion reactor will go into wild imbalance, and within thirty seconds it will explode."

Mr. Esmeralda took out his handkerchief and dabbed at his forehead. It was infernally hot and rancid inside this room; and his equilibrium wasn't helped by the fact that he was so hungry and that Kappa was so repulsive to look at. Neither was he consoled by the thought that Kappa's wild and malevolent scheme to blow up a nuclear-power station was only two days away, and very real. When he had first met Kappa in Japan, all that time ago, it had seemed like a joke; at the very worst, a nuclear scare like Three Mile Island, with hardly any real damage to be done to anyone. But here, today, Kappa was talking about blowing up Three Arch Bay the day after tomorrow, in a 150-megaton nuclear blast, seven thousand times more powerful than Hiroshima. It was absurd, and unimaginable. He couldn't even think what a 150-megaton blast could possibly look like, or sound like, or do. Yet Kappa fully intended to set one off: not just once, but over and over again.

"I gather you're leaving Los Angeles, then," said Mr. Esmeralda. "You were afflicted by one nuclear blast; I'm sure you wouldn't want to go through another."

"I want you to rent me a private boat," said Kappa. "It should be comfortable, well appointed. I will take the minimum of crew with me and sail northward to San Francisco, in order that I may witness the devastation from a safe distance."

"What time are you planning on letting the Tengu loose?"

"At nine o'clock in the evening, the day after to-morrow. It will hinder rescue services even more if it is dark."

"When will you pay me the money that you promised me?"

Kappa was silent for a moment. Then he asked, "Do you think I should pay you at all?"

"You should, unless you want me to call a SWAT squad the moment I walk out of the door."

"You are trying to say that I must either pay you or kill you?"

Mr. Esmeralda took a deep breath. "You could put it like that, if you so wish. But, if nothing else, I have always taken you to be a man of your word."

"Very well," said Kappa. "You will be paid. All the remaining money that I agree to pay you will be credited to your bank account by tomorrow morning. But I expect you to remain in Los Angeles until the Day of Fate to make sure that the Tengu goes and that all possible arrangements for the destruction of the reactor have been completed. If I were you, I would arrange for a private plane to fly you out of Los Angeles as soon as the mission begins. You can fly far enough and fast enough in a single hour to avoid the main effects of the blast.''

''I suppose there is some comfort in that.''

Kappa said, ''You have no word of Sennett yet?''

''The boy is still being held at Pacoima Ranch. But, no, his fahter hasn't responded yet.''

''Gerard Crowley is supposed to be in charge of capturing Sennett, is he not?''

Mr. Esmeralda nodded. ''He would have succeeded immediately if Sennett had been at home. He sent in Yoshino and Toshiro, and they took the boy without anybody noticing. Crowley was supposed to contact Sennett with instructions for the boy's release this morning, but so far I haven't heard of any developments. Crowley will catch him, I am sure of that. Sennett isn't the kind of man who would risk his son's life, not for anything.''

''Is that what you think?'' asked Kappa. ''Then what if I were to tell you that Sennett has been to see Nancy Shiranuka?''

Mr. Esmeralda stared at him, at that hideous, nearly smiling mask. ''Sennett has been to see Nancy Shiranuka? But how? He doesn't even *know* her.''

''I do not understand how, I can only surmise,'' said Kappa. ''Either Sennett knows more about us than we think; or else somebody in this little group of ours has betrayed us. According to the *Oni* who watched Nancy Shiranuka's apartment last night, Sennett arrived there late yesterday evening and stayed until the early hours of the morning.''

''Was Gerard Crowley there?''

''No, although I *do* know who spent the night with Gerard Crowley's wife.''

Mr. Esmeralda asked, ''You've been watching *me*, too?''

''Of course. You don't think that you're exempt from

my suspicion, do you? Nobody is."

"But Gerard Crowley was supposed to go to Nancy Shiranuka's to brief her about the attack on Rancho Encino Hospital, and work out new plans for Doctor Gempaku."

"Crowley didn't arrive," said Kappa. "One of my men went to check Crowley's apartment, where he was fortunate enough to see *you* arriving; then he checked the Bonaventure Hotel, where Crowley has been keeping a room; and the house on Packard Street, where Crowley's mistress lives. No Crowley. No mistress, either."

"I'll check on it myself," said Mr. Esmeralda. All the time he was thinking: My God, not Crowley, too. Crowley had already threatened to go to the police and try to plea-bargain his way out of trouble. Why hadn't he gone to Nancy Shiranuka's, as he was supposed to? And what had Jerry Sennett been doing there? The treacherous group that Mr. Esmeralda had assembled to carry out Kappa's "bodyguard" project was proving even more treacherous than he had ever imagined. Kappa was right to bring the Day of Fate forward to the soonest date he could manage. And even so, Mr. Esmeralda was beginning to wonder if they could pull it off before the police discovered what they were up to. There was no honor among entrepreneurs.

Kappa said harshly, "I want you personally to drive Doctor Gempaku to Rancho Encino so that he can perform the necessary rituals. Then, I want you personally to make sure that Sennett is snared, and that both he and his son are killed. You can leave Crowley and Nancy Shiranuka to me—and Commander Ouvarov, too, when we find him. They have all been useful in their way. They have enabled us to bring into America all the people and all the equipment we needed. But now, they are growing restless; and restless servants are dangerous ones."

Mr. Esmeralda asked, "I can go now?"

"Yes," whispered Kappa. "But don't think that I have forgiven *your* mismanagement and *your* carelessness. You

will only be able to purge your errors by making sure that
the rest of my program is fulfilled without a single
mistake. And, to make certain that you have the necessary
incentive, I have already taken your Chinese chauffeur as a
hostage. You will have to drive yourself from now on,
until this mission is successfully accomplished. We will
take the girl on the boat with us when we sail to San
Francisco, and we will release her only when the atomic
sun rises in the southern sky. Otherwise, she will die. My
Oni have many diverting ways of killing women, some of
which take several days.''

Mr. Esmeralda felt as if cold leeches were sliding down
his back. There were a dozen angry things he could have
said. If he had been younger, fitter, and more reckless, he
might have tried to seize Kappa and throttle him. But he
had been surviving for too many years, staying alive in
cities and situations where more impulsive men had died
violent deaths, and he had lost the instinct to do anything
rash.

''Promise me that you will release her when the power
station blows,'' was all he said. ''Promise me on your
honor.''

''I promise,'' said Kappa, and his eyes glistened behind
his mask like the eyes of a hermit crab peering through the
shell of a long-dead host.

CHAPTER SEVEN

David was dreaming about sunbathing on the beach at
San Luis Obispo when the screen door slid back and
Doctor Gempaku stepped in. Just behind him stood one
of the black-masked *Oni* with an oblong lacquered tray,
on which there was a bowl of *oshi-zushi*, pressed rice with

ham and prawns and cucumber. Doctor Gempaku bent over David, shook his shoulder, and said, "Breakfast, young sir."

David blinked, rubbed at his eyes, and then sat up awkwardly. He was naked, covered only with a thin gray blanket, and there was no sign of his clothes. He said, "Has my father called yet?"

"You must have patience," said Doctor Gempaku. "Your father does not yet know where you are, or what we are expecting of him."

"You're out of luck if it's money you want," said David. "Dad's practically bankrupt."

"Oh, no, we're not after money," smiled Doctor Gempaku. "We're looking instead for *silence*."

"Silence? What's that supposed to mean?" David watched out of the corner of his eye as the *Oni* adept set down the breakfast tray, and then retreated to the doorway. The Japanese went no further, though, and it was obvious that he intended to keep a sharp watch on David until Doctor Gempaku's visit was over and the door could be locked again.

Doctor Gempaku said, "Your father knows about things that ordinary men like him should never really have had the misfortune to discover."

"This is something to do with Japan?" queried David. "Something to do with the war?"

"You're a bright young fellow," said Doctor Gempaku. "If you had been born Japanese, you would have gone far. But, well, things must be different. A very great pity."

"You're not going to harm my father?" asked David.

Doctor Gempaku reached across to David's breakfast tray, crumbled off a piece of oshi-zushi, and began to nibble at it. "Do you know what your father did in the war? Do you know why he still has to have psychiatric treatment?"

"Sure," frowned David. "He was on a mission for Naval Intelligence, and all his friends got killed by the

Japanese, right in front of his eyes.''

"Do you know what the mission was?"

David shook his head. "Something to do with—I don't know—spying out landing sites for American aircraft to invade the Japanese mainland. That's what he told me once.''

Doctor Gempaku took out a clean handkerchief and industriously wiped his hands, and then his mouth. "Your father has been lying to you; or, at least, not telling you the whole truth. Under the direction of a special Naval Intelligence task force, a task force of only fifteen men and yet a task force which was considered so important by the U.S. Joint Chiefs of Staff that it was put under the direction of an Admiral—Admiral Knut Thorson—your father was parachuted into Japan to detect, with a high-powered radio, the exact location of a very special Japanese military training center.''

"What's so special about that?" asked David.

Doctor Gempaku ruffled David's hair. "You do not understand at all, do you? That military training center was devoted to the creation of a special kind of Japanese soldier; a soldier who would be religiously as well as patriotically inspired, to the point where he would no longer feel pain, no longer feel fear. It was one of several attempts to protect the Japanese homeland. As futile as all the rest, perhaps; as futile as arming women and children with sharp bamboo sticks. But you cannot blame any nation, when it is isolated and afraid, for seeking to survive.''

"What happened?" asked David. He was hungry, but he still hadn't touched his *oshi-zushi*.

Doctor Gempaku shrugged. "The usual American over reaction. A fierce and unreasoning desire to avenge Pearl Harbor, perhaps. Something like that: who can understand the American psychology? The American mind is a mixture of cloying sentimentality and hideous brutality. Who can possibly reconcile the contradictions of Los Angeles, a city in which nearly eight hundred people are murdered every year, a city in which there are nearly two hundred rapes every month, and yet a city which can gleefully produce *The Great Muppet Caper* and *On Golden Pond*. You smile? Perhaps you find it amusing that a nation can publicly exalt the human spirit while at the same time wallowing in the deepest slough of moral degradation in civilized history.''

David said, ''I don't really understand what you're saying.''

''Let me tell you what your father did in Japan. Then you may grasp what I am trying to get into your head. Your father located the training center at Hiroshima, and sent back to the American high command a signal which he *knew* was the go-ahead for the dropping of the first atomic bomb. Although he was quite aware that his signal would lead to the instant and horrible deaths of thousands of civilians, he said, ''Do it''; and they did it. You know that your father goes to a psychiatrist, of course. Well, now you know why.''

David stared at Doctor Gempaku in disbelief. ''That's crazy,'' he said. ''They wouldn't have dropped the atomic bomb just to wipe out one training center.''

''They considered it necessary,'' said Doctor Gempaku. ''By their own lights, they considered it worthwhile.''

''But they dropped the atomic bomb to shorten the war. Japan was never going to surrender. They were going to fight until the very last man. I mean, the war could have gone on for *years*.''

Doctor Gempaku helped himself to some more of David's breakfast. ''How readily the young absorb the lies of their parents,'' he said. ''By May of 1945, Japan was already defeated, and even the most fanatical of her leaders knew it. The Japanese merchant navy, on which the whole country depended for food and supplies, had been reduced from ten million tons to one million. Over forty percent of all of Japan's sixty major cities had been destroyed by bombing. Her navy and her air force were shattered; what remained of her fleet was immobilized for lack of fuel. In May, we attempted to discuss peace with the Americans, using the Russians as mediators. But the Americans relentlessly insisted on unconditional surrender, *unconditional*, and failed to make it clear to the Japanese people that our Emperor, who is divine, would not be treated as a war criminal, and would be allowed to remain as Emperor under any Allied occupation force. This failure by the Americans to understand even the simplest fact of Japanese life and religion was what prolonged the war beyond the early summer of 1945. And through the hand of your father and his military henchmen, it was this failure that eventually led to the dropping of the first atomic bomb.''

David was silent. Doctor Gempaku stood up straight, then walked across to the window. ''I am sorry if I have been lecturing you. But you should know why you are here.''

''Do you want to kill my father?'' whispered David.

Doctor Gempaku made a face. ''I do not *want* to kill him,'' he said.

''But you're going to?''

''Almost certainly. And you, too.''

David stared at Doctor Gempaku, shocked. He felt as if all the blood had drained out of his body; he was ice-cold and empty.

''They'll catch you,'' he said unsteadily.

''Who will?''

''The police. The Los Angeles police.''

Doctor Gempaku turned around. ''By tomorrow night, there will be no Los Angeles police. More than that, there will be no Los Angeles.''

David couldn't think of anything else to say. He chewed nervously at his lip, and looked at Doctor Gempaku against the diffuse light of the window.

Doctor Gempaku said, ''It will be interesting to see how brave this man who killed so many thousands of Japanese during the war can actually be.''

CHAPTER EIGHT

Gerard Crowley looked unshaven and tired as he pushed his way between the crowded tables of Zucky's deli-restaurant a little before noon. His tie was loosened, and his shirt was crumpled and dirty. He was halfway through his second cigar of the day.

Jerry, in spite of his anxiety and his nervousness, had felt hungry when he had arrived at Zucky's, and had ordered himself a turkey sandwich and a cold beer.

Gerard Crowley, when he arrived, stood a foot or two away from Jerry's table with his hands in his pockets, his cigar between his lips, an expression on his face that was half cautious and half apologetic, like a man who has cornered a wounded Doberman and doesn't quite know whether he ought to try to bind the dog's foot or run for his life.

"Listen," he said, "I'm sorry about what happened. I'm sorry about all of it."

Jerry couldn't think what to say to that. The last thing he had expected from Gerard Crowley was an apology. The waitress came back with Jerry's sandwich and asked Gerard, "You're eating, sir?"

"Just give me a Scotch for now," said Gerard. He took the cigar out of his mouth and sat down next to Jerry, tugging the sleeves of his jacket down to cover his grubby cuffs. All around them, the deli was noisy with talking and laughter and music. Gerard said, "I don't suppose you want to shake hands."

"I just want to know how to get my son back," Jerry told him.

Gerard said, "The last I heard, an hour ago, your son's safe. You know why they're holding him, don't you? It's *you* they want. It's you they wanted right from the very beginning. Sherry Cantor died because they wanted you."

"The Tengus?" asked Jerry.

Gerard nodded. "They were afraid you'd guess. It looks like you did."

Jerry said tightly, "What's this all about? What the hell's going on? Nancy Shiranuka said something about bodyguards."

"That's a blind," said Gerard. He crushed his cigar out in the ashtray and wiped his mouth with the back of his hand. "I don't know what they're really into, but I can't believe it's anything to do with bodyguards. When they first approached me, they said it was nothing more than a moneymaking scheme for protecting rich Arabs and nervous *mafiosi*. Killer bodyguards, each one worth a million dollars of anybody's money. That's what they *told* me. They offered me the kind of money that nobody in his right mind would possibly turn down; and they backed up the carrot with a big stick. They knew about some contraband business I'd been involved in, and they said that if I *didn't* help them, they'd fix me up."

"Because of that, you agreed to murder?" asked Jerry. He tried to keep his voice as level as possible, but he was seething with frustration and anger at David's kidnapping, and at Gerard Crowley's impossible weakness. He was weak himself, he knew it. He still hadn't been able to find a way to face up to his own past. But Gerard's weakness was of an even more insidious variety: Gerard's weakness was a steady and unstoppable corrosion of the spirit. In Gerard's life, there was no hope of redemption, only meaningless apology.

Jerry thought it was ironic that their names were so similar: Jerry and Gerard. They were like the two faces of Dorian Gray, the unspeakably corrupt and the falsely innocent. They were different victims of the same human problem: an inability to cope with the utter immorality which was the prerequisite of success or even survival.

Gerard said, "The hits didn't seem like anything very special at first. They were a way of trying out the Tengus, proving that, as a market commodity, they worked the way they were supposed to. I know you find that difficult to swallow, but you haven't been working for twenty years in the import-export business like I have. You can believe me—anything that turns a buck gets sold. Drugs, fertilizers, chemicals, guns, surface-to-air missiles, tanks, mines, spirits, tobacco, pornography, girls, animals, boys. If you have enough money, you can buy anything, from anywhere. Let me tell you something, my wife thinks I'm a cold fish, unreachable. But if you're going to keep yourself alive and moderately wealthy, you have to keep your soul under lock and key, and that's what I've been doing. They told me to hit you, and that's what I arranged to do. They told me to kidnap you, take you out to the mountains, and dispose of you; so, I found that you weren't at home, I took your son instead."

"It was *you*?"

Gerard nodded. "I arranged it. I was told to flush you out, and that seemed like the best way."

Jerry was dumbfounded. "So now what?" he said. "I'm supposed to forgive you, or something? *Now* what? I want my son back, and that's all there is to it."

"Would you give up your life for your son? If I said you can have him back, but only if you allow me to kill you, what would you say then?"

Jerry stared at him. "Are you serious? Are you asking that as a serious question?"

Gerard didn't even blink.

Jerry put down his turkey sandwich. His throat was drier than ever. "If that's the way it has to be . . . then yes. If that's the only possible condition for David's release."

Gerard smirked, and then let out a grunt of a laugh. "You're even more innocent than I imagined," he said. "Do you really think that anybody who wanted to kill you would actually honor this agreement, and release your boy? Your boy's being kept alive for one reason only: you're still alive. Once you're dead, why should anyone bother? Your boy will be knocked off, too. You're not likely to come back from the grave and argue about it, are you? And your boy will be far too damning a witness for us to let him go."

Jerry was silent for a long time, staring at Gerard in

hopeless anxiety. Then he said, "You've come to meet me for a reason, right? Either to have me killed, or to put up some kind of a suggestion."

"That's right," said Gerard. The waitress brought his whiskey, and he paid for it with a $20 bill. "You see, everything was fine until yesterday night. Then, they sent out a Tengu to kill Admiral Thorson, who is the only other man apart from your good self who might have jeopardized the Tengu project by recognizing what the Tengu actually are and by helping the police to trace them back to where they came from."

"Admiral Thorson was in a coma. He had been for months. Why should they bother to send out a Tengu to kill him?"

"They're *crazy*, that's why," said Gerard. "And, besides, they're Japanese. Although they won't admit it, a whole lot of what they're doing has got something to do with the ancient Japanese principles of revenge and honor. You and Thorson knew about the Tengus: you had to die. Don't ask me why. The whole thing's like some kind of nightmare."

Jerry said, "I get the feeling you're trying to tell me that you're changing sides. You're not trying to threaten me, are you? Or are you? You're trying to find out if I'll forgive you enough for what you've done to help you."

Gerard took out another cigar and clipped off the end. "This Tengu project isn't what it seems, believe me. There's something really heavy going down; and when I say heavy, I mean *heavy*."

Jerry picked up his sandwich, looked at it, and then put it down again. He said, "You took my son, right? All I want to hear from you is that you're prepared to help me get him back again."

Gerard briefly closed his eyes, to indicate his assent.

"I don't *trust* you," said Jerry. "For Christ's sake, how can I trust you? It was you who took him in the first place."

"I'm not asking for anything," Gerard said. "Not

sympathy, not forgiveness, nothing. I'm just asking you to believe that in the past twenty-four hours, I've changed my mind about the people I work for, and I've begun to change my mind about myself. The motivation has been completely selfish. I'm scared, if you want to know the truth. I've never been scared of anyone or anything in my life, but I'm scared now. And the reason I'm scared is because I'm in love. I've been dating my secretary, Francesca. I was supposed to go back to Nancy Shiranuka's place last night and talk about the Tengus, report on what we'd been doing out at Rancho Encino. But I didn't go. Instead, I took Francesca to L'Ermitage, where nobody was going to find us, and I spent the whole night talking myself out. My past, my present, and my future. The whole Rancho Encino thing went wrong, it all turned into a massacre. I can't live with that. When you're really in love for the first time, you realize you can't accept half the things you accepted before. You've got a responsibility to yourself, and to the person you love."

He smoked, and rubbed at his forehead, and then he said, "I can't erase what's happened, you know? I can't bring Sherry Cantor back to life. But I would if I could. And I'll do whatever I can to help you get your son back. I thought I was a frigid, emotionless tough guy before any of this started, and the fact is that I'm not. I don't think anybody is, when you really take it down to the bottom line. You can't be a lover and a killer at the same time. And that's why I said I was sorry when I first came in."

Jerry said, "Nancy Shiranuka told me they were holding David at some ranch near Pacoima."

"That's right."

"What goes on there? When you say 'they,' who do you mean? How many people do they have there?"

"The ranch at Pacoima is where they're creating the Tengus," said Gerard. "The head guy there is Doctor Gempaku, he's the guy who actually develops the Tengus, brings them into being. Then there's ten or eleven guards; they all wear black masks on their faces, so you can never tell which is which. But they're all armed, and they're all skilled in *Oni*, which is some kind of ancient martial art.''

"I know about *Oni*," said Jerry.

"In that case, you'll be quite aware that these guys are totally deadly," said Gerard.

"Yes," said Jerry. He felt awkward with Gerard, suspicious of him. And yet at the same time he could recognize that Gerard was going through an inner turmoil that, if he only allowed it to, could bring him out of a life that had been shallow and cynical and exploitative, and into an existence that would be honest even if not particularly profitable.

Jerry hadn't been at L'Ermitage, during those hours in which Gerard had drunk whiskey after whiskey, and talked, and argued, and made love to Francesca in ways that had been both tender and fierce. Jerry hadn't seen that the news from Rancho Encino had shocked Gerard more than Gerard was prepared to admit, even to himself. Wheeling and dealing was one thing. Hearing secondhand stories about hits on treacherous Chinese dope dealers was chilling, but not personally alarming. But the slaughter at Rancho Encino and the kidnapping of David Sennett had made Gerard Crowley realize at last that he was out of his league. In spite of his apparent remoteness, in spite of his cynicism, he was a man who needed to feel that he was loved; and with loving and being loved came morality, and with morality came hesitation.

"The only way you can rescue your son alive is by hitting Doctor Gempaku when he's least expecting it," said Gerard. "Do you own a gun?"

Jerry shook his head.

"You'll need something heavyweight," said Gerard. "These *Oni* guards have Israeli Uzis, and they won't hesitate to use them if they think that something's wrong. I can get you an M-60E1 and a couple of Ingrams. You have some friends who could help you?"

"I have some friends, for sure," said Jerry. "But whether they'd help me or not . . . Are you suggesting I *storm* this place?"

"What else are you going to do?" asked Gerard. "The minute those people see anything that looks like a police car, they're going to kill your boy stone dead. My suggestion is that I take you in there, like you've given yourself up, and then two or three of your friends bust into the place and go through it with machine guns until there's nobody left."

Jerry said, "You're out of your *mind*! First of all you tell me, quite calmly, that it was *you* who kidnapped my son. Now you're telling me that you're prepared to help me rescue him by blowing all your fellow kidnappers away. I'm asking you, Crowley, are *you* nuts or am *I*?"

Gerard looked away. Then he said quietly, "This has all come too late—my conversion, if you want to call it that. Too late for any kind of sensible action. I'm just making a suggestion, that's all. If you don't like it, if you can think of something better, then do it. I won't stand in your way. But I'm going to have to ask you one thing."

"What's that?" asked Jerry.

"I'm going to have to ask you to plead on my behalf, if this ever comes to the law. I'm in love with a beautiful girl, Sennett, and I don't particularly feel like spending the next ten to twenty years in the penitentiary. That's why I agreed to meet you today; that's why I'm trying to help. It's got to be a deal or else it's no deal. You speak on my behalf; I'll help you get your son back."

Jerry finished his beer, taking as long as he could, watching Gerard Crowley all the time.

"You'll get me the guns?" he asked at last.

"An M-60E1, easy," said Gerard. "Do you think you'll know how to use it?"

"I was trained on a Browning during the war."

"You'll manage. I'm not so sure whether I can get the Ingrams, but I'll do my best."

Jerry said, "Surely the police can manage this better. Maybe the SWAT team. I'm an old man, Crowley. Well, not *old* exactly, but getting on. I'm not even sure that my friends will want to help me."

"If you call the police in, I'm finished," said Gerard.

"Not only that, but your son will be too. You know how ham-fisted the cops can be, when it comes to a confrontation like this. It'll be blood and dead bodies, and that's it."

"You can show me where this place is, at Pacoima?"

"Sure," said Gerard. "Only I have to have your promise that you'll back me up in court."

Jerry pressed his hands together in a mimickry of prayer. Then he said, "In principle, okay. In practice, I don't know. I'll have to go talk to my friends first. You're asking me to risk *my* life so that you don't have to risk *yours*."

"I'm supposed to tell you that your son has thirty-six hours to live," said Gerard. "Either you come out to Pacoima Ranch by midnight, or David dies."

Jerry said, "You're a bastard, you know that?"

"Sure I'm a bastard," Gerard replied. "But every bastard has his moment of glory."

Jerry pushed his away his half-eaten sandwich. The world seemed suddenly strange, and cold, and threatening beyond belief. "Glory," he said, mostly to himself. "Some glory."

CHAPTER NINE

Francesca was still at L'Ermitage, pinning up her hair, when Gerard and Jerry said goodbye to each other on the sidewalk outside of Zucky's and walked off in opposite directions. She looked at herself in the mirror and thought: Francesca, you'd better not fall in love. Whatever else you want to do with your life, don't fall in love. Not with Gerard Crowley.

Last night, she had seen a side of Gerard which she

hadn't even realized existed. Gerard afraid. Gerard
sensitive. Gerard thinking about nothing but her, and
pleasing her; with champagne, and gardenias, and breast
of duckling with Bordeaux sauce.

She brushed out her long auburn hair in front of the
mirror. She was naked except for a white lace G-string
from Janet Reger of London. She had developed expensive
tastes in the three years she had worked for the CIA, first as
an undercover agent, and then as a kind of highly paid,
high-class callgirl-cum-entrapment-operative.

Gerard Crowley was not a particularly big fish. But
Crowley Tobacco Imports was the central clearinghouse for
five or six heavy smuggling operations, particularly the
heroin business operated by the Jonas brothers, and the
Metaxas weapons-smuggling ring which supplied machine
guns and missiles to the terrorist groups of the Middle
East. It had been Francesca's job to gather sufficient
evidence against Gerard Crowley to persuade him to testify
against Billy and Nathan Jonas, Salvatore Mazzarino, and
Giorgio Scarantino.

She hadn't reckoned with the surprise bonus of Mr.
Esmeralda; but although she had reported back to her
local CIA chief of operations everything she could find out
about Gerard's dealing with him, she hadn't yet been able
to decide exactly what it was that Mr. Esmeralda was up to.
Gerard was obviously frightened of him; and did whatever
he told him to. But whenever she tried to question Gerard
about him, Gerard said nothing at all, or very little of any
interest, and quickly changed the subject.

Last night, she had known that Gerard was frantically
worried. Instead of meeting her at the Bonaventure or her
apartment, he had insisted on taking her to L'Ermitage,
where he had booked a room for two and ordered up the
most lavish meal on the menu. Then, he had talked for
hours about his childhood, and about his days in Cuba,
and how life had tricked him and trapped him into being a
stooge. ''How can you have any scruples when society
expects you to be rich instead of poor, and yet makes it

impossible for you to be rich by honest and honorable means?''

He had made love to her four or five times, urgently and violently. She liked him because, over a period of several months, she had made an effort to like him. This was her third "secretary-mistress" operation, and she had learned that she had to do everything she could to see the best in her "marks," no matter how brutal and coarse they were. There were some nights when she had lain in the dark with a man's semen leaking out of her, as tackily as drying blood, and heard him snoring on the pillow next to her, and known that in two weeks' time she would be standing in court testifying against him. And still she liked him.

She didn't know whether she was actually capable of love.

She knew that Gerard had invested all of his affections in their relationship: that his marriage had fallen to pieces, and he was looking to her to provide him with his future. But she didn't feel sorry for him, or guilty. One way or another, one day or another, with or without her, he would be caught for smuggling or milk extortion or drug-running or arms dealing or pimping. He was one of those men who had been born without a future, no matter how hard they tried. Next month, Francesca would be smiling seductively at a new employer, and Gerard Crowley would be forgotten altogether.

She finished brushing her hair, then walked across to the closet where her dress was hanging up.

"Poor Gerard," she thought. "My God, poor, lonely Gerard."

CHAPTER TEN

After the killings, the staff of Rancho Encino Hospital had moved Admiral Thorson to the next wing, to a lemon-yellow room with a reproduction of "Some Steps in the Hospital Garden" by Van Gogh on the wall above his bed. Admiral Thorson was still shocked by what had happened, and by the realization that his wife was dead, but he was conscious and coherent. During the day he spoke three or four times to hospital staff, and to Harry Calsbeek, the Chief of Detectives from Encino police headquarters.

There was little he could say: his wife had screamed, he had woken up to see a dark, flailing shape through the plastic of his oxygen tent. Then he had heard a salvo of gunfire, and blood had splattered in front of his eyes like an action painting. "I can tell you this, though," the admiral had said hoarsely, "I shall never forget my Mary screaming until I leave this earth. I shall never forget it, ever."

Sergeant Skrolnik and Detective Pullet arrived at Rancho Encino during the evening, tired, vexed, and arguing with each other. Detective Pullet had been attempting some more bursts of lateral thinking, and had come up with the idea that the killer might be a failed Japanese restaurateur with a grudge against American naval officers. Maybe they had patronized his original restaurant in Tokyo, but hadn't taken the trouble to patronize his new restaurant in Los Angeles? Skrolnik had had enough of lateral thinking, and had told Pullet to keep his mouth shut and his mind on the facts.

Calsbeek was waiting for Skrolnik outside Admiral Thorson's room.

Calsbeek was heavily built, red-haired, with a face that looked scraped, like a raw rutabaga. His tweed suit hung around him in fold after fold, each pocket crammed with pieces of paper, rolled-up magazines, clips of .38 bullets, chewing gum, Life Savers, Swiss Army knives, loose buttons, and string. But while his appearance may have been gentle, sloppy, and shuffling, his mind and his tongue were as abrasive as sandpaper.

"You should have been here three hours ago," he told Skrolnik. "I've talked to the man all I can, there's nothing more to be done."

"You took notes?" asked Skrolnik.

"Of course I took fucking notes."

"By the way, this is Detective Pullet," said Skrolnik. "Detective Pullet is our number one deductive thinker."

"I see," said Calsbeek. "Well, maybe he can deduce why three loony Japs and a white man decided to burst into Rancho Encino Hospital and slaughter everybody in sight, because sure as hell *I* can't."

Pullet said, "You have to go back to the fundamental reasons why anybody kills anybody else. Believe it or not, there are only *eight* reasons why people kill other people: robbery, rape, jealousy, self-defense, violent disagreement, pity, revenge, and to keep them quiet. Well . . . nobody wanted to *rob* Admiral Thorson, because he didn't have any money on him. Nor did they want to *rape* him. I doubt if *jealousy* was the motive, because he didn't have a particularly distinguished career, and he certainly wasn't fooling with anybody's wife."

Skrolnik said, "Will you get to the point, Pullet?"

"Sure," said Pullet. "Nobody killed him after a violent disagreement, because he was in a coma, and unable to argue with anybody. It's unlikely that anybody attacked him so violently out of *pity*. That leaves us with *revenge*—which, considering his record in the Pacific theater of war against the Japanese, could well be likely. Or, the motive of keeping him quiet."

"He was in a coma, what could he say to anybody about anything?" asked Skrolnik. "Why should anybody want to keep him quiet?"

"You're right," said Pullet. "So what are we left with? Revenge. A Japanese attacks a World War Two admiral, presumably with the intention of revenging Midway, or

Leyte Gulf, or whatever. It's my guess that when you manage to identify this turkey, you'll find that his father or his older brother went down with the *Hirvu*, something like that."

"Takes your breath away, doesn't it?" said Skrolnik, turning to Calsbeek.

Calsbeek said, "You can question the admiral at midnight, when they wake him up to give him his medication. Don't press him too hard, you know? Give an old, sick man an even break. He's just lost his wife and it hasn't sunk in yet."

"We understand," said Skrolnik. "Now, can we see the bodies?"

Pullet said, "I'll wait here, you know, stand guard."

Skrolnik said wearily, "Come on, Pullet. You've got all the theories, you've got to see the bodies, too."

Calsbeek led the way to the hospital morgue. A pale-faced young man unlocked the door for them, and they trooped reluctantly into the chilled, fluorescent-lit room where the hospital kept the remains of loved ones who had passed away during their stay.

"Drawers eight, nine, and six," the young man told them.

Skrolnik, without hesitation, rolled out No. 8. It was Kenji, the Japanese who had been stabbed by Commander Ouvarov. His face was still locked in a ridiculous grimace of pain.

"You can't say that *he* died a serene death," remarked Skrolnik.

They opened the next drawer, No. 9. It was the Japanese who had been hit pointblank by one of the hospital security guards. The bridge of his nose was blown away, and his eyeballs were collapsing toward the middle of his face, giving him a ludicrous but horrifying squint.

"You didn't tell me this hospital had been attacked by Ben Turpin," said Skrolnik laconically. Neither Pullet nor Calsbeek could find it in them to laugh. "Number six," instructed Skrolnik, unperturbed.

The body of the Tengu lay on the slab with his arms tucked neatly beside him, his bloodstained loincloth already black and fetid, his chest and thighs gaping with anemic wounds. There was no head: only the protruding trachea, and a tangle of muscles and tendons and nerves.

"Well, your boys certainly put paid to him," said Skrolnik. "What do you arm them with, howitzers?"

"We killed him before he could kill Admiral Thorson," said Calsbeek acidly. "That's all you need to know."

"Has the coroner been over this body yet?"

"He's taking it tomorrow. There was a mass poisoning two nights ago at Strawberry Drive, up by the reservoir. His slabs are kind of crowded right now."

"Well, life's busy in Encino right now," remarked Skrolnik. "What are you trying to do, beat out the Los Angeles homicide statistics?"

"Believe me, this is the last thing I want," grated Calsbeek. "Encino's supposed to be quiet and neighborly. Neat yards and law-abiding suburbanites. Up until now, the worst crime we've had all year has been inconsiderate roller-skating on the sidewalk."

Skrolnik rolled back the drawer, and the Tengu's mutilated body disappeared from sight. "Do you want some coffee?" he asked Calsbeek. "Stiffs always make me thirsty."

Calsbeek gulped a few mouthfuls of scalding machine-made coffee with them, and then left. Skrolnik and Pullet sat for the next two hours in the reception area, listening to the splash of the illuminated fountain and the syrupy warbling of Muzak, and leafing through copies of *Reader's Digest* and *Encino*.

"I never realized that Encino was such a goddamned dull place," said Skrolnik, tossing one of the magazines back onto the table.

Just after midnight, a short, bespectacled doctor with a shock of black wavy hair came scuttling into the reception area to tell them, blinking, that Admiral Thorson would now be available for a short period of police questioning.

"As long as you understand that he's a very sick man, you got me?"

"Yes, sir," grunted Skrolnik. "Aren't we all?"

Considering the trauma that he had been through, Admiral Thorson looked remarkably fit. He was no longer the old "Inch-Thick" of Navy days. His eyes were sunken and shadowed. But when Skrolnik and Pullet were shown into his room, he nodded to them alertly and said, "What's this? More damn fool questions?"

Skrolnik smiled uncomfortably and perched his rump on the edge of an uncomfortable stacking chair. Pullet went across to the other side of the bed and peered with almost morbid interest at the admiral's cardiopulmonary monitors and electroencephalograph. Skrolnik said, "We won't keep you very long, sir. We know that you've been through a lot. But what happened here at Rancho Encino bears a close resemblance to a homicide we're investigating in Hollywood."

"I'm sorry to hear it," said Admiral Thorson. "Would you mind passing me that glass of lemonade? A man gets damn thirsty all wired up like this, tucked up in bed like a damned invalid."

Skrolnik passed him the lemonade, and the old man took four or five sips and then handed it back. "Used to be bourbon and branch, in the old days," he grunted.

Skrolnik said, "What particularly interests us, sir, is that your assailant was Japanese. Detective Pullet here has been theorizing that maybe the attack has something to do with your war record. We've had one or two cases of white people attacking Japanese because they lost somebody they loved during the war; usually when they're drunk or depressed or suffering from some kind of nervous collapse. But on the face of it, your assailant was psychotic, to say the least, and Detective Pullet thinks that maybe . . ."

Admiral Thorson looked from Skrolnik to Pullet, and then back again. "Anything that I did during the Second War is faithfully and fully recorded in my memoirs, sergeant. *From Saipan to Kyushu with Admiral Knut*

Thorson, published by the Institute for Naval Studies. Rather than interview me, and wear out what little there is left of me, I suggest you go buy yourself a copy.''

Skrolnik wedged his fingers together and raised his eyebrows toward Detective Pullet in an expression of testy patience. ''What I was trying to get at, Admiral, if you'll forgive me for pressing you, is whether you were involved in anything personal or private that may have excited some Japanese fruitcake to try to get even with you. I understand that the Japanese have very severe codes of honor and duty; maybe you inadvertently trod on someone's face during the war, upset them more than you'd meant to. Something to do with a woman, maybe? I'm not trying to pry.''

Admiral Thorson was silent for a moment. Then he gestured toward his bedside cabinet and said to Skrolnik, ''Open the top drawer. Take out the letter you'll find in there.''

Skrolnik did as he was told. He lifted out the faded V-mail envelope and opened it.

''Read it,'' said Admiral Thorson.

> *How can a love so gentle be so fierce?*
> *How can a soft caress grip with such strength?*
> *How can your tenderest glance so quickly pierce*
> *My heart its very depth, my life its length?*

Sergeant Skrolnik said cautiously, ''It's poetry.''

''Yes,'' said Admiral Thorson. ''I wrote it to my wife in October 1944, just before the battle of Leyte Gulf. It was one of many. Let me ask you if a man who writes poetry like that to his wife is likely to get involved with a Japanese woman?''

''I'm sorry,'' said Skrolnik. ''But you understand that I have to chase after every possible idea.''

''Admiral,'' put in Detective Pullet, running his hand through his tangled hair, ''was there any other operation you were in charge of, during the war, anything that maybe didn't get into your memoirs?''

"Anything that didn't get into my memoirs was excluded for reasons of national security," Admiral Thorson answered. "There were one or two operations I was able to write about in the revised edition of my book, in 1968, but since then nothing else, as far as I know, has come off the top-secret list."

"Was there anything that might have motivated an attack of revenge—the kind of attack that happened here last night?"

Admiral Thorson said, "I can't discuss anything that isn't in my memoirs without a specific security clearance from the Secretary of the Navy. I'm sorry."

Pullet sensed something, he wasn't at all sure what it was. But the way in which Admiral Thorson had abruptly invoked the rulebook aroused his nose for the obscure and the unusual. Admiral Thorson had an inkling of what had happened to his wife, and why. Pullet was sure of it. And if Pullet knew anything at all about the psychology of retired military commanders, Admiral Thorson wasn't refusing to discuss it because it was secret. He was refusing to discuss it because he was afraid of being ridiculed. The attack on Rancho Encino Hospital had been pretty wacky, as homicides went, and Pullet was convinced that Admiral Thorson had an equally wacky theory about it.

He said, "This guy who assaulted your wife and the rest of the hospital staff. Did you ever see anyone who looked like him before? All those wounds on his body? Would you have any idea what they were?"

"I'm afraid I can't answer that," said Admiral Thorson.

"Then you *do* know something about it?" demanded Pullet.

"I didn't say that. I simply said that I can't answer your question."

"You can't answer the question because it's a matter of national security?"

"That's correct. Now, please—"

Pullet dragged over a chair and sat astride it, frowning at Admiral Thorson with scruffy concern. "Admiral," he said, "there was a multiple homicide here last night.

Your own wife was among the victims. Now, if you refuse to discuss what happened here because you believe that it's going to be an infringement of national security, then you must have some kind of notion what it was all about. I mean, otherwise, how do you know that it's likely to be an infringement of national security?''

"I'm tired," said Admiral Thorson. "I'm tired and you're playing with words. I don't have anything to say to you."

"Admiral—"

"The man is *dead*, isn't he?" Admiral Thorson demanded. "He's been caught, and executed on the spot. What's the purpose of investigating any further?''

"Admiral," said Skrolnik as gently as he could, "It's conceivable that there might have been a conspiracy to attack you, involving a considerable number of people. So far, we don't have a single clue *why*. But we believe there are men still at liberty who were concerned in the killing of your wife. We want to catch those men.''

Admiral Thorson shook his head. His voice was hoarse now, and desperate. "You'll have to leave me alone for now. I'm too tired. Please—will you call the doctor?''

Skrolnik took a deep breath and stood up. "Okay, Admiral. If you don't want to help, then I guess I can't force you. Pullet, will you push that bell, please? We're going to leave the admiral to think things over, see if he can't come up with some kind of surprise recollection. Something meaningful to add to his memoirs.''

The doctor came in and asked, "All finished now?''

"I hope not," said Skrolnik.

"You haven't upset him?" asked the doctor.

"He's okay, *I'm* the one who's upset," Skrolnik complained.

Skrolnik and Pullet left the hospital and walked out into the warm night air. Skrolnik's car was being repaired in the police workshop, and he had borrowed a dented black Lincoln Continental from his next-door neighbor. He had parked it on the far side of the hospital parking lot, and so he and Pullet had to cross almost to the perimeter of the hospital to reach it. They were almost there, walking side by side in irritated silence, when Pullet said, "What's that? Do you see something?"

"Where?" asked Skrolnik.

"Out on the road there, beside those bushes. No—you see that low stone wall. That's it. There."

Skrolnik strained his eyes in the darkness, and made out the shape of what appeared to be a man, kneeling in the road. As Skrolnik took two or three steps nearer, he saw that in front of the man there were two smoking bowls, and he also glimpsed what looked like two shiny crossed swords.

Skrolnik immediately hiked out his .38 revolver and released the safety. Pullet did the same. Without a word, Skrolnik ducked down behind the nearest parked car, ran the length of it with his head bent low, and then crossed the hospital lawn at a quick canter, making obliquely for the bushes beside the road, but keeping a screen of shrubs and trees in between himself and the man with the smoking bowls and the swords.

As he neared the road, Skrolnik waved his arm behind him to indicate to Pullet that he should circle around on the other side. Then, without any hesitation, he hurled himself straight through the bushes, with a crash of leaves and broken branches, and struck a knees-bent stance on the road, his gun held in front of him in both hands, and yelled, "Police! Freeze!"

There was a shot from the other side of the road, and Skrolnik felt the wind of a bullet flash past his cheek. He dropped to the ground and rolled himself back into the bushes again, firing off a quick diversionary shot that hit something on the other side of the road with a sharp *spang*! of metal.

The man who had been kneeling on the roadway had already scurried crabwise to the protection of the low stone wall. Skrolnik gingerly raised his head and shouted, "Pullet? Where the fuck are you?" but before Pullet could answer there was a roar of an engine starting up, and a large limousine backed out of the trees on the other side of the road, reversed wildly up to the stone wall, its tires smoking and its suspension bucking, and Skrolnik knew that their mysterious suspect was about to make a fast getaway.

He knelt among the dust and the leaves, steadied his hand, and fired off four shots, in what he hoped was a tight cluster, toward the limousine's front window. There was a crackling of broken glass, but the limousine gunned its engine, and took off down the road with its tail snaking from side to side and its tires screaming like slaughtered pigs.

"Get on the radio!" Skrolnik bellowed at Pullet. "Get an alert out on those jokers! Go on, *move*!"

Pullet pushed his way out of the bushes and went running back across the lawn to the parking lot, trying to stuff his gun back into his trousers as he went. Skrolnik meanwhile walked along to the place where the man had been kneeling and hunkered down to examine the evidence that he had left there.

One of the bowls had been tipped over, and its contents were strewn across the blacktop. It was still smoldering, though, a grayish powdery substance that looked like incense or charcoal. There was a light, sweetish smell around, which reminded Skrolnik of something he couldn't immediately put a name to. Something unusual and exotic and, for some reason, very disturbing. He licked his finger, touched the powder, and tasted it. It could have been dried flowers or the burned gum from some species of tree.

He recognized at once what the two crossed swords were. Samurai swords, curved and sharp and decorated with lacquer and silk bindings. He didn't touch them; he wanted them photographed and fingerprinted first. But they confirmed what he and Pullet had just been saying to Admiral Thorson. The attack on Rancho Encino had been connected with Thorson's war record, and his assailants almost certainly wanted revenge. What for, Skrolnik couldn't even begin to guess. He reloaded and holstered his gun, and planted his fists on his hips in a gesture of thoughtful determination. It was a pose that everybody in Skrolnik's department recognized as a sure sign that Skrolnik was now going to get tough.

Pullet came running back, breathless.

"You're out of condition," said Skrolnik. "Why don't you take up jogging? Listen, run back to the car and get my accident signs, will you? I don't want any of this stuff moved until Rabinowitz's boys have had a go at it."

Pullet said, "What the hell do you think he was doing? Are those swords?"

"Samurai swords," Skrolnik nodded. "Whatever he was up to, it was something to do with that attack on Admiral Thorson. Just, for Christ's sake, don't ask me what."

"I'll get the signs," said Pullet; but the moment he turned around, every floodlight in the hospital grounds was suddenly switched on, and the alarm began to bellow through the trees. Skrolnik said, "*Thorson*," and took out his gun again.

CHAPTER ELEVEN

They arrived at the doors of the hospital puffing and blowing. But Skrolnik forced his way in, past a screaming nurse and a dazed security officer who was waving his gun around at nobody and nothing, and jogged heavily down the corridor toward Admiral Thorson's room.

Another security officer came cantering toward them, shouting, "Get back! Get back!" but Skrolnik and Pullet simply dodged aside to let him run past, and he didn't even attempt to clear them out of the corridor.

"That guy's frightened," remarked Skrolnik.

"Aren't you?" asked Pullet.

They turned the corner and collided with Admiral Thorson's doctor. His hair seemed to be standing on end, and his eyes were as wild as Harpo Marx's.

"What the hell's going on here?" Skrolnik shouted at him, with all the coarseness he could muster. "What the hell is everybody running for?"

"It's that *thing*," garbled the doctor. Then he tore himself free from Skrolnik and ran off toward the hospital lobby.

"That *thing*, huh?" asked Skrolnik, wiping his nose with the back of his gun hand. "This is beginning to sound like some kind of monster movie. The Thing from Rancho Encino."

Pullet said, "We'd better go take a look in any case."

"I was afraid you'd suggest that," Skrolnik retorted. "You're becoming far too conscientious for a rookie."

They turned the last corner, into the corridor that took them directly to Admiral Thorson's room, and Skrolnik froze. At the end of the corridor was a wired-glass door, and through the distorting, refracting glass he could see a short, bulky shape, like a man with his head bent forward in contemplation. Skrolnik said, "The Thing?" and Pullet shrugged. "How do I know? I never met a Thing before. Challenge it."

Skrolnik raised his .38. "You!" he shouted harshly. "You, behind that door! Come out of there with your hands on your head!"

For a long moment, the bulky silhouette remained motionless. Skrolnik said, "Cover me," and took one or two apprehensive steps forward, his gun still raised.

"Do you hear me?" he shouted. "Come on out from behind that door with your hands on your head! You don't have a chance!"

The silhouette raised its arms, slowly and deliberately. "He's giving up," said Pullet, with relief, half-lowering his revolver. But then, with a terrifying, rending smash, the silhouette thrashed its fists into the glass door, tearing it apart in a wreckage of tangled wire, broken glass, and splintered wood.

"Oh, Jesus," said Pullet.

The creature that forced its way through the broken door may have been human once, but it was human no longer. It was the Tengu from the morgue, revived, and walking, mutilated not only with the scars of Doctor Gempaku's hooks, but with the gaping bloodless bullet wounds it had sustained from the Encino police. The worst thing of all, though, was that it had no head, only that raw pipe that rose from between its shoulders and the gristly remnants of its neck.

Skrolnik said, "It can't be. Pullet, that damned thing can't *be*."

The headless Tengu took one heavy step after another, dragging itself clear from the glass and the wire, heading toward Admiral Thorson's door. It may have been an optical illusion, but Skrolnik could have sworn that he saw tiny blue flames dancing in the air around the Tengu's shoulders.

He fired into the Tengu's chest, twice. Dead, white flesh flapped up as the Tengu's body absorbed the bullets, and the Tengu appeared momentarily to hesitate. But then it continued to shuffle toward Admiral Thorson's door, and at last it bumped against the oak veneer, its mutilated but muscular shoulder cracking the wood, its hands clawing toward the handle.

Skrolnik, white-faced, sweating, fired two more shots, only an inch apart, into the area of the monster's heart. The Tengu jolted with the impact and swayed, but then continued to beat dully against the admiral's door. Smoke from the bullets that had entered its chest cavity rose from the open pipe of its severed neck.

Pullet shrieked, "You can't kill it! For God's sake, it won't die!"

Hesitantly, Skrolnik approached the creature, his gun

held out in front of him. He fired two more shots, from pointblank range. One of the bullets went right through the Tengu's stomach and exited from its back. The other hit it in the chest. Neither bullet seemed to make any impression at all, except that the fires which flared around the Tengu's shoulders seemed to roar and grow fiercer.

Skrolnik, sickened and scared, but high on the adrenalin of sheer danger, tried to reach out and seize the monster's arm. But with a sideways chop, the Tengu knocked him aside, so that he collided heavily with the opposite wall of the corridor and twisted his ankle.

With six or seven splintering blows, the Tengu tore down Admiral Thorson's door and stepped into the dimly lit room. Skrolnik, wincing with agony in the corridor, knew now that there was absolutely nothing he could do. He also recognized that for the first time in his life he was up against something completely unstoppable; something which refused to obey any of the laws of nature, or at least the laws by which Sergeant Skrolnik organized his life and his police work. This thing, whatever it was, was supernatural, a ghost or a ghoul or a zombie, a thing that was undead and couldn't be killed by any conventional weapons, or defeated by any conventional prayers. Skrolnik knew that for certain: his brain had been spinning with frenzied appeals to the Lord his God ever since the Tengu had burst through the glass door.

"Pullet!" shouted Skrolnik. "Break open that fire cabinet down there! Get me that fire ax!"

Through the doorway, Skrolnik could see the Tengu approaching Admiral Thorson's bed; standing there, headless, swaying slightly as if it were recovering from a great and painful effort of will. The blue flames still jumped and blazed around it, but now it appeared to have a dark glow of its own, a frightening and almost visible aura, like a torturing iron that has just lost its red-hot radiance but is still capable of searing a man's flesh.

"Admiral!" bellowed Skrolnik. "Admiral, if you can manage it, get the hell out of there!"

Skrolnik limped on his one good ankle to the torn-apart doorframe. Now he could see Admiral Thorson sitting up in bed, his face papery and wrinkled, his sunken eyes bright with fear.

"Admiral!" shouted Skrolnik.

But the admiral's eyes were on the Tengu alone. The Tengu took one shuffling step nearer after another, until it was standing right up against the admiral's bed. Knut Thorson stared at it in horror and recognition.

"I never believed it could be real," he whispered. "Not even then."

Skrolnik said, in a determined hiss, "Admiral, I want you to roll off that bed, roll away from the monster onto the floor. Then dive right under the bed and leave the rest to me. Pullet, where the fuck's that fire ax? For Christ's sake, move your ass."

Whether he had heard Skrolnik or not, the admiral stayed where he was, propped up on his pillows, his monitoring equipment betraying every overstimulated beat of his heart, every jump of fear in his brain. He gave no indication that he had understood a single word, nor that he was going to try to save himself. But just then, Pullet came jostling up with the fire ax and handed it clumsily to Skrolnik, as if it were the baton in an amateur relay race.

"Stand back," grunted Skrolnik, and took one limping step forward into Admiral Thorson's room, swinging the long-handled ax in both hands.

Admiral Thorson shouted, "*Mary*!" at the top of his quavery voice, and then Skrolnik whirled the ax around and chopped it deep into the Tengu's severed neck, splitting its breastbone with an audible crack. Skrolnik stumbled backward on his twisted ankle, toppling Pullet over as well, but there was nothing they could do to save Admiral Thorson now. With the ax handle still sticking out from its back, the Tengu seized Admiral Thorson by the neck and wrenched him out of his bed, half lifting him in the air. Admiral Thorson hung in the headless creature's powerful hands, awkward and powerless; his cardiopulmonary monitor giving one last screech as the monster wrenched the wires loose.

With one flailing tear, the Tengu ripped off the admiral's hospital nightgown, baring his scrawny, ribby body; then, without hesitation, it plunged its fist through the flesh of the admiral's stomach, in a spattering welter of blood and fluid, and seized the admiral's backbone as if it were grasping the skeleton of a snake. Soundlessly, wordlessly, because it could never speak, or hear, or see—because whatever it could do, it could do only through the possession of the ancient demon Tengu—it pulled the admiral's spine right out through his torn-open belly, virtually turning his body inside out.

Skrolnik was utterly unable to speak, or even to think. All he knew was that the headless Tengu with the ax still stuck between its shoulders was throwing the admiral's gory corpse aside, so that nerves and intestines and tendons slid in bloodstained strings onto the floor, and that now it was turning toward him.

"Pullet," he said. "I do not want to be here."

Together, they scrambled to their feet, and with Skrolnik leaning his weight on Pullet's shoulders, they hopped and hobbled and half ran down the corridor to the hospital lobby, closing and locking the last door behind them. A crowd was already gathering there—nurses and medics and police, including a furiously disgruntled-looking Harry Calsbeek.

"Why do you foreigners always bring trouble?" he snarled. "What's going on here?"

Skrolnik caught Calsbeek's sleeve and pulled him aside, shoving away an inquisitive reporter from the *Encino Star*. "What I'm going to say I'm only going to say once," he told Calsbeek, scarcely opening his mouth as he spoke. "That creature you shot last night is still alive, and still walking around. It's just burst into Admiral Thorson's room and tore the poor old guy to very messy shreds. I don't know how it can still be alive. I don't know why. Maybe it's all just a nightmare. But if it is, then you're in

it too, and you're going to have to act accordingly. My best
suggestion is that you go get a couple of cans of gasoline,
and as soon as the creature appears, we set fire to it."

"We can shoot it, can't we?" asked Calsbeek. Then,
"What am I talking about? I don't even *believe* you. Are
you off your head or something? What's going on here?"

He was answered almost immediately. There was a
screech of tearing wood and ripped-off hinges. Then a
massive smash, and a low moan of fright among the
hospital staff and patients gathered in the lobby. One of
the nurses screamed, and then another, and then everybody was rushing for the main doors, jostling and pushing
and knocking over potted plants.

"*Don't panic!*" yelled Skrolnik, the veins standing out
on his neck. "*Don't panic, or somebody's going to get
crushed!*"

Calsbeek said, "Oh, my God."

The door to the lobby came sailing over their heads,
tumbling and turning, to crash noisily into the ornamental
pool. Dark, and yet still radiating that awesome aura, the
headless Tengu stood in the open doorway, the ax protruding from its neck, its scarred and mutilated chest rising
and falling with the breath of one of man's oldest and
most terrible enemies, a devil even more vicious than
Lucifer.

Skrolnik said, "*Now* will you get the gasoline?"

"Evans!" bellowed Calsbeek. "Guttierez! Get out to
the wagon and bring in those spare cans of gas, and do it so
damn fast I don't know you've gone!"

Calsbeek's two officers elbowed their way as quickly as
they could through the last stragglers pushing each other
to get out of the hospital, while Skrolnik and Calsbeek and
Pullet retreated toward the reception counter, drawing
their revolvers and watching the Tengu warily. For a while,
the Tengu stayed where it was, in the doorway, no flames
dancing around its shoulders at the moment, no movement to suggest what it might be considering next. But as
Evans and Guttierez came clanging back with their heavy

cans of gasoline, the Tengu took one clumsy step forward and raised both arms as if it were feeling its way across the lobby, sensing the presence of vulnerable humans through the nerves in the palms of its hands.

To Skrolnik, the Tengu looked like a bloody carcass of beef, headless and gutted; or the hideous human corpse in Goya's painting of Saturn devouring his children. The body was human, but the missing head had taken away all its identity, all its humanity.

"Get your men to splash as much gas on that thing as they can," said Skrolnik. "Just tell them to keep out of its way. Once it gets hold of you, you're dead beef."

Calsbeek gave the order, and Evans and Guttierez opened up two of the gasoline cans and began circling the Tengu cautiously, swinging the cans back so that they could slosh as much fuel over the creature as possible. The Tengu didn't even flinch, but kept walking slowly and deliberately across the lobby toward the reception counter. Skrolnik and Calsbeek retreated from the counter, and climbed clumsily around the edge of the ornamental pool to keep as much distance between themselves and the Tengu as they possibly could.

The Tengu hesitated for a second or two, confused by their movement. Then Skrolnik saw the tiny foxfires glittering around its severed neck again, and it swung toward them, its hands still extended, a grisly caricature of Frankenstein's monster. Skrolnik thought, *I'm going to wake up in a minute. I'm going to wake up and find that I'm late for breakfast. Oh, holy Jesus, please let me wake up in a minute. Or preferably sooner.*

Pullet reached across to the low coffee table in the middle of the waiting area and picked up a copy of *Los Angeles* magazine. He attempted to rip it in half, but because this was August, it was the 404-page restaurant-guide special, and he couldn't do it. "For Christ's sake," said Skrolnik. "Tear out individual pages, roll them up, make a torch."

Step by step, they backed off toward the open hospital

door. Evans and Guttierez splashed the last of the third
can of gasoline over the Tengu, until the creature was so
drenched that it gave off rippling fumes. Pullet had made
his torch now, and was lighting it with a book of matches.

The paper flared up. The Tengu suddenly made a
volent and unnervingy accurate rush toward them. The
ghostly blue fires around its shoulders roared up like a
locomotive roaring through a tunnel. Calsbeek said, "Oh,
shit," and collided with the doorframe as he tried to
scramble his way out. Skrolnik yelled, "*Throw the goddamned torch, Pullet!*"

Pullet threw it. It fell immediately to pieces and
fluttered into separate blazing pages. Skrolnik thought for
one dreadful second that Pullet had missed altogether, but
then a wayward draft from the open door blew one of the
burning pages up against the Tengu's chest.

The Tengu stumbled toward them, arms outstretched,
groping for them, but then the burning paper ignited the
gasoline on its chest and fanned a pattern of orange flames
across its ribcage. There was a dull, breathy, thumping
noise, and the gasoline that Calsbeek's two officers had
splashed into the Tengu's lungs and stomach through its
wide-open neck exploded, and blew chunks of flaming
flesh across the hospital patio.

The Tengu staggered, burning fiercely from thighs to
shoulders. It took one slow step forward, then another,
even though Skrolnik could see right through its charred
ribs to where the fire was blazing inside its chest, and its
bones were crackling and popping with heat.

Unnerved, Calsbeek fired off two shots, but they made
no impression on the Tengu at all. It stood where it was,
fiery and defiant, a walking corpse that refused to bow
down, even to immolation. It was only when the flesh of
its thighs had actually burned through to the femur that it
spun around and collapsed onto the paving stones with a
noise of flaring fat.

Skrolnik limped closer, and stood over the guttering
body with horror and relief. As the flesh burned away from

the neck and upper cheset, the ax blade suddenly dropped onto the patio with a clunk, and he jerked back in involuntary shock.

Calsbeek was calling harshly on his radio for reinforcements, so that the hospital could be screened off. The hospital administrator, with a great deal of shouting and bustling about, had already arranged for the patients to be moved to different rooms, away from the intensive-care unit where Admiral Thorson had been murdered. The night was echoing with whooping choruses of sirens, and the trees around the hospital were alight with the flashing of red-and-white police beacons.

At last Calsbeek came over and stood beside Skrolnik with an expression that put Pullet in mind of a cartoon bulldog who has discovered that bones can fly. "I don't know how the hell I'm going to report this," he said. "I've already filed a memorandum saying the guy's dead. Now I've got to file another one saying he came to life again, and we killed him for a second time."

Skrolnik watched the Tengu's corpse sputter and glow, and the ashes blow away in the evening wind.

"Shit," he said, and limped back to his car, followed by a silent Pullet.

CHAPTER TWELVE

The *Los Angeles Times* carried the headline ADMIRAL SLAIN BY 'DEAD' KILLER—ASSASSIN, 'FATALLY' SHOT BY POLICE, REVIVES TO FINISH OFF THWARTED MURDER MISSION.

Mack Holt read the story carefully, sniffing from time to time, and then passed the newspaper back to Jerry Sennett with a shrug. "I agree with you. It sounds like this Tengu stuff is all true, and it's happening here. But what am *I* supposed to do about it? I cared for Sherry, you know that. I really cared about her a lot. But it's not my responsibility, any of it. I mean, what moral justification can there possibly be for me to attack some farm somewhere, out at Pacoima, and start shooting up a whole lot of Japanese I've never even met?"

Jerry pointed to the penultimate paragraph in the news story. "Sgt. Skrolnik revealed that certain Japanese artifacts, including two samurai swords, had been discovered close to the scene of the crime. He expressed the opinion that they were directly linked to the murder of Admiral Thorson, although he was not yet prepared to say how or why."

Mack settled back on his saggy sofa and crossed his ankles. Olive was sitting beside him in a yellow UCLA T-shirt and nothing else, idly scratching and stroking at the blond curls at the back of his neck with her clawlike fingernails.

Jerry said empthatically, "The only two people the Tengus have tried to kill so far are Admiral Thorson—who's dead, at the second attempt—and me. As far as I know, Admiral Thorson and I were the only two surviving servicemen left in the entire United States who knew right from the very beginning, what the whole Appomattox mission was all about. And even *I* didn't know everything that was going on until the A-bomb had actually been dropped. There must be plenty of senior officers in the Naval Intelligence Command today who have access to the files on Appomattox; and I'm sure that successive Presidents have been alerted to what went on. But, as of last week, only two people in the whole damned country could have known *immediately* what was happening if they heard on the news about Japanese killers who were impervious to bullets, and had the strength of five men put together. Me, and Admiral Thorson. And that must be why they went for us."

"I still don't understand," said Olive, running a nail around Mack's earlobe. "Why should they want to kill you or something which happened such a long time ago? Supposing you *did* find out that someone had been making these Tengu-people? So what?"

"I don't know," said Jerry. "All I can guess is that they're intending to use the Tengus for something really spectacular. A bank robbery, maybe. Or maybe they want to assassinate the President. The President's supposed to be taking a vacation at Rancho Cielo next month, isn' he? Maybe it's some kind of weird retaliation against American trade restrictions on Japanese cars. I just don't have any idea. All I knnow is that they wanted both me and Admiral Thorson dead, presumably so that we couldn't tell any tales."

"Didn't Crowley know what was going on?" asked Mack.

Jerry shook his head. "He suspected there was more to the Tengu program than building up a team of body-guards, but he didn't have any coherent ideas about what it might be."

"You believe him?"

"I don't think I have much choice."

Mack said, "You really want us to help you break into that place, and rescue your son?"

Jerry pulled a noncommittal face. "I can't *force* you to help me."

"But that's really *dangerous*, man," said Olive. "Any one of you could get killed."

Jerry said, "It's a risk I've got to take. My son's in there and I've got to get him out. I can't see that I have any choice."

"You won't be much good to your son if you're dead," said Olive.

"No, I won't," Jerry agreed. "But the way Crowley sees it, they're intending to kill me anyway, and David, too, no matter what I do."

"You trust Crowley? The same guy that actually kid-napped your son?"

Jerry raised both hands in a gesture of mute acceptance.

Mack, with his arm around Olive, shook his head in disbelief—more at the fact that he was sitting here listening to what Jerry had to say, than at the absurdity of Japanese samurai possessed by ancient devils. "This whole thing's insane, you know. What can you possibly do about it, as a defenseless, untrained, private citizen? Your best choice is to call the police, and you know it. I mean, that's my advice, and you know what *I* feel about the police."

"Crowley said that David wouldn't stand a chance if I called the police."

"Kidnappers always say that," said Mack dismissively.

"How many kidnappings have *you* been involved in?" Jerry demanded.

"Well, none."

"Let's take this particular kidnapping on its own particular merits, then, shall we?" asked Jerry. "Crowley is my only contact; and whether he's lying to me or not, he's the only person who's suggested a way in which I might conceivably get David back unharmed."

Mack and Olive were silent for a while, uncertain of what to say. They saw before them a tired middle-aged man who had already lived through thirty-eight years of guilt for annihilating thousands of innocent men, women, and children; a man who secretly felt that he was solely responsible for turning nuclear theory into nuclear practice. Until he had said *go*, the idea of dropping an atomic bomb over a populated city had been no more than that: an idea. In the Chugoku Sanchi, alone, under a summer sky more than a third of a century ago, he had singlehandedly initiated the age of nuclear confrontation, an age which Mack and Olive took for granted because they had never known anything else, but which Jerry regarded as a Dark Age of his own making.

Now he was faced with an equally bitter choice over just one life: that of his only son, the only child he and Rhoda had conceived together. If Jerry himself were to die, David would never know from Jerry about all those times when his mother was young. He would never hear the explanations behind the photographs in Jerry's albums—this is the moment when your mother saw a goose chasing a woman across a barnyard in Massachusetts, that time just before you were born when we decided to take one last second honeymoon; this is the time a young black man offered to take our picture overlooking Niagara Falls, and took the best damned picture of two ordinary people in love that there ever was.

Mack said, "You really think Crowley's going to get you a machine gun?"

"He said he'd try. An M-60 and a couple of Ingrams."

Mack slowly shook his head. "This whole business is crazy."

At that moment, Maurice Needs appeared in the bedroom doorway, naked to the waist, scratching his head and yawning. "Boy, did I sleep good," he said, flexing muscle after muscle in turn. "Is there anything for breakfast? Eggs, maybe?"

"Eggs, he says," remarked Olive sarcastically. She climbed off the sofa, and stalked bare-bottomed to the kitchenette, watched with a mixture of pride and jealous annoyance by Mack. Jerry glanced after her, too, and then turned back to Mack and smiled.

"She's some woman, isn't she?" asked Maurice. "Dynamite. Doesn't care a two-bit shit for anybody."

"She loves her husband," Mack corrected him.

Maurice shrugged, with a big bunching of muscles. "Well, that's good. I always did believe in fidelity."

Jerry stood up and picked up his coat from the floor. The sleeves of his wrinkled gray shirt were rolled up, and the brown leather belt around his pants was cracked and worn. There was something defeated about him, which made Maurice look quickly over to Mack and frown, as if he were asking a question: Something's wrong here, what's happening?

Jerry said, "You know that if you don't help me I'll try to do this myself."

Mack said, "You're putting me in a position, aren't

you? You know, deliberately, you're putting me in a position.''

"What position? What? What are you talking about?'' asked Maurice.

Mack briefly, with expletives, explained about the Tengus, Gerard Crowley; and how David had been kidnapped. He also told about Gerard's offer of an M-60E1 and two or three Ingrams.

Maurice made a face. "An M-60? Jesus, that's a brute. My older brother used one in 'Nam. Six hundred rounds a minute. You could cut a guy in half with one of those.''

"He's offered one,'' said Jerry. "He's agreed to call me at eleven o'clock this morning to talk about delivery.''

"*I'll* come with you,'' said Maurice. "Jesus, what the hell. It's better than bending iron bars in a goddamned circus.''

Olive came into the room, holding a plate of scrambled eggs with bacon strips. "Do I pamper you or do I pamper you?'' she asked Maurice, setting the plate down on the table. Jerry couldn't help noticing the plump black lips of her vulva, shaved smooth and glossy as a King's Country plum. He thought: I'm in another age, another morality, another existence. He felt as if the atom bomb had obliterated for ever the world of zoot suits and Plymouth Road Kings and "Mairzy Doats,'' and beached him like the hero of some 1940's radio comedy on an unknown planet. He thought, my God, that's what Hiroshima did to me. It suspended me in 1945, a man in amber, and I don't think I've grown a day older since.

He said to Maurice, "Do you know something, there used to be a show called *Duffy's Tavern*, and every program started with this guy on the phone saying, 'Duffy's Tavern . . . Archie the manager speaking. Duffy ain't here. Oh, hello Duffy.' ''

Maurice stared at him, and nodded. "When was that?'' he asked, just to be polite. "I don't think I ever saw it.''

"Radio,'' said Jerry. "Sometime before you were born.''

"Oh," said Maurice.

The telephone rang. Mack said, "Answer it, will you, Olive?" but Olive was in the bedroom now, dressing. Mack picked the receiver up and said, "Duffy's Tavern . . . Archie the manager speaking."

There was a pause. Then Mack held the receiver out to Jerry, his face serious. "Did you give my number to Crowley?" he asked.

Jerry said, "I'm sorry. You know how urgent it is. I left a message on his recorder."

"Well, feel free," said Mack. "I just hope the guy isn't a psychopathic killer, like the rest of his friends."

Jerry took the phone and said, "Mr. Crowley?"

"That's right. I'm at the office right now. Did you hear the news?"

"Yes," said Jerry. "I'm not sure what it means."

"It means that this whole thing's falling apart, that's what. If there's something big in hand, they're going to try to do it quick, or else they're not going to try to do it at all. They're going to be pulling out of Pacoima within the week, believe me, and that means you've got to get your boy out of there just as soon as you can."

Jerry asked, "Have you told them you've been in touch with me?"

"I told them we've arranged a meet for later on today. I've told them you're willing to do any kind of a deal to get your son back, and that I should be able to cajole you back to the ranch."

"You've got the guns?"

"I've got the M-60 and six belts of ammunition, as well as two spare barrels, although you probably won't need them. I couldn't get any Ingrams, but I've got you a Canadian SMG and a couple of Browning high-power automatics."

"Sounds like enough for World War Three," said Jerry. Across the room, Mack raised his eyebrows and lit up a handrolled cigarette. Maurice was already mopping up the last of his egg.

"Just listen," said Gerard. "All the guns are in the trunk of a white Grand Prix, parked at the Chateau Marmont, on Sunset. All you have to do is go to the desk and ask for Mr. Wisby's keys. You got that? Mr. Wisby's keys. They'll give you the keys and you can go straight down to the parking lot and drive the car away. Then I'll meet up with you at the intersection of Van Nuys Boulevard and San Fernando Road, by the Whiteman Air Park, at three o'clock on the button. You with me? I'll be driving a Riviera, but I'll see you before you see me."

Jerry was silent. Then he said, "How do I really know that I can trust you?"

"You *don't* know," Gerard retorted. "But if someone gives you a heavy-duty machine gun and a heap of ammunition, and offers to help you get your son back, free of charge and with no strings attached except a good reference, well, that could be a sign that he isn't entirely antagonistic, wouldn't you say?"

Jerry said, "Okay. I'll meet you at three."

He handed the phone back to Mack, who hung it up and stared at him, with smoke blowing evenly out of his nostrils. "Well?" Mack asked him. "That sounded like all systems go."

"He's got the machine gun," said Jerry. "We're going out to Pacoima at three o'clock this afternoon."

Olive came in, wearing lemon-yellow jeans and a loose crocheted top. "Don't ask Mack to go with you," she said. "Please, I'm scared."

Maurice said, "*I'll* go. No problem. Just so long as I get to use the M-60. Can you imagine my brother's face when I tell him about it?"

"You probably won't *live* to tell him about it," said Olive.

"Aw, come on, Olive," grinned Maurice. "Where's your good old American sense of humor?"

"That's right, sweetheart," put in Mack. "Haven't you learned that it's *fun* to kill people, especially when they're of different racial origin? These are Japanese. We killed millions of them in World War Two. What's half a dozen more?''

Olive looked at him warily. "Don't tell me you're going, too?''

Mack puffed at his cigarette and nodded. "You think I'm going to let Maurice use an M-60, and I'm not even there?''

"But you said just a minute ago that—''

Mack stood up, and reached for his wornout cotton-twill jacket. "Forget what I said a minute ago. These guys killed Sherry, right? The least I can do is help to wipe them out.''

"Oh, *John Wayne*," said Olive sarcastically. "When I started going out with you, I thought I was getting into a free-and-easy laid-back Hollywood hanger-on situation, bed and avocado-burgers and a little late-night music. I didn't realize I was joining the Green Berets.''

"It's pronounced *berays*, not *barettes*," said Mack, kissing her on the forehead. "And, believe me, I'll stay way out of trouble.''

"Do you have to go *now*?" Olive wanted to know. "It's only eleven-thirty.''

Jerry said, "I think it would be a good idea if we all went around to my place and picked up some maps. I'd like to go get my own gun, too, in case of problems.''

Olive lowered her eyes. "All right. If that's the way you want it. But I can't guarantee that I'm going to be here when you get back. *If* you get back.''

"*Sweetheart*," Mack appealed.

"Sweetheart my fanny," retorted Olive.

"You see what being married to a sailor does to a girl?'' asked Mack.

CHAPTER THIRTEEN

Outside, in the sunshine, Detective Arthur was standing beside Jerry's car, his notebook tucked under his arm, inhaling violently from a Dristan nasal spray.

"Good morning, officer," said Jerry. "How's the allergy?"

"Worse," said Arthur. "Some other damned plant has started pollinating now. It's killing me. And yesterday they gave me a case near a eucalyptus grove."

"What can I do for you today?" asked Jerry.

"Sergeant Skrolnik wanted you to know that Lieutenant Edward Smith is assuming overall direction of the Sherry Cantor case, after that thing out at Rancho Encino last night. Sergeant Skrolnik was out there himself, twisted his ankle or something. Now he's hobbling around like an alligator with a jalapeño pepper up its ass. Having to report to Lieutenant Smith isn't helping his temper much, either."

Jerry asked, "Is there anything else? I was just about to go home."

"Well," said Detective Arthur, wiping his nose again and then opening up his notebook, "Sergeant Skrolnik did want to ask you if knew anything about some sort of Japanese ritual where you have two blue-and-white porcelain bowls . . . that's what he's written down here in my notebook . . . and two crossed samurai swords. The bowls are supposed to contain some sort of stuff like ash or incense."

Jerry frowned. "It isn't like anything that *I've* ever heard of. But I'm not an expert on Japan. I was just there during the war and the occupation."

"He wanted you to think about it, that's all. He also asked me to advise you not to leave town, not for a day or two."

"So Sergeant Skrolnik thinks there's some kind of connection between Sherry Cantor's murder and Admiral

Thorson's murder?" asked Jerry. "Some kind of Japanese connection?"

Detective Arthur put away his notebook, and spent a long time trying to push the clip of his ballpen into the torn lining of his inside pocket. "The guys who tried to knock off Admiral Thorson were all Japanese except one, who was an unidentified Caucasian. Three of them were killed: one by security guards at the hospital, one by police, and one by this unknown Caucasian."

Jerry asked, "The killer who was supposed to have come to life again and killed Admiral Thorson last night—he was Japanese, too?"

"That's what I said. They were all Japanese except one unidentified Caucasian."

"It doesn't say in the *Times* that he was Japanese."

Arthur sniffed, and shook his head. "If you want to know the truth, Skrolnik's playing the whole thing so tight to the chest that *nobody* knows what's going on. I can tell you something, though, a few heads are going to roll for what happened out at Rancho Encino last night. A killer was supposed to be dead and he wasn't? He actually got out of the morgue and attacked his victim for the second time? I'm glad *I* wasn't in charge, believe me. Poor old Harry Calsbeek's been put on suspension—he was the officer responsible. They'll probably bust him without a pension; and Skrolnik's not much safer, either. They'd probably suspend him, too, if they had the manpower."

"What's Skrolnik doing now?" asked Mack.

"Putting the shit up the whole Japanese ethnic community, that's what," said Detective Arthur. "He's got foot patrols going around to every *sushi* bar, every teriyaki joint, every tempura restaurant, you name it. There isn't a *tatami* mat in town that's going to go unturned. He's already had complaints from the Japanese community-relations people. They still remember what we did to the Issei and the Nisei during the war. But the guy's desperate. Two spectacular buchery cases and nothing to show for it. He's even been around to the Japanese Culture

Department at UCLA, asking about those porcelain bowls and those swords. If it's got anything to do with Japan, Skrolnik's going to shake it down. Karate clubs, flower-arranging classes—he's hitting them all.''

Jerry turned back to Mack and raised his eyebrows. Mack shrugged noncommittally. They'd just have to hope that Skrolnik didn't locate the ranch out at Pacoima before this afternoon.

Jerry said to Detective Arthur, "I'll keep in touch, okay? Right now I'm going home. If I can think what those bowls and swords were all about, I'll call you.''

Detective Arthur went back to his car. Maurice said to Jerry, "Do you actually know what those bowls and swords could have been?''

"I don't have any idea," said Jerry. "But Nancy Shiranuka may know. Perhaps if you guys could go pick up the car with the guns on it, and drive it back to my house, you could drop me off at Alta Loma Road on the way, so that I can talk to her.''

They climbed into Jerry's Dodge, with Maurice taking up most of the rear seat. Jerry heard the suspension groan as El Krusho made himself comfortable.

Jerry drove to Alta Loma Road and parked outside Nancy Shiranuka's apartment house. "If I'm not back out again in two or three minutes, just drive off and get the Grand Prix," he told Mack. "And for Christ's sake, be careful. I don't want Olive's worst fears to come true.''

"Me neither," said Mack, sliding across behind the wheel.

Jerry went up to Nancy's apartment and pressed the bell. After a little while, he heard the slap of her slippers on the polished wood floor, and she opened the door herself. "Jerry," she said, with mild surprise. "Why don't you come in? I'm on the telephone.''

Jerry took off his shoes and followed her into her serene living room. He sat down on a *zabuton* and waited while Nancy spoke in Japanese to someone who was obviously a girlfriend of hers.

"Well," she said when she had finished. "I didn't expect you back so soon."

"I saw Gerard Crowley yesterday."

"He told me. He also told me what he plans to do."

"What do you think about it?" asked Jerry.

"About attacking the Tengus? I think it is very dangerous. But there are ways of protecting yourself."

"You think it's better not to call the police?"

Nancy nodded. "The *Oni* at the ranch would kill your son and everyone else if they even so much as glimpsed a police car or a uniform."

"You say there are ways of protecting ourselves?"

"Of course. The world is populated by good *kami* as well as black *kami*. It is possible to invoke their help against any of the demons, including Tengu."

"How?" asked Jerry.

Nancy said, "The greatest protection of all is the bond between two people who have been physically and mentally unified. The apotropaic spirit of that bond can be contained in any token or artifact that belongs to the person with whom you have joined. Do you have a lover?"

Jerry blew out a little tight breath of anxiety. "No," he said. "Not exactly. There was only Rhoda, my wife, and as you know she's—well, you know what happened."

Nancy looked at Jerry with those dark, liquid eyes and said nothing. Jerry tugged at his leg, in an attempt to tuck it under himself Japanese-style, but his knee was too stiff. He said, "Out of practice. Out of practice in lots of things, I guess."

Nancy said, "The bond must necessarily be with a living person. Once the person is dead, his *kami* has left for another plane of life altogether, beyond the gates of heaven."

"Then I guess I'll just have to do without it. I haven't been with anyone since Rhoda."

Nancy thought for a moment or two, and then stood up. "Come," she said, and held out her hand for him. He stared at her, uncertain of what it was that she expected of him. But then he took her hand, climbed up off the *zabuton*, and followed her along the corridor to a plain, wood-floored anteroom. Its walls were hung with a collection of five erotic woodblocks in the style of Kiyomitsu, beautifully dressed Japanese women in flowing silk robes, their clothes only slightly lifted or parted to vreveal the huge gnarled penises that were penetrating their vaginas.

Without a word, Nancy loosened Jerry's necktie, and began deftly to unbutton his shirt. Jerry stayed still, his hands by his sides, watching her with a feeling of unreality but also, for the first time since he had heard that David had been kidnapped, a feeling of peace. As he had noticed the last time he had visited her, Nancy had an extraordinary quality of inner tranquility, a calm that reminded him of the still lake around the Gold Pavilion in Nara, of walking along the little alley called the Path of Philosophy by the Old Canal in Nanzenji, when the rows of cherry trees silently blizzarded their blossoms into the water.

In a matter of moments, with humility but also with dignity, Nancy had stripped him naked. His penis rose higher with every heartbeat. She ran her hands down his bare chest, making him shiver, and down his thighs. Then she loosened her own pale-pink silk robe and let it slide on to the polished floor. She was slim and small-breasted, naked except for an embroidered ribbon of white silk that was fastened around her waist and between her legs, tied so tight that it disappeared into the cleft of her sex.

She untied the ribbon, and drew it off herself, to reveal that it had been keeping in place, inside her, a miniature jade figure of a baldheaded deity carrying a peach, the symbol of the female vulva. Without comment, she set the figurine aside, and then took Jerry's hand and led him into the bathroom.

Under a sharp, needling shower, Nancy soaped his shoulders, his back, and his buttocks. She cupped his balls in her hand for a moment, while she soaped up and down the shaft of his erection; but not for too long. The true stimulation would come later. Then she stood with her eyes closed, her long dark hair spreading wet across her shoulders, as Jerry slowly and firmly lathered her back, her breasts, and her slender thighs. The water dribbling between her legs turned her dark heart-shaped pubic hair into a tail.

Afterward, fresh and dried, they closed themselves in the bedroom, where a large soft *futon* lay on the floor. Nancy insisted that Jerry close his eyes and lie on his back. She massaged him with lightly scented oil, and spoke to him monotonously and matter-of-factly about the mystical power of yin and yang, the sexual union; and of the nutritive powers which wise men could gain from drinking "the medicine of the three mountain peaks" from the women they couple with. The first juice was the juice of the Red Lotus Peak, saliva from the tongue; the second juice was from the Double Lotus Peak, milk from the breasts; the third was the most nourishing juice of all, and should be imbibed by men in the greatest quantities possible, the precious juice of the Mysterious Geteway.

Jerry lay back on the *futon*, feeling Nancy's fingers working at his muscles, feeling her naked skin against his, and although his anxiety for David never left him, it became tempered with a new determination, more resolute and more balanced. He began to feel that if he had gone to Nancy Shiranuka for help, instead of his shrink, he might have forgotten Hiroshima years ago.

At last, with exceptional elegance, as beautifully curved as a bamboo-brush painting, Nancy lifted herself over him, and took his penis in her hand, so that she could couch it in the slippery curves of her vulva, and, with a musical sigh, sink down on him, so deeply that she trembled with a sensation that was part pleasure and part shock.

She was like no other woman, Caucasian or Oriental, that Jerry had ever slept with. She seemed to give herself to him totally, surrender her pride and her personality without any reservation whatsoever. She rose up and down on him as if she were conjuring the very soul out of him, through his penis; and at the instant of his first climax she withdrew herself, only by a fraction of an inch, so that they could both witness the jets of semen anointing her open lips.

They were locked together in the bedroom for an hour and a half, and during that time she brought him to three climaxes, opening her body up to him in every possible way. Yet, when it was finished and she lay next to him on the *futon* smoking a cigarette, he felt as if he had been through a mystical rather than a physical experience. He understood now what she had meant about the bond between two living people, the knot tied between their spirits, as if every movement had twisted one silken cord around another, as if each act of intimacy had tightened the ties.

When they were quiet again, when their breathing was gentle and even, Jerry said, "There's something else I have to ask you."

Nancy lay beside him, her face so close that he could scarcely focus on it. He'd been growing increasingly far-sighted with age, and he found that he was reading newspapers at arm's length these days. Eyeglasses, bridgework, baldness—how the human body decayed. Nancy didn't know how much of a gift of youthfulness she had given him by making love to him this afternoon.

"The police say they found two bowls and two samurai swords out at Rancho Encino Hospital. Blue porcelain bowls, containing incense or ash. And the swords were crossed. They've drawn the obvious inference that they were part of some sort of Japanese ritual, but they don't know what, and neither do I."

Nancy was silent, stroking Jerry's shoulder. Then she said, "The police shot and mortally wounded the Tengu who was sent to kill Admiral Thorson the night before last. It would have required a magical ceremony close to the Tengu's body to draw back the demon and revive the Tengu. The ceremony with the bowls and swords is called

the Hour of Fire. It directs the Tengu back toward the
dead meat of his previous host, and encourages him to
bring it back to life again. A Tengu can be revived even if
he has been burned to ashes. The Hour of Fire is specifically forbidden, not only by the priests of Shrine Shinto
themselves, but, by secret agreement, by the Japanese
police. Anyone who is thought to be trying to perform the
ritual of the Hour of Fire is arrested and imprisoned, and
usually meets with a fatal accident while in police
custody.''

''They take it *that* seriously?''

''They take the Tengu seriously,'' Nancy corrected him.
''The Tengu is the darkest of all Japanese demons because
he thrives on the weakness and corruption of the human
soul. The purer the soul that the Tengu can corrupt, the
greater the social and ethical damage to Japanese society,
and the greater the Tengu's increasing strength. The
company boss who takes a bribe after twenty years with a
spotless record; the hardworking man who decides to steal;
the woman who murders her husband—they are all victims
of the Tengu. Has it never occurred to you why Japanese
society is structured like it is? Why large companies act so
paternally and protectively to their workers? They are
shielding the people for whom they are responsible from
the madness and violence that the Tengu always brings
with him; the madness of war, the madness of murder, the
madness of cruelty. The Tengu has affected Japanese
thinking for hundreds of years. *I* believe it, no matter how
much you smile at me. Some Japanese learned to control
his influence: the samurai warriors, for instance were
always balancing between strict morality and utter violent
insanity. They courted possession by the Tengu, and
hoped that they could control him. But the Tengu
eventually brought Japan to war with the United States,
which was the ultimate madness, politically and
historically and socially. Japan recovered, but the Tengu
lives on, and always will, to haunt and taint the Japanese
spirit. You must forgive us for many things, Jerry. We are
a people possessed.''

It was nearly a quarter to two when Jerry dressed again, and called a cab to take him back to Orchid Place. Nancy had warmed him a little deluxe saké, the saké with the gold leaf floating in it, and they sat facing each other in the living room, drinking and enjoying each other's satisfaction and warmth.

At last, she opened her sleeve, and gave him a small porcelain box, decorated with erotic paintings and perforated with elaborate holes.

"What's this?" he asked her, turning it over and over.

"That is your keepsake for what we did today. That is your talisman. It will help to protect you. All you have to do is have faith in it, and have faith in the joining-together we achieved this afternoon."

He said, "If I thought that it was possible for a man to fall in love with a woman after meeting her only twice, I'd say that it has just happened to me."

Nancy smiled. "I have loved too many men, and been used by too many men. I have become because of my many experiences the *symbol* of a woman, rather than an individual woman whom you could love as a mistress or a wife. Would you really like to kiss every morning as you leave for work the lips of a woman who has fellated a whole forest of penises, white, black, and yellow? Would you really like to make love to a body that has been used and abused so many thousands of times? Sex to me has become something spiritual, something close to the very heart of the meaning of my existence. It is no longer a way of forming an attachment with one man. I don't care if I have one man or many men. All that I care about now is understanding my life, and reaching the peaks of sensory excitement that help me to do so."

Jerry looked at her without speaking for almost a minute. Then he looked down at the porcelain box she had given him and asked, "Can you tell me what this is?"

"It's a cricket cage," she said. "Chinese ladies used to catch singing crickets and put them inside, and then store the cages inside their sleeves, so that wherever they went walking in their gardens, they were accompanied by the singing of crickets."

"There's no cricket in it now," said Jerry.

"No," said Nancy. "But instead I have put inside it something even more attractive, and protective. A *koban*-sized *shunga* print, a *kachi-e*, a victory picture for you to carry into your conflict. It shows a highborn lady having intercourse with her lover in front of a mirror. It is by Shunchō, and it was printed in the mid-1780's, as one of a series called *Koshuku-zue júni-kō*. It represents the acts which you and I have performed this afternoon, and it will guard your life against the Tengu."

Jerry held up the cricket cage in his hand. "I wish I could believe that."

"You *must* believe it. If you doubt it, think to yourself: Why did this woman who is almost a total stranger make love to me today, if it were not to form a bond of strength against the demon?"

Jerry looked at his wristwatch, the same gold wristwatch they had given him when he left the Navy. His prize for bombing Hiroshima. He said, "I have to go now."

Nancy held his wrist and placed his hand inside her silken robe, against her breast, so that he could feel her nipple rising against the palm of his hand. "I come from the *ukiyo-machi*," she said. "You must never think of me as a lover, but only as a bond. Someone with whom you formed a sexual and a mystical union."

Jerry leaned forward to kiss her, but she turned her head to one side. "When you have defeated the Tengu," she said, "come back here at once and drink your fill of the juice of the Mysterious Gateway, to restore your strength. Until then, you should thirst."

Jerry went to the door and opened it. "You're a very strange and beautiful person," he told her. He felt moved by what had happened to him in the past two hours. Nancy remained where she was, striped by the brilliant sunshine through her venetian blinds, her black hair shining, one breast still bare.

The cab was waiting for him. Jerry said, "Eleven Orchid Place, please."

CHAPTER FOURTEEN

Gerard was shrugging on his coat, and reaching for his keys and his pen, when Francesca came back into the office from lunch. "Gerard," she said, "you didn't tell me you were going out."

Gerard gave her an evasive grin. "Listen, I won't be long, okay? I have to see Chatfield about those Dutch cigars."

"Henry Chatfield called yesterday. It's all cleared up. He's probably back in New York by now."

Gerard stared at her coldly. "Listen," he said, "if I have to see Chatfield about those cigars, then I have to see Chatfield about those cigars. You understand me? Jesus Christ, you're not my wife."

Francesca raised her head a little and looked at Gerard through long, mascaraed lashes. "Gerard," she said, "I have to know where you're going."

"I'm going out, okay? Out of the door and along the corridor and down to the parking lot, and out."

Francesca said, as gently as she could manage, "That's not enough."

"What do you mean, 'That's not enough?' What are you talking about?"

Francesca sat down, crossing her long artificially suntanned legs. She looked Gerard directly in the eye, with a look he hadn't seen before. Almost *official*. She said, "This morning you went to the Avis desk at the airport and rented a white Pontiac Grand Prix in the name of Hudson Foss. Afterward, you drove to a lock-up garage in Westwood, which is rented from Westwood Star Properties by someone who calls himself P. B. Sexton. That garage contains a number of contraband items, including video equipment, pornographic viedeotapes and magazines, cocaine, whiskey, vodka, men's apparel, and weapons, one of which was an M-60E1 machinegun complete with ammunition and spare barrels."

Gerard was silent as Francesca continued. "You were

seen to load the M-60 machine gun and other weapons into the trunk of the Grand Prix, and then drive it to the Chateau Marmont hotel on Sunset Boulevard, where you checked into one of the bungalows in the name of Wisby. Then you immediately caught a cab and came back here.''

Gerard looked down at the polished surface of his leather-topped desk, and then back up at Francesca. All of a sudden, he saw what she was. Hard, certainly: but with that implacable well-trained hardness of a law-enforcement officer. Aquisitive, yes, but only for facts and figures and damning information. A gold digger who was digging for convictions, not diamond bracelets. She had gone to bed with him not for himself but for evidence. Everything he had boasted about, every extravagant gift he had bought her—it had all gone down in a notebook somewhere, to be given as meticulous information for the prosecution when he was eventually brought to court.

"Well," he said, "it seems like I've made quite a fool of myself."

Francesca said, "You can still save yourself a lot of trouble if you tell me what's going on. You're involved in something, aren't you, with Mr. Esmeralda? Something more than forming a team of karate bodyguards."

Gerard struck a match and slowly began to feed a cigar. "What are you?" he asked her. "U.S. Customs? What?"

Francesca didn't answer. All she said was, "There's only one way you can save yourself, Gerard. You have to tell me what's going on."

Gerard asked, "You've reported any of this? The guns? Do your bosses know what's going on?"

"They will."

"They *will*, huh?"

"I have a certain amount of discretionary power when I'm operating undercover in the field."

Gerard slowly shook his head, like a man who has watched his favorite hockey team let in eleven goals in a row. "So, going to bed with me was 'operating in the field,' was it? I'm glad to know that romance is not yet dead."

"You've been running guns and you've been smuggling narcotics," said Francesca. "You've also been dealing in industrial and military information. You didn't really expect the CIA not to show *some* interest in you, did you? You're not that modest?"

"I don't think modesty has much to do it," said Gerard frostily. There was a feeling inside of him like boiling oxygen, the kind of freezing steam that surrounds a rocket just beore its launch. "I was actually stupid enough to believe that you were my lover. I run a few deals, sure. You know that. You've helped me to organize some of them. A caper here and a caper there. Something to keep the cashflow flowing. But is it really worth *this*? Is it really worth your sleeping with me, pretending to love me, taking me away from my wife? Wouldn't you call than entrapment? Well, maybe you wouldn't. It seems like your morality is a whole lot different from mine."

"Gerard, I have to know what the guns are for."

Gerard shook his head. "No, Francesca, you don't have to know what the guns are for. You're going to get the hell out of this office, and get the hell out of my life, and if I ever set eyes on you anywhere near me again, I'm going to bang you one right in the nose. You understand me?"

"Do you want me to have you arrested?" asked Francesca. "I can do that just by picking up the phone."

"Go on, then," said Gerard. "Pick up the phone."

Francesca stayed where she was. "Gerard," she said, "you're making this too difficult."

"It's easy," Gerard told her. He lifted up the receiver and held it out to her. "Here it is. Dial. Have me arrested."

"Gerard—"

Gerard slammed the phone down again. He was furious, shaking with temper. "You dumb bitch! Either bust me or leave me alone! If you've got the goddamned nerve to go to bed with me, at least have the goddamned nerve to finish the job and pull me in!"

"Gerard, I need to know about Esmeralda. I need to know about the guns."

"Well, fuck you," shouted Gerard, "because I'm not going to tell you anything about either of them without a formal arrest and without a lawyer. And if you're not going to arrest me, or question me formally, then you can get the hell out of here because you're *fired*, as my secretary, and right now you're trespassing."

Francesca stood up. "All right," she said. "Don't say that I didn't give you a fair chance."

"If your name never passes my lips again, baby, that'll be far too often for me. Now, out."

Francesca hesitated for a moment, looking at him, trying to appeal to him. But he rammed his hands into his trouser pockets and stalked to the window, staring out over the Avenue of the Stars and smoking his cigar in steady, furious puffs.

She said, "It wasn't all business, Gerard. I can't turn around now and say that I wasn't fond of you, or that you weren't any good in bed. You're selfish, and you're distant, but you know how to give a woman what she wants."

Gerard said nothing, but continued to puff at his cigar.

"So long, then" said Francesca.

She opened the office door, and it was then that the Tengu burst in, half tearing the door off its hinges, knocking Francesca right back against Gerard's desk, sprawling over the top of it in a shower of calendars, pens, photographs, paper clips, and letters. She didn't even have time to scream.

Gerard shouted, "*Who the f—!*" but then he saw the white Nō mask, the brutally scarred, half-naked body, the wealth of snake and dragon tattoos, and a sensation of utter cold dread soaked through him like ice water soaked up by blotting paper. He knew what it was all about. He knew why the Tengu was here. Esmeralda had sent it around to silence him, and to punish him for his failure in arranging the death of Jerry Sennett and Admiral Thorson. The deal was up, the game was over. He had been right from the very start. Esmeralda had particularly selected him and Nancy Shiranuka and all the rest of the team because they were dispensable, murderable, easily disposed of at the end of the day's work.

Panting heavily behind his mask, the Tengu circled the office and stalked toward him. Gerard backed off, reaching for the wall behind him, his cold eyes darting from side to side, calculating, checking distances, looking for any way to get out. Francesca was climbing slowly to her feet, dazed, her skirt torn open to the waist.

Gerard moved round behind his desk, keeping his eyes on the Tengu all the time. He coaxed open the top right-hand drawer, and there was his .357 Python revolver. He curled his finger into the drawer and hooked the gun out by the trigger guard.

Francesca screamed, "Gerard!" as the Tengu made a sudden and inexorable rush toward him. Gerard cocked his revolver, held it high with both hands, and fired. The bullet went right through the Tengu's chest in a splatter of blood, and the impact of it made the Tengu stagger. But it raised its masked face, with a question mark of its own blood splashed onto one cheek, and kept coming toward him, more slowly, more cautiously, but just as threateningly.

Gerard raised his revolver once again and carefully squeezed off a shot at close range, into the Tengu's face. The bullet was fired so near that the varnish on the Tengu's Nō mask was burned black on one cheek by flaring gunpowder. From the neat hole in the papier-mâché, the slug must have drilled straight into his left cheekbone. But still the Tengu kept coming, grunting with pain and effort, and it was clear to Gerard that nothing would stop it. Hadn't Mr. Esmeralda told him, with a warm smile, that the Tengu were unstoppable?

Tense, sweating, Gerard reached for the arm of his high-backed leather swivel chair and drew it cautiously between himself and the Tengu. The Tengu raised his hands, ready to seize Gerard and tear him to pieces. Francesca said, in a high, almost hysterical voice, "Gerard, what shall I do? Gerard, *tell me what to do*!"

Gerard didn't listen to her. Instead, he pulled back his chair as far as he could against his legs and gripped it as tightly as possible, until white spots showed on his knuckles. He licked his lips, his mouth dry, judging his moment, judging his distance.

"Francesca," warned Gerard, "move away from the window. Get over toward the door."

Francesca, panicking, said, "What?"

"Just do what I tell you, get away from the window."

But then it was too late. The Tengu rushed forward, and Gerard couldn't think about anything but shoving his chair toward it as fast and as powerfully as he could, catching the Tengu right in the knees, sweeping it into the rolling castored chair with the sheer momentum of his desperate forward run; half wheeling, half forcing the Tengu clear across the room and driving him straight into the floor-to-ceiling window at a careering, uncontrolled pace, right into the net curtains, until there was an awesome creaking of glass, and then an explosive shatter. The Tengu hurtled straight out into the afternoon sky, followed by the black leather chair, and both dropped 27 floors, 332 feet, the Tengu spread-eagled, surrounded by glittering tumbling glass, and taking slightly less than four seconds to hit the ground. They heard the bang of flesh against concrete, even from so far up, and the clatter of the chair.

Francesca held Gerard very tight, clinging, almost clawing. Her face was so tense that it was ugly. Time passed, thirty seconds, a minute.

"Gerard," she said.

Gerard covered his mouth with his hand. Then he said, "Listen. I know what you think you've got to do. I know you're supposed to arrest me, and all of that. But just give me twelve hours. Can you do that? You've given me plenty of rope until now. Give me twelve hours more."

Francesca said, in a jumbled voice, "I don't love you, you know. I don't love you enough to want to stay with you."

"Francesca, I just want the *time*."

She released her grip. The sound of police and ambulance sirens was already echoing across the plaza below them. The wind billowed the nets and sent letters headed CROWLEY TOBACCO IMPORTS snowstorming across the room. "All right," she said. "But call me tomorrow morning, when you've done whatever it is you have to do. Don't fail me, Gerard, because if you do, I'll have to send them out looking for you, and you know they'll find you. They may even kill you."

Gerard said nothing, but went to his desk and took out a handful of cigars, which he pushed into his inside pocket. He gave Francesca one last look, and then he walked out the torn-open door, and through the reception area. In the corridor, he met two breathless policemen.

"Hey, did you see which office that guy fell out of?" one of the cops asked him.

Gerard pointed two doors down, along the corridor, HERMAN & GUBLENIK, ATTORNEYS AT LAW. "I think it was that one," he said. "Those two are always fighting, Herman and Gublenik. It wouldn't surprise me if one of them pushed the other out of the window. Either Gublenik or Herman, who knows?"

"Okay, friend," said the cop, and went hurrying on.

Gerard walked along to the elevator, stepped in, and pressed the button for the lobby. When the doors closed, his eyes closed, too. Only his cold self-control prevented him from trembling like a newborn foal.

CHAPTER FIFTEEN

The ambulance had been quick, but Mr. Esmeralda, who had been parked in his limousine by the curb on the Avenue of the Stars, had been quicker. With one of Kappa's nameless Japanese to help him, he had shouldered his way through the crowds which had surrounded the Tengu's fallen body and dragged the Tengu off to his car. A man had protested, "I'm a doctor. You can't take that man off like that. The police are going to want to see him."

Mr. Esmeralda had smiled at the doctor, all teeth and Latin charm. "You must understand that *I* am this man's personal physician," he had lied. "If he had fallen from a window, it is necessary that I examine him before the police. Ethics, you know."

The doctor had started to protest again; but with a kick to the kidneys that was so fast that it was practically invisible, the *Oni* paralyzed the doctor where he stood, so that the doctor could do nothing but grasp in agony at his back and gasp for breath.

Sweating, Mr. Esmeralda had humped the Tengu's body into the back of his limousine, slammed the door, and driven off in a howling U-turn toward Santa Monica Boulevard. Just as he had reached the traffic signals, a Doheny Medical Services ambulance had come howling around the corner, its red lights flashing. Mr. Esmeralda had put his foot down and barged his way into the east-west traffic, provoking a chorus of very non-California hornblowing. Then he had roared off westward, as fast as he could, toward Eva Crowley's apartment.

Now Mr. Esmeralda glanced in his rearview mirror at the dead Tengu, propped up in the back seat, where Mr. Esmeralda himself used to sit, before Kappa had detained Kuan-yin as a hostage. Mr. Esmeralda had imagined when he was younger than when people fell from tall buildings, they were smashed into pieces; it was only when he had

seen *Life* magazine's celebrated picture of a 23-year-old
girl who had thrown herself 86 floors from the observation
deck of the Empire State Building, to lie peacefully and
apparently undamaged on the dented roof of a limousine,
that he had realized how peculiarly calm a death it was.
You fall, you stop falling. That was all.

It had been essential, however, for him to rescue the
Tengu's body before the police and ambulance arrived.
This was the last Tengu who was anything near to
readiness, and, as it was, Doctor Gempaku was going to
have to perform the Hour of Fire again to revive him. Considering they were supposed to attack the nuclear-power
station at Three Arch Bay at eight o'clock tomorrow night,
that didn't leave Doctor Gempaku very much time. Mr.
Esmeralda silently cursed Kappa and his penchant for
hiring the weak and corrupt and dispensable. But then he
thought: Kappa hired me for the same virtues, or lack of
them. Perhaps there is some method in his madness, after
all. It was doubtful whether anyone who wasn't weak and
corrupt and constantly live in fear of his life would ever
contemplate helping Kappa to destabilize a nuclear-power
station and extinguish half of California. To perform such
actions needed a particular kind of personality deficiency;
and while Gerard Crowley and Nancy Shiranuka and
Commander Ouvarov might all be dangerously inefficient
and unreliable, at least when the moment came to set off
the final explosion, they would none of them have serious
moral qualms. Nor did Mr. Esmeralda have any qualms
about killing them.

He was unsure what had happened to Gerard Crowley.
Perhaps the Tengu had killed Crowley before he fell from
the twenty-seventh floor, perhaps he hadn't. In any event,
there was no time to find out. It had been difficult enough
taking the Tengu into the building and up in the elevator,
draped in a long Mexican blanket to conceal his Nō mask
and his scarred body, an insane pantomime. Now all Mr.
Esmeralda wanted to do was get the Tengu back to
Pacoima Ranch.

There was only one stop he had to make, now that things were heating up so much, and that was to Eva Crowley's, to collect his living insurance policy. He pulled into the front driveway of the Crowleys' apartment building and said to the *Oni*, "Keep your head down. I won't be longer than five minutes."

Eva was still wrapped in a towel, fresh out of the shower, when Mr. Esmeralda rang the doorbell. Kelly and Kathryn were home, too, playing backgammon.

"Carlos," said Eva, surprised. "I didn't think I was going to see you until tomorrow."

"Well," said Mr. Esmeralda with an elasticated little smile, "you see me now. How soon can you get dressed?"

"Carlos, I'm sorry I can't go out—I have to meet some friends of mine for a bridal shower this afternoon, and the girls are coming with me."

Mr. Esmeralda glanced down at his gold wristwatch. "You have three minutes to put something on. Anything, a dress, a pair of slacks."

"Carlos, I've told you. I'm going out. Now, it's very good to see you. I'm delighted you came. Girls, Carlos is here, if you want to say hello. But really, Carlos—"

Mr. Esmeralda raised both his hands to silence her. "Please, Eva, listen to me. You have no choice. You have to come with me, right away; and the girls too."

Eva blinked in astonishment. She said, "How many times do I have to—"

Mr. Esmeralda reached to the waistband of his white tropical pants and brought out a small .32-caliber automatic. It was like a gesture out of a 1940's gangster movie.

"Put that away," Eva told him, shocked. "Carlos, how can you—?"

Mr. Esmeralda said, "Eva, my dear lady, you have two minutes to put on some clothes. If you are not dressed and ready to come with me by then, I will shoot you and kill you. Now, move."

Behind Eva, Kelly and Kathryn had now stood up, and were staring at Mr. Esmeralda and his gun with undisguised alarm. Mr. Esmeralda said, "If you do what I tell you, there is no personal danger. But, please, for your own sakes, be quick."

Kelly reached for the telephone, but Mr. Esmeralda swung his pistol around so that it was pointing directly at her. She froze.

"This is going to be my first and only warning," said Mr. Esmeralda. "I have killed people before, for being far less troublesome, and if you cause me any problems, I will not hesitate to kill *you*. Believe me. I also have to tell you that I am not going to explain why I am taking you with me, or for how long. So do not trouble to ask me; I will not answer you. All that I require from you is silence and obedience and calmness. Those three things are all that will protect you in some trying times."

Eva said, "I suppose it's no good appealing to your better nature."

"You are right," said Mr. Esmeralda. "I do not have a better nature."

CHAPTER SIXTEEN

They reached the perimeter fence of Pacoima Ranch shortly before four o'clock in the afternoon. It was warm and breezy in the hills, one of those golden California afternoons when the sun turns the grass to sparkling fire, and the mountains lie wrinkled and dry and orange as terra cotta under a dense blue sky. They had left the Little Tujunga Road, and driven out over rough country to the southeast side of the ranch, down a narrow and stony *arroyo secco*, and then up through a sloping grove of white firs. At last they halted beside a split-rail fence, and

Gerard stopped his Buick and climbed out. His first move was to light a fresh cigar.

"Well," he said, as Jerry and Mack and El Krusho got out of the white Grand Prix, and walked up the slope to join him, "this is the boundary. From here, it's going to be all on foot."

"How far are the ranch buildings from here?" asked Jerry.

"A mile, no more," said Gerard. "But they don't have any defenses at all on this side. It's steep, and it's difficult going, and in any case they're not looking for anybody to hit them. They may be nervous about the police, but the police have a way of storming right up to the front door. They certainly won't be expecting anybody to come creeping in from the side."

"If you say so," said Mack, who had taken a sharp dislike to Gerard Crowley from the moment he had first met him. Mack was not at all enthralled by men who smoked large cigars and dressed like loan sharks.

Gerard ignored him and turned to Maurice. "Do you think you can carry that M-60?" he asked. "It doesn't weigh more than twenty-five pounds. Mr. Holt, if you don't mind carrying the belt box."

Maurice, his muscles bulging under his tight white T-shirt, lifted the long-barreled M-60E1 machine gun out of the trunk of the Grand Prix and hoisted it over one shoulder, complete with its bipod. Mack reluctantly took the box of 7.62-mm. ammunition, while Jerry carried the Canadian SMG, a very light submachine gun rather like the old British Sterling, and three magazines of 9-mm. Parabellum bullets. Gerard stuffed the two Browning high-power automatics into the pockets of his suit.

They climbed over the split-rail fence and began to scale the hillside at an angle of 45 degrees. The mountain air, as they walked, became gradually cooler. Gerard at last drew up close to Jerry and said, "They tried to finish me off this afternoon. They sent a Tengu around to my office."

"What does that mean?" asked Jerry, wiping the sweat

from his face with his hand. "You've outgrown your use-fulness to them?"

"I guess. I didn't stop to find out."

"You got away from the Tengu?"

"I shoved him out a twenty-seven-story window."

Jerry raised his eyebrows, but said, "That doesn't necessarily mean you've seen the last of him."

Gerard looked at Jerry without any expression on his face. "A couple of weeks ago, I would have said you were pulling my leg. Now I know you're telling me the truth. Those damned Tengus are indestructible."

"Not *totally* indestructible," said Jerry. "That was why we dropped an A-bomb on them in the war."

Gerard took his cigar out of his mouth, and spat. "That's all we need, then? An A-bomb? You should have told me. I would have stocked up."

It was nearly five o'clock by the time they crested the ridge which overlooked Pacoima Ranch from the south-east. They sat among the scrub, sharing the water bottle Jerry had brought along, the same one he had used in the mountains of Japan, while Gerard briefly outlined the ranch buildings to them and pointed out the dilapidated barn where the Tengus were concealed.

"In my judgment," Gerard said, "someone has to go in there and lock all those reinforced doors, so that the Tengus can't be released. That will give us *half* a chance of storming the place successfully, at least. Now, Doctor Gempaku's quarters are over there, in the main farm-house; while your son, Jerry, is being held at the back of that outbuilding. My feeling is that you should take the SMG and go straight in there on your own, with the sole purpose of getting your son out. Leave the rest to us."

"How many Japanese guards are there?" asked Mack.

"It varies. Never fewer than five, often as many as seven. Then there's a cook and a housemaid. It would make life more pleasant if we didn't wipe *them* out as well, but for God's sake don't risk anything on their be-half. He who cooks for the devil should use a damn long ladle.''

They discussed the attack for nearly a quarter of an hour. Then Maurice and Mack carried the M-60 down toward the southern side of the ranch, keeping as close as they could to the scrubline, and positioned themselves behind an outcropping of rock about a hundred yards away from the main ranch buildings, well within the range of their machine gun, which could fire effectively for over three-quarters of a mile. Once they had settled, they waved back up the hill to Jerry and Gerard to show they were ready.

"I'll go down and see if I can lock the Tengus in," said Gerard. "You skirt around the back and see what you can do to get your son out of there. The signal for the attack to start will be three quick pistol shots, one after the other. Then we just go in there, giving them everything we've got."

Jerry said, "You didn't have to do this, did you?"

"What do you mean?" asked Gerard.

"You didn't have to help me rescue my son."

Gerard took out one of his automatics and checked the clip. "I'm doing this for myself," he said. "If I don't waste these people now, they're going to be after me for the rest of my life. I don't know who they are, or what they're into, but they're the kind of people who never let go."

Jerry said, "Are you really such a self-centered shit?"

Gerard got to his feet and smiled. "Yes," he said. "When it comes down to it, we're all busy looking after number one, aren't we? And don't tell me that sons and wives and lovers don't count as number one, too. You look after your own. That's what *you're* doing here, and that's what *I'm* doing here."

It was 5:18. Without saying anything else, Gerard tossed away his cigar and made his way down the eastern side of the slope that led toward the ranch. Jerry watched him for a while, with extraordinarily mixed feelings—part anxiety, part confusion—and then cocked his machine gun and slid and skated down the stony slope himself, circling even farther to the east.

There was no sign of life in the ranch, no clue that it was being used to develop the most brutal warriors that the world had ever known; nor that it was being guarded by armed and fanatical men. It could have been a quiet, normal, Tujunga horse ranch late on a summer afternoon; the kind of place where Roy Rogers might have tethered Trigger, or Rin-Tin-Tin might have returned home for his Gravy Train. Jerry ducked low as he ran through the thorn-bushes toward the outbuilding where David was being held, feeling surprisingly self-conscious with his machine gun. He wondered fleetingly what he would do if someone stopped him and challenged him: how he would explain the fact that he was running around on private property with a very lethal weapon. But then he looked quickly down toward the barn, and saw Gerard Crowley dodging toward the open door with an automatic raised in his right hand, and he knew that what they were doing was not only deadly serious but deadly. Nobody was going to stop him and ask him what he was doing. They would probably shoot first.

Down in the barn, Gerard stepped quickly and nervous-ly toward the prefabricated building where the Tengus were kept, his pistol held high, his eyes wide, his whole body wired with tension. He ran up the steps to the door-way of the prefabricated building and tried the handle. It was locked, which meant that Doctor Gempaku was not inside. He swung back the two lock covers, and then went back down the steps to scoop up a handful of dirt and gravel from the barn floor. Spitting on the dirt to make it more pliable, he pressed it into the locks, liberally mixed with gravel and grit, so that Doctor Gempaku would never be able to get his key inside—at least, not in a hurry. The Tengus would never be able to get out, either. That door was four solid inches of carbonized steel.

Once he had jammed up the locks, Gerard ran the length of the prefabricated building until he reached the far end, where the electric cables ran inside to power the air-conditioning and lights. The ideal conditions for imbuing a man's soul with the evil *kami* of the Tengu were 55 degrees of cold and an atmosphere low on oxygen. In the ancient magical days of the samurai, warriors had opened up their souls and their minds to the Tengu by sitting on the upper slopes of Shirane-san, overlooking Chuzenji-ko, sometimes nailing one of their hands to a board inscribed with occult characters, to hasten their possession by the most terrible devil known to man. The samurai never climbed Fuji-san, though—despite the fact that it is nearly 1,000 feet higher, and much nearer to the gods. The climb up Fuji-san was, and remains, a recreation for ordinary people, and the upper-class samurai would never deign to go any farther than the Sengen Shrine at the mountain's base.

Gerard located the power cables, and didn't hesitate. With three or four grunting tugs, he pulled them free of the generator, in a shortcircuiting fritz of crackling electricity. From inside the prefabricated building, he heard the air conditioning whir to a stop; and from the generator he heard a cough, and a stutter, and finally silence.

The Tengus were locked inside, without air or light. Most of them were in a painful and suspensory trance, so they wouldn't notice. But the few who *did* notice, and discovered that they were gradually suffocating from lack of oxygen and stiffling with heat, could beat on the door all they wanted. They would never get out alive.

Gerard ducked out of the barn, raised his automatic high, and fired off three shots. They cracked loudly in the still mountain air and echoed from the distant ridges.

It took only seconds for five *Oni* guards to come running from the main ranch building. They caught sight of Gerard as he ran around the back of the barn,. They paused, aimed, and opened up a quick burst of fire with their Uzi submachine guns. Suddenly the afternoon was applauding with echoes.

One of the *Oni* called to the others that they should circle the barn and prevent Gerard from running away. But just as he said that, Maurice and Mack, who had been crouching patiently behind their rocks with the M-60E1, opened fire on them from what—to a general-purpose machine gun with a muzzle velocity of 2,800 feet per second and a cyclic rate of 600 rounds per minute— amounted to point—blank rage.

All five *Oni* jumped and danced like marionettes. The ground around them pattered with bullets, and dust rose up in scores of tiny spurts, until they spun and collapsed, awkward, disjointed, and lay dead.

Gerard appeared from the other side of the barn and shouted, "Okay! There can't be more than one or two of them left! Let's get in there!"

El Krusho hoisted up the machine gun, followed by Mack with his ammunition box, and together they loped down the lower part of the slope and across the ranch compound.

Meanwhile, Jerry had reached the window of the out- building. He flattened himself against the wall and took a quick, darting look inside, the way the Marines had taught him before he had been dropped into Japan. He could see David lying on a cot in there, mercifully and miraculously alive; but he also glimpsed a Japanese guard in a black silk mask standing by the door. Jerry had two distinct ad- vantages, however: surprise, and the fact that he was holding a submachine gun, while the guard appeared to be armed with nothing more than a holstered revolver.

Jerry thought, *I'm too old for this. Too slow, too tired.* But all the same, he curled himself backward, like Kent Tekulve winding up for one of his odd submarine pitches, and then he rolled himself, shoulder first, through the window of the outbuilding, with a smash of glass and rotten wood framing, and across the floor.

The Japanese guard snatched for his revolver, but he was split seconds too late. Jerry slammed off a deafening burst of 9-mm. bullets, almost a whole magazine, and the guard's chest and legs and belly turned into pulped tomatoes.

There was an odd silence. The room was filled with sharp, gunpowdery smoke. The guard turned, uttered a very Japanese-sounding sigh, and fell to the floor. David said, "*Dad—*"

Jerry raised a hand, indicating that David should stay where he was, keep quiet. "Are there any more of them?" he whispered.

"Five," said David, wide-eyed. "Six altogether."

It was then that they heard the deep, bronchial rattle of the M-60E1. Jerry stood up, and changed the magazine of his SMG, recocking it, ready for more killing. David had never seen his father like this before. Not cold and ruthless and efficient, handling a machine gun as if he handled one every day. He began to understand at that moment that war was something you never forgot. There are bespectacled insurance assessors in Cleveland who can still strip an M-3A1 without hesitation.

Jerry said, "Are you okay, David? They haven't hurt you?"

David, frightened, shook his head.

"All right," said Jerry. "Let's get out of here. Out the window. Then turn sharp right, and run like hell, up the slope, toward the treeline. If you hear any firing at all, dive for the ground and stay there. I'll be right behind you, but just remember that you can run faster than me."

David climbed cautiously out the window. "It's okay, Dad," he said. "There's nobody out here."

Jerry climbed after him, stiffly, wondering how the hell he had ever managed to roll through the whole window-frame. Then the two of them ran side by side toward the trees, keeping their heads well down. Within a minute, they were safe in the bushes, behind the rocks. Jerry panted, "It's okay, we can stop here. Stop, we're all right."

From the hillside, Jerry saw what happened next from a bird's-eye view. Mack and El Krusho were still jogging across the ranch compound—Maurice with his machine gun angled across his shoulders—when a silvery-blue Lincoln limousine appeared, speeding toward the ranch with an ocher-colored plume of dust rising up behind it. Almost simultaneously, Gerard came into view from behind the barn, shouting something to Mack and Maurice, and waving his arm toward the Lincoln.

David said, "What's happening? What are those guys doing?"

"Those guys helped me to save you," said Jerry tersely.

The Lincoln swerved around in the front yard of the ranch, scoring a wide semicircle in the dirt with its tires. As far as Jerry could see, there were at least four or five people in it, two or three of them women. He faintly heard Gerard Crowley shouting, "Mack—for Christ's sake, don't shoot—that's my wife! Those are my daughters!"

Then, from the ranch house, a man came running, sprinting toward the Lincoln with his head down. Gerard raised his automatic and fired two sharp shots at him, missing both times. But the man dodged and weaved and stumbled, and only just made it to the limousine as it gunned its engine and began to speed back the way it had come. A door flapped open, and a hand reached out to drag the man inside the car. He almost missed, desperately clawing for the door handle to give himself leverage. But then the Lincoln slowed momentarily, and he managed to scramble in.

Gerard raised his pistol once more, but as the Lincoln roared away down the drive, he realized that he probably wouldn't hit it anyway, and pushed his gun back into his pocket.

Jerry and David stayed where they were for five or ten more minutes, while Maurice and Mack and Gerard searched the ranch. At last, Gerard called, "It's clear! You can come down now!"

Stiffly, slowly, Jerry and David came down the slope to the ranch house. Maurice and Mack were already on the veranda, their machine gun propped against the rail, both of them looking scared, a little shocked, but satisfied. Gerard was puffing noisily at a cigar, and pacing up and down with his hands thrust into his pockets.

"You didn't see that, man," said Mack to Jerry. "Five of them, in five seconds. I couldn't believe it."

"My brother's going to eat shit," said Maurice.

Gerard asked, "How's your boy, Jerry? Okay?"

"I'm fine, sir, thank you," said David. He paused, and then he said, "And thank you, for everything you did."

"I'm afraid my motives weren't entirely philanthropic," said Gerard, his cigar glowing in the twilight. "Apart from which, it looks like the one who actually rescued you was your dear old papa. I saw that guard, Jerry. Squashed canteloupe isn't in it."

"Who was in that limousine?" asked Jerry. "I thought I heard you say your wife and daughters."

Gerard puffed, blew out smoke, and nodded. "That limousine belongs to Mr. Esmeralda, the guy who originally employed me to work out all the finances and building work that this program was going to take. I was also responsible for bringing Japanese workers and recruits in from Kobe. They're not all here now, although I always had to make sure that they were delivered here.

"As far as my own personal experience with him goes, Esmeralda is a snake. The kind of guy you'd pay quite a lot of money to have nothing to do with. I don't know what the hell he's doing with my wife and daughters. Maybe he's holding them as hostages. But you may as well know that I've been living apart from my wife—well, most of the time—and I don't get on very well with Kelly or Kathryn. I guess when they're older, I might. But not right now."

"Who was the man who ran from the ranch and jumped into the limo?" asked Jerry. "He looked Japanese to me."

"*That*," replied Gerard, "that was the one man we should have captured or wasted. That was the man who's been running all of this Tengu business, Doctor Gempaku. Gempaku claimed that he'd once discovered a way to make Japanese athletes into the best in the world—faster and stronger and totally tireless. Well, they banned him from the Toyko Olympics because he was using weird and unethical training methods. But you can understand what kind of a guy he is: dedicated, peculiar, unethical, very old-style Japanese. He would have gotten on well with Yamamoto, all those guys.''

Jerry said, "What's going to happen to the Tengus? How many was he trying to prepare?''

Gerard smiled. "Six altogether, I believe. But they're all contained in that prefabricated building now, without air and without cooling. They're probably feeling pretty damned uncomfortable right about now, and if you ask me, I think they deserve it.''

"What are you going to do?'' asked Jerry.

"Do?'' said Gerard. "I'm going to leave them there. They're shut in behind four inches of reinforced steel, and there's no way at all that they can get themselves out.''

Jerry said, and his voice was unsteady, "They're men. They're people. You're just going to let them die?''

Gerard snapped, "They killed Sherry Cantor, didn't they? They killed Admiral Thorson. They damned well nearly killed me.''

"So you're going to be their judge and executioner?''

"For fuck's sake,'' said Gerard, "you've been watching too many episodes of *Kaz*.''

There was an explosion from the direction of the barn. Glass was knocked out of the ranch-house windows like afternoon sleet, and the ground itself, hard-baked as it was, felt as if it were recoiling from a seismic shock. They rushed to the windows in time to see the huge rolling column of fire that was all that was left of the prefabricated Tengu building, and the flaming chunks of timber and aluminum which turned over and over in the sky.

"What the hell happened?'' said Mack.

Gerard watched the sparks showering down. His face was blank, far away, the face of a man who has almost managed to achieve what he always wanted. Revenge?

Satisfaction? It was impossible to tell.

He said, "I don't know for sure. There was an oxygen pump there, designed to take some of the oxygen out of the air in the building, make it thinner, you know? That's what they asked me for when I arranged to have it built. I disconnected the generator wire; maybe the sparks from the wire ignited the oxygen."

Maurice Needs watched him with a frown, as he said, "Anyway, we did what we set out to do, didn't we? Huh? Those Tengus are broiled burgermeat by now."

Gerard said, "That's not enough. We've still got to get Gempaku, and Esmeralda, too, if we can."

"I think it's time we left this to Sergeant Skrolnik," said Jerry.

"Are you kidding?" snapped Gerard. "Do you think the police could have pulled off an attack like this one, and still brought your boy out safe? That's my wife and daughters that man has there, and even if I don't particularly get on with them, I don't want to see them hurt, either. What's more, if we let even *one* of those Japanese bastards live, they're going to keep after us until they kill us. How would you feel if Gempaku or Esmeralda were caught by the police, and then released on bail? I know how I'd feel. I'd feel like leaving the goddamned country, and fast."

David held Jerry's hand. "Do you think we could go home now?" he asked.

Jerry ruffled his hair. "Sure. I think we're finished up here for now. Gerard? Can you guide us back?"

Gerard nodded and ran his hand through his hair. "Okay," he said. "I think we did the best we could. Let's go."

They were just about to leave when they heard a telephone ringing. Jerry said, "Leave it. Don't answer it." But Gerard opened the front door of the house, listened, and then ran quickly upstairs to Doctor Gempaku's office. He snatched up the phone and said, "Yuh?"

A man's voice said, "Mr. Esmeralda?"

Gerard hesitated, and then answered, "Yes. That's right. Who is this?"

"You don't *sound* like Mr. Esmeralda."

Gerard said, in what he hoped was a strong Colombian accent, "Of course this is Mr. Esmeralda. Who else do you think is going to be sitting out here in this godforsaken ranch at this time of day?"

"I'm sorry," the man said. "This is John O'Toole, from the Tahiti Way pier at Marina del Rey. I've fixed up the yacht you wanted. I was lucky, the guy who was renting her this week suffered a heart attack, and had to bring her in early. She's really neat, you'll like her. The *Paloma*. Real luxury through and through. Television, air conditioning, waterbeds."

"Is she going to cost extra?" asked Gerard, taking a blind stab at a businesslike question.

"Thirty bucks a day, that's all. And that includes all the paraplegic facilities we're putting in, the ramps, and the special toilet."

"Paraplegic facilities?"

There was an awkward pause. Then O'Toole said, "You did ask for paraplegic facilities, didn't you? Don't tell me I've gotten hold of this goddamned special toilet for nothing."

"Oh, sure," said Gerard. "I was distracted. Somebody just came in. Sure, the paraplegic facilities are great. Well done. Terrific."

"I got all the Japanese food, too," said O'Toole, a little uncertainly. "I'm up to my ears in bean curd and *harusame* noodles. You're going to want that? My secretary spent the whole afternoon shopping for it."

"Yes, we'll want all that," said Gerard. "Now tell me, what time did I say we'd want to sail?"

There was another pause, longer. "This *is* Mr. Esmeralda, isn't it?" O'Toole asked again.

"You think I'd be asking you all these questions if I wasn't?" Gerard demanded.

"*You're* not Mr. Esmeralda," insisted O'Toole, and

banged the phone down.

Gerard sat for a moment in silence. Then he came downstairs to find Jerry Sennett waiting for him inside the house.

"What was it?" asked Jerry.

"A call from Marina del Rey, of all places. The guy thought I was Esmeralda. Apparently, Esmeralda's renting a yacht called the *Paloma* from the Tahiti Way pier—when and why, he didn't say. But he did confirm that the yacht was stocked with Japanese food, and he also said that it was specially fitted out for a paraplegic."

"A *paraplegic*?" Jerry frowned.

"Don't ask me," said Gerard. "I never knew there were any paraplegics involved in this."

"But Esmeralda obviously does," said Jerry. "And when Nancy Shiranuka sent Kemo to find out who it was that Esmeralda was seeing—you remember, after he'd met you at Inca's restaurant—Kemo was killed by one of these *Onis*."

"I don't see what you're trying to say," said Gerard.

"Somebody powerful is running this Tengu business, that's what I'm trying to say. Somebody who has kept his or her identity secret the whole time, using Esmeralda as a go-between. Esmeralda's not the top guy, is he? I mean, he's made it clear to you that he's only passing on instructions, rather than initiating them. Kemo was killed because he tried to find out who the top banana was, and it's my guess that the top banana is this paraplegic."

"Well, well," said Gerard sarcastically. "Sherlock Holmes."

"Nothing of the kind," Jerry retorted. "We have an organization here that consists mainly of *Oni* adepts, and that means young, physically fit men, the fastest and the most deadly exponents of any Japanese martial art ever devised. Those guys can make kung-fu adepts look like idiots, as you well know. They have to go through six years of shadow-training before they're even allowed to fight each other. So what is a paraplegic doing among people like this? He obviously can't compete with them on a physical level, so he can't be one of the regular gang. The only way in which he can possibly compete is on a mental level, and that means to me that he's probably the boss."

"Jerry," said Gerard, unexpectedly putting his arm around his shoulders, "you are a genius. The only problem is, what is this dictatorial paraplegic up to, and why, and where the hell is he?"

Jerry said, "He must be here in Los Angeles, otherwise Kemo wouldn't have been killed so quickly when he tried to locate him. Second point: if he's going to do anything soon, like assassinate the President or the Governor, then he's going to have to do it pretty damned quick, because he knows that we're on to him, and the police are, too. Why do you think Esmeralda was renting a yacht for him? To make his getaway, I suspect, when his assassination or robbery or whatever it is starts going down."

"A getaway, by *yacht*?"

"It makes sense. The first place that the cops cordon off is the airport, followed by the highways, followed, as a distinct afterthought, by the seaways. You're probably fifty times more likely to get away with a crime if you escape by water than by any other means."

"You've carried out a survey?" asked Gerard sharply. "Maybe I should rob a couple of million from Wells Fargo and flush myself down the toilet. I'll be floating off to Hawaii in the company of ten tons of soggy toilet tissue before the police even know that I'm gone."

Jerry let out a short, testy breath. "You don't buy this, do you?"

"I don't see why I should," said Gerard. "There could be a thousand reasons why Esmeralda wanted equipment for paraplegics on a cruise to Panama. Maybe his sister has polio. Who knows? You can't read anything into it until you know the truth."

"By that time," said Jerry, "it all may be far too late"

Gerard said, "This is ridiculous. Let's start heading back to the cars."

"Just a minute, listen," insisted Jerry. "We've got ourselves a paraplegic, right? And the odds seem to be that he's Japanese. For some reason, he's involved in a series of unusually violent killings, either against Americans in particular, or Americans in general. Who does he hit? First me, unsuccessfully, killing Sherry instead; then an innocent policeman who's only trying to do his duty by busting a couple of Nipponese lunatics for running a red light. Then, *en masse*, the security and intensive-care staff of Rancho Encino Hospital and Admiral Thorson. What's he trying to do? He's one of the most eclectic killers I've ever come across."

"We were supposed to be trying to keep you quiet," said Gerard. "Esmeralda said that if you'd heard about Tengus on the media, you'd have immediately warned the authorities."

"Yes, but why *should* I have heard about Tengus in the media?"

"I don't know. They were supposed to have been killer bodyguards for very wealthy people. Don't tell me *that* isn't a story. 'Richard Burton buys Liz Taylor a million-dollar Japanese martial-arts expert, just to keep would-be admirers out of her hair.' "

"If it was all going to be *that* innocuous," said Jerry, "why bother to keep us quiet at all? Or maybe there's something heavier going down?"

"Search me," said Gerard uncomfortably.

Jerry held his arm. "Wait a moment," he said. "If this Japanese is a paraplegic, and he's been trying to take his revenge on American people, then he must have been doing it for a reason. Maybe it's *our* fault, maybe it's *my* fault, that he was born a paraplegic."

From the veranda Mack called impatiently, "Come on, you guys, it's a long haul back to the cars."

"Just a minute, Mack," Jerry called back. Then to Gerard, "Listen, there have been nearly ten deaths in the past few days, but all of them have been connected with your attempts to kill just two people: me and Admiral Thorson."

"That's right," agreed Gerard suspiciously.

"Admiral Thorson and I have one thing in common: we are the only two surviving members, as far as I know, of a Naval Intelligence team that gave President Truman the go-ahead to bomb Hiroshima."

Gerard stared at Jerry. Then he said slowly, "You've been talking about revenge, right? A Japanese paraplegic taking revenge, because of Hiroshima? Could that be it? Maybe he was crippled by the A-bomb. Maybe he was radiated with gamma rays when he was still in the womb and born deformed. "That happened to thousands of babies—thousands."

Jerry beckoned to Mack. "Mack," he said, "Gerard and I are beginning to think that this whole Tengu business has something to do with what I did at Hiroshima."

Mack glanced at Jerry suspiciously. He knew that Jerry had been to a psychiatrist, and the last thing he wanted to do was set off in hot pursuit of another man's neurosis. But Gerard gave him a quick, quiet nod of the head, which meant to Mack that Jerry was probably still quite sane.

"Olive's husband works for the naval records department, doesn't he?" asked Jerry.

"Sure. He's a whiz on Pacific war history. He can tell you the whole of the battle of Midway, in detail, like it's some kind of drama. The *Kaga* sunk at 7:25 P.M., the *Akagi* was scuttled at five o'clock the next morning. He's amazing. He's also amazing to trust me with Olive."

Jerry said, "Is there any way that Olive can get in touch with him?"

"Sure, he's on the phone. The area code for Honolulu is 808. She calls him once or twice a week. At the Navy's expense, I hasten to tell you, not mine."

"Right," said Jerry, "call her now, from the phone upstairs, and ask her if she wouldn't mind contacting him as soon as she can, and asking him to check if there were any clubs or organizations formed after the war to help Japanese people injured or deformed by the atomic bomb. Can you do that?"

"You think this guy is going to belong to the Happy Disabled Club of Tokyo?" asked Gerard.

"No," said Jerry. "But anyone who has been severely handicapped has to come into contact at some time or another with official organizations, even if he's only seeking advice or equipment. It's likely, anyway, even if it isn't a dead certainty."

Gerard said to Mack, "You want to give it a try?"

"Okay," breathed Mack. "But I think you're wasting your time."

Gerard dry-washed his face with his hands. "Just do it," he said. "Then we can all go back to the city and get ourselves a drink."

CHAPTER SEVENTEEN

It was a bad break, the worst of an operation that had been nothing but a whole series of bad breaks. He should never have listened to that voice on the Kii-Suido ferry; he should never have been tempted by Kappa's money or Kappa's beguiling voice. But everything that he was doing now had a terrible flawed inevitability about it; as if the foundation stone of an ancient Mayan ruin had cracked, and the balance of tons and tons of decorative stone could do nothing but crack and crack and eventually collapse.

He had driven Doctor Gempaku and the dead Tengu to Laurel Canyon, and left them there. Doctor Gempaku had been unsympathetic and ungrateful for being rescued. He blamed Mr. Esmeralda for all the inadequacies of the security arrangements, and was furious that six *Oni* adepts had been shot dead so easily. He didn't yet know that the Tengu building had blown up, and that half a dozen prospective Tengus had been blown into lumps of meat and bone. None of them was yet fully possessed by Tengu, and so their remains would never rise, not even for the Hour of Fire.

When he left Doctor Gempaku and the Tengu at Laurel Canyon, Mr. Esmeralda was told that Kappa himself was sleeping, in preparation for tomorrow's big day, and was not to be disturbed. If ever Mr. Esmeralda had felt like storming into Kappa's inner sanctum, shaking the little toad awake, and twisting his head off his neck, it was then; but he knew that the *Onis* who guarded Kappa were faster than the human eye, and that he wouldn't even have laid hands on Kappa before he was dead.

As a Catholic, the kind of death that the *Onis* gave out to their victims appealed to Mr. Esmeralda very little. He did at least want to go to his grave intact. He mumbled, "Everything is completely under control," and drove off before they could argue with him.

He was alone now. He had left Eva Crowley and her twin daughters locked in the bedroom of his house on Camden Drive—all of them naked in case they felt like trying to escape—and an *Oni* guard at their door. Kappa didn't realize that one of his own men was helping to protect Mr. Esmeralda's own insurance policy, his ultimate protection against the wrath of the Tengu. Mr. Esmeralda whistled "La Cumparsita" as he drove. Then, at the intersection of Laurel Canyon Boulevard and Sunset, at a red light, his foot accidentally slipped from the brake pedal and he noisily rearended a large Mercury station wagon.

The driver of the station wagon climbed out, a ginger-haired woman in upswept eyeglasses.

Mr. Esmeralda let down his window. "Madam," he said, "I take full responsibility. I apologize. I am a clumsy idiot."

"You could have *killed* me, you know that?" the woman demanded. "As it is, you've whiplashed my neck. Do you have any idea how much it's going to cost in doctor's bills to straighten my neck out? Can you *imagine*?"

Just then, a young motorcycle cop came over. "Is anything the matter here?"

"It was all my fault," said Mr. Esmeralda. "Usually, my chauffeur drives this car. I slipped on the pedal. My foot. I will pay for any damage to this lady's automobile."

"This is your car, sir?" asked the cop.

"Mine, in a sense," said Mr. Esmeralda. "It belongs to my company."

"May I see your driver's license, sir? And your registration?"

Mr. Esmeralda opened his black alligator wallet and produced his license. The young cop said, "Will you wait here a moment, please?"

"I'm in a hurry," said Mr. Esmeralda. "I have an appointment."

"I won't keep you longer than I have to, sir."

Mr. Esmeralda sat sweating in his seat as the cop walked back to his motorcycle, and began to read his license-plate and driver's-license numbers over his radio. The woman whose car he had hit remained beside him, saying, "It's going to cost a *fortune* to straighten my neck out. I know it is. A *fortune*."

The cop came back, his eyes invisible beneath the peak of his helmet. Esmeralda tried to smile, but the cop unbuttoned his holster and said, "I want you to get out of the car, sir, please, keeping your hands in sight."

"I don't understand, it was an accident," protested Mr. Esmeralda.

"This has nothing to do with the accident, sir," the cop told him in that same even voice. "You're under arrest for attempting to murder a man named Gerard Arthur Crowley."

CHAPTER EIGHTEEN

It was nearly seven o'clock the following morning before Olive's husband called back from Honolulu and told them what they wanted to know. He sounded tired, and more than a little slurred. "I've been drinking all night with this Japanese guy, Hachiro Nakamata. Suntory whiskey on the rocks. Hachiro used to work for the memorial museum in Hiroshima, indexing and filing the names of survivors. He knows more about the people who escaped from that blast than anybody. What happened to them, how they tried to live their lives afterward."

Olive said, "Did he know anything about societies for crippled people?"

Robin Nesmith burped into his first, a burp that carried 2,000 miles, and said, "Sorry. Yes, he did. He knows all of them. The Society for the A-Bomb Handicapped, the Hiroshima Benevolent Group, dozens of them. But he particularly mentioned something that I'd never heard about before, the Circle of Burned Doves."

"The Circle of Burned Doves? What's that?"

"It's a group of people who were born deformed because of the effects of gamma radiation when the bomb dropped. All of them, in one way or another, have become wealthy and influential, and they apparently have wealthy contacts in several of the largest and best-known Japanese industries. When you consider that many of the chairmen and managers of the big Japanese industrial combines were officers in the Japanese forces during the war, it's not surprising that they've been diverting some of their money and energy into getting revenge. The Japanese are not as fatalistic as many Western people seem to think; they're fiery and emotional, and they *never* forget. The general feeling in Japan is still, even today, that the dropping of the atomic bombs was unnecessary and unjustified, apart from all the moral questions involved. And the Circle of Burned Doves is dedicated to making America pay for what she did—through economic attack and through any other means at their disposal. According to Hachiro—although I can't say how true this is—our car industry was sunk almost entirely through the economic planning of the Circle of Burned Doves.''

Jerry, who had his ear pressed to the phone so that he could hear what Nesmith was saying, asked Olive, ''Find out what 'any other means at their disposal' might mean.''

Nesmith said, ''I asked Hachiro that myself, but he was incredibly vague. All he said was, 'It could mean an eye for an eye.' ''

''You mean dropping an atomic bomb on America?''

''He wouldn't say.''

Olive gave Robin her love, and then put down the phone.

''Well,'' said Mack, ''where does this get us?''

''Nowhere at all, much,'' said Jerry. ''Have you heard of the Circle of Burned Doves, Gerard?''

Gerard hadn't slept very well on Jerry's sofa. His eyes were ringed with dark circles, and he was breakfasting off crackers, cheese, and Chivas Regal. He shook his head. ''It doesn't ring any bells.''

Maurice said, ''I'm going out for some muffins and stuff. Anybody want anything? Olive?''

''No, thanks, Maurice.''

Jerry, rolling up his shirtsleeve and nervously scratching at his elbow, walked across the window and stared out at the sunshine. ''It looks as if we've been guessing right up until now, but I still don't see why they've brought back the Tengus. They didn't spend all that money and set up that center just to kill off me and Admiral Thorson. They've got to have something really catastrophic in mind.''

At that moment, the phone rang again. It was Sergeant Skrolnik, sounding as tired as Robin Nesmith. ''Mr. Sennett? I thought you might like to know that we've arrested a man in connection with the murder of Sherry

Cantor, and with several other murders."

"You've arrested someone? Who is it?"

"I'd like you come down to headquarters, if you don't mind, and take a look at him. His name's Jesus Carlos Esmeralda, he's a Colombian. We picked him up after a tipoff from the CIA."

Jerry said, "I'll be right down," and hung up the phone.

"What's going on?" asked Gerard.

"That was Sergeant Skrolnik. He's arrested your man Esmeralda. Apparently he was tipped off by the CIA."

"*Francesca*," snapped Gerard angrily. "She agreed to give me some goddamned time."

Jerry said seriously, "Come on, Gerard, I think this is the time for us to throw in our hand with the police. We've come so far, but there isn't very much else we can do, not on our own. If they've picked up Esmeralda, the police must be quite close to clearing this up themselves. Maybe we could help them."

"They didn't say anything about my wife and daughters?" asked Gerard.

Jerry said, "No. They just said Esmeralda."

"Fucking Esmeralda," said Gerard.

Mack put in, "Jerry could be right, you know? Maybe there's some clue that we have that the cops don't know about. And maybe they've got a whole of information that *we* don't know."

Gerard opened his cigar case and found that it was empty. He tossed it onto the table, and stuck his hands into his pockets with undisguised glumness. "All right," he said. "But you realize that I'm heavily implicated in all of this? If I go down to police headquarters with you, they're going to bust me, too."

"You stay here, then," said Jerry. "Maybe you can do me a favor and keep an eye on David; although why I'm entrusting you with the same boy you just kidnapped, I don't know."

"You can trust me," Gerard told him. "Just give me a

call if you hear anything about Eva and the girls."

"Sure," Jerry told him. "Mack? Maurice? Olive? You want to go?"

Down at police headquarters, accompanied by a sweaty and pasty-faced Skrolnik, who was exhausted after a long and futile night of questioning, arguing, and delicatessen coffee, they stared at Mr. Esmeralda through the two-way mirror in the side of his cell. Jerry said with certainty, "That's the man I saw at Orchid Place, the day Sherry Cantor was murdered."

"You're sure of that?" asked Skrolnik.

"Positive. He was standing in the street, watching my house. I remember thinking that he looked like somebody out of an old Humphrey Bogart movie."

"We think he's the ringleader," said Skrolnik.

Detective Pullet came into the room just then and gave Maurice a funny, half-apologetic smile. "We're still getting in data from the CIA on Esmeralda's activities abroad. Apparently he's been dealing with arms and drugs and stolen antique furniture like he's Ralph's or something. Hello, Mr. Needs. Glad you could be here."

"The pleasure's mutual," said Maurice. "How's the lateral thinking?"

"Still going strong," said Pullet. "We'll crack this business before you know it."

"Not if you think that Esmeralda is the ringleader," Jerry told him.

"What's that supposed to mean?" Skrolnik demanded.

Jerry said, "Is there some place where we can talk? In private?"

"Sure," grunted Skrolnik. "Come across to Welch's and watch me eat breakfast. You like corned-beef hash? They do the best."

CHAPTER NINETEEN

Mr. Esmeralda was released on $50,000 bail at two o'clock that afternoon, and told that he was not to leave the city of Los Angeles. His attorney told Judge T. N. Slattery that his client was "a pillar of international goodwill." The prosecution raised no objection to the granting of bail, especially since Mr. Esmeralda had no previous criminal record in the United States, and had once been decorated by President Sukarno of Indonesia for "services to the people of Djokjakarta and Surakarta."

Immediately after he left the courthouse in the company of his lawyer, Mr. Esmeralda caught a taxi to his address on Camden Drive, where he stayed for two hours, until just after 4:20 P.M., talking on the telephone. All of his conversations during this period were tapped by the police, under the jurisdiction of a special warrant.

His first call was to Mercury Custom Air Services, at Torrance Municipal Airport, confirming his booking of a Gulfstream III for 7:45 that evening. Destination: Liberal, Kansas.

"Liberal, Kansas?" asked Skrolnik, wrinkling up his nose.

Pullet said, "I'll check with the private air services at Liberal. He's bound to be using it as nothing more than a stopover."

The next call that Mr. Esmeralda made was to Twentieth-Century Bandbox, a dry-cleaning company, asking them to send over his two white suits and six shirts.

The third call was more mysterious. It was traced to the number of a house in Laurel Canyon. Mr. Esmeralda said, "Tell Kappa I was picked up by the police for a traffic offense. A rearender, nothing serious. I'm out now, and everything's fine for tonight. Everything's arranged. Kappa can leave immediately away for Marina del Rey. Yes, I know. But tell him everything's fine. I'll come to the house at seven precisely and make sure that everything's going smoothly. How's the Tengu? You did the Hour of Fire? He's fine? Okay, doctor. Okay. That's good. Tonight's the night, then. I'll see you when I see you. Just one thing—Kuan-yin's all right? What? You're sure about that? Very well. All right. Take care of that Tengu.''

The fourth call was to a man called John O'Toole, of O'Toole's Luxury Yachts, at Tahiti Way, Marina del Rey.

''The yacht is ready, Mr. O'Toole? That's excellent. My clients will be ready to leave in less than an hour. Very well. No, you have no need to do that. Good. And, listen, you don't have to worry about yesterday. I know who that man was, the one who answered the phone at the ranch. You have nothing to worry about. Yes. That's right. Thank you.''

Skrolnik listened to the last conversation and sat back in his swivel chair. ''Tonight's the night, then? And they're going to do something with that Tengu of theirs?''

''That's right,'' Jerry nodded.

''He didn't give any indication, did he? No indication at all.''

''I'd bust him now, if I were you,'' said Mack.

Skrolnik shook his head. ''I've learned my lesson often enough, Mr. Holt. You don't jump on anybody until they're actually involved in the commission of a crime, *in flagrante*. The times I've gone to court with wiretaps that would make your curly hair stand on end, and had them thrown out because *conspiracy* to commit a crime, without the crime having actually been committed, is one of the hardest imaginable offenses to prove. All Esmeralda has to do is say, 'I was joking, Your Honor. I was fooling around with a friend.' And anyway, you take a look at a transcript of those conversations, and you won't see *nothing*, nothing indictable. He spent most of his time saying 'yes' and 'no' and 'okay,' and unless you can establish exactly what it was he was talking about, you won't get anywhere.''

Jerry said, ''What are you going to do?''

Skrolnik grimaced. "I'm going to do my duty, Mr. Sennett. Ordinary, functional police work. I'm going to have Esmeralda tailed, and arrested if he attempts to leave Los Angeles in contravention of the terms of his bail. I'm going to assign a team to track down that house in Laurel Canyon and follow the Tengu wherever he goes. Any attempt by the Tengu or any of his assistants to commit any kind of violent crime, and *shazam*! I'm going to throw his tail in jail."

There was a silence. Then Mack said, "How?"

"How what?" asked Skrolnik crossly.

"How are you going to throw the Tengu's tail in jail? I thought the Tengus were pretty well unstoppable. Look what you had to do at Rancho Encino. The thing was dead, supposedly, and it still came after you."

"You weren't there at Rancho Encino," said Skrolnik.

"No, I wasn't. But from what Jerry's told me, it sounds like these Tengus are pretty invincible characters."

Skrolnik stood up, wrapping his beefy arms around his chest. "Let me tell you something, junior," he said. "When that Tengu came for me at Rancho Encino, it had no head."

"No *head*?" asked Jerry.

"That's right. Calsbeek's men had blown its head clean off its shoulders. But that didn't stop it. It came right on in there, headless. We burned it, but if we hadn't, it would probably have torn us to pieces. So I know what I'm talking about, and when I say that I'm going to throw that Tengu's tail in jail, that's exactly what I'm going to do."

"What did you do with the ashes?" asked Jerry.

"What?" frowned Skrolnik.

"Even a Tengu's ashes are capable of being revived by the appropriate ceremony," said Jerry.

Skrolnik made a dozen faces, each one more grotesque than the last. "Just leave this fucking thing to me, will you? That's all I ask. If I make a mistake, let it be *my* mistake, not yours. You got me?"

"You'll keep us in touch?" asked Jerry.

"Sure, I'll keep you in touch. Now, why don't you get back home and watch the whole thing on television. You'll be warmer and safer, and you won't be getting under my feet."

Mack said, "Wait a minute—" but Jerry took his arm and raised a finger to tell him that he should keep quiet.

They went across the street to Welch's, and ordered hamburgers and beer. Jerry went to the pay phone and called David. Gerard was being the prefect babysitter, David told him. They had been playing checkers together, and so far David was ahead by nine games to six. "He told me what he did in Cuba, and all about the time when he was a boy on a tobacco farm."

Jerry said, "Underneath that frozen exterior, I think a nice guy may be thawing out. Take care, David. I love you, and I'll see you later."

When he got back to the table, Maurice said, "I've been thinking, you know?"

"You've been *thinking*?" Mack teased him. "Do you mind if I call the networks?"

"No, seriously," said Maurice. "They've got one Tengu left, okay? But even if there's only one, the cops don't have much chance of stopping him, do they? They don't have much chance of knocking him off before he does anything really serious."

"It took an atomic bomb to wipe out the first community of Tengus," agreed Jerry.

"Right," said Maurice. "But supposing the Tengu met up with another Tengu—an even stronger Tengu?"

"Maurice,' you're talking through your ass," said Mack. "If there's only one Tengu left, where's this other Tengu, this even stronger Tengu?"

Mack knew what Maurice was trying to suggest even before he'd finished speaking, but the idea of it was so stunning that there was nothing he could do but sit there with his half-eaten cheeseburger in one hand and his mouth open and wait for Maurice to point to his own

T-shirted chest and say, "Right here. *Me*. I could be a Tengu, couldn't I?"

Jerry said intently, "Maurice, you don't even know what you're suggesting. The only way in which anybody can open themselves up to being possessed by the Tengu is through excruciating agony. That, and all the necessary invocations and rituals."

"You've got that Japanese woman, don't you?" asked Maurice. "That Nancy Shiranuka. She'd know all the rituals."

"Well, I guess she would, but—"

"But nothing. Let's go over there and ask her to do it."

"Are you *crazy*?" Jerry hissed at him. "To turn yourself into a Tengu would mean pain so great that you wouldn't even know where you were. Besides, once you've been possessed, it isn't that easy to become *un*possessed, to be exorcized. Nancy Shiranuka almost died when she was purified of one of her Japanese demons. And that demon was nothing compared to the Tengu. The Tengu is absolutely the worst demon ever."

Maurice put down his avocado-and-bacon burger, his second. "Listen," he said quietly, "what you guys don't seem to understand is that I'm just a strongman in the circus. El Krusho, nothing else. Can you imagine what it's like, being El Krusho? Even my fucking name's a joke. I bend steel bars in my teeth, and pick up fat ladies, one in each hand, and if I accidentally slip a finger up their snatch when I'm lifting them, they love me forever. I'm *nothing*, man. A pile of muscles, a freak show. If I'm lucky, I'll get a different pretty girl every Saturday night, and a $20 bonus to buy myself a steak dinner at Charlie's. I run a creaking '69 Corvette, and all I own in the world is three pairs of sneakers and about 108 T-shirts."

"So?" Mack challenged him.

"So, I want to do something *exciting*, *weird*, *different*. What we did yesterday, attacking that ranch—that was a blast. I haven't done anything like that in my whole life.

Listen, you think I'm afraid of some *pain*? Have you tried lifting weights, working out in a gym? You want to talk about pain, when you're lifting 350 kilos of solid iron?''

"Maurice," said Jerry, "this is something different. This is *spiritual* pain, too.''

"So what are you going to do?" Maurice demanded. "You're going to let this Tengu character run around killing people? Or what?''

Jerry looked across the table at Mack, and suddenly he didn't feel hungry anymore. Mack shrugged. Maurice was one of those plain people who were impossible to convince of anything, if they didn't want to be convinced.

"We don't have too much time," said Jerry. "A couple of hours, at the most. That may not be long enough. You may go through a whole lot of pain for nothing.''

"The sooner we get started, the better, huh?" said Maurice.

Mack said, "For Christ's sake, Maurice. You want to be a martyr or something?''

"I don't know," said El Krusho. "Maybe. Anything's better than being El Krusho.''

CHAPTER TWENTY

In Nancy Shiranuka's apartment on Alta Loma Road, Maurice Needs went through the pain and the ritual required to make him a Tengu.

Gerard Crowley and Jerry Sennett tied his wrists and ankles, and then left him in the bedroom with Nancy. Mack Holt had already started on the Gekkeikan saké, and they silently joined him, sitting on *zabutons* with their legs uncomfortably crossed, trying not to think of the agonies

Maurice was voluntarily suffering in the next room.

Nancy had reduced the light in the bedroom to a single crimson candle. She was naked, except for the tight silk ribbon which she wore around her waist to keep her carved jade *harikata* in place. Her skin was shiny with perfumed oil, and her hair was tied tightly back from her forehead.

She sang to him "The Song of the Lost Warrior" and then "The Night Forest." As she sang, she began to scratch his chest with steel skewers, gently at first, more irritating than painful; but then deeper, until his chest and his stomach were scored with their points, and the blood began to break through the skin in rows of crimson beads. For the first time, he closed his eyes and gritted his teeth.

There was one advantage that Nancy Skiranuka had over Doctor Gempaku: she had been possessed by a demon herself, and she had been a member of the Shrine of the Seven Black *Kami*. She knew what the world of the demons *felt* like. She could sense when she was getting close to that dark, fluttering, cloud-world of evil beings. She could summon them by name. She knew what each of them sounded and smelled like: O Goncho, the wolf-howling bird of Yamahiro; Jinshin Uwo, the beast of earthquakes; Kappa; and Raiden, the thunder devil. They were stylized and fanciful beings in Japanese literature and art. Millennia of educated priests had changed their faces and distorted their legends. But Nancy knew they were real. She had experienced the ghostly shadows of their malevolence inside her head. Their ill will had twisted her body, and their corruption had almost destroyed her.

She chanted the longest of the devil-summoning rituals of the Shrine of the Seven Black *Kami:* the Calling Down. In the next room, Jerry and Gerard and Mack looked at each other in subdued silence, and poured out another round of Gekkeikan. Whether this was right or wrong, it was more than they could bear.

Mack unexpectedly began to recite the 23rd Psalm. Gerard didn't join in, but he closed his eyes and lowered

his head, and when Mack had finished, he said, "Amen."
Only Jerry remained stiff and quiet, with his eyes wide
open.

Nancy slowly twisted and dug the skewers into the
muscles of El Krusho's arms and chest. There was a
crackling, tearing sound as she lifted the pectorals away
from his chest. She didn't have the ritual silver claws that
Doctor Gempaku had used, but she was capable of inflict-
ing sufficient pain to rouse up the Tengu.

"Tengu, come into your slave," she chanted. "Tengu,
possess your slave. Tengu, O emperor of all that is violent
and corrupt, come into him." As she chanted, she lifted
herself slightly up and down, so that her heel pushed the
jade dildo in and out of her. She closed her eyes in a
mixture of ecstasy and agony.

Outside, Gerard said, "I don't know why the hell
Esmeralda kidnapped my wife and daughters. I don't
know why the hell he did that."

Mack said, "You'll find out soon enough."

"Well, I don't know whether I will," said Gerard,
patting his pockets in search of cigars which he knew very
well he didn't have.

In the bedroom, Nancy leaned over El Krusho's
bleeding chest and slowly sliced the point of a Japanese
cooking knife deep into his upper arm. She had seven
knives in all, representing the Seven Black *Kami*, and with
these she pinned El Krusho's flesh to the wooden floor of
her apartment. El Krusho twitched and groaned out loud,
but his eyes were closed now, and he was already approaching the first levels of a deep trance.

Now, with El Krusho crucified to the floor, Nancy lit
incense. The sacred smoke trailed over him, and perfumed
the air with rare and expensive spices, in a way which
would entice a demon. Her voice became so high-pitched
and strange that Mack, in the next room, raised his head in
bewilderment. "What the hell's that woman *doing* in
there?"

Another hour passed. It was well past seven. Outside the

apartment, the sun was sinking into the evening smog of the Pacific shoreline like an angry and sullen god. Jerry leaned against the window and watched the skyline over downtown Los Angeles slowly turn purple, the color of grape jelly stirred into cream of wheat. He had telephoned David a half-hour ago, and David was fine.

Gerard checked his watch. "If this takes any longer, we'll be too late," he said. He turned the saké flask upside down, but it was empty. "Mack," he said, "go take a look in that liquor cabinet. See if Tokyo Lil's got any more saké."

Jerry shot Gerard a sharp, critical look. Gerard shrugged and said, "I'm sorry. I'm just edgy, is all."

CHAPTER TWENTY-ONE

Eva Crowley had never felt so humiliated. Nor had she ever felt so frightened. Not just for herself, but for her children. After a day's naked captivity in Mr. Esmeralda's apartment, without food or water or sanitary facilities, hours in which they had alternately wept and talked and argued with each other, sometimes hysterical, sometimes calm, sometimes vengeful, they had at last been let out and told to dress themselves under the unblinking supervision of their black-masked *Oni* guard. They hadn't argued. The guard had kept his Uzi machine gun raised at them the whole time they were dressing, and had then hurried them out of Mr. Esmeralda's house into his waiting Lincoln limousine.

"I hope you have not had too uncomfortable a day," Mr. Esmeralda had asked Eva smoothly, as he drove out into the evening traffic.

Eva had said nothing. She had been shaking with rage and fear and embarrassment. Now, as they cruised softly southward on the San Diego Freeway, past Culver City and Inglewood, she sat with her face close to the limousine's tinted window, watching the sun set beyond the airport, and the red-and-amber lights of the cars overtaking them on either side. Kathryn silently cried, she hadn't stopped crying since this afternoon. Kelly tried to comfort her, but she too was stony-faced with shock.

"Have you ever been to Kansas?" Mr. Esmeralda asked, turning off the freeway onto Hawthorne Boulevard, heading directly south through Torrance toward the airport.

"Kansas?" asked Eva, confused.

Mr. Esmeralda glanced at her in his rearview mirror and his eyes smiled. "We're about to take a little flight."

He drove up to the wire airport gate which led onto the tarmac. There was a high-pitched whistling of executive jets, Learjets and Canadairs, and an oily smell of aviation fuel on the wind. The security guard came out of his hut, and Mr. Esmeralda showed him his pass.

"Mercury Custom Air Services down there to your left," he said.

A black van had drawn up behind Mr. Esmeralda's limousine. "This is my baggage," Mr. Esmeralda smiled.

"You got a pass for your baggage? I'm not supposed to allow baggage vehicles on the field without a pass."

"Of course," said Mr. Esmeralda. "Just go ask the driver."

Mr. Esmeralda waited, his eyes fixed on his rearview mirror, while the security guard walked back to the van. Eva said, "Carlos, what's happening? We can't go to *Kansas*! For God's sake, what's happening?"

Mr. Esmeralda smiled. In his mirror, he had seen the flying fist of one of Kappa's *Oni* adepts drop the security guard to the ground. He tugged the Lincoln's gearshift into drive and turned left along the perimeter fence.

The Gulfstream III was waiting for them on its apron, a

large executive jet with its lights flashing and its engines already warming up. As they drew up to the side of the tarmac, Mr. Esmeralda said to Eva and her girls, "We are going to alight from the car now, and we are all going to be smiling. You understand me? This is going to be a happy family flight to Kansas. I have my gun in my pocket, and if any one of you attempts to make a fool of herself, like shouting or signaling or trying to run away, then I shall instantly shoot to kill. Believe me, this is not a jest."

A steward from Mercury Custom Air Services opened the limousine doors for them, and they stepped out into the warm and breezy evening. "Mr. Esmeralda? Right this way, please. This way, ladies. Fine evening for a flight, isn't it? You should have a wonderful view of the city as you take off."

"I shall be just one moment," said Mr. Esmeralda. The van had now parked behind his Lincoln, and flashed its lights just once. "I have to speak to my employees before I leave."

He took two steps toward the van, and he knew that it was all going to go wrong. The arrangements had been for the Tengu, in the company of Kappa's last three *Oni* escorts, to follow Mr. Esmeralda down to the airport for a final briefing, before driving farther south to Three Arch Bay, and their ultimate destination—the nuclear-power station. But Mr. Esmeralda had felt in his bones, right from the very beginning, that the Tengu needed no further instructions, any more than Kappa's vicious *Onis*. And when he heard the rear doors of the van banging open, and one of the *Onis* screeching "*Tora! Tora! Tora! Tora!*" he hesitated for only a split second before he turned around and began running toward the jet, shouting at the Mercury Air representative, "Get this plane off the ground! Now!"

Kathryn and Kelly screamed. For as Mr. Esmeralda ran past them, the Tengu appeared in the lights which flooded the Mercury Air apron, both arms raised in a ritual greeting to the devils which swarmed in the night air. He was even more grotesque than the previous Tengu: his body was not only gaping with the wounds from Doctor Gempaku's silver claws, but smashed and misshapen from his 27-story fall from Gerard Crowley's office window. His eyeballs were totally white: he did not need to see, not in the ordinary sense of the word. He was already dead, although not yet dead, and he strode toward Mr. Esmeralda with all the purpose of a creature that is possessed by a hideously powerful devil.

Mr. Esmeralda was halfway up the steps to the jet's cabin, leaving Eva and the girls on the tarmac, when the Tengu reached the foot of the steps, grasped them in his hands, and shook them violently, until they rattled and thundered.

"*Take them*!" shrieked Mr. Esmeralda, pointing to Eva and her twins. "Take them instead! They are yours, as a substitute!"

The Tengu raised his face blindly toward Mr. Esmeralda, then hesitated, turned, and groped the air. Eva and the girls stood where they were, mesmerized by fright.

"Take them!" screamed Mr. Esmeralda. "Take them!"

Still the Tengu hesitated, but then he took one or two uncertain steps toward Eva, his hands raised, his wounds glistening blue in the airport lights. Although Mr. Esmeralda couldn't hear her above the whistling of the Gulfstream's engines, she stepped forward to meet the Tengu and whispered, "You can have me. But not my daughters."

With one sweeping blow, the Tengu knocked Eva's head sideways and snapped her neck. She stood where she was for a second or two, her head at a sickening angle, and while she did so, the Tengu wrapped his arms around her, dug his hands into her lower back until he had seized her ribcage, and then, with one grisly and explosive wrench, opened her chest out like the ribs of an opening umbrella. Stomach and guts splashed onto the concrete apron, and even Mr. Esmeralda stood on the steps of the jet and stared in horror.

Without even looking at Kathryn or Kelly, the Tengu stalked back toward the black van. Two of the three *Onis* were waiting, arms folded, to receive him and help him back into the van. The third *Oni* was hidden in the shadows, although what he was doing, Mr. Esmeralda couldn't tell.

"I want to get out of here," he said to the stewardess who was standing behind him, white-faced, in the cabin doorway.

The stewardess couldn't speak. "We have to leave *now*!" snapped Mr. Esmeralda. "We have to!"

The stewardess shook her head, speechless, too shocked by the murder she had witnessed to move.

"Where is the captain?" Mr. Esmeralda demanded. "We have to go!"

There was a sharp swishing sound, and a flash, and Mr. Esmeralda halfturned to look back down toward the van. That was the last conscious movement he made. The third *Oni*, resting against the hood of the van, had fired a single antitank round from an 84-mm. Carl Gustaf rocket-launcher, a 5.7-pound high-explosive projectile which penetrated the fuselage of the Gulfstream close to the wing and instantly exploded.

Fully loaded with fuel, the plane blew up in a huge, rumbling burst of orange fire. Pieces of incandescent aluminum were hurtled into the air like a fireworks display.

The black van was already speeding away, without lights. But as it reached the perimeter of the airport and turned south again on the Pacific Coast Highway, it was picked up for the second time that evening by a beige Cutlass, driven by Detective Pullet. Beside him sat Sergeant Skrolnik, and in the back seat were Detective Arthur and a police marksman named Woschinski, who had blotchy red acne and a habit of sucking peppermints, but who could hit a moth at 250 yards and clip only its legs off.

Skrolnik rapped into his radio, as Pullet followed the van. "Something's happened at Torrance Airport. A damned great explosion. As soon as you get any word on it, let me know. Meanwhile, what about that call to Sennett? Did you get through? Did you tell him to get down here? I want him *down* here! He knows what the hell's going on, all this Japanese crap, which is more than I do. Tell him to take the Long Beach Freeway as far as the Pacific Coast Highway, and then head south. Tell him to get his ass in gear. Does he have CB? Well, that's one goddamned relief. Tell him to get down here fast. This is it. The balloon's going up.''

CHAPTER TWENTY-TWO

Four miles out of Marina del Rey, a U.S. Coast Guard cutter intercepted the yacht *Paloma* and hailed her to heave to. The yacht immediately cut her engines and wallowed for almost ten minutes in the water, without navigation lights, without putting down her anchor. After hailing the yacht four more times and raking her from stem to stern with floodlights, the Coast Guard captain finally decided to send aboard three armed enlisted men.

They discovered, on the foredeck, still alive—but only just—a tall Japanese who was later identified as Doctor Gempaku. He had knelt by the rail, and in the ritual manner of *seppuku*, and sliced open his own stomach with a razor-sharp samurai sword. Down below, in the galley, they found a Chinese girl who had been killed by being garrotted with a redhot wire. There were signs of her breasts and buttocks of severe sexual assault.

In an inner cabin, dead, were three young Japanese men

wearing black silk masks. They had all committed suicide
by thrusting sharp knives, one in each hand, into their
own eyes and deep into their brains.

It was in the very last cabin, though, that they found the
greatest horror of all. Sitting in a cushioned basket,
surrounded by hundreds of burning candles, a small deformed figure, naked, like a glistening fledgling that had
fallen featherless from its nest before it could learn to fly.
The heat and the stench inside the cabin were over-
powering, but the tiny figure smiled at them as they
stepped in, their eyes wide with caution and fright, their
carbines held high.

"Holy shit," said one. "Holy shit, this isn't even *real*."

The tiny figure continued to smile at them. The most
unnerving thing about it was that, on top of that deformed and twisted body, it had a perfectly normal head,
the head of a handsome 37-year-old man.

"Good evening, gentlemen," it whispered. "It seems
that you have caught me at a disadvantage."

One of the Coast Guardsmen nodded; and, ritually, in
return, the tiny figure nodded too. It's heavy head
dropped forward onto its chest, and for a moment it
whined, and whined again, and then fell silent.

"What's the matter with it?" asked one of the Coast
Guardsmen. "Do you think it's okay?"

"Would you think *you* were okay, if you looked like
that?"

"Jesus, I don't know. Why don't you go take a look."

"I'm not taking no fucking look."

The other man glanced behind him, to make sure that
no other Coast Guardsmen had boarded the yacht. Then,
with the barrel of his carbine, he knocked five or six
lighted candles onto the blankets and cushions that lay on
the floor. He watched them for a second or two, to make
sure they were well alight. Then he closed the cabin door
and struck at the lock with the butt of his gun to jam it.

"We didn't even go in there, right?" he asked his companions.

"We didn't even go in where?"

The man checked his watch. "Let's give it ten seconds," he said. "Then we'll shout fire."

The *Paloma* burned for less than twenty minutes before listing over to port and quickly sinking. Kappa, the water devil, had returned at last to the water. There was a smell of steam and oil and charred varnish on the wind.

CHAPTER TWENTY-THREE

They reached the power station at Three Arch Bay only five minutes after Sergeant Skrolnik. Jerry parked the Dodge beside Skrolnik's Cutlass, and turned immediately around to look at El Krusho. Wrapped in a blanket on the back seat, alternately nursed and tortured by Nancy Shiranuka, Maurice was in a state of feverish trance, twitching and mumbling and murmuring. Mack and Gerard, both in the front seat with Jerry, glanced at him uncertainly, as if they weren't at all sure they should continue.

"This isn't going to kill him or anything?" asked Mack. "I've known that poor sucker for years."

"He is completely possessed now," said Nancy. "Nothing will hurt him, not even bullets."

"Nothing?" asked Gerard. "Not even another Tengu?"

Skrolnik came over to their car and slapped on the roof. "Esmeralda's dead," he told them. Jerry lowered the window to hear what he was saying. "He was trying to escape in an executive jet at Torrance Airport, and it seems like these Japanese bastards fired some kind of rocket at him. The whole plane went up. Six, maybe seven people killed altogether. Most of the corpses haven't even been identified yet.''

"My wife—my daughters," said Gerard. "Any news of them?''

"You're Gerard Crowley?" asked Skrolnik.

"Yes, sir.''

Skrolnik raised his head, so that his face couldn't be seen from the interior of the car. Then he said, "I'm sorry, Mr. Crowley.''

Gerard said, "Jesus. Did they suffer?''

"Not as far as I know.''

Gerard was silent after that. Jerry said to Skrolnik, "If they're attacking this power station, then presumably they're going to try to set off some kind of nuclear explosion.''

"That's what I thought," agreed Skrolnik. "They've parked their van around the side there, not far from the beach. We're keeping them under close observation, and I've already called for reinforcements. They won't even get close, I promise you.''

"Don't count on it," said Jerry.

Skrolnik peered in through the open window. "Is that Needs you've got in the back?''

"Yes, sergeant.''

"What's the matter with him? He looks sick.''

"He's okay. He needs some air, is all.''

Detective Arthur came over and said hastily, "Sergeant, they want you around at the fence.''

"Okay," said Skrolnik, and then to Jerry, "Don't wander away too far. I may need you.''

"Okay," said Jerry.

Once Skrolnik had gone, Jerry and Mack and Gerard climbed out of the car, opened the rear door, and helped El Krusho onto the grass. He coughed and swayed, 325 pounds of entranced muscle, a human machine possessed by a violent spirit. Jerry could have sworn that he saw tiny blue fires twinkling around El Krusho's head, but he guessed it was fatigue or reflections from the power station.

The power station was floodlit now: a compact collection of white concrete buildings with a tall red-and-white striped chimney, a battery of shiny aluminum ventilator shafts, and a cylindrical roof over the fusion reactor itself like a huge sailor's cap. Plumes of steam rose from the slender chimneys that exhausted the power station's cooling plant, and the deep reverberating thrum of generators was carried toward them by the evening wind.

"Tell Maurice to go in there and kill the Tengu," Jerry instructed Nancy.

Nancy said, "You are sure this is what you want?"

"It's what Maurice wants."

"Very well, then," said Nancy, and spoke rapidly to Maurice in Japanese.

"He's going to understand that?" asked Mack. "He doesn't even understand English."

"I am speaking to the Tengu, not to Maurice," said Nancy.

She had to pause for a moment while a police helicopter flackered overhead, its searchlights running across the ground like a frightened ghost. Then she finished her incantation and bowed to Maurice with the respect of one who recognizes extreme power when she confronts it.

There was shouting from the far side of the fence around the power station, and a sharp crackling of gunfire. Nancy said to Maurice, "It's started. You must go. Kill the Tengu. Kill it swiftly."

Without hesitation, Maurice seized the wire of the perimeter fence and ripped it apart like unraveled knitting. He stepped straight through it, followed closely and anxiously by Jerry and Mack. Gerard stayed behind with Nancy.

As they came around the corner of the cooling plant, they saw a double cordon of police and security guards, all armed, facing the Tengu across the parking lot. Every floodlight was lit, giving the scene the brilliant unreality of a movie set.

But there was no question that the Tengu was real. He came slowly forward, toward the main doors of the power station, his head bound tightly with a scared sweatband painted with magical characters, his eyeballs white as boiled eggs, his body damaged and scarred and torn so viciously that the naked sinews showed through his wounds. *God,* thought Jerry, *you can see the blood pulsing through his arteries.*

Nobody challenged the Tengu. The police had bullhorns, but they didn't use them. Instead, an officer simply said, *"Fire,"* and there was an ear-spitting fusillade of carbine and pistol shots.

The Tengu was hit again and again. Bullets blew lumps of raw flesh from his shoulders and his chest. One bullet turfed the skin and muscle away from the left side of his face, so that his jawbone and teeth were bared. But he didn't waver. He kept advancing on the ranks of police and security guards, his arms raised above his head, even when a sharpshooter hit his forearm and elbow, smashing the bone and digging up the muscle.

The police cordon began to waver and break, unnerved. *"Fire!"* demanded the officer, but none of them did. They watched in horrified fascination as the Tengu, bloody and maimed, walked right through their ranks, up the concrete steps of the power-station entrance, and then burst open the doors with a single blow of his fists. Before anybody could react, he had disappeared inside.

Skrolnik ran forward, screaming, "Stop him! For God's sake!" but the confusion and panic were too much. Most of the officers stayed where they were, unable to admit to themselves that they had seen a man hit by seventy or eighty large-caliber bullets and still walk. Jerry and Mack guided El Krusho up the concrete steps to the broken doors of the power station, and although one policeman challenged them and asked, "What are you doing?" nobody else stood in their way.

In a moment they were inside, following the spatters of
blood which the Tengu had left behind him on the floor.
Inside the power station, it was coolly air-conditioned, and
lit with dim, greenish fluorescent lamps. The floor was
polished vinyl, as reflective as water, and the walls were as
white and sterile as a hospital.

Skrolnik, at the smashed door, yelled, "Sennett! What
the hell do you think you're doing?"

But Jerry and Mack kept pushing El Krusho onward, up
a flight of steel stairs, along a steel latticework catwalk, and
around at last to the main hall where the fusion reactor was
housed. Mack pointed down to the reactor itself and said,
"There he is. For God's sake, he's playing around with all
those switches!"

The fusion reactor was quite small, the first of America's
experiments in nuclear fusion. It was no more than 20 feet
high, shaped like a giant metal donut in a frame of
pipework and valves and electrical wiring. The control
console was a white upright cabinet, no bigger than a
Space Invaders game, with five power-indicator dials, and
a circular screen to indicate the build-up of nuclear energy.
The Tengu had already flicked down a whole row of
switches, and the fusion reactor was beginning to hum as it
built up the extraordinary charge of power necessary to
raise its internal temperature to 100 million degrees
Celsius.

Skrolnik came banging along the catwalk, followed by
six armed policemen and the scientific director of the
Three Arch Bay complex, a young but balding man with
hornrimmed glasses as heavy as Clark Kent's.

"He's *tampering* with it, for God's sake," shouted the
scientific director. "He's started it up!"

"Cut the power, then!" snarled Skrolnik.

"I *can't*! If I shut off the power now, the whole damned
thing will go unstable!"

"Shoot him!" Skrolnik directed his officers. "Blow his
goddamned head off!"

"No!" insisted the scientific director. "One stray

bullet, and the whole reactor could blow up!"

"Well, *what* then?" screamed Skrolnik in utter frustration.

"Go, Maurice," said Jerry in a gentle voice. "Go kill him."

Everybody watched in morbid fascination as Maurice strode purposefully along the catwalk and down the steps which led to the main floor of the reactor room. The Tengu, at the reactor's console, neither saw nor acknowledged him, but he must have sensed that he was there, since both of them were possessed by the same evil spirit. Different manifestations of the same spirit, invoked for different reasons—after all, like the demons of Christendom, the devils of Japan were legion—but the same fundamental spirit. The atmosphere within the nuclear-reactor hall crackled with evil and with the huge power of the fusion reactor, as it steadily amassed incredible power.

"Kill him!" shouted Jerry, and Mack leaned over the rail of the catwalk and yelled, "Sic him, Maurice!"

El Krusho stepped forward and seized the Japanese Tengu by the neck. His bruised and lacerated muscles bulged with power as he wrenched the Tengu's head this way and that, and then twisted the Tengu's arms around behind his back. But the Tengu, for all that he was lighter and less muscular then El Krusho, had been an *Oni* adept when he was alive; and as El Krusho tried to claw back his head and break his neck, he twisted powerfully around, and threw El Krusho against the metal staircase.

El Krusho lurched to his feet again and tore into the Tengu with the madness of a wild animal. He dug his fingers into the Tengu's wounds, and ripped yards of red muscle away from the Tengu's bones. He butted the Tengu repeatedly with his skull, and at last the two of them became locked together in the clinch which, in *Oni*, is known as the Fatal Embrace. It is one of the few slow moves in *Oni*, a twisting together of arms and backs which can be fatal to either antagonist, or both.

There were three or four minutes of grunting strain, as the Tengu pulled against El Krusho and El Krusho pulled back. Then, with enormous effort, El Krusho staggered to his feet, carrying the Tengu on his back like the carcass of a slaughtered bull, and walked with him, step by agonized step, out of the reactor hall and out toward the huge pool where spent nuclear fuel was kept submerged, prior to re-processing.

The pool hall was as cold and echoing as a swimming pool. Beneath the deep-turquoise water, lit by underwater floodlights, stood rack after rack of tubular steel where the fuel rods were stored.

At the very edge of the pool, El Krusho and the Tengu wrestled and chopped and grappled with each other. The Tengu at last seized Maurice by the neck and flailed him from one side to the other, howling with a weird echoing howl that sounded as if it had come from hell itself.

There was a moment of physical ballet, a moment of strain and tension and ultimate pain. Then both of them, Tengu and El Krusho, toppled and fell into the radioactive pool.

Mack and Jerry stood by the edge, watching the two figures claw at each other beneath the surface, their bodies distorted by the water, a huge burst of bubbles rushed to the surface from El Krusho's lungs, but still neither of them came up.

It was then that Skrolnik came through and urgently touched Jerry's arm. "Listen," he said, "the reactor's gone out of control. It's like a runaway train. The director doesn't think he's going to be able to control it."

Jerry looked down into the depths of the pool, where El Krusho and the Tengu were struggling their last among the racks of plutonium and U-235. He could already feel the deep hum of the fusion reactor reverberating throughout the building. He glanced at Mack, and then at Skrolnik again.

"Hiroshima," he said. "That's what this is all about.

Goddamned Hiroshima.'' He felt a crunching of broken porcelain in his pocket, and realized it was the cricket cage.

CHAPTER TWENTY-FOUR

At 8:27 P.M., the sun rose over San Juan Capistrano, just south of Los Angeles. The explosion of the reactor at Three Arch Bay was exactly similar to the detonation of a hydrogen bomb, since the release of neutrons caused by the fusion of the reactor led to fission of the plutonium and uranium waste in the used-fuel pool, and the discharge of violent radioactivity.

The evening turned to daylight as an immense white fireball ascended thunderously into the sky, and then hung there, rumbling, glowing with malevolent heat and power. A young starlet who was prancing out of her car on Santa Monica Boulevard was immortalized in the glass of the Palm Restaurant window. A famous producer who was drinking his tenth collins of the day looked southward from his Bel Air balcony when he first saw something flashing, and was evaporated where he stood.

Within seconds, a roasting wind blew through Garden Grove and Anaheim and Lakewood, turning Disneyland to fiery wreckage, melting the dummies in the Hollywood Wax Museum, melting human beings, too. Dreams and reality both died that day. Reels of movies waiting to be edited at Twentieth-Century Fox and Universal Studios flared up in seconds.

David Sennett was watching television when he heard the first crack and rumble. Then a terrifying flash filled the room, and the drapes billowed out as if a hurricane had caught them.

"Oh, Dad," he thought. He knew what had happened. "Oh, Dad, Oh, God."

THE CHILLING NOVEL OF THE ULTIMATE *PSYCHO*-LOGICAL CRIME

SWITCH

from the award winning
WILLIAM BAYER

The two murder victims had little in common – one was a lonely call-girl, the other a prim schoolteacher.

But there was one brutally tantalising connection – their killer had decapitated them both and then switched their heads . . .

Riveting. It is a novel in which the grit and madness of New York are palpable. It does high honour to the grand tradition of the American psychological thriller.'' Thomas Keneally

Very exciting. The plot is impeccable. I recommend it highly.'' *The Spectator*

0 7221 14958   CRIME   £2.50

THE HYPNOTIC POWER OF SOUL-CHILLING TERROR . . .

Death Trance

Graham Masterton

Respectable businessman Randolph Clare, president of one of Tennessee's largest companies, is challenging the bureaucratic Cottonseed Association with lower prices and greater efficiency. But then tragedy strikes – his wife and children are savagely and brutally murdered . . .

In desperation Randolph makes contact with an Indonesian priest who claims he can help him enter the world of the dead. But there demons await, hungry for those who dare make the journey. Not only do they want Randolph's life, but are eager to condemn his family's souls to a hell of agony far beyond all human imagination . . .

Don't miss Graham Masterton's other horror classics:
REVENGE OF THE MANITOU   THE WELLS OF HELL
THE DEVILS OF D-DAY   THE HEIRLOOM
CHARNEL HOUSE   TENGU
NIGHT WARRIORS

0 7221 6124 7   HORROR   £2.99

BETWEEN THE BALANCE OF POWER AND GLOBAL
CHAOS, ONE MAN WALKED THE KNIFE EDGE . . .

THE MAN WHO
WAS SATURDAY

DEREK LAMBERT

Moscow treated defectors from the West with kid-gloves. That is, until
they had outlived their usefulness. But the American Calder was different.
He had defected to Russia with information so explosive that even the
iron-clad regime of the Kremlin shook with fear. It had kept him alive. Until
now. For Calder is desperately keen to return to the West . . .

So they place the ruthless and scheming Spandarian on his trail, a KGB
chief with a mind as sharp as the cold steel of an ice pick. And as back-up
they unleash Tokarev, a professional assassin who kills for pleasure . . .

0 7221 5374 0   ADVENTURE THRILLER   £2.95

A selection of bestsellers from Sphere

FICTION

THE PANIC OF '89	Paul Erdman	£2.99 ☐
WHITE SUN, RED STAR	Robert Elegant	£3.50 ☐
A TASTE FOR DEATH	P. D. James	£3.50 ☐
THE PRINCESS OF POOR STREET	Emma Blair	£2.99 ☐
WANDERLUST	Danielle Steel	£3.50 ☐

FILM AND TV TIE-IN

BLACK FOREST CLINIC	Peter Heim	£2.99 ☐
INTIMATE CONTACT	Jacqueline Osborne	£2.50 ☐
BEST OF BRITISH	Maurice Sellar	£8.95 ☐
SEX WITH PAULA YATES	Paula Yates	£2.95 ☐
RAW DEAL	Walter Wager	£2.50 ☐

NON-FICTION

INVISIBLE ARMIES	Stephen Segaller	£4.99 ☐
ALEX THROUGH THE LOOKING GLASS	Alex Higgins with Tony Francis	£2.99 ☐
NEXT TO A LETTER FROM HOME: THE GLENN MILLER STORY	Geoffrey Butcher	£4.99 ☐
AS TIME GOES BY: THE LIFE OF INGRID BERGMAN	Laurence Leamer	£3.95 ☐
BOTHAM	Don Mosey	£3.50 ☐

All Sphere books are available at your local bookshop or newsagent, or can be ordered direct from the publisher. Just tick the titles you want and fill in the form below.

Name _____

Address _____

_____

Write to Sphere Books, Cash Sales Department, P.O. Box 11, Falmouth, Cornwall TR10 9EN

Please enclose a cheque or postal order to the value of the cover price plus:

UK: 60p for the first book, 25p for the second book and 15p for each additional book ordered to a maximum charge of £1.90.

OVERSEAS & EIRE: £1.25 for the first book, 75p for the second book and 28p for each subsequent title ordered.

BFPO: 60p for the first book, 25p for the second book plus 15p per copy for the next 7 books, thereafter 9p per book.

Sphere Books reserve the right to show new retail prices on covers which may differ from those previously advertised in the text elsewhere, and to increase postal rates in accordance with the P.O.